HOMO

ACTION

LOVE

STORY!

D1570678

For Maggie,
the original Boots McHenry
!

AUTHOR'S NOTE

Homo Action Love Story! takes place in a medically advanced future, where the only health risk for two people who go to bed together is the risk of a broken heart.

This is not our world.

Always be safe.

Use
condoms /
.

HOMO

ACTION

LOVE

STORY!

a tall tale

Ben Monopoli

PART 1

Splatter

Chapter 1

When I kiss him the stadium erupts in hooting and cheers — a stomping, thundering, rattling riot 40,000 happy spectators strong. Feet pound concrete steps, hands ricochet in wild clapping. Streamers, party hats — the works. They're loving this, and who can blame them? Not me. Dude's body is banging and it's laid out right here like a smiling, naked gift, to me and every onlooker. But mostly to me.

He smiles at me as he breaks the kiss and leans up. I know the toothy grin's as much for them as it is for me, though. He laughs, lets go of his paintball rifle so it lands with a hollow clang on the gleaming roof of the tractor trailer where we're sprawled. We're in the Industrial Zone, I guess, though the trailer has the Forest Zone's trees looming willy-nilly around it. He's sitting on my crotch, hard in the scruff of blond fuzz surrounding my belly button, legs tucked back against my thighs, toes wedged under my knees. We've kissed during games but obviously we've never made love on the field, as all our fans are desperate for us to do now. *Do it, do it*, the crowd chants gleefully in at least three languages. A few people behind the Smalltown Zone stand and throw their hands skyward to initiate the Wave, which gets halfway around the stadium before petering out.

When Ryan drops down to kiss me again a curtain of his shaggy brown hair folds over my goggles and my senses are reduced by one. The others heighten. I become more aware of the crowd's applause, of its rises and falls as they alternate between cheering us on and hushing in anticipation when they think the magic's about to happen. And of the hot sun beating on my bare skin, and of my dick cupped in the soft valley of Ryan's ass cheeks.

I tell him to let me in.

"Boots," he laughs mid-kiss, and I can taste his sly grin. He leans up again and pulls off his goggles, throws them over the edge of the trailer; fourteen feet down they clap pavement.

Then he spits into his palm and holds it out for me to spit too, and with my eyes closed I can feel the hot wetness he suddenly applies to me.

"Will you do me good?" he says.

"*Pfft*, don't I always?"

At this the crowd laughs, all 40,000 of them in giddy unison.

"Cocky, isn't he?" Ryan says to the many-faced mass, and I see a stadium's worth of nodding heads.

With their encouragement he rocks back a little, shifting his weight from my groin to my thighs, his dick bumping back and forth across my abs. He flexes his ass cheeks, rocks back farther, and I see on his face his focused intensity as he prepares to receive me.

The crowd knows it's finally happening. As a mass they lean forward, 80,000 elbows on knees, on railings, on shoulders of the spectators in front of them. Like a hurricane of anticipation they all inhale deeply. And hold it.

Hold it.

Hold up. Stop. Wake up.

Breathlessly I slap at the blaring sat-radio alarm clock and silence it before any lame pop choruses can lodge in my brain. My heart is pounding. Shit. If I don't open my eyes maybe I can fall back into the dream. My boner is raging, lifting a drafty tent of silver silk sheet over me. I squeeze it through the sheet, try to relieve the horniness the way you squeeze a stubbed toe to ease pain. Doesn't work—makes it worse, actually. Makes it throb. I turn and the silk tugs across the head and I gasp. I roll over a few times between the sheets to cross the vast expanse of pillow-top mattress, eager to press myself against Ryan's smooth and fuzzy curves. And, you know, finish what we started in my dream.

But my hands find Ryan's half of our bed empty, a barren field of wrinkled sheets. I open my eyes for the first time and look up at the mirror on the ceiling. I'm in bed alone.

"Ryan?" I lean up on an elbow. "Hey. Ryan?"

I lay my hand on his pillow, find the notch his head made during the night still warm. I toss the sheet back and slip out of bed.

The hardwood floor is cold on my feet. I yawn and scratch my armpit and walk over to the big balcony doors, pull them open like I'm in a commercial for erotic fabric softener or something. The California sun is warm on my bare body, the morning breeze cool. Babbling in the backyard is the perpetually-spitting Poseidon statue-fountain-thing Ryan insisted we install near our kidney-shaped pool. Across the patio from the pool is our guesthouse; beyond that our big expanse of manicured lawn. The tang of freshly-cut grass makes my nose itch.

"Where are you, Ryan?" I muse, a detective on the case. "Hmm. I know where you are."

I turn, break into a sprint, re-enter the bedroom, grab the edge of the mattress and fling my legs up over it—my bare hip and thigh glide across the silk as though the mattress were the hood of a flashy car.

I land on my feet on the other side, feeling cool.

As I near the master bathroom the floor grows warmer. I know Ryan's close. Steam spills from under the door. I grab its steel handle and slide it open. A fluffy cloud of hot air smelling of eucalyptus envelopes me, licking my skin.

When it clears I can see his tall blurred shape in the all-glass shower stall beside our enormous bathtub. From time to time his ass and shoulder bloom squeaky against the steamed-up glass, sending cascades of droplets sliding down after they pull away. Now the door opens and he peers out. Soapy water falls from his chin and darkens the slate floor.

"Hey," he says, voice echoey in the stone-and-tile room. "Come in." He holds out his dripping hand and I take it and join him in the shower, turning on my own showerhead once he's closed the door. He likes his water hot-hot so I keep mine cool to balance it.

"You're up early," I say, leaning into the stream and smoothing back my hair.

Without responding, he picks up a bar of soap and starts washing me, a thing he used to do more often. He starts with my back, works my neck and shoulder muscles with strong hands.

"Not that early," he says finally, turning me around to wash my armpits and pecs. He molds my chest hair into short, sudsy spikes like pornographic armor. My boner is springing back to life and he notices it, smirks, flicks it.

"Usually I'm dragging you out of bed on game days," I say.

"I slept lousy last night for some reason." He smooths down my spikes but doesn't touch my boner again.

"Pre-game jitters?"

"This fucking interview," he says, stepping back into his own stream. "You know I hate the TV stuff."

"It's not that bad. And it comes with the territory."

"Yeah, well —"

"Don't worry," I tell him, "I'll handle the talking, if you want. You can just sit and look pretty for the cameras."

He laughs.

When I'm clean and rinsed we shut off the water and stand in the scented steam with our arms around each other — just a few quiet moments we try to steal every morning. This morning, though, I'm not as content to be still. Rubbing my groin against his, I tell him maybe I could relax him a little.

"Tonight," he laughs. "For sure."

"When the alarm went off I was in the middle of a dream about you, you know." I trace a circle around his nipple.

"Good dream?"

"We were in the stadium during a game. Very naked. And about to make love. The crowd was insane for it. So much cheering."

"Oh god," he groans.

"What?"

"The crowd, the stadium. Symbolic much?"

"Symbolic of what?"

"C'mon, Boots, our relationship has always belonged to the fans as much as to us. Don't you think it's only fitting that they'd eventually watch us fuck?"

"That's silly," I tell him. "You belong to me and only me."

He smirks. "Yeah, well. So did we finally give them what they wanted?"

"No time. The freaking alarm."

He rolls his eyes and touches his chin to my shoulder.

It would be easy to get something going now, I'm sure, but there'll be time for sex tonight after we bring home a win against the Panthers. Victory sex will be even sweeter. Right now I just want to hold him.

I whisper to him that I love him.

"You really do," he says, and I can hear a smirk in his voice. I fake-punch him in the gut and then reach for a towel.

Ryan Kroft and I, in addition to being hot-and-heavy boyfriends, are teammates on the Warriors of Thebes, California — one of the most popular teams in the North American Paintball League and winner of last year's Splatter Cup. Ryan and I like to tease each other about who's the bigger superstar of the Warriors, but the truth is it's a close call. Our simu-kill rates are never more than one or two apart. The other Warriors love us, our coach Lucinda Skullcrusher loves us, the fans love us, and we love each other. Drafted to the Warriors from separate colleges, it was love at first sight between Ryan and me that day in the locker room. After team orientation we went home together and haven't been apart for more than a few hours since. That was more than two years ago. Sometimes it feels like minutes. Other times, in more stressful times, it feels longer.

Like now. Ryan, dressed in jeans and a white leather jacket, is fidgeting in his chair while we wait for the interview to start — fidgeting in ways probably only I would notice. For one, he's aggressively making a new hangnail. He keeps touching the plug in his right earlobe. He's already firmly declined to remove his reflective sunglasses and the studio techs are busily rearranging the lights to keep them from sending lens flares into the cameras.

"I don't know why I still get so nervous," he whispers, pretty brown eyes hidden behind the shades.

"It's cute," I assure him, and give his hangnail-finger

a squeeze. Like a boulder on his knuckle is last year's Splatter Cup ring. "You're a killing machine in the stadium but behind the cameras you're just a bashful little boy."

"Shut up, poo face."

I rub the back of his neck and he touches the bridge of his nose to keep his shades in place. I wish he'd ditch them—viewers might suspect he's hiding a sign of domestic abuse or something crazy like that. One fan's online speculation could bloom into a global scandal before this interview is over.

Behind and beneath us is a field of green-screen. In front of us is a fluttering curtain of flexiglass monitors and people standing around with earpieces and tablets.

Across from us the interviewer, a dude named Alan Bosco (a bag of bones recently imported from the all-but-dead football league), is having his makeup retouched, watching the process in a mirror he holds at arm's length. When he's satisfied he pushes the stylist away and turns to us to make pre-interview small talk. I roll with it, but Ryan entirely ignores. It's normal for him to be quiet during these things but it's not like him to be rude. I give him an *Are you OK?* look and he nods.

Still, during the ten-second countdown before we go live, I can feel him tensing up. I should've just blown him in the shower. Would've relaxed him a bit.

On the newly-rigid flexiglass monitors the green-screen suddenly morphs into glossy 3D animations that make it look like we're sitting on floating chainlink cubes containing basketball-size suns. When the red lights on the cameras blink on, I'm still thinking of blowing Ryan, and I hurriedly wipe off the grin.

"Boots McHenry, Ryan Kroft, a million thanks for stopping to chat this afternoon. This epic afternoon. A victory today will mean there's only one game standing between the Warriors and the whole enchilada. The Splatter Cup. Today's game is make or break. How are you boys feeling going into it?"

"Feeling good," I say, looking to Ryan, who tilts his head but doesn't add anything. "Feeling rested. Feeling good. Feeling ready to send a Panther to exile."

"Love your confidence. It's a heck of a season record to maintain. Do all the successive wins make each new game more intimidating? Does it build in your brainboxes?"

"Each game's its own game. There's nothing else. But it's been a good season, no doubt about that. And it'll continue."

"It *has* been a good season for the Warriors," Bosco says, "though if you remember, in last week's game against the Pelicans you had a near-death moment, Ryan Kroft."

On the monitors I see the cameras jump to a close-up of Ryan but his shades reveal nothing.

"It may have *looked* like a near-death to people at home," I say, "but we're professionals. To us it wasn't close. We work in fractions of inches. By that measure he had miles."

"We're— We're showing the clip," Bosco says. "In super slow mo. Over on this monitor here." He points; Ryan and I look. "And clearly Ryan Kroft was about to take a direct hit to the throat—"

"Maybe," I say.

"Oh," Bosco says, leaning forward, "you don't think so?" As if to bolster his argument an animation appears, demonstrating the probable path of the paintball bullet. A semi-transparent representation of it hits the on-screen Ryan in the Adam's apple and spreads translucent yellow over his face and chest. It gives me the willies.

"All I know," I say, trying to keep my cool, "is that

regardless of what your cute little cartoons show, in real life Ryan's just fine."

"If you'll let me be so bold, Ryan Kroft, in that near-death moment it seemed your head was somewhere else. Somewhere far away from the game."

Ryan sighs and looks away. Usually he's more professional than this. Sure Bosco's a jerk but it's nothing we haven't dealt with a hundred times before.

"Well he's still here, isn't he?" I say, wishing Bosco would just drop it.

"All thanks to your teammate, Piper Pernfors."

"Pernfors pushed me out of the way of the bullet," Ryan says, speaking for the first time. His voice sounds as though he knew this was coming. "Of course I'm zilla grateful."

"And it would've been a *direct hit* otherwise," Bosco prods.

"So would *this* have been," Ryan growls, raising his fist, "if I actually hit you, Alan. But I'm not going to. So that means it's not actually a hit at all. No connection, no hit. See the difference?"

Bosco clears his voice, smooths the tablet in his lap. "Let's move on?"

"Wait a second," Ryan says. "What are you implying about the non-hit? That I was slipping up? Off my A game?"

"We're a team," I say, reaching over and squeezing Ryan's knee. "Teammates look out for each other. Ryan sent a Pelican to exile later that game. Reduced them to a rookie line-up for next year. And in the one moment when Ryan wasn't kicking huge amounts of ass, Piper had his back. Everything worked how it's supposed to work."

"Kind of ironic then, Boots McHenry," says Bosco, "that your old boyfriend would end up rescuing your current one?"

"I don't see what's ironic about it. Piper and I dated in college. Then we stopped dating. Now we're teammates. This isn't some kind of romantic triangle."

Bosco smiles. Ding ding ding. I want to slap my hand over my mouth. Without even realizing, I've said every gossip peddler's favorite words: *romantic triangle*. He seems satisfied, or at any rate willing to let it drop for now. I wonder if that's what he was trying to get from us all along. Romantic subplots are always big; there's a ton of downtime during NAPL games and the commentators need something to go on about. Bosco is, after all, trying to make a name for himself in the NAPL—why not prove his worth by muckraking?

Whatever. It doesn't matter. This might just be revenge on Ryan for forcing them to rearrange their lights.

"You two had your anniversary the other week?" Bosco says, changing course.

"Yeah," I say, looking over at Ryan. "Two years."

"So the Warriors have been good to you. I mean since you met on the team."

"I like to think I would've met Ryan otherwise. Fate and stuff. But yeah, the day I saw him getting fitted for his uniform and those pretty eyes flashed over at me, I knew he was the one for me."

To Ryan he says, "What's it like having a lover as a teammate?"

"I'm not sure it affects the game."

Bosco turns to me for clarification and I add, "It makes us stronger. Better. Any of us guys will go to bat for another, but with Ryan and me it's even deeper than that. If Ryan were to get hit and go to exile, I don't know what I'd do. Five years with zero contact would be a hell of a long time."

After we've left the studio and are making our way fifteen floors down to the locker room, I ask Ryan if he knew Bosco was going to bring up the near-death thing.

"Figured it was likely."

"Is that why you were dreading it?"

He shrugs.

"I don't know why it's such a big deal to everyone."

"Oh, they know the Warriors are cake-walking to another Cup and they just want to manufacture some drama along the way. Doesn't mean I have to like it."

"Then let's give them something better to talk about today," I say. "Hey, maybe we can reenact my dream!"

"You horndog," he smirks. "Keep your mind on the game, Boots."

Mind on the game. Right. Before entering the Warriors locker room I always remind myself of that very thing. I never have a problem once I'm inside—I have a boyfriend and, more importantly, I'm a professional. But the locker room requires a frame of mind I need a few deep breaths to get into. A controlled mindset that's able to ignore the gleaming muscular bodies going into and out of the showers and the casually discarded t-shirts and underwear that litter the concrete floor.

We descend the blue metal staircase and then split the Warriors' white-and-yellow *W* logo in half as the big glass doors it's painted on part for us.

The first Warrior we encounter today is Rufus Wong. He's standing near the entrance (where all the action is), wearing only a towel, fixated on the lipstick-size microphone a young journalist is wagging in his face. Rufus is a hot tamale, so they say, and he acts as though God created him on the first day, even ahead of light. The tabloids constantly showcase him in the company of various men and women (sometimes both at the same time) and there's nothing phony or drummed-up about these affairs. Chances are good Rufus will get with this skinny blond journalist after the game. Assuming he hasn't already.

Ryan socks Rufus's shoulder as we pass, gives him a quick "Hey." Early last season that simple gesture would've sent the media into a feeding frenzy. For some reason they were fixated on the idea of Ryan and Rufus getting together—maybe because of the neat alliterative pairing of their names (headline writers like things tidy). Eventually, though, they accepted that the team romance was between Ryan and me.

"I guess what bothers me most about that interview," I add as we arrive at our lockers, "was how Bosco was trying to make it seem like Piper doing his job meant you weren't doing yours."

Ryan shrugs, takes off his jacket, hangs it in his locker. He pulls off his shirt and unbuckles his belt. "Let's let it go, Boots. It's probably just the romantic triangle storyline they're going for." He pulls down his pants.

"Probably."

"And like you said, there's a Panther that needs putting down today."

He tosses his balled-up jeans and underwear into his locker. He's naked now and the bright lights illuminate every inch of his body—and maybe I'm biased but it's pretty much the perfect body. He's six-one (an inch shorter than I am), and lithe and thin, less beefy than I am. If we were born before the rise of pro paintball I most likely would've quarterbacked a football team, whereas Ryan probably would've run track. His muscles are hard, chiseled, and he puts a lot of work into them every day in our gym.

He rakes his fingers through his shaggy hair and ties it back with a rubber band. His armpits sport a brown fuzz that dapples his pecs and belly and ass too. Since I'm sitting on the bench, his dick is at eye level and it's everything I can do not to lean forward and —

Soon, I tell myself. *There's a time and place. After the game he'll be all mine. We'll finish my dream.*

"Looking good today, Kroft," says a familiar voice, flirty but with a shade of sarcasm. I turn and see Piper. He's zipping up his uniform, a thin, navy-blue neoprene bodysuit emblazoned on the front and back with his #5 and our team's *W*. I'll admit, reluctantly, that his blue eyes can light up any room. His head is shaved on the sides and he's got a shock of blond hair running down the middle that sticks up here and there and hangs in his eyes — it makes him look like a Comanche warrior by way of Sweden. His goggles are slung around his neck recklessly like a bandanna. Add in his chunky utility belt and he looks like some kind of Old West superhero.

"Look, Boots," Ryan says, punching Piper's shoulder with his free hand while stepping into his own uniform, "it's my knight in shining armor!"

"Hey Piper," I say.

I met him when we were eighteen; it was lust at first sight. We dated for three years, then we stopped. Among other things, I caught him in bed with both of my roommates. At the same time. Enough said, right?

"Shining armor?" Piper laughs. "What'd I do now?"

Ryan tells him about the interview. He laughs again. "Guy saves his teammate's ass and it *has* to be because he wants to snuggle up to it, right?"

Ryan finishes pulling on his uniform, the thin fabric stretching over his muscles, and zips it up the side. The uniform's hard codpiece covers his dick. I ball-up my t-shirt and pull down my boxers. It always feels weird to be naked around Piper now, so in the locker room I'm quick about it. It has to be done, though: nothing can be worn under these uniforms, lest you get unsightly underwear lines. Things like that are easy to spot in 3D-HD.

When we're dressed, the ten of us Warriors stand in a line, spread-eagle like clones of Da Vinci's Vitruvian Man while teams of handlers weigh us down with our weaponry and ammo. I glance over at Ryan, who smiles at me and then resumes fiddling with his goggles.

In addition to the skintight uniforms (which ride up in the ass but which at least offer the codpiece to obscure the erection I inevitably pop when Ryan's on fire), we wear light but sturdy shoes and a pair of self-cleansing goggles. A utility belt goes around our waists — a bag of bullets jangles from one side and a pistol is holstered on the other. A magnetic strap that runs from shoulder to belt can hold our rifle if we need both hands free, but that's not often — a paintballer's rifle is never far from his hands. To prevent rapid fire, and to keep things interesting for the spectators, both rifle and pistol hold only one bullet at a time. Plenty of guys in exile were losers in the race to reload.

Over the hubbub of the handlers and clicks of weapons checks I can hear the crowd thundering in their seats as the intro music starts blaring. The sounds remind me of my dream and get me a little heated. But it all dims when my handler presses a com-piece into my ear. After a static crackle I hear our coach, Lucinda Skullcrusher, give her usual pre-game pep-talk from the coach's box where she sits high above the field. We do roll-call, each of the ten of us announcing our numbers — I'm six, Ryan's nine (a happy accident) — to make sure we can all hear each other and Lucinda.

"Good to go, boys. Kick some ass out there. Bring us

another win. And watch your back, and your mates'. Especially Rufus's. He's a target today, since apparently he can't keep his cock under wraps." I'm not sure what she means by that but whatever it is, it fits Rufus's character just fine. "We haven't had a simu-death all season and I want it to stay that way. All the chattering class is wringing their panties about how we're the favorite for another Cup this year, and for once they're right. Just thinking about it makes me wet. Get us one step closer, boys. Be in touch. Skullcrusher out."

The day is bright and blue and I shield my eyes with my hand waiting for my goggles to darken in response to the sun. I look up at the thousands of roaring fans that surround us in rows of seats that begin a hundred feet above the field. There are even more of them than there were in my dream. It's always a personal thrill that I never feel dwarfed by them. This stadium is my house and they're all just guests.

Ryan and I wave in general directions at the tiny faces as we jog to our assigned position in the Forest Zone, one of the four zones mirrored on each half of the field. There's also the Industrial Zone (last encountered in my dream) full of dumpsters, barrels, and the tractor-trailer truck. Smalltown is based on a little desert town, with all the cars, recycling receptacles and ads you'd expect. Seaport is a mazelike series of docks built over a pool with a simulated tide. The terrains abut each other with sharp edges — pine-needle-strewn forest floors turn to pavement or water with no transition. Crossing from one to another has the jarring effect of stepping from a sitcom living room to a naked television studio.

Dividing the field along what was the fifty-yard line back when this stadium was still used for football, is a gigantic curtain that permits each team to arrange itself on the field free from the other team's view.

Hunkering down behind some bushes, Ryan and I wait for the curtain to rise and for the game to begin. Over the com Skullcrusher is making last-minute adjustments to some other players' positions. She can't seem to settle on where to put some of the close-combat Warriors. Through the trees into Industrial I can see Rufus Wong hopping up and down behind the truck, psyching himself up, spinning his rifle around his finger as though it were a giant six-shooter.

Touching my com to make sure I'm not broadcasting to the whole team, I say to Ryan, loudly to combat the roar of the crowd, "What's the story with Rufus today? Skullcrusher said he's a target?"

"You didn't hear? He got caught with the wife of #2 on the Panthers. Specifically, with his head between her legs."

"How Rufus of him."

"Number 2 wasn't thrilled, as you can imagine. All eyes are on them today. It's personal."

"So the commentators already have their storyline for today."

"Maybe. They probably expect a paintbath."

"That means they won't be watching us as close."

"I hope so."

"Maybe I'll toss you up onto that trailer truck and find out what's under your codpiece."

"Too bad it takes ten minutes to get out of these suits."

I can't help but grin. The interstitial music stops and in its weighty absence the crowd begins to roar even louder and stomp the stands in that time-tested *We Will Rock You* rhythm. Far ahead the curtain dividing the teams shimmers in the sunlight and begins to rise.

"This is it," Ryan says, gripping his rifle, taking a

breath.

"Stay safe."

I kiss him and our goggles knock together. Mine mistake the bump for a slap of dirt, and water squirts across the polycarb.

Chapter 2

Stomp stomp clap

  Stomp stomp clap

Certain people are born to do certain things. You know? Some are musicians, some are soldiers, some bake the best apple pie you've ever tasted. I'm a pro paintballer. It's what I do and it's who I am. Ryan is my teammate, my boyfriend, and he means the world to me. There have been moments with him, just the two of us alone, when I've felt totally complete. But if I'm really honest, nowhere in the world is Boots McHenry more Boots McHenry than on this field, with a rifle in my hands and the crowd in my ears. It makes me smile. I was made for this. This is war. And it's *on*.

It's a scramble from the get-go. Just as Ryan and I are starting to push forward through Forest, Skullcrusher's voice crackles in our ears. She's rearranging us already. From her vantage point in the coach's box she can tell Rufus is going to face some heat right away.

"Lord, #2 over there looks like a rabid pitbull," she groans. "All the pussy in the world, Wong, and you had to go for his wife's."

Ryan smirks.

"Wong, hang back," Skullcrusher adds, "we'll let their #2 get careless. Man literally has *steam* coming out his ears. Pernfors and Kroft, you boys head down into Upper Smalltown. McHenry, fall back to Lower Forest; Santiago, you join McHenry there — I'm putting you boys in the trees. Wong's ass needs plenty of sniper cover."

Ryan hefts his rifle as Piper comes jogging up beside us. He's got his rifle stowed; he's a close-combat guy and prefers the pistol.

"Looks like we're on, Kroft," Piper flirts, but like always there's a touch of sarcasm too.

Ryan gives me a kiss and we split up, him and Piper heading to Smalltown and me falling back.

I'm pretty sure Santiago was in Seaport somewhere and it may take him a minute to get to me. But he's an incredible sniper and I'm always glad to work with him.

Alone the forest feels dense around me. I take a breath and smack a branch away from my face. Being separated from Ryan on the field always gets my hair up. I don't like not being there to have his back.

Reaching Lower Forest, I pull myself up into the bottom branches of the tallest tree, a towering faux-ganic elm whose top is almost level with the first row of spectators. I climb up and up. The tone of the cheering deepens and becomes less echoey when it starts hitting me from all sides. The cheering's like fuel. I climb faster, up through the leafy canopy of the surrounding trees. I settle in about thirty yards off the ground, and from here I can see the entire field. It's a good position but dangerous too — while you're watching the field, the other team's sniper could be chilling in his own tree, filling his crosshairs with your heart.

So I try to focus on everything all at once. I *feel* the field. I think I'm OK. Still, I won't feel comfortable until Santiago is with me.

From my perch I see two or three naked-eye flashes of green Panther uniform right away. I'll take a shot if I get a clean one, but protecting my fellow Warriors is my main job at the moment. I touch the rifle scope to my goggles to get an image-link and scan the field more closely. My heart's pounding; it always pounds hardest when I'm not seeing anything. If the Panthers' coach has alerted his players that I'm up here they could be taking cover, and it could be quiet until some of the close-combat Warriors force them out of hiding. I settle in.

It's kind of bizarre to me how popular pro paintball is as a spectator sport. It's thrilling to play, but watching it should be like watching grass grow. Games go for two hours or until the first simu-death. Only one simu-death is allowed per game, and sometimes there isn't one at all. When the cost is as high as five years in exile, completely cut off from the rest of civilization, nobody takes it lightly. Maybe that's why audiences watch—not for the action, but for the tension. Since it's so risky to be a showman, the showmen (like Rufus and sometimes Piper) seem all the more exciting. Those of us who are more careful wait and watch. You take your shot when you have one, lie low until you do. Sure, there's plenty of running and chasing, but a lot of the time it's just like this, especially for us snipers: muscly dudes in tight uniforms, chilling in trees. Highly-paid muscly dudes, I should add.

Over my com comes a player-to-player beep, then a voice: "McHenry. Coming up behind you. Don't get excited." It's the voice of Clemente Santiago, our #4. I look down and see him climbing. To disguise the wobble of the branches caused by his weight he ascends a few branches at a time during gusts of wind. He's good. After watching him for too many seconds I reestablish my image-link on the field and cover him while he gets into position on a branch a few feet above mine. Settling in, he scrapes his shoes against the branches, sending crumbs of faux-ganic bark falling past me. He glances down as he places his rifle butt against his shoulder.

"Spying anything fun?"

"Nothing yet."

He has short, messy black hair and a scruff of mustache that looks pretty cool. A white lollypop stick hangs out of his mouth. He's my age, twenty-four, got promoted to first string mid-season last year after Anders Kaplan ate it in a game against the Icebergs (our only simu-death last season, and Santiago was the lucky beneficiary — or maybe it was the team who got lucky: it was Santiago's well-aimed bullet in the next game that took us to the Cup).

"Looks quiet down there," he says, tonguing the lollypop from one side of his mouth to the other while he scans the field.

"For now. I think Coach's going for a spook-and-snipe."

"They spook em, we snipe em," he says around the pop. "Sounds good to me. I'm fine with letting the close-combat nerds do the dirty work, get all sweaty."

I smirk and imagine getting a sweaty Ryan back into our silvery bed. I wonder if straightboy Clemente has ever been with a guy — if he has, no doubt it was Rufus. It seems like every straight guy who's ever messed around with a guy has messed around with Rufus.

"Company, McHenry," Clemente says suddenly. "Sniper. Our tree, opposite. See him?"

I squint, then blink up to a higher zoom on the image-link.

"He's hidden pretty good," Clemente adds. "But I saw a tell-tale rustle that went against the wind."

"I love a tell-tale rustle. Don't see him yet."

"Little higher than our position."

I zoom out a little. And there it is, a tiny fleck of

green bodysuit behind the leaves. "OK. Should we take the shot?"

Clemente raises a finger to his com. "Coach. Santiago. Clear line on the dudenheimer in the tree over there. Should we take it?" After a moment he says to me, "No answer."

"She still working out the spook, maybe?"

"Could be," he says.

"We could just go for it, finish the game off early."

"Let's give it a second," he says. "He's covered pretty good. We miss, he'll fire back while we're reloading."

Clemente's right, but he also has a tendency to be overly cautious. He never fires until he's sure. One well-placed bullet could end this game quick, though. And I could have Ryan all to myself.

"If you want to go for it," I say, "I'll clean it up if you don't get him. Surprise from your miss will kill his chameleon act, make it easier for me."

He tosses the lollypop from cheek to cheek, considering. I can practically feel the intensity radiating off him. He's preparing to send a dude to exile and that carries a lot of weight every time. "OK. I'll get him. Aiming for his nuts."

"You bitch," I laugh.

A moment later there's a foghorn-like blast and all the lights in the stadium go blue. In surprise I pull off my goggles and naked-eye the field.

I look up. "Did you—?"

"No," Clemente says, lowering his rifle. "Isn't me."

I don't know what Panther got simu-killed. I don't know who did the shooting. But the game's over. That means Ryan and I can spring out of our uniforms and go home and finish my—

"Fuck!" Clemente is yelling, punching the tree trunk into a plume of faux-ganic bark.

Maybe I'm in denial. Maybe it's just that over the course of our two winning seasons I got so used to the lights signaling a Warrior victory that I failed to sense anything wrong. But with a shiver my daydream evaporates and I realize the simu-death has been on our team. One of the Warriors is down.

Clemente and I look at each other, nervousness filling his big brown eyes. Is he thinking what I'm thinking? Fearing, for my sake, what I'm fearing? The worry in his eyes— Is it for Ryan?

Last season when Kaplan got simu-killed I was nearby and I witnessed it; when the blue lights started flashing there was no moment where I had to wonder if they were flashing for Ryan. This not-knowing feeling is new and I hate it.

Over my com I hear Skullcrusher swearing. "Shit! Shit! Shit!"

Clemente's got his finger at his com: "Who'd we lose?" But no one's answering; it's radio silence. After a minute he drops down to my branch and puts his arm tight around me. "Only one-in-eight it was your boy, McHenry. Let's go see."

Startled into action by his touch, I descend ahead of him and jump the last six feet painfully to the ground. After dodging shrubbery and leaping stone walls, and finally running down Smalltown's deserted main street, I find the other Warriors grouped near our entrance to the field. They're standing in a loose circle. Skullcrusher is there already. I can see Ryan from behind; the back of his uniform is clean and that means he's at least fifty percent not dead. Piper, facing me from the other side of the circle, catches my eye briefly before looking away. When Ryan sees him see me he turns around, turns slowly, a look on his face of overwhelming sadness. I feel my heart rend and break. Across his left pectoral is an explosion of green paint.

I slump to my knees in the sandy street. Ryan runs and drops to the ground in front of me, puts his arms around me, swapping paint onto my uniform—it may as well be blood.

I whisper into his hair, "How?"

"It was so fast. So much shooting. I was just in the wrong place at the—"

"No. You can't go away. You can't leave. This is stupid. You can't."

"Shit, Boots, I have to. It's in the contract. You know there's no way."

I can see myself twenty feet tall on all the monitors that are normally filtered out by our goggles, holding on to him for the last few seconds I'll get to hold on to him.

We are pro paintballers, employees in the biggest sports-entertainment industry in North America. We are worshipped and overpaid. We're paid to win, of course, but from time to time we're paid to disappear—because people care most about winning when there are terrible consequences for losing. We're paid to disappear from everyone—family, friends, spouses, everyone—to a place that's on no map, to a place so guarded by every legal means no one can say for sure that it even really exists. A disappearance so complete it's come to be known as simulated death. No Internet, no care packages, no visitors, no phone calls, nothing. For five fucking years.

After a hit, simu-death is carried out fast—already I can hear the sounds of the helicopter. In moments it'll land in the stadium and, as a dozen cameras look on, Ryan will have to get on.

As he said, it's in the contract.

"Now it's going to be fine, Boots," he's saying, moving

tears away from my eyes with his thumb. Guys with cameras are swarming us for close-ups; the ref is pushing through them, coming for Ryan. I want to kill them all. "Don't worry. Just carry on. You can still win the Cup."

"I don't care about the fucking Cup!"

"Boots." He smiles gently.

"Kroft, I need you to come with me," the ref says sharply, but Ryan ignores him.

"Listen to me." He squeezes my face in his hands. "Listen to me, Boots, my sexy guy. We signed up for this. We always knew it could happen someday. Listen. You need to make sure my parents get my checks, OK?"

The chopper is landing in the empty no-man's-land at the middle of the field. In the wind Ryan's hair comes out of its elastic and blows against his face.

"Boots. I love you and always will. Five years. Five years. I promise you'll be OK."

And then he's led away.

Since a simu-death is easily the highest rated part of any game, the NAPL stretches it out as long as possible while still keeping it fast enough to be brutal and shocking. Often the broadcast goes split-screen, showing ads for beer, cars, and summer blockbusters alongside the winning team celebrating and the losing team sulking. Because our relationship makes it extra poignant, Ryan's simu-death is stretched to almost fifteen minutes, plenty of time to beam my tears onto millions of acres of flexiglass — TVs, phones, tablets — worldwide.

While Ryan's video retrospective is playing I overhear Rufus Wong say something to Piper about our chances at the Cup being blown to shit now. That fucker. Piper knows enough to hold his tongue, and drifts to the edge of our circle. Clemente squeezes my shoulder supportively a few times, but he looks deep in thought and clearly has no idea what to say.

The coach is the one who says the final goodbye—that's how things are done. Lucinda Skullcrusher, grim-faced and pissed, shakes Ryan's hand. I hate it. I hate having to stand so far away from him, no more significant now than any other Warrior, while Ryan makes his long, solo walk across the field to the waiting chopper. I feel an arm hug me: it's Piper.

In the helicopter Ryan turns and looks directly at me. I realize he's saying something, maybe trying to get some last message across, but his voice is drowned out by the roar of the blades, and the wind is blowing his hair in his face, obscuring his mouth. Then he pats his chest, near his heart, near where he got hit.

"What'd he say!" I cry, pushing past Wong. "Did anyone see what he said?"

"He must've been saying goodbye," Piper says.

"Seemed more than goodbye," Clemente says, shaking his head. "Check the playbacks later, McHenry, you might be able to see."

Then, as the cameras look on, the chopper, bound for exile, lifts my sweet Ryan into the sky. And it feels like all of me that matters goes with him.

Chapter 3

Young people think they're invincible or some shit. That's why they don't believe in seat belts or bike helmets. It's why they didn't use condoms back when there were still things you could catch. And it's why the risk of losing five years of your life is small beans compared to the perks that a contract with the North

American Paintball League brings with it. It's always going to be someone else who gets simu-killed, not you. *Pfft.* Never you.

The difference between two years ago, when I put my thumb-print on that contract, and now, is that in those two years someone else began to matter to me more than myself. Exile would've been a small price to pay if it were just me: I would toil in idleness at whatever secret facility the NAPL has set up, and I would come out, a mere twenty-nine years old, to a huge if dusty house, a flush bank account, perhaps a job as a commentator.

Young people think they're invincible, that nothing bad will ever happen to them, and then something changes: they fall in love. And the world begins to seem a lot more fragile. And the odds of things going terribly wrong double. Because it's not just them anymore. Until it is.

For the first time I enter the post-game locker room without Ryan at my side. The other Warriors are there but I barely notice them. And the mood must be grim but I barely notice that either. As if I care about the Cup. My handlers scurry over to me and start pulling equipment off me — taking my rifle and pistol, unbuckling my belt, pulling my goggles off over my hair — but I never stop walking. Finally they give up and stand holding my gear as I slouch to the showers.

I enter the big tile room still wearing my uniform, choose a showerhead from one of the many that protrude from the walls, crank the knob and stand under the hot stream. The water makes a funny-sounding patter on the skintight neoprene. I hear it but barely. I'm looking down at the paint that came from Ryan's uniform, running down my belly and legs in diluted streams, streaking across the tile floor like vomit and swirling down the drain in the center of the room.

Finally I unzip my uniform, from my neck down across my shoulder, around my armpit and down my side. The zipper ends at the hip. At the best of times the uniform is hard to get off, but sopping wet it's impossible. Squeaks echo off the tile walls as I yank my arms out of the clinging sleeves; deep *thocks* vibrate the air as I struggle fruitlessly to pull the legs off over my feet. I'm naked from the ankles up but my feet are trapped in the spongy, twisted fabric.

"*Fuuuuck!*" I yell loud enough to make my vocal cords sear with pain. I'm about to punch the wall too but some part of my brain goes into survival mode and spares my knuckles. Instead I slump clumsily to the floor and bang my head against the wall. Water rains on my chest and thighs.

I hear a voice say, gently, "You OK in here?"

Piper is standing in the entrance to the showers, wearing a towel and a worried grimace.

I look at him. "Think I'm stuck." I rub water and tears out of my eyes.

"Looks that way." With nothing more than a lift of his eyebrows and a slow extension of his hand, he asks if I want help.

I look at him. I don't want to be seen, especially not by him. I look down the length of my body at my missing feet. At my shriveled dick. And croak, "OK."

He walks across the showers, feet slapping the tile, and kneels in front of me so we're eye to eye. With a cautious finger, as though he's examining the victim of a bear-trap, he pokes the mass of wet neoprene swallowing my feet. This is as close to my bare dick as he's been since our college days but he seems to respect that I'm in no mood for jokes.

"Quite a pretzel you've got here, B."

I shrug.

He looks up, reaches past me, and shuts off the water. "I think we can get you free, though."

He pushes his fingers down between the suit and my ankles to try to right the inside-out mess, but it isn't working.

"Were you there?" I ask.

"Where?" he says, tugging at the suit.

"When Ryan got hit. Were you nearby? Did you see it happen? Why did no Panthers take credit?"

"*All* of the Panthers are taking credit, Boots. Practically all. It was like a firing squad. We may never know which one actually scored the hit."

The idea that Ryan was ganged-up on makes me feel even more angry. "Why didn't you save him?"

For a moment Piper just looks at me. "I wasn't close enough, B. There was nothing I could do. I would've. Last week I *did*, remember?"

I nod.

He ends up tugging my uniform with all his might. "Heave!" he groans, trying to be funny but having a genuinely tough time. The wet floor offers zero traction against my back so he ends up dragging me halfway across the showers before the suit finally lets go. Like the victim of some kind of attack I lay naked and wet in the middle of the floor, a forearm over my eyes. I can't help but smirk, too, knowing how I must look. Piper drops the sopping pile of uniform and when it hits the floor it squirts water in all directions. Then he offers me his hand.

"It's going to be OK, you know," he says, dusting off my shoulders. "Don't you worry your pretty head. You're going to come back from this. The team will come back from this."

"I hope so."

"I know so. Now," he says, looking me up and down with a glimmer of nostalgia, "let me go find you a towel."

On my first Ryan-less night I lay in our bed looking at myself in the ceiling mirror, and see how tiny I seem in the huge expanse of shadowy sheets. The big bed looks so pompous now and I can't believe how naive we were in buying it. Naive because we never imagined it would ever hold less than the both of us. That *invincible* crap. I wonder where he is. What he's doing. And, crazily, whether he's forgotten me yet.

I spent all evening watching the video. There are precious few — or maybe mercifully few — pixels of Ryan getting hit. Most of the cameras were devoted to the showdown between Rufus fucking Wong and the Panther he cuckolded, a showdown that resulted in a firefight on the border of our Industrial and their Seaport. Guys from each team were involved. Ryan was there. The landscape started blooming blue and green as paintballs were fired. The one that found its mark first, found Ryan. I've watched the video fifty times. A second before the hit he looks up, gapes in surprise; it looks as though he saw it coming. Somehow that's more comforting than if he got shot in the back or while he was down.

But what kills me is that I have no one to blame. Was it their #3 who got him? Probably. But it could've easily been their #1 or #6. Even #9 looks to me like he was at the right angle to be the villain. But I don't know for sure; no one does, not even the Panthers themselves. The video coverage is shit. So I have no one to focus my rage on. The effect of this is that it gives me one more loose string in what's going to be five fucking years of loose strings.

At some point I roll over to Ryan's side of our bed, to the shallow groove in the mattress where he slept, and fall into a dreamless, restless sleep.

Chapter 4

The next time I have to be in the locker room is a lazy day, a practice, mostly a chance for us Warriors to build back some morale after Ryan's simu-death two days ago. It's four days until our next game, the one that'll decide whether we move on to the big enchilada. Lucinda Skullcrusher, never one to let slip a chance at the Cup, is intent on getting us back into shape with the new guy, Ryan's replacement, whoever that turns out to be.

In the locker room when I arrive for practice I first see Rufus Wong talking to Clemente, sizing him up in that way Rufus is always sizing up anything with a heartbeat. I want to kick Rufus in the cock. In the absence of having any Panther to blame, Rufus may as well get all my rage. When I walk by them without saying anything Clemente ditches Rufus and follows me to the lockers. He has his practice uniform halfway on, hasn't pulled on the sleeves; they're flapping against the backs of his legs. He has a spray of fine black chest-hair and a bright, multicolored scorpion tattoo; its big-clawed body covers his left pectoral and its pointed tail twists up onto his shoulder. It's abstract, like a cave painting. Sexy.

"We were wondering if you were going to show," he teases, putting a foot on the bench that runs along the lockers.

"I want to go over there and knock Wong's teeth out,

Clemente."

"And why would you do that, McHenry?" He crosses his arms over his chest but his face is sympathetic.

"Because it was his fucking antics off-field that got Ryan killed."

"Simu-killed. Remember that. And you know punching Rufus would be the *wong* thing to do."

I look at him blank-faced.

"*Wong* thing. No? Nothing? Tough crowd." He hits my shoulder and steps off the bench. "How you been doing, McHenry? No one's seen hide nor hair since the game."

"I've spent the past two days sulking."

"Awh. Well I guess that's OK. You had a shitty turn of luck. But it's up-and-at-em now, right?"

I nod but I'm not sure how it'll feel, getting up-and-at-em without Ryan. It's not going to be the same. It might even be terrible.

"Hey," Clemente continues, "did you watch the playbacks from when Ryan was in the chopper?"

"A million times."

"Anything?"

I shake my head.

"I gave it a look too. Damned if I can figure out what he said. His hair's whipping around and covers his lips." He tugs on his mustache to illustrate. "Anyway. Thought I'd give you a heads-up." He gestures with his chin to the guy changing his shirt at one of the farthest lockers. "Skullcrusher chose our new #9."

Number 9: Ryan's number on some other dude. Sure it was inevitable that a second-stringer would get bumped up. I knew the team would absorb the loss and basically act as though Ryan never existed. But still.

"Marius Tumble, eh? Lah dee fucking dah for him."

"McHenry," Clemente chides, squeezing my shoulder—he's one of those guys who's always touching you, never in the way you hope for, though. He looks at me with gentle brown eyes. "Don't bring it to the field. Marius had squat to do with Ryan. He's just here to fill the void."

"But what about *my* void?" I say it seriously but we both catch the unintentional double entendre and look at each other blankly for a second before breaking into dumb grins.

He squeezes my shoulder again. "Seriously, though. Don't take it out on Marius."

I nod because of course he's right. We're a team; in every game Clemente's ass is on the line too, and he wants my head where it should be. And ultimately he wants his hands on the Splatter Cup—same as me, if I can remember what it was like to want anything other than Ryan.

Clemente returns my nod and then stretches around to yank up the top half of his uniform. Then he punches his fists through the sleeves and starts to zipper up. Watching him, I find myself idly wishing he'd pull down his uniform again and make slow love to me here on the floor of the locker room. Anything to take my mind off of Ryan for a minute.

"Speaking of whom...." Clemente nods at our company and tells him congrats before moseying away.

Marius Tumble is six feet of lean, blackboy muscle. His eyes and teeth are blinding white against skin the color of coffee beans. He's got his shirt off but he's still wearing his jeans, a brand that if we win the Cup he'll no doubt get paid to wear.

Bashfully he rubs his buzzed scalp while holding out his other hand. "We've met and everything. But I wanted to say hi again."

I shake. "Hi, Tumble."

"And just say that, you know, I'm sensitive to the situation."

"Thank you."

"He was—is—a damn good baller. I'll do my best to honor the number."

"Thanks, I appreciate that. And congrats."

"Look, it's Six and Nine, together again," Piper announces. He's still in his street clothes: a pair of jeans and a white sleeveless tee. After shaking Marius's hand he slips an arm across my bare shoulder, where I feel the soft prickles of his short blond pit-hair (trimmed with No. 4 on the clippers if he still uses the same setting he did when we were together). The skin-to-skin contact feels nice, but I think it's best if I continue focusing my erotic energies on the lost cause of Clemente Santiago. Piper is a more complicated situation I don't want to fall into again. A hunky ex-boyfriend whose pit-hair length you still remember is a dangerous person to be around when you're getting over a simu-death and your bed feels way too big.

Practice is easy. We run through some raid patterns, do some sniper practice on targets festooned with the Vigilantes logo. Skullcrusher and her assistant coaches pace around the field, shaken by the loss and making calculations for our much-reduced chances at the Cup. My performance is fine but Lucinda Skullcrusher is a good enough coach to know when someone's going through the motions, however efficient those motions might be. When I come out of the shower after practice she's leaning against my locker, making notations on a tablet. She looks up. I secure the towel around my waist.

"Join me in my office for a minute, McHenry," she says.

"OK. Uh. Should I get dressed first, Coach?"

"It'll just be a minute. Walk with me."

She turns and I follow her. To any casual observer it must look like I'm stalking her—she barely comes up to my nipples and probably doesn't top 120 pounds. And yet when Lucinda Skullcrusher says jump, you jump, and when she talks, you listen up.

In her office she drops into the leather captain's chair behind her desk and I settle into a less-comfortable one in front of it, crossing my legs inside the towel like a dude in a kilt.

"Before you say anything," she says, holding up a callused hand smeared with whiteboard ink, "yes, your performance was OK out there today, considering."

"I'm just—"

"But OK isn't going to beat the Vigilantes. Fire will beat the Vigilantes. Passion will beat the Vigilantes. Where were those?"

"Want the truth?"

"Always."

"My fire and passion are on some mysterious island in the South Pacific somewhere, if the legends are true. In exile."

She lifts her eyebrows.

"I love him. Is it such a surprise?"

"From a professional? Yes. Honestly, yes."

"I gave you the professional, Coach. The professional is here in front of you. The joy came from Ryan."

She shakes her head. "Don't feed me that horseshit. I watched you play when you were in college. You had the passion and the joy, and Kroft wasn't even a blip on your radar yet."

"My *heart* is broken, Coach."

She sighs, leans back in her chair. "It's five years, Boots. This is the game. You both always knew there was a chance this might happen. It's only five years."

"Easy for you to say, Coach. You're what, fifty? I'm twenty-four. We've only been together two years. It won't be long before we've been apart longer than we were ever together. What will it even *mean* in light of that? It makes everything pointless. I don't know how he feels. It would be easier if I just went too."

At that last part she sits up straighter and peers at me with narrowed eyes. "I *hope* you're not getting any *ideas*."

"Meaning?"

"You know what I mean. Self-inflicted exile."

"Suicide?"

"Call it what you want. I call it fucking stupid."

I sigh. "To be honest, Coach, I've thought about it. The nights go on forever."

She clenches her jaw. "You know, McHenry, I have every right to kick your ass off this team just for saying that much." She shakes her head. "You can go as crazy as you like when the off-season comes but for now you'll do as I say. And if I even *suspect* you're thinking more about self-inflicting, you'll be out of the NAPL so fast your head'll spin faster than a fucking—uh—fucking pinwheel on a car antenna driving at two hundred M P H. With a lawsuit for violation-of-contract that'll have you rooting bottles out of the trash like a plastic pirate just so you can buy a goddamn turkey sandwich for lunch."

I stare at her, unblinking, chastened. She breaks eye contact and looks down, just briefly—I'm pretty sure it's the only time I've ever seen her demure—and she sighs.

"But I know I would never have to threaten that, much less do it. Because I know you, McHenry, and you are part of a *team*." The word *team* sounds holy the way she says it.

"I know. I'm sorry. I would never really do it."

"Don't tell me. *Show* me. Better yet, show the goddamn Vigilantes. Biggest game of the season — I know I say that every game, but this one *is*. Do your job. Get us to the Cup, McHenry. Find the joy. I promise you, it's still there."

When I come out of Skullcrusher's office I'm vaguely stunned. I hadn't actually been thinking about committing self-inflicted exile until she mentioned it — but the idea was born and squashed with a quickness that's somehow left the five years looming in even starker relief. There's no escape now. No possible alternative, not even the fantasy of one. Just loneliness and that empty bed.

I sit down on the bench in front of my locker, rub my sweaty palms on the towel stretched across my thighs.

I want to get out of here. I need a beer. I need someone to talk to. I wonder if Clemente has left yet. Maybe I can still catch him.

I drop my towel and as I'm turning to my locker I spot Piper on his way out the door, duffel bag slung over his shoulder. With one hand he slips on his sunglasses, and he opens the other to me in his customary Piper wave.

I've called out to him before even thinking about doing it. He stops with the big glass doors open. I swing the towel back around me.

"Feel like, I don't know, grabbing a beer or something?"

He flashes me a surprised smile. "Yes."

"Let me just get dressed."

Now he smirks a smirk that says, *Don't bother*.

I don't acknowledge it. While I'm slapping on some deodorant I notice him pull out his phone and start tapping. He's cancelling other plans, I'm sure.

I wonder what I'm getting into.

Actually, I *don't* wonder—I know, and that's why I'm doing it. Familiarity. I know the kind of place he'll want to go, I know the kinds of things he'll want to talk about. And most importantly, I know the precise moment to hit the brakes to keep us from ending up in the sack.

"Dude, hurry up," he says, drumming his fingers on the glass.

I take my own car and follow him to a pot bar called El Gaucho, where in the welcoming haze the conversation revolves mostly around work. And work—inevitably for me and reluctantly for Piper—leads to Ryan.

"I just don't know why it happened, though."

"Sometimes these things just happen, Boots."

"I mean I watched the playbacks. I saw the hit. But I can't help but feel that if I'd been with him instead of in that fucking tree, I could've saved him."

"You couldn't have. Know how I know? Because *I* was there. And *I* saw it happen. And if *I*, the magnificent Piper Pernfors, couldn't save him, then certainly mere mortal Boots McHenry couldn't have either."

"Bitch."

He grins. "But seriously, if it was doable I would've done it. Ryan's a good guy or whatever but I would've done it for you. Heck, I *did* do it. The week before. I saved the guy's ass, remember? So, really, I bought you one extra week with him, which I think is a pretty big deal."

"Never thought of it that way."

"Well you should. Because if you do you'll see you owe me."

"I owe you, huh? What do I owe you, exactly?"

He laughs. "I take sexual favors and all major credit cards."

From El Gaucho we go to a brightly-lit IHOP where over big plates of pancakes we talk about movies, then premium cable, then actors, then sex scenes, then what was the craziest place we've done it since we were last together. And when he starts being lewd with his sausage I know it's getting close to the moment where I'll need to step on the brakes.

"You know, Piper, if you hadn't cheated on me so many times we could've had a lot of fun together," I say, wistfully because of the pot.

"We did have fun together, B."

"Yeah, right." I pick up my fork and resume eating.

"Am I wrong?" he prods.

"I mean a maintainable fun, Piper. A fun that didn't end the way it finally ended."

"I told you you could join the three of us," he laughs. But when I don't reply he frowns and whispers, more seriously, "I'm older now."

"And your looks aren't what they used to be," I say. It's dumb and low and isn't even true—if anything, he's hotter—but I want to hurt him so I go for the easy hurt.

What I really want to do is to keep him from asking me to go home with him. But it doesn't work, and when the bill is paid and he finally asks, I find myself not saying no.

And by the time I really realize what's going on, I'm shoeless on his couch and he has his hand under my shirt, swirling his thumb in the hair around my belly-button, the way he used to do. He's got a two-story condo in a highrise on Thebes Harbor—I'm looking through the giant windows at the boat-dotted ocean rendered in dark pastels. The whole thing's like a postcard. Kissing him feels familiar and I'm in the mood for something comfortable. If Ryan's gone, why not just take the runner up?

"I've missed this so bad," he whispers.

Where my hand lies in his lap I can feel the cock I've sucked countless times. I slip my hand down the front of his pants and feel its familiar hardness between my fingers, get a slippery smear of pre-cum across my palm.

He's taken off his shirt and is using the force of his kiss to push me back against the arm of the couch, while tugging off my shirt too.

"I knew we'd never lose the chemistry," he says.

He pulls my hand out of his pants and brings it to his mouth, licks his pre-cum off my palm, sucks my fingers one by one. Then he kisses up along my arm and lets my hand fall against his cheek and along his throat and down along his chest.

And it's his chest hair that makes me realize that for all the familiarity, this isn't three years ago—that time has passed and lives have been lived. When I was first with Piper he was eighteen, his chest still naturally smooth; but since we broke up his body has filled out and his chest hair has filled in along with it. In the space between that smooth chest and this one, was Ryan and my entire time with Ryan. And I think of Ryan on the helicopter, his words obscured. What was he trying to tell me? What am I about to do? I'm a young man and I won't be able to go five years without sex. Ryan will understand that. But at the end of the five years, do I really want to tell him that within days of his exile, I ran back into the arms of my ex-boyfriend, Piper Pernfors?

Piper is kissing around my belly button while rubbing my cock through my underwear. I desperately want the blowjob I know is only seconds away, but if it goes that far I won't be able to stop it from going all the way. This is my last chance. It's either the brakes or the accelerator.

For better or worse, I choose the brakes. Then I

choose the accelerator as I floor-it out of Piper's underground garage. Then I choose the brakes again when I squeal into the back of a Foodmart parking lot to relieve a pair of balls that are ten shades of blue. Four strokes and I'm shooting into a coffee cup that's been in my car for a week. It isn't as cozy as Piper's ass would've been, and my jizz sloshing around with a quarter inch of stale French vanilla makes for a funny-smelling ride home, but it's a story I'll feel OK telling Ryan when the time comes. It's a story Ryan will like.

Chapter 5

Last practice before the game against the Vigilantes. Piper and I mostly ignore each other. It goes without saying he wasn't thrilled to be ditched on his couch with his shirt off and his dick out.

Nobody notices our cold war, though, because Marius Tumble is the talk of the Warriors today. Guy's got moves. It's hard for me to get too excited when he's wearing Ryan's number, but when I see him somersault off the hood of the tractor trailer, dive over a barrel, and put a bull's-eye right on Rufus Wong's plucked unibrow (technically illegal but too impressive for anyone to care), all in one unbelievable motion, I can't help but feel a renewed craving for the Splatter Cup. Maybe Skullcrusher was right: I loved this game before I met Ryan; maybe I can love it again. Maybe I just have to find the passion.

Maybe, but I don't get much chance to look.

We lose the game against the Vigilantes. Actually, it's a draw—plenty of paint is exchanged but no one on either side is hit by any, and we run out the two-hour clock. But a draw is definitely a loss when it means the Vigilantes are going to the Cup and we aren't. It's them over us because we had a simu-death this season and they haven't.

In a way, I'm glad Ryan's exile has now definitively cost the Warriors something. His absence can't be swept under any rugs just by bumping Marius Tumble up from second string, because in the end we couldn't get to the Cup without him.

"Next season, right McHenry?" Clemente Santiago says, clapping me on the back as we head to the locker room for a round of post-season interviews. "We'll have it going *on*."

What are the things I do when that last game's just a memory? Well, I don't shoot any commercials or go on any talk shows—not that I have any choice, since all offers and endorsement deals evaporated the moment we lost. What I do is I make use of the Internet and consume enough 3D porn to make the studios blush, because sex makes me forget that I'm lonely. I watch a lot of TV too, but carefully, because for the first few days it's wall-to-wall coverage of the Cup—which in terms of public consciousness gives the old Super Bowls a run for their money. I sit on the balcony and read (you know you're in a tough place in your life when you decide now's a good time to start *Moby Dick*). I do push-ups and sit-ups and myriad other exercises because I know that if I lose my body I'll be even more depressed—I do them until sweat stings my eyeballs. I soak my muscles in hours-long baths. I order take-out. I sleep.

The thread that connects these post-season activities is that I do them all in my bedroom. I have fourteen other rooms but, like, why bother? I don't want to deal with it. I don't want to deal with *outside*.

But OK, I'm grumpy, I'm sad, I'm lonely—I'm not crazy, I'm not completely losing my shit. So when I realize it's been almost a week, I shave, throw on some jeans and a t-shirt, and, after hesitating a second, grab the keys to Ryan's old red Mustang.

Just a drive. At first just a drive. But when the top's down and the warm evening wind is playing a percussive symphony through my t-shirt I start to feel a blossom of something that, if I'm really careful, I might be able to nurture into something resembling OK. So I drive for hours. I drive and drive without stopping, up the coast practically to Oregon and then back down. And all that driving has made me thirsty.

So when I come upon a particular bar on the far side of Thebes from the stadium—a place where Warriors sometimes retreat to get smashed, a place where nobody gives a shit about paintball and the TVs are always tuned to Mixed Martial Arts Club (MMAC) fights—I pull in and park. The bar has the curious name of Yon's Kneecaps, but we Warriors usually just call it *the place where no one gets in your face about paintball*.

I head inside and, sure enough, the TV over the bar is showing two BILFs (brutes I'd like to fuck) going at it in a steel cage. I know a bit about mixed martial arts because Ryan's baby brother Colby was the Junior MMAC champ last year (the same year Ryan himself won the Splatter Cup—a good one for the Brothers Kroft).

Yon's is full of rugged types shooting the shit. Lots of leather, lots of tattoos, lots of cursing.

"What'll I get you, McHenry?" the barkeep asks as I'm grabbing a stool at the end of the bar. I tell him a Sam Adams. He uncaps a bottle for me and pushes it across the scratched wood on a black napkin.

I'm nursing the Sam, watching the BILFs sweat on each other, when a peanut out of nowhere pegs the tip of my nose. I look up and then over just as Clemente Santiago is zinging another one at me from the far end of the bar. I try to dodge this one and it gets my ear.

"Shitty reflexes for a sniper," he shouts.

"Snipe it up your fat ass, Santiago," I call, getting up with my beer to go sit by him.

He's wearing a gray suit-vest over a white v-neck tee. He flicks a peanut off the stool beside his and pulls it out for me. "You've emerged?"

"It's an experiment. Don't want to overdo it. I'll probably head back to the cave soon. How you been?"

"For a guy with no endorsement deals?"

"Companies are fickle bitches, aren't they?"

"Truth."

"They only want us when we're winners."

"Fickle bitches is right. Under Armour was like, *Adios!*"

"Bummer. It's not my top concern though, lately. Endorsement deals don't fill a house."

"Right," he says. "I know. Sorry."

"Don't sweat it." I take a sip of my beer.

Onscreen BILF #2, pinned beneath and entwined throughout BILF #1, is frantically tapping #1's thigh (the only place he can reach) to signal surrender. BILF #1 looks almost disappointed that he's won without being able to snap anything. I once saw Ryan's brother dislocate the shoulder of a particularly stubborn jock who just would *not* tap out.

Clemente takes a swig from the bottle of hard cider in front of him. "Had my money on the other guy."

"You made a bet?"

"Nah. Just saying."

"That cider good? You're always drinking that stuff."

He holds up the bottle, spins it around, lets it catch the neon light from the signs above the bar. "Yeah. Can't get enough."

"You paid to say that?"

He laughs. "If I was I wouldn't be anymore. Nah. Just got a boner for it for some reason. I like the taste."

"You're surly tonight."

"*Surly.* I like that. Nah. This is my rough-n-tumble bar persona. All these guys." He leans closer to me. "They make me nervous but I like them."

"Yeah. These toughsters."

We're quiet for a while. On the TV parts of the earlier fight are being shown again in slow motion while men in suits commentate.

"Maybe you should get a dog," he says. "Keep you company."

"Maybe."

"What's the worst change?"

"About living alone?"

He nods.

"Lots of things. I don't know. Sleeping alone. Not being touched. Sex or lack thereof."

"Ah, you must be getting to that point where you want to stick your dick into anything that moves. When's that happen, second week after splitsville, I guess?"

"Splitsville. God, I don't even know if it *is* splitsville. We never talked about how we would handle exile. I don't know jack shit about anything—that's another bad change." I consider whether to tell him about it, then do: "I almost nailed Piper last week."

"Pernfors? No way."

"The one and only."

"Wow."

"Why *wow*?"

"Guess I always think *wow* when I hear about two dudes going at it. Part of me's always surprised people actually do that on a regular basis."

"OK."

"I don't mean it bad or anything."

"I know."

"Just like how I'm always surprised there are actually rocket scientists."

I laugh. "Honestly, it's not so different from these MMAC fights, except that there's jizz at the end."

He laughs, dribbling cider out of his mouth and wiping it away. "So go on. You almost nailed him?"

I shrug. "We hung out after practice and went back to his condo. We were messing around in his living room. Got to the point where messing around was going to turn into sex, and I didn't want to go there. You know our history."

"Sure, you guys were all married and stuff."

"We weren't *married*."

He smirks. "Then why not just go for it? Get touched. Seems safe."

"I *wanted* to. Well, I wanted sex, just not with Piper. Not with my *ex*. I feel like it would hurt Ryan's feelings. I don't want to do that even if he'd never know about it."

"You're a victim of your morality, McHenry."

"Bite me."

He laughs, swigs some cider. "You can't be planning on going five years without getting laid." He's incredulous.

"That's not realistic. No."

"So at least you still have your sanity." Another swig.

"What fucking sucks the most about this simu-death thing is that— I mean, are Ryan and I splitsville or what? Are we on hiatus? Should I be dating other guys?

Potentially *falling in love* with other guys? I know we should've discussed this beforehand but we never did. Isn't that crazy? We thought we were invincible or something. So I'm in a holding pattern. And for the foreseeable future I don't want to do anything that Ryan wouldn't think was kind of awesome."

"Until?"

"Until—I don't know—enough time passes that I don't care anymore? God that sounds so horrible." I take a long swig of beer.

"And sleeping with someone you had a long relationship with would not be awesome to Ryan."

"Exactly."

"So you turned him down."

"Piper? Eventually. We were pretty far into it before I bailed, though."

"Ouch."

"The poor bastard. We were just about naked. I think he thought I was joking at first."

"You're a cocktease, McHenry." He takes a slurp.

"Wasn't easy, Santiago. I had to jerk off in a Foodmart parking lot just to make sure I wouldn't turn around and go back."

"What a perv." He smacks my shoulder. "So you just want to get your rocks off, basically. Easy peasy."

"You make it sound like I'm trolling around for it. But I guess it would clear my head if it happened, for sure."

"Then why not just go online or whatever?" he says. "Arrange a hookup."

"Yuck, everyone knows me. There's so much baggage with that. The whole *fuck a pro paintballer* thing. Nah."

"I love that baggage. I've gotten so many chicks with that baggage."

"You like the fans more than I do."

He shrugs. "OK, so if not a stranger, then someone you know. A friend with momentary benefits. Piper's out. How about Rufus? Rufus wouldn't turn down a fling."

"Ugh, not Rufus. That's gross."

He nods. "Yeah, you'd probably end up in the tabloids."

"Plus, he's not my favorite person these days."

"Right, you blame him for Ryan."

I nod.

"So then you're looking for a peer who's not Piper or Rufus. Thought about the new guy? Does he swing homo?"

"Clemente, you're lousy at this," I laugh. "Marius is Ryan's replacement. Think about that for a sec."

"Oh god, yeah. Awkward symbolism. People would think you have a fetish for the number nine."

I laugh. "I don't want any emotional baggage. I don't want anyone asking me to autograph their cock. I don't want a relationship. Just a roll in the hay to clear my head. That would be nice."

"Right. Well."

"So who to ask...." I drum my fingers on the bar, flick a peanut.

"Right. Who to ask...." He takes a sip of cider.

"Yeah, who to ask."

"Right...."

I laugh. "There's really only one other guy on the team I'm really friendly with." I feel something swirl in my gut as I watch his lips freeze on the bottle.

"Yeah," he says, putting down his cider, "I was just thinking that."

"Oh yeah?"

He looks at me kind of sideways, a quick glance.

"He's straight, though, McHenry."

I laugh. "That's why he'd be *perfect*. No strings whatsoever. One and done."

"What are you saying?"

"Why, what are *you* saying?"

"I just want to be sure I—"

"Sure of what?"

This has already gone on longer than I know what to do with.

He looks away from me across the bar. "Uh." He smooths his mustache with his thumb and index finger, then roughs it up again. "Am I being propositioned?"

I look at him, then drop my eyes and take a quick sip of beer. Basically I crumble. "Sorry, Santiago, that was stupid of me. I was only playing."

"No, no," he says, opening his hand on the bar in a forgiving gesture. "It's fine to *ask*. Don't worry about it."

"I should've known you wouldn't want to."

There's a long pause. I don't know whether he's thinking or watching TV or flat-out ignoring me.

"I haven't said I *won't*, McHenry," he says finally. The entire bar seems to fall silent but of course it's just my imagination. "But I'll need a few more drinks before there's any chance of me hopping into bed with *your* sweaty ass."

I laugh, tingling, consumed, for the first time in a week, with something other than Ryan. Clemente picks up his empty bottle and slams it down on the bar, sends it skidding past the bartender.

"Barkeep," he says, "give me enough so's I can do something crazy."

Chapter 6

When he seems to have a decent buzz going but not much more, Clemente announces he's ready to get this show on the road. This is a surprise. I figured he would keep drinking until he passed out, or at least until I felt like sleeping with him would be taking advantage.

"You drive," he says, "I can't," and as we step out into the night he tosses me the heavy keys to his motorcycle. It's an old-fashioned 1970s Honda, all clean lines and chrome, refitted with a fancy electric engine. Hot bike. He gets on behind me and puts his hands on my hips, his fingers near what's rapidly becoming a real throbber.

"Think in all that back and forth I forgot what I actually agreed to here," he laughs.

"Me too."

"Just so there's no disappointment, McHenry, I'll do the best I can for you, but I don't know how much Little Clemmy's going to cooperate with this."

"No pressure," I say, and I kick-start the bike. "Whatever happens is just for fun."

Since the rest of my cavernous house is as dark and vacant as ever, I bring Clemente straight to the sanctuary of my bedroom. You might think he'd see this as a cheap ploy to get him near my bed as quickly as possible, but when he walks into my room he says, "*Brrr*, is it me or did it feel almost haunted out there?"

He looks around. There's a pizza box on the floor, a scattering of fan-mail (sympathy cards, mostly) on the bureau, the pile of dumbbells I carried up from the gym.

"Kind of thought you were kidding about living in your bedroom," he says.

"Dead serious," I say, dropping his keys on a table by the couch. "Want anything to drink or anything?"

"Glass of water? Bike dries me out."

I go down to the kitchen to get it. As I stand filling the glass, I wonder if he'll be naked when I get back. Naked and maybe lying on my bed, big Latin cock at attention, ready to plunge into whichever of my orifices I offer up first. That's assuming he can get his big cock (or *Little Clemmy*, as he called it) up at all. Hopefully this'll be fun but it occurs to me that sleeping with a straight guy is a self-esteem minefield. I could primp and preen for hours and none of it would matter if the sight of a schlong stops him cold. I need to remember not to take it personally if he can't get anything going.

With water sloshing out of the glass and dripping off my knuckles, I take the big winding staircase three steps at a time, as much to escape the rest of the house as to return to my waiting teammate.

"My cave," I sigh as I shut the door.

He laughs. He isn't naked, though he's slipped off his Converse and is sitting on the couch opposite the bed, barefoot in his great jeans and white v-neck with vest. He has one leg folded under his butt and is bouncing the other foot gently in the air. He holds out his hand for the glass and says thanks.

I sit down beside him, close but not *let's fuck now* close, not even *let's kiss now* close, and rest my arm on the back of the couch, just where it can lightly touch his shoulders. With my thumb I stroke the back of his neck. As his muscles tense he smiles bashfully and gulps water. The glass is empty in seconds but he holds it near his belly.

"How upset were you that we didn't go to the Cup?" I ask.

He bounces his bouncing foot, stretches it out, lets it

bounce again; there are fine black hairs across the top of it.

"Disappointed," he says, "but not exactly *upset*. It's a money thing with me. I like winning just fine, but I don't exactly need the rush of victory to be happy—I'm a pretty secure guy. And I've never had the—should I say *love?*—the basic love of playing you seem to have. Or had." He rubs some of the condensation off the glass. "Feel mad in the way I used to feel when I worked at the pizza shop and got turned down for a raise. Now the difference is just between whether I can buy ten pizza shops or a thousand. No big deal."

"I get that."

"You?"

I'm still stroking his hairline but his neck has relaxed under my thumb. "Cup or no Cup, I'd still be coming home alone. Guess winning would've been a nice distraction, though."

"Yeah."

"But I feel distracted now, so that's cool."

He laughs. "Glad to be of service, etc."

There's a long pause. I notice a few curls of black chest hair springing from the depths of his neckline, and near his collar bone is the tip of the tail of his scorpion. Even though I've seen him shirtless dozens of times, seeing him shirtless tonight will somehow be a discovery. I'm still not sure he's really going to show me.

"Done with this?" I say, offering to take the water glass.

He lets it go, but bashfully, as though he's giving up a security blanket. Because he's been holding it near his crotch, his crotch seems suddenly revealed. With my heart pounding I reach out slowly and touch him there, press the stiff metal teeth of his fly, feel him flaccid beneath the denim. He lowers his eyes; I'm not sure whether he's embarrassed by his softness or whether he's hoping he stays that way to prove a point.

"Look at me," he says quietly, eyes still lowered, and I know now he's embarrassed, "supposed to be Mr. Big Man, Mr. Super Jock, and I can feel my face turning pinker than a little girl's." He looks at me and shrugs.

"We don't have to do anything," I say. "We could play video games."

"Maybe, but I think— I'm OK. Let's see."

I'm about to reach for his crotch again but instead I scoot closer so our shoulders are touching and slip my hand around his upper thigh. I kind of want to rest my head on his shoulder but, less romantically, I slide down and rest it against his armpit. It's like we're at the movies.

"I should let you drive Ryan's Mustang some time. It's fun. I was out cruising before I stopped at Yon's."

"That baby running electric or hydrogen?"

"All hydrogen," I say.

"Power, yum." He laughs.

"Outside the city, along the coast— I just opened it up. Felt so nice."

"Yeah. Bet so."

As I've been kneading his upper thigh his cock has slowly filled the crotch of his jeans. It's a relief. Physically, at least, he'll be able to do what I'm hoping for. But I feel like I'm coercing him, sweet-talking him— *I shall distract you with cars while I casually give you an erection*— and that isn't how I want this to go. I don't want him to be embarrassed afterward. Maybe I shouldn't have brought up the Mustang; there's already too much Ryan in the air, too much sexual mourning. I don't know why Clemente's here, but he's here. He deserves to have fun.

"Hold on," I tell him, thinking of a way to lighten

things up.

"OK." He sits up straighter, glances down at his pants as if realizing for the first time that he's hard.

I hunt around for something I can use for what I have in mind — anything tubular — and settle on the TV remote. I hold it by the bottom and aim the other end at my mouth.

"My name is Boots McHenry, and I'm coming to you live live live from the exotic location of my own bedroom. I'm here with Clemente Santiago, star sniper of the Theban Warriors."

"What are you doing?"

"You all know Santiago, but here, we'll put his stats up on the screen." I hold my open hand beside his face to mimic a computer-generated stat orb. "Six feet of pure power, ladies and gentlemen." I lean closer to Clemente so we can share the mic. "Tonight's the night, folks. The Warriors' star sniper is on the precipice of his first sexual encounter with a man! Santiago, how are you feeling going into this? Are you pumped?"

"Are you nuts?"

"Just play along."

He rolls his eyes — and grins. "Uh. Feeling pumped, McHenry. Sure. Feeling pumped."

"Feeling ready?"

"Got a little buzz going, which is nice. Got a little bit of a boner, it seems, so that's encouraging."

I give his boner a squeeze through his jeans. "Yes, he does have a boner, folks. So, Clemente — "

"Do you?"

" — Do I what?"

He lowers his eyes to my crotch. "You know."

"*Pfft*, since Yon's, dude."

"Oh." He purses his lips, impressed, maybe pleased with his powers.

"Getting back on track— Clemente, is this something you've been training for? Is experimenting with a dude a longtime goal of yours? What kind of prep have you done to get in shape for tonight's event?"

"Hasn't been a goal, McHenry, nope. Can't say it's been a goal. I'm flying blind. But I think so far the pre-game's going OK, so, you know, God willing...." He raises his hand ceilingward.

I give his erection another squeeze. "So, ladies and gentlemen, he's feeling pretty hard under his fashionable jeans. Think it might be time to ditch them and see what's underneath?" Though I've seen his dick almost as many times as I've seen him shirtless, I've never once seen it hard. And I'm eager to change that. "Clemente, what do you think?"

A pause. He's not sure. His cheeks flush. He shrugs. And then: "We can try."

"What was that?" I push the mic closer, cup my free hand around my ear.

"Uh. I say we lose the jeans!"

It's as if his words have lit a zooming fuse that can only end in an explosion of nudity. He jumps up, bare feet plunging into the leather cushions, and tugs at his belt and fly. Then he pushes his jeans and his white square-cut briefs down to his knees in one sudden swoop. His hard cock bounces away from his treasure trail like a spronging diving-board and aims itself at me. I see him look from his cock to his bunched jeans, as though in disbelief that he's actually just done this. Then he sits down somewhat demurely on the arm of the couch, fuzzy knees together and cock pointing up from between his thighs.

I struggle to find my voice.

"Ladies and— Ladies and gentlemen, we're witnessing Clemente Santiago's dick now, and it's pretty much perfect. I'll put its stats up on the screen." Without taking my eyes off it I wave my hand around beside his face somewhere and then drop it to his knee. "It begins with, really, the cutest treasure trail I've seen in a long time. And the trail gathers into, really, the uh, nicest-looking bush anyone who's ever undressed a man could hope to find. Clemente, do you have anything to add?"

"Just sort of taking it slow, Boots."

"He's, uh— I guess I should describe the shaft, ladies and gentlemen. It's nice and thick and long and smooth, not all veiny like some of the ones you see. It's tan brown with a darker seam running up the underside. And, uh." This can't really be happening, can it? But somehow it is. "Really it's the head of this dick that's the miracle, ladies and gentlemen. Clemente, has this feature earned you a lot of praise?"

"It's been mentioned once or twice, Boots." And then, believe it or not, he salutes!

"It really is the pinkest, prettiest cockhead this humble reporter has ever seen." His dark foreskin seems to be bowing away from the head as if offering me a gift. "Soft looking and it looks so sweet too, like it's made out of bubble gum. Clemente, I really would like to give our audience the fullest picture possible. Would you mind if I—?" I wiggle my tongue.

"I think— Heh." He slaps his hand over his eyes. "That might be a prudent course of action."

"Here, you hold on to this," I say, offering up the mic, which he takes.

He's been sitting on the arm of the couch with his knees touching. His jeans and underwear are still bunched around his calves and I have to pull them off before I can open his legs and shimmy closer to his erection. Before I do, though, I take off my shirt so I'll be able to feel his hairy thighs against my ribs. His legs are just *everywhere*, thighs thick and hard when I clamp down on them with my arms.

He doesn't move as I approach.

I start at the base of his cock, near the ticklish balls, and work my tongue up along the dark seam, lapping up a string of sweet, sticky pre-cum that's on its way down. I run my tongue around the pinkness at the top, savoring it for as long as I can stand, and then with a hungry grunt I sink the whole thing deep into my mouth. It hits the back of my throat and I bury my nose in his dark hair and inhale as best I can this new scent of other man, of my teammate Santiago. This is my first time with another guy since meeting Ryan and I marvel at how something so practiced can feel so new and exciting because of nothing more than a different scent.

"That is— That is—" He's talking into the remote. I peer up and see his eyes closed and a dopey grin on his face. "That is what we call a blowjob, McHenry. That is, holy moly, that is definitely a— Wow."

With one hand I cup the tight sack of his balls and stroke them with my thumb. With the other I squeeze the base of his cock while I work the head with my tongue. Pre-cum is sticky salty-sweet on my lips.

"Ladies and gentlemen," he continues, "McHenry's really showing a mastery of proficiency at working with the balls. This is, uh, this is something that can sometimes go overlooked but Jesus."

I deep-throat him again so I'll have my hands free to unbutton my own jeans. I sink one hand into my boxers and feel my pubic hair slick with what must be a gallon of pre-cum. I wiggle out of my jeans and get them down around my knees.

Clemente starts narrating again, with a wary voice as though he's just noticed a hornet in his car: "The audience should be made aware that another penis has entered the field. And it's big and looks really hard and, uh— Now there are two penises here and it can safely be said that this—that this has definitely started to become very manly, with two penises here. It can be said that Clemente Santiago's first experience with another guy is very much underway. Oh man."

I pull his boner out of my throat. "Two penises OK?"

"Two penises, hey, whatever, I'm rolling with this. Keep on doing what you're doing and I'll roll with this till the *cows* come home."

I grin and resume sucking him. I smooth a palm-full of pre-cum along my own shaft and give it a few tugs, but not too hard. I wouldn't want to hit the point of no return by mistake.

Suddenly there's a squeak I take at first for microphone feedback and Clemente's cock yanks out of my mouth, pulling a gooey string of pre-cum and spit along with it. His thighs pound painfully up into my armpits. The ass-on-leather squeak rings again as he loses more traction on the arm of the couch. He's grabbing at the back cushion trying to hold himself up. My upper body keeps him from fully backflipping heels over head, but in a kind of slow-mo fall he ends up hanging upside-down against the side of the couch. I kneel up to peer over him. His head is bent at an uncomfortable-looking angle against the hardwood floor, but he's smiling. And he's still holding the mic. "Wipeout," he says into it, and laughs.

"Shit, Clemente. You OK?"

"Just fine." His heels are pointed ceilingward behind me. I secure his thighs with my armpits to begin letting him down slow, but suddenly I don't want him to move any farther: Here before me is a beautiful taint and two finely-haired ass cheeks that, if parted, will reveal everything Clemente Santiago can ever show me.

"I promise you," I say as I lower my face toward him, "you're going to want to stay in that position for a little longer."

"What're you—?"

But I'm not hearing him. When I push apart his firm cheeks I find a wrinkled pink circle that looks designed as singularly for pleasure as a man's nipples, as though it's never been used for anything else. I let a pool of spit gather on my tongue and then dribble it, *plop plop*, onto the only smooth place in a landscape dappled with black fuzz. When the pinkness glistens with my spit I tickle it with my tongue, gently at first and then more forcefully pressing into the smooth folds.

"Holy spaceman, ladies and gentlemen!" Clemente gasps amid a series of giggles. I assume he's still speaking into the mic. "What is *that*?"

"Ith a wimhob," I mumble, slapping with my tongue while rubbing my nose up and down his smooth taint. I know it's beyond precious to describe the taste of Clemente's asshole as something I'd squeeze out of a little plastic bear, but that's what it makes me think of: the musky tang of honey. I'm sure the mesmerizing scent alone could give me a hands-free orgasm.

"Fucking miracle," he says with a gasp, and gasps again when I squeeze his cock, which it occurs to me I've been neglecting.

I'd be content to continue eating him for hours but I can tell from the tension building in his legs that this isn't the right position to do it in. When his ass is slick with my spit and I finally come up for air, I tell him, "Letting you down now, OK?"

Gently I lower him until his tailbone touches the floor; his calves are still across the arm of the couch. I almost kiss the bottom of his foot but that seems like too much. I look down between his legs at the half-naked

Clemente Santiago, who in addition to his t-shirt and vest wears a dazed smile and a lot of my spit. He moves the mic to his lips, just habit by now or maybe some kind of security blanket, and says, "That was nice. And now?"

"Well, ladies and gentlemen, now we're going to kick things up a notch. We're going to find out what Theban Warrior Clemente Santiago is really made of."

I tug my jeans the rest of the way off and walk over to the big silvery bed, my erection bouncing in front of me. I lie down on my back and lean up on my elbows. He's standing near the couch, looking all the more naked, somehow, because he's dressed from the waist up. He's twisting the remote in a way that hints he might be going back into bashful mode.

But then he drops it on the couch, pulls off his vest and shirt, and stands up straighter, shoulders back and chest puffing out, colorful scorpion growing as he inhales. Something has changed in his mind — I don't know what or why but I'm glad — and he's going to roll with this. Suavely he walks across the room, a pro-athlete rooster, his cock leading the way. He reaches the edge of the bed and without breaking stride steps up onto the mattress and towers above me, head nearly grazing the ceiling mirror. He has nice plump muscles, not the chiseled, angular things you see on some guys; Clemente's are soft, natural. As he steps around to keep his balance on the pillow-top his pecs jiggle just slightly in a way that makes me want to, I don't know, do good things for the world.

"Killer view," I say, looking up at him, at the muscles of his thighs and the soft grooves of his abs. He has an appendix scar. I'm not sure what'll happen now — or if he has any idea either. I hold my hand up to him but instead of taking it he kneels down beside me, and with a what-the-fuck smirk lies down on top of me. Our cocks touch for the first time. I can feel his feet on mine. I raise a knee between his legs, feel his balls slide along my thigh. I look into his eyes — his face is three inches from mine — and smirk.

"Shut up," he laughs. "I'm doing my best here." His breath smells of hard cider. "I'm going to try something."

His mustache whisks like a brush against my nose and upper lip and then he kisses me. It's tense at first but he loosens up when we start rubbing our tongues together. I clasp my hands against his smooth back and work my pelvis against his, rubbing our dicks together in big slow hairy circles. His pecs are pressing so hard against mine that I might have the same scorpion tattoo by the time we're done. His weight feels good on me. I've always loved this, what silly people disregard as humping but what aficionados call *frottage*—this feeling a guy over every inch of me, forehead to toes.

"How am I doing," he says during a pause, "with everything?"

"So far Clemente Santiago definitely has what it takes."

He drops his head and presses his forehead into the mattress above my shoulder. I can hear him laugh, and he's still rubbing his crotch against mine in a gentle, absentminded rhythm an old high school boyfriend of mine called *microhumping*.

"What's funny?" I ask.

"Dudes doing this," he says. "Inherently funny."

"Wait'll we start to fuck, Clemente. It's comedy gold."

He lifts his head off the mattress and looks at me. "Fuck?"

"Since this is a one-and-done, I want my money's worth."

He smirks, but I can tell he's still not sure.

"Don't worry," I add, "you're pitching."

"OK." Then he laughs. "*Whew.*"

"You're so straight it's painful."

"Fuck you."

We both laugh and, lifting his pelvis up off mine, he punches me in the dick with his dick.

Once the prospect of fucking has been introduced (and the straightboy has been reassured that he'll be the top) everything else pales in comparison. He's only lying on top of me for another few seconds before I push him off and scramble for the lube.

"Pistol Oil?" he says, smirking at the label on the bottle I've given him. "Do all dude-lubes have cool names like this?"

"Use plenty," I say, lying down on my back. "It's been a while for me."

"We should be shooting an ad for this," he says, crawling over one of my legs so he can kneel between them. He pops the cap and squeezes lube on his fingers. "Maybe we can get an endorsement deal. *When the Theban Warriors fuck each other, they always choose Pistol Oil brand personal lubricant.*"

I laugh. "Maybe! Let's see how good you are first."

"You won't be complaining, McHenry."

"Oohhh, he's a tough guy!"

"Oooohhhh!"

"Oooohhhhh!"

"Ooooohhhhhh!" He's laughing. He's actually having fun.

I swing my legs up over his shoulders, one calf on top of his scorpion. With fingers that seem suddenly nervous he lubes my ass and then starts covering his dick.

"Don't worry," I tell him, "this is the easy part."

"My big secret is that sometimes I get performance anxiety and lose the boner."

It's sweet that he's told me. "*Pfft.* The game's over. This is your victory lap now."

"My victory lap, eh?"

"Shut up and fuck me, Santiago."

He grins. "That's what they all say." And his damn face is too far away for me to kiss, or smack.

He rocks side to side on his knees, finding leverage on the pillow-top, adjusting my calves on his shoulders. For a second he strokes my inner thigh with his thumb and seems amused, but not quite put off, by the hair. He feels for my hole with his finger and guides his dick past my balls to the spot. It takes us a minute but when things line up right and he starts to push that pink cockhead into me I can feel my pulse pounding in the tight skin around it. Then, not realizing he's going too fast, he pushes the rest of the way into me, filling me to his balls in one stroke. From my face and the hand I press to his belly he knows to slow down, and he does. But after a few minutes and two more applications of lube we've got a killer rhythm going.

And we're sweating like mad.

I can feel his wet pubes tickling my balls, love the steady slapping of his groin against my ass, am in awe of the sweat beading on his brown chest and belly and shoulders. Crazy how wet this suddenly has become — how sopping, dripping wet.

"Wow," he gasps between thrusts. "Good for you?"

"Best. Don't stop."

I love that the wetness makes it all the more intense, erotic, dirty. How the wetness makes it truly sex, truly *fucking*. The droplets of sweat that are falling from his hair and nose and chin and pattering my chest like a prelude to sperm. The lubey hands with which he's clutching my thighs almost tight enough to hurt. It's not something that could be dashed off in a broom closet or an airport bathroom. Not something tidy or utilitarian. I wanted a distraction and propositioned the guy I thought could make it the most simple and the most casual but I never expected to truly fuck, beyond the cliché word, that word people throw around to mean almost anything, but to truly, epically *fuck*.

"I am fucking this dude," Clemente yells, genuinely *yells*, pounding away at me with bravado, knees buried deep in the mattress. "I am fucking the bejeesus out of this dude!"

I don't know whether he's marveling at the experience or simply continuing to narrate for the imaginary mic he left on the couch.

With a sound that startles us both the silk sheet that has been stretched too tight between his knees shreds and I tell him, as he gapes down with raised eyebrows, "It's fine. Don't stop. You're hitting my spot."

"Your spot?"

"You're nailing it." My words feel all slurred in my mouth, as though my voice is half spit. Most of my brain is in sensory overload.

I can feel his pink cockhead slamming deep inside me, can taste his sweat on my lips. I can smell his honey-sweet ass on my face, too, and I only wish there was some miraculous karma sutra position that would let me continue eating it while he pounds me to smithereens. In my own hand my cock feels ready to burst.

"I'm getting close," I tell him, gasping. I try to think of paintball.

"Me too!" He runs his forearm over his face and then *fwaps* a line of sweat at the sheets. "When I come where do you want me to come?"

You don't look nearly turned-on enough to come, straightboy, I think sarcastically, but I'm being pounded way too hard for sarcasm.

He looks down at me and adds, "It's gonna be buckets!"

"Oh my god. Wherever you want. In me. On me. Anywhere."

"I'm gonna come, McHenry. I'm gonna come. We're going to have had sex!"

The attention paid to all this talking has brought us both away from the precipice, though, and for that we're awarded another glorious minute or two. He spends it drilling me hard, leaning into me and pushing my right leg down so my shin almost touches my face. With my free hand I rub my palm down his chest, sending streams of sweat gliding across his abs. Then he pushes my hand away from my cock and seizes it and almost at the same time pulls out of me and seizes his own. A couple of strokes and we're both gushing in shuddering, yelping unison like a pair of squealing pigs. The bed slams the wall, the sheet rips even further. Tendons stand out on his neck, his teeth clench, bubbles of spit froth on his lips. And when it's over I'm drenched in the new hot wetness of our mixing-together jizz.

"Holy," he says, dropping his head forward when he's done shuddering. Sweat snaps out of his hair and hits my face; I touch my tongue to my lips. Then my tired legs slide off his shoulders and along his wet arms. "Holy mother of god." He looks down in apparent surprise at the streaky white mess we've made together on my abs and chest.

Then he releases my cock, which until now he was squeezing, and rolls away from me and hits the bed on his side, long arms and legs clattering across the mattress like a drunk falling out of a moving car. For a minute or two our heavy breathing is the only sound in the room. Then he sighs and says, "Gee whiz."

I laugh. "Thank you for that."

"No sweat." Then he laughs and flicks his fingers at me. "Well, some sweat."

I remember our game. Holding up an invisible microphone, I say, "Well ladies and gentlemen, the deed is done. Number 6 of the Theban Warriors, Boots McHenry, and #4 of the Warriors, Clemente Santiago, have just completed an event that before this evening neither one saw coming. Let's go to Santiago for some final words before the team hits the showers." I hold the mic over to Clemente. His hair is sticking up, wet and slick as though he's just stumbled through a carwash.

"Well, McHenry, going into tonight I'm not sure I knew what to expect. I was glad to be able to help a fellow Warrior take his mind off some things, but to be honest I assumed I'd have to do a lot of imagining to get through it. But then you opened that mouth of yours, and uh— I mean the first quarter was great, but then right before halftime you unleashed the rimjob and it was, it was—"

"A miracle, I believe, was the word you used."

"A miracle! Sure. Then, you know, halftime, wasn't sure again. But hey, I rolled with it, and in the end I guess I actually had fun."

"Me too."

"Right on."

He reaches out with a jizzy fist and I bump mine against it.

We don't shower together. I'd like to, but I don't suggest it. He's done what I asked him to do and I don't want to push my luck. The mic might've blown up in the water, anyway—the mic or whatever accompanying mental devices that are required for a straightboy to fuck his teammate and be cool with it afterward. So I offer him the master bath and use another bathroom down the hall. Fifteen minutes later when I return to the bedroom he's sitting on the couch, dressed and tying his sneakers.

"You OK to drive?" I say. "You're not buzzing anymore?"

"Nah. It was just a buzz. And do you realize we were at it for like two hours?"

"Two hours?" I glance at the clock in disbelief. It's only been ninety minutes but I love that he rounded up.

He stands up, shoes tied. "Nuts, right?"

"Totally."

"So yeah. Hey, have you seen my keys?"

I point to where I dropped them on the table. He walks over and puts them in his pocket.

"Hey, what'd you mean," I ask, "when you said *We're going to have had sex.* Right before we finished. That was some impressive tense work."

He laughs. "I don't know. Guess I just meant there was a line coming up fast and on the other side I'd be a dude who's slept with a dude. Because it's never really sex until someone squirts."

"So you're on the other side now."

"No worse off for it. That good enough?"

"Thanks. Hey. Want me to walk you out?"

"Nah. I know my way around a mansion."

He leaves the room and I sit down on the bed, listening to him bounding down the stairs with concussive footsteps that are proof he's taking them two or even three or four at a time. Is he in a hurry to escape?

Never mind. I feel too good to worry about it. I can still feel him inside me and I want to savor it. I flop back on the bed and sigh.

Then I remember, as I hear his motorcycle roar to life,

that I drove it here myself. Which means my car's still at Yon's. I sit up quick, ready to chase him down for a ride. But in the end I let him go. He's done me enough favors tonight.

A little while later I call a cab and go get my car.

Chapter 7

Next day, early afternoon. I'm sitting on the floor of my room in my boxers flipping through TV channels eating a dry bagel when my phone rings. I expect it's one of Skullcrusher's assistant coaches again, reminding me to clean out my locker (and Ryan's) before the annual locker room hose-down, but when I see the animation on the flexiglass screen, I quickly pick up and say hey.

"Dude."

It's Santiago. The call is voice-only. I want to ask him to switch to video but there's no reason for me to need to see his face — aside from, I don't know, nostalgia.

"My back's killing me today," he says, though he doesn't sound very miserable. I recall him hanging over the arm of the couch, feet skyward, head bonked against the floor.

"Guess that's my fault," I laugh.

"Remember that game against the Icebergs? When I was chasing what's-his-name through Smalltown and went face-first over that bench?"

"I saw about fifty replays of it."

"This feels like that."

"I think you'll survive."

"Not complaining, just saying. Hey. Did you get your car? I totally forgot we left it at the bar."

"I grabbed a cab over there."

"Ah. OK, good." There's a pause. "So what's up today? Your location says you're at home. You should get out of that bedroom, get some fresh air or whatever. Must stink of dick in there."

"I like it."

"You would." There's a pause. "You clean your shit out of the locker room yet? I went over this morning."

"Skullcrusher's goons keep calling me about it. I have to do Ryan's too. I've been putting it off."

"Ryan angst?"

"Ryan angst."

"Guessing last night didn't kill it off?"

"Don't take it personally. It was a nice distraction."

"Yeah, well. Why don't you go take care of the locker shit, McHenry. And hey. Give me a buzz when you're done. We should meet up. I think there's something I want to talk to you about."

"You think?"

"I'm feeling it out. It's solidifying."

"Solidifying?"

Now I really wish I'd clicked us over to video — maybe his face would be telling me something his voice isn't. It's odd for Clemente to be calling me at all today, odder still for him to want to hang out. I mean, isn't it? Clemente's the first straight guy I've been with so I'm not exactly versed in their psychology, but I expected he'd need a cooling-off period while he reasserts his heterosexuality. I expected to be avoided, if not outright ignored. Now he wants to chill? WTF, as the old-timers say.

After we hang up I shower and shave and put on jeans and a black tanktop. I take Ryan's Mustang again — I've always liked this car and it's not like Ryan's using it. The afternoon is bright and the air has a cleanness to it that's perhaps the lingering rosy glow that comes from two hours of playtime with a naked and curious straightboy.

As I approach the stadium — that bowl-shaped behemoth that seems to make the air around it twitch like jittering, old-fashioned movie effects — I find all but one of the dozen lots empty. It's like driving through a heat-hoarding desert of asphalt. The one lot in use is the one nearest the stadium; trailer trucks are lined up and I remember that The Hush, one of our niche-market culture's last surviving stadium bands, has three nights of shows next week. Out with the paintball, in with the rock and roll.

I lower the window and wave a keyfob at a sensor to gain access to lot A-1. And here I park in space #6. All the other Warriors' spaces are empty except #5, which means Piper's here too. Wonderful.

I enter through the secret personnel-only door that's always made me feel like the stadium is my second home, twist along the concrete-and-glass corridors, and arrive in front of the locker room.

The door doesn't open for me, which I guess means it's locked. Through the glass there's only that security-light glow to light the benches and lockers and empty laundry carts.

With the heels of my palms I try to part the glass doors but they don't budge.

I look around, see nothing but my reflection. The place looks deserted, a loser of a ghost town. No sign of Piper or anyone else.

As I'm getting out my phone I hear the faint crackle of talk radio from around the corner. It grows louder and soon is accompanied by the rattling wheels of the maintenance man's pushcart. Demetri, a bull of a guy of about sixty in faded blue coveralls, an unlit cigar perpetually hanging from the corner of his mouth, comes around the corner. He's listening to the weather.

"Boots McHenry," he says, looking up. "What brings you around?" His voice is part growl. I half expect him to give me a play-by-play about what we did wrong in the Vigilantes game, but he spares me.

"I'm here to clean out my stuff. And Ryan's. But it looks like the locker room's closed up?"

"Shame about Ryan," he says, letting his cigar droop in cartoony sadness. "Would've been us at the Cup if he'd been playing."

"Thanks."

"To lose five years. Well—" His cigar perks up. "Them's the stakes."

"Them's the stakes," I repeat, nodding. "Think you could do me a solid and let me inside?"

"Having some kind of photoshoot in there," he says. "Pernfors is. Some calendar or magazine or some such. Strictly private. That's why it's locked. Lighting or whatever. Do not disturb. *Sshh.*" He chomps on his cigar.

"Ah, well it'll just take me a minute. I've been dreading this and now that I've got up the gumption I want to get it done."

"Aye, I hear you. Wasn't easy when I lost my Dolores, either. No simu-death there, though. The real thing." He clears his voice. "Keys. They're around here somewheres." Multiple sets jangle from loops on his belt. He removes a ring and separates one key on it, letting the others slide to the bottom. "This one here."

"Thank you."

"Lock er up when you're done. I'll be around front, cleaning up after some dingus exec who doesn't know how to clean up after his mutt."

As Demetri crackles away down the hall I fit the key in the locks at the top and bottom of the double doors.

They part, revealing that yellow-tinged darkness inside. The locker room feels like a tomb, one of the many Ryan lives in now. I flip a few switches and the overhead lights tinkle on with that fluorescent chirping. Brighter now, but still a tomb.

Our lockers contain most of the same things, but while mine are worn-out junk, all of Ryan's seem precious. Precious simply because they're the last. I pull out the #9 t-shirt he wore during practices. I feel an urge to put it on, but don't, not here. I do, however, hold a pair of his boxers against my face, fill my entire respiratory system with the scent of his stale sweat. If scent is composed of tiny particles I imagine these particles filling my lungs and entering my bloodstream, becoming part of my own body. I inhale the smells of his body so deeply that soon I can't smell them anymore. Either I've used up the smell or become immune to it. Both thoughts are sad.

Using a trash bag seems loaded with terrible symbolism, but I didn't have the foresight to bring anything more respectful and it's all I can find. I fill it with our things, the mixture of our NAPL careers, and then shut the lockers. I'll be using mine again next season; Ryan's will stay empty.

As I'm about to leave I remember what Demetri said about Piper being here for a photoshoot. I haven't seen or heard any sign of him, though. I drop the bag by the doors and walk to the other end of the locker room, past the massage tables and media green-screen and down the long concrete hallway that leads to the showers. There's light at the end of this hallway—clean white photoshoot light. The porous concrete muffles sound but before I've gone too far down the hall I can hear the patter of water hitting the floor. I stop and peer around the corner. Two shower heads are raining water onto the floor; on the dry end of the room are a camera bag and a scattering of clothes. Tripod lamps running on battery power throw light at the walls and floor, which glisten colorfully like a gasoline spill. On the floor in the middle of the room Piper is lying nude on his back in much the same way I lay on the day he wrestled my uniform off me. But Piper's arms are spread and his knees are raised; the soles of his feet are flat on the floor. The position gives him leverage to bounce the guy, also nude, who's bouncing on Piper's pelvis. Piper is sucking two of the dude's fingers the way he sucked mine on the night I aborted our sex. His eyes are closed; without opening them he lifts his hands and grabs the guy by the hips, guiding him up and down more smoothly. He quickens his rhythm as the guy riding him gasps and smiles.

I feel my dick start to harden. I know that if I'd made another choice in Piper's living room it would be me riding him rather than some nameless magazine photographer. And there's nothing keeping me from joining them, of course. If I did, the photographer would be an afterthought in a heartbeat.

The photographer arches back and moans with pleasure, and Piper's eyes spring open in what looks like surprise. Why surprise? The photographer's moaning can't be an unexpected sound. Was it because the voice didn't match the face Piper was imagining behind his closed eyelids? Could that imagined face have been mine?

I drop my hand to my crotch and feel my hardness straining my jeans. When I look up again Piper is looking at me. Still bouncing the photographer, but looking at me, staring me down through the low cloud of steam that surrounds them. On his face is an odd stew of embarrassment, anger, and desire.

Without saying anything I turn and retreat down the

hall. While Piper presumably finishes with the photographer, I leave the locker room with a boner and a trash bag full of my simu-dead boyfriend's smelly old underwear.

On my way out of the stadium I toss the key to Demetri and call Clemente. He tells me to meet him at the bar.

Is it becoming a cycle? My awkward longing for Piper is absorbed instead by Santiago and diffused harmlessly by his uninterested beauty. It's as though Clemente's the gorgeous homo and I'm the shy fag-hag, shooting my ill-defined lust at him without fear of it returning or even ricocheting anywhere dangerous. Clemente can absorb it and be indifferent to it too. The fact that we've already fucked and apparently nothing has changed between us is only evidence of how much I can throw at him.

When I join him at Yon's he's nursing a bottle of his hard cider and watching the MMAC on one of the many TVs. A bowl of pretzels sits near his elbow; he dips his hand in and removes a handful.

"How's your back?" I tease, dragging a stool up beside him.

He slaps his palm against his open mouth and bangs in a handful of pretzels. "Better," he says through the doughy paste that clings to his white teeth. "Vicodin."

"Nice."

"Left over from my Icebergs spill."

With a raised finger he signals the bartender, from whom I order what Clemente's having.

"Locker cleanout done?" he asks. He swallows a wad of pretzel paste and washes it back with cider.

"Yeah. Thanks for the push."

"Couldn't have been easy." He touches my shoulder gently and squeezes. It catches me off guard until I remember that Clemente is the kind of guy who's always touching you, and only once in the way you hope.

"Yeah, well. I suppose they'll hose it out now. Easy come easy go."

He looks at me and frowns. He's nice enough not to call bullshit.

I take a sip of cider. "So you said there's something you want to talk to me about? Or something you *think* you want to talk to me about?"

"Yeah."

"Has it *solidified?*"

"You're such a mess, McHenry, that yeah, I think it has."

"What?"

"Now that the season's over," he says, "I'm thinking of getting out of Thebes for a while."

Ah. Of course. He really was taking the stairs four at a time last night. And now he's hopping, skipping, jumping right out of town.

"Kind of an extraordinary measure just to reassert your heterosexuality, no?" I say sardonically and gaze up at the BILFs kicking the shit out of each other.

"What?"

"You need space, Clemente, I get it. I expected it. It's fine."

He looks at me funny. "Space from what?"

"From my ball-sack?" I feel irrationally angry.

"What? McHenry—"

"It's OK, Santiago," I say, patting his wrist, "I said one-and-done and I meant it. We're cool. You don't have to run away."

"Boots, would you pull the dick out of your ear and let me complete a sentence for once?"

I take a sip of cider and look at him.

"I'm not running away, McHenry. I want you to

come *with* me."

Cider stops in my throat and I have to make a conscious effort to swallow it down. It makes a gaggy sound in my neck. Him calling me this morning was surprise enough. Now he wants us to go vacationing together?

"Actually," he continues, "if you don't come, there's no point in me going either. So. Up to you."

"Where?"

"Not exactly sure! Which is what makes it an adventure."

"You want to throw a dart at a map?"

He sips some cider. "No, no. It's a destination, I just don't know the location yet. Got to find out."

"Sounds... vague?"

"The secret's well protected."

"OK." I laugh; I don't know what else to do. "I'm confused."

"It's just an idea."

"What is? What, Clemente, what?"

"Less an adventure. More like a *mission*."

"A mission now? Not a vacation but a mission?"

"I'm thinking somewhere nice. Tropical." He pauses. "An island. A mysterious island."

"A mysterious island.... Don't tell me you're—"

"Yes. Very serious." He narrows his dark eyebrows and his ironic mustache suddenly looks the most kickass thing I've seen in my life. "*That* mysterious island."

Chapter 8

For an hour I'm pressed against Clemente with my arms around his middle but totally alone with my thoughts, and my thoughts are of an island. The roar of his motorcycle prevents any further discussion, so I play in my head over and over the rest of what he told me at the bar:

That he thinks it's—"no offense, dude"—kind of pitiful that I'm living in one-fifteenth of my house. That it is—"again, dude, no offense or anything"—really sad how I had such trouble clearing out Ryan's locker. It's tugging his heartstrings something fierce, he said, seeing me like this. This kind of stasis isn't healthy, he added. And although he enjoyed our sex more than he expected to, he thinks I might need a more significant remedy in my life than a quick one-and-done.

"So that's our mission," he told me at the bar. "To get you a real goodbye or whatever. To find out what the fuck Ryan said to you from the chopper. To tie up the loose strings. So you'll know how to proceed. So you can move on."

Clemente—bold, brash, perhaps borderline nuts Clemente—wants to help me get to exile island so I can see Ryan, so I can have the time and freedom to talk things out, to make decisions about how we want to spend the next five years. To decide whether to wait it out, or end things.

"It'll be good for you," Clemente said about the mission, but I know he meant it would be good for him too. All of his major endorsement deals backed out after the Warriors screwed the pooch in our last game, and now the commercials he planned to spend his off-season shooting will star someone from the Vigilantes. Dude wants adventure.

"And you need one," he told me.

He wants action.

"And you need some of that too," he said.

Problem is, no one knows how to get to exile

island—assuming it really is an island—and the people who know aren't talking. There are nondisclosure agreements on top of nondisclosure agreements. It's all part of the contract.

"Isn't it hard to get to a place that officially doesn't exist?" I said.

He grinned. "Boots, you make it sound like it's Area 51 or some shit. This is just a paintball league we're talking about."

"OK, Sherlock, then what's our first clue?"

"I know a guy," he said slyly. "He's been there, and I think he'll tell me where it is."

Now, because my teammate Clemente Santiago *knows a guy*, the night's flashing cold and dark around us as we blast up the coast on his motorcycle. Against me he feels warm and full of purpose. From time to time over the wind I hear him making the electric guitar *boweeow weeow* sounds that must be his personal theme music or something.

Like the entrance to Xanadu the steel gates stand tall, ivy-smothered, and vaguely menacing before us. Far beyond the gates, at the end of a winding driveway, a house, veiled in shadows, stands atop a hill. The sky seems darker above it, as though the house has its own weather system, a perpetual thunderstorm.

Clemente brings the Honda to a stop and lowers his sneaker to the gravel. When I let go of him and hop off the bike my body creaks with stiffness.

He pushes his glasses up over his hair.

"Probably should've called first," he says, getting off the motorcycle and dropping the kickstand. He walks over to a panel on the stone wall beside the gate, and presses a button. "Hope he's still up."

After a minute a bright light in the panel blinks on,

seeming to examine us like a cybernetic eye. I know enough about home security systems to know it's a camera and that our image is appearing somewhere inside the creepy house.

"Yesss?" It's a male voice, breathy. Either breathy or full of static.

"Coach, it's me. I was in the neighborhood. You home?"

"Of courssse I'm home."

The voice is indeed breathy, as though air is being pumped through the man's teeth as he speaks.

"I'm here with Boots McHenry, my fellow Warrior. Can we steal a moment of your evening?" He looks at me and smirks.

As the gate is grinding open we get back on the bike and ride it up the long driveway, leaving it near one of the doors of the garage. The house isn't as big as it looked from the street, or as big as you might expect from the fancy gate out front. Mine's bigger. And although floodlights are now gleaming from the eaves, the house remains subtly haunting. Eye-teasing shadows flicker over the well-kept lawn.

As we're walking up the steps the huge front door opens inward—a portal to another, warmer dimension. Standing in the entry with her hand on the knob is a blue-eyed girl of about six or seven, with a smile suited more to a romantic comedy than to the suspense thriller the outside of the house suggests. She has a blond ponytail, a pink t-shirt, and pajama pants patterned with cartoon daisies.

"Hey Beyoncé," Clemente says. "Dig the daisies. This feller here's my friend Boots."

"I know you from TV," she says, daintily holding out her little hand, which disappears into my own.

"Thank you."

"You're here to see my Grampy?" she says to Clemente.

"I know it's late," he replies. "Just for a minute."

"OK," she shrugs; for kids the clock means jack shit. "He's in his liberry. I know the way."

She shuts the door behind us and looks back over her shoulder a few times to make sure we're following.

"Who's Grampy?" I ask Clemente.

"My mentor."

"And he knows how to get to the island?"

"Did his five years back in the day. Everyone who's ever been knows, or at least has an idea. I think he has a lot more than an idea. And I think he might be willing to tell. Kind of owes me a favor."

Skipping, ponytail swooshing to and fro, Beyoncé leads us down several hallways to a smoked-glass door. She slides it open and skips into the library. The place is wall-to-wall books, colorful old-fashioned hardcovers and paperbacks, and various types of sports memorabilia. Two paintball rifles hang in an X over the fireplace. Across the room Beyoncé climbs into a wheeled armchair that's facing away from us. Resting against the back of the chair I notice the top of a salt-and-pepper head. Slowly the chair rotates to face us. Beyoncé is sitting on the old man's knee, petting the Corgi that lies asleep on his lap.

The man's sallow face is crisscrossed with clear tubes delivering oxygen into his nose. He wears slippers and a garish, lime-green tracksuit. His eyes are watery and hooded by loose eyelids, but they have a certain spark.

The chair hums toward us carrying all three passengers. When it jerks to a halt Clemente approaches.

"Nice threads, Coach," he says, shaking the old man's hand, and then comically shaking the sleeping dog's paw. Beyoncé covers her mouth to stifle a giggle. I realize suddenly how obvious it is that she has a crush on Clemente. "This is Boots," he says.

"My condolencesss," says the old man, nodding, "on your boyfriend."

"Thank you."

"So the reason we're here," Clemente continues, "is there's something Boots and I want to ask you."

"Oh?" The old man smirks, waiting. The Corgi looks around sleepily before returning its head to the drooly spot on the old man's knee.

"Actually—" Clemente says, "Boots, would you mind giving us a second?"

"Uh. OK, yeah."

I'm not sure where to go so I meander to the other side of the library. The place isn't so big that I can't hear as Clemente begins telling the old man about Ryan— which feels weird on multiple levels. I keep one ear on them as I scan the library walls. Among the sports memorabilia is a series of framed photos of the old man—a much younger man when most were taken— posing with bleacher-rows of boys of about six or seven in paintball uniforms. Little P-Ball. I wonder if Clemente is one of these six-year-olds wearing one of these ill-fitting chest-guards. Probably, but I can't pick him out. Maybe if the boys were wearing mustaches....

"He's in this one over here," says Beyoncé, who's suddenly standing beside me, barely as tall as my waist. "See?" She's on her tip-toes pointing, making grunting noises as she stretches.

"Which one?"

"Lift me up," she says, and I do, hoisting her by the armpits. She reaches out and pokes one of the photos, putting a tiny fingerprint on the face of a six-year-old Clemente Santiago. "Look at his *glasses*," she teases.

"Nerdy, huh?"

"I like him both ways," she says thoughtfully. "A boy and a grown-up."

"He come here a lot?"

"Only every *week*," she boasts, popping her hand onto her hip.

Across the room Clemente must have gotten to the point, because the old man suddenly shouts, as loudly as he's probably capable, "The *island? Fu – !*"

The dog, startled, springs to its feet on the old man's lap.

"We want to go there, Coach," Clemente says calmly, as though he was expecting the outburst. He touches the dog's head. "So Boots can say a proper goodbye to Kroft."

"A proper goodbye! Clemente Erick Santiago, WTF? Man alive!" Oxygen sizzles through the old man's tubes with an intensity that makes me afraid they'll rupture. He puts his hand on his forehead and closes his eyes for a moment before looking over at me and the girl. "Beyoncé, sssweet, why don't you go get the movie ssset up and I'll join you in a jiff."

The girl skips out of the library, waving at us from the doorway before she bounds away.

"If there's anything you can tell us," Clemente continues, "we'd appreciate it. Anything would help. We're starting from zero here."

The old man still seems like he's trying to contain himself. "You boysss must realize I can tell you absolutely nothing. There are nondisclosure agreements *about* nondisclosure agreementsss. And that's already sssaying too much."

"If you can't tell us anything about the island – is it an island? – then just tell us what direction to go. Where to look. A hint."

"*Pffft.* A hint? They'd sssue me if it ever came out."

He looks at me, including me in the explanation, so I go and join them. "You can guess from my sssircumstances that I'm dependent upon the residual luxuriesss of my time in the NAPL. My medical care doesn't pay for itself, and the girl has no one left but me— And I've got another few years in me, max." He sighs. "I have to provide for her after I'm gone. I can't risssk losing that."

"I thought we agreed that *I* would provide for her after you're gone?" Clemente says. It's news to me, though somehow not quite a surprise. It's also, I can see, Clemente's main bargaining chip here.

The old man looks up at him, narrowing his watery eyes. "Ah. I see. A quid pro quo. Tricky."

"Just give us a hint, Coach," Clemente says. "No one will find out. Even if they do they'll never trace it back to you."

The old man creaks forward in his chair, as though to impart a great secret. "And what about you, Clemente Erick? Sssay I do help you and you get caught and lose everything. What happens then?"

"Future worst-case scenario? I'm kicked out of the NAPL and I have to raise a six-year-old on, I don't know, a gym teacher's salary. No one's ever survived *that* before."

The old man laughs, a sound that seems to reverberate through all of his tubes, down to the hissing tanks beneath the chair. "It means that much to you?" He's looking at me. "Just for a goodbye?"

"This was *his* idea," I say, holding up my hands.

The old man touches his lips with a wrinkled fist and looks from me to Clemente. "And what's *your* motive?"

"Mine?" Clemente says. "I don't know. It would make a good essay on what I did on my summer vacation?"

The old man rolls his eyes. "Come here so I can slap

you."

Clemente lowers his face, grinning, but the old man doesn't so much slap as swat. Then he inhales dramatically, as though gathering his secret up through the tubes. "I was injured on the island."

"So it definitely *is* an island?"

"Clemente Erick, *hush*. I was injured. I won't say how. I may have fallen off a cliff; I may have been attacked by wild boars; I may have been put down by snipers while trying to escape. I won't ssspeak of it. When I regained consciousness I was in a helicopter— what woke me was the sound of numbers, digitsss, crackling over a radio. Numbers that represented my return from death, both sssimulated and literal. And ssso they've been burned in my memory ever since. I remember them well."

"What are the numbers?"

"It took me months to realize they were coordinates. And either I'm going sssenile or else an old man still wants the youngsters to think he's cool, but whatever, it's your lucky day. I'm going to tell them to you. They're a hint. Do with them as you will."

He writes the numbers, longitude and latitude, on a torn strip of paper no bigger than my thumb. The island's address. Ryan's address. And then, with a conspiratorial wink, he tells us to sssscram.

"Did that really just happen?" I say as we're walking Clemente's motorcycle back down the driveway. Shadows from scraggly branches spike the pavement. "Or was that some kind of fever dream?"

"Oh, it happened for sure, dude," Clemente says, patting his t-shirt pocket where the scrap of paper is stashed. "But it was way too easy. Which means it's going to get a lot harder."

"Think so?"

"Ever seen a movie, Boots? That's just how these things work."

"Like in the movies, huh?"

"Sure."

What we encounter at the bottom of the driveway on the other side of the gate probably isn't the kind of difficulty Clemente was referring to, and it isn't that out of the ordinary, but it's a pain in the ass nonetheless. The paparazzi. Two cars (probably from competing websites) with photographers leaning against them snap to attention when they see us.

"They must've followed us here from Yon's?" Clemente says to me.

"Two jocks on a motorcycle speeding into the night? How could they resist?"

"Santiago! McHenry!"

Blinding LEDs ignite to illuminate the scene as microphones plunge into our faces from the other side of the steadily opening gate.

"Not as fun as the last mic I had in my face," Clemente teases me matter-of-factly before turning to the paparazzi. "Folks!" he grins.

"You two were seen leaving Yon's Kneecaps together earlier tonight. Anything the world should *know*?"

"That we're defecting to the MMAC?" I say, raising my forearm and gently but firmly moving some little dude aside so we can get through the gate. He hops backward but comes right back at us, all microphone and sharky grin. I suppose these people are just trying to earn a living, but aren't there better ways? "I don't know what else you could be implying."

Clemente mounts the bike and I get on behind him. "I know what they're implying, McHenry," he says, loud enough for the mics to get it. "They think we're getting sexy together. Now that you're solo and all."

"So that means it's *true?*" the little dude with the microphone cries, voice rising at the prospect of a scoop.

"I should *be* so fucking lucky," Clemente laughs. "Don't forget to bleep that." Then he kick-starts the bike and we're off.

He's really flying to put some distance between us and the paparazzi. My hands are clasped against his belly, a necessity I avoided in front of the cameras. But after a few minutes I think we've outrun them. While I'm busy wondering how Clemente's old coach got into the shape he's in, Clemente puts his hand on my clasped hands and shakes them against his abs, his t-shirt sliding between my palm and his skin. It surprises me and my heart skips. But it's just that he wants me to hold tighter. When I do, he lets go of my hand and jerks his thumb behind us. I turn. The paparazzi are catching up with us, each trying to outrun the other for the first shots of Clemente Santiago and Boots McHenry at high speed together. If they like jocks on a motorcycle, they adore jocks on a motorcycle at high speed.

The winding road is narrow and the screeching paparazzi are ignoring the solid yellow line—their game of trying to pass each other is a sure-fire recipe for disaster. Clemente touches my hands again, and then with a jerk he knocks back into me as I knock back against the low backrest. The road beneath us becomes even more blurred, but it's a smooth road—the vibration of Clemente's back against my chest is because he's laughing.

I turn and look back again, air forcing my face into a smile I'm too nervous really to be feeling. The cars are gaining on us, taking up both sides of the street. Quickly I turn to look for oncoming traffic but the road's clear for now. Popping bursts of LEDs capture still photos of us, and I'm sure video's being recorded too—it'll be on the Internet in minutes. One car, driving in the wrong lane, is straining to get beside us for a close-up. Clemente only accelerates—trees and signage go by looking like abstract art. I wish there was a way to communicate with him, to tell him to let them get some video before somebody gets killed. But over the wind and the high-pitched purr of the motorcycle it's hopeless. I wonder if, despite his showy attitude earlier, he doesn't want to be documented with me.

That's dumb, right?

Without warning, the bike's high-pitched purr drops a few octaves and Clemente becomes a brick wall I'm crashing into—my cheek pounds the back of his head and my balls slam his tailbone. He could've told me he was going to clobber the brakes!

The paparazzi unwittingly roar past us, one on either side, both still accelerating, and it must be their surprise at our sudden disappearance that makes them drift inward. Their side mirrors collide in an explosion of plastic and sparks. Horns blare—two, then three. The car in the right lane careens to the shoulder, small trees disappearing underneath and springing up mangled on the other side. The car in the wrong lane follows just in time to clear the road for an oncoming pickup.

Clemente lowers his foot to catch us when we finally come to a halt. Behind us in the red taillights a black streak on the road extends from the bike far away into the darkness.

"Fancy driving," I say.

"We'll go another way," he laughs, then he turns us around and follows the pick-up.

He drops me back at Yon's, where Ryan's Mustang is

still parked. My butt's sore, and after climbing off the bike I do a few squats to stretch while Clemente laughs and calls me a pansy. Fight sounds and cheering waft from the bar, and I'm toying with asking him inside for another hard cider.

"They think we're sleeping together," he laughs. "If they only had any idea what we're *really* up to!"

"But we did—"

"But that was just a one-and-done."

"Sure. Of course."

"That's not the big scoop. That's Rufus on a slow day."

"Hah. Right."

"The big scoop— They'll never know."

"I hope you're right."

"Be in touch," he says, settling back on the bike. "We need to start planning. Transportation, stuff like that. Logistics. We should come up with another couple guys to round out the team. So think about who. People we trust."

"Clemente," I say before he kick-starts the bike. "You never really answered your coach. Why are you doing this? What's your motivation for this whole thing?"

"Motivation? Like for finding a mysterious secret island to facilitate a romantic/sexual reunion between my two teammates?"

I laugh.

He touches his mustache in contemplation. "Well let's see. I'm twenty-four. I have more money than God. I have zero endorsement deals. No girlfriend. And four months off with jack shit better to do. What more motivation do I need?"

It makes sense, of course. The better question is, what more motivation do I *want* him to have?

"Later Boots."

The bike purrs to life and he speeds off.

I watch him until the night envelopes him. Then I unlock the Mustang and get in. On the passenger seat, like a crinkling memento, is the trash bag full of Ryan's things. I'd totally forgotten about it but now it's all rushing back.

Chapter 9

After getting home I notice that soon after I left Clemente's coach's house (probably around the time we were giving the paparazzi the slip), Piper called me and left a video message. I don't watch it right away. I drop the phone on my bed and kick off my shoes.

I make a quick run to the kitchen to whip up some mac and cheese while the house's silence throbs like a migraine. Then I'm back in my bedroom, my sanctum, the door shut tight behind me. Am I pitiful for huddling in here, as Clemente gently suggested? I don't like to think I'm afraid of anything but it's tough to deny I'm treating this room as a safehouse.

Forking macaroni into my mouth, I watch Piper's message on my phone a few times. Then I flick it to the TV and watch it life-size.

He's sitting on his black leather couch (the one I bolted from), barefoot with swooshy white basketball shorts and a ribbed tanktop that hugs every curve of his chest and leaves his hard arms bare. It's an outfit perfectly appropriate for around the house, but Piper remembers full well how horny those swooshy shorts make me, and his wearing them isn't coincidental. A lamp glows behind his head, giving his shock of blond hair a saintly shimmer. But I'm filled with raunchy thoughts. I recall the scene in the locker room earlier today, the view I had of his golden-haired inner thighs and of his cock plunging in and out of that photographer — and the blue eyes that caught me watching. I look into those eyes now while he speaks.

"Hey Boots. I just wanted to give you a call and say that, you know, I'm sorry about this afternoon. I'm sorry you saw that. Of course I wish you would've— Well no, no I don't, you were right to walk away. It wasn't the place for it." He looks down at his hands. "It didn't mean anything, in case there's any chance you're wondering. I don't know if you even care anymore. I feel like maybe I'm really screwing up here, first with the other week and now today. That maybe fate's given me an opportunity to mean something to you again and I'm blowing it. I just want you to know that today, that guy, it wasn't anything. It just happened. You know how it is. It was just for fun. So, you know, we should hang out again some time, and I'll keep my hands to myself. We could grab a beer or hit up a club or something. We have to keep working together, Boots, and I don't want you to think I'm a total motherfucker. And I *do* want you to think—god I shouldn't even be saying this—I *do* want you to know I still love you. So. I guess it's your move."

Though I kind of feel bad for doing it, all I can do is roll my eyes. At the tortured explanation. At the passive-aggressive declaration of love, meant to appear tacked on at the end but clearly the whole point. But watching him onscreen in those shorts has turned me on, and one perk of living alone is there's no one to judge me. So I put the video on repeat. I set my dinner on the floor, lay back on the bed, push down my pants. My boner springs out, the head still crusted with the pre-cum spilled while I watched Piper's shower scene. As I watch him now (he appears to be sitting across my room; these are the glories of floor-to-ceiling TV) the memory of him nude and hard (both today and during our college days) fills my mind even as the crystal-clear image of his bare arms and legs fills my bedroom. Doesn't take long for me to get close, but it's long enough to make me feel guilty. Guilty in a way that getting fucked by Clemente didn't. Because with Piper it still feels wrong, for all the same reasons that made me bolt from his couch. It'll always feel wrong; it's just disrespectful of Ryan. So I mute the video, pull my pants the rest of the way off, walk across the room. From the trash bag I grab Ryan's underwear, then I return to our bed. I hold the underwear over my face—the sharp smell of sweat is deliciously vibrant again. I remember how he used to squirm with glee when I nibbled my lips up and down his cock, how he loved to have his nipples stroked while I fucked him. I think of these things while I jerk off holding his underwear against my mouth. But to be honest I'm still darting my eyes to the life-size image of Piper, too. I come all over my chest but the underwear tastes stale in my mouth even before the orgasm is over. Meanwhile Piper's living room looks bright, and beckons. *Your move,* he mouths.

I turn off the TV.

If we'd had time to talk, Ryan and I, things would be so much different now. If I really knew what he wants me to do during the five years he'll be away, it would be so much easier. Simu-death, like real death, leaves you no time to prepare. It's just as spontaneous as real death can be. But simu-death's promise of the person's eventual return opens an enormous window of uncertainty in a survivor's life. In that way it's almost harder to move on from than the real thing. Do I wait? Will *he* wait? There's no way to know.

Only, there *is* a way to know. And the first step is

written on a scrap of paper tucked in Clemente Santiago's shirt pocket. For the first time—really the first time—since he proposed our incredible mission, I begin to believe in it. And I know I have to see it through.

Chapter 10

A new morning, and today I wake up happy for the first time since Ryan's exile. The big bed may still be empty and I may have somehow, during the night, caught my leg in the giant hole Clemente put in the sheet, but I'm happy. I sing in the shower. I eat breakfast in the kitchen rather than sneaking it up to my room. Sunshine streams through the windows. No cartoon birds land on the sills, but I wouldn't be surprised if they did.

I call Clemente and ask where and when he wants to discuss the logistics of the mission. He tells me his place, whenever I want, and he flicks his address to my phone's GPS. I've never been to his place—our socializing is usually done either on the field or at Yon's—and I'm curious to see what it's like. I know he lives alone, and since I also know how much his NAPL contract brings in, I suspect the house is big. *What does a straight man's castle look like?*, I wonder as I drive. My mind conjures something that's entirely garage and gym, with a giant grill on a big brick patio surrounded by rainproof TVs. A team of busty supermodel maids to suck his dick and do his laundry. A stern, grandfatherly butler to throw open the curtains in the morning and make him W-shaped pancakes before games.

When I stop my daydreaming and focus on the road I realize my phone has guided me to a pretty unlikely part of town for the place I've been imagining. This is a lower–middle class neighborhood with pot-holed streets, porches with peeling paint, and lawns strewn with Playskool playground equipment. Here and there kids ride bikes, eyes glued to the Mustang as I cruise by. I look skeptically at the phone. Finally it tells me my destination's on the left and I tell it it's wrong, but I slow down anyway. I pull up in front of a tiny blue single-story ranch with a white chain-link gate and a cracked concrete walk leading to the front stoop.

I look around. I call Clemente. He answers.

"Dude, you flicked me the wrong address."

"Did I? Fuck, sorry. Where are you?"

"Parked in front of a little blue house."

"Wait— What?"

As he's saying this the front door of the little blue house opens and a mustachioed face peers out. Clemente lowers his phone and I lower mine too.

"Oh fuck." My forehead hits the steering wheel. I'm such a shit-heel.

Standing on the front stoop, he raises his phone back to his ear. I do the same.

"I get it," he says, "you were kidding me about being lost. Har har har."

He's being generous, letting me off the hook, and I'm grateful for it. My embarrassment cools a little.

I let myself in the front gate. The guy next door is mowing his lawn in a tanktop and slippers. As I'm coming up the walk a yellow face, wizened with gray around the muzzle, pokes out from between Clemente's jeans-clad legs. An ancient yellow lab plops down the three steps and bumbles toward me, tail going back and forth as fast as he can probably manage it, big grin spread across his rubbery lips.

"Who's this?" I say, rubbing the dog's ears as he licks

my hand and pushes his nose into my balls.

"That's Trooper," Clemente says.

"Didn't know you had a dog."

"Gotta have a dog, McHenry." He throws a dishrag over his shoulder. He has on a faded gray Warriors t-shirt and his hair is wet. "Come on, Troop, leave Boots's crotch alone."

"How old's this guy?"

"Sixteen. Had him since I was eight."

"Jeez."

"Coming in?"

I take the screen door from him and follow him in. Trooper, after struggling on the steps, follows me. As I close the door he goes and lays down on the linoleum under the round kitchen table.

"I'm really sorry," I say. "That was beyond douchey of me just now, about the house."

"Don't worry about it. Seriously. We're big-time, you know what I make, you had expectations."

"I shouldn't've assumed we all waste it on empty rooms."

"Forget it, really. Coffee or something?"

"Sure." I sit down at the table and Trooper sniffs at my sneakers. The kitchen is tiny, all cupboards and stove and fridge, with a sliding glass door that goes out to a sun-bleached deck. A foam dog bed leans upright against the railing. "Let me guess: you grew up here."

"Ding ding."

"That's cool. Where's your mom live now?"

He has his back to me; there are dark spots running down his spine where he didn't towel off enough before putting on his shirt. He turns slightly, showing me the side of his face, and the side of a smile. "In a mansion."

I laugh.

"Actually in a condo. Same building as Piper."

"Ah. Nice. On the harbor."

"Yup." He puts a mug of coffee in front of me. "Milk and sugar or whatever? Never think to ask because I like it black."

"I'll get it."

His fridge is stocked with two six-packs of his hard cider, a carton of eggs, a bunch of vegetables, a loaf of oatmeal bread, three ham steaks. I grab the soymilk.

While I'm pouring and stirring he takes a chair at the table. He pulls a flexiglass tablet out from under some papers and snaps it stiff. He pokes at it with one hand while sipping his coffee.

I sit down across from him, accidentally kicking Trooper, who doesn't seem to notice.

"I was trying to make a list," he says, "of things we need to consider for the mission."

From across the table it's easy for me to read his list—even upside down—because it has only two items: *Transport* and *Recruits(?)*.

"Don't worry, I was more productive with the mapping," he laughs, poking the screen and bringing up another window. "I searched the longitude and latitude Coach gave us and this is what I got. Take a gander." He spins the tablet around and slides it toward me.

There's an orange pin-marker sunk in one of two green landmasses in the middle of an expanse of animated blue waves. I zoom out a little and find that the pin-marker is far at the western end of a very familiar-looking archipelago.

"Exile island is in *Hawaii?*" I say.

"Past what people would probably think when they think of Hawaii—but technically, yup."

"Why'd I think it was Fiji or something?"

"I thought Fiji too. Everyone does. Why? Is there a reason or is it just habit? Does the brain hear *exotic island*

and automatically think Fiji?"

I take a minute to look at the map, spin it beneath my fingertips. "Your coach said he heard the coordinates in a helicopter."

"Right."

I tap the pin-marker. "But what if the coordinates aren't exile island? What if they're where he was being taken to?"

Clemente frowns, takes a sip of coffee. "Go on."

"He gets hurt, wakes up in a helicopter, hears the pilot reading these coordinates. What if they're the coordinates of where they were *going*, not where they were coming from? Maybe they flew him out of Fiji to the nearest American hospital."

He bumps his knuckles against his chin a few times, thinking. "Good point. Except why this island? Hospitals would be on the big islands. This one's rinky-dink. Unpopulated."

"Is it? What do satellite images show?"

"Unblemished paradise, basically."

"That's easy to fake these days, though. A few image scramblers perched up high.... Could be a prison camp underneath and the satellites would never know it."

"It's exile for prima donna athletes, McHenry, not punishment."

"Feels like punishment."

He shrugs. "So either exile's in Fiji, and on this island there's a secret NAPL hospital disguised by image scramblers. Or else Ryan's here." He taps the pin.

I laugh. "Occam's razor, I guess, right? Simplest explanation, etc."

He taps his temple, winks.

"But one thing's for sure," I say.

"What's that?"

"Your coach remembered the coordinates right.

Because what are the chances messed-up ones would still point to a tiny uninhabited island?"

He grins and knocks back the last of his coffee. "I was afraid I was going to key them in and get Patagonia or Siberia or something."

"Seriously."

"More coffee?"

"Sure, top me off." I smirk at the double entendre but he doesn't seem to catch it. He gets up and fiddles with the French press.

From where I'm sitting I can see through the living room into his bedroom. Crooked pennants line a wall, and a framed photo of our championship team lineup hangs over his unmade bed. The room is kind of a mess, but a cute mess. At the foot of the bed is a plastic basket of laundry with socks and t-shirts hanging over the side. On top is a pair of square-cut briefs that might be the ones I removed from him the night we had sex. The messy bedroom, the dog, the childhood home: I kind of wish I knew these details about him when we were in bed together. To what effect I'm not sure. No way it could have been better than it was. But maybe it would've been sweeter, or something.

He puts the French press on the table along with the sugar, stands touching his mustache before saying, "Ah, milk." He gets the container of soymilk from the fridge and sits down again.

"So back to your list," I say as I pour.

"The list. Transportation."

"That's important. We can't swim there."

"No, swimming's out. Too many sharks." He smirks. "Should we fly?"

"That's the obvious, unless you want to go by boat. Should we sail?"

"We'll have to go by boat to get way out there, even

if we fly to Honolulu. Sailing the whole way would be more discreet. I don't know how to sail, though. You?"

"Nope."

"Then that leads us to the second item. Recruits. Do we want to do this alone? *Could* we do this alone?"

Going it alone has a certain appeal and would be good for secrecy, but getting on and off exile island relatively unseen may take some expertise.

"Given our line of work," I say, "we're probably both more accustomed to working in a team."

"That's what I was thinking," he says. "Better to have a couple extra guys to watch our backs. Since we don't know what we're going to find when we get there."

"Yeah."

He leans forward and, touching his mustache with his thumb, looks into my eyes. "So," he says with a grin, "who do we take?"

The last time Clemente and I started discussing the qualifications of various people, weighing their pros and cons, I ended up with his dick down my throat. As much as I'd welcome that happening again, for this I figure it's better to cut to the chase.

"This time *I* know a guy," I tell him, coyly slurping my coffee. I pick up my phone to check the potential recruit's location status. "Looks like he's at work. Want to pay him a visit?"

So Clemente puts on some flip-flops, gives Trooper a handful of treats, I start up the Mustang, and we're driving. Aviator sunglasses cover his eyes but I can tell by his smile that he's excited. Crisp air billows our shirts.

"You and I are snipers," I say while we wait at a light. "So to balance us out, we should have a close-combat guy. Just in case we need to fend off any muscle-head security or anything."

"And your guy fits the bill?"

I tell him my guy comes to mind immediately when I think *ass-kicker*. "I've witnessed him in action. He's a mixed martial arts champ."

"Fancy."

As the light changes, Clemente, with his arm slung behind my headrest, leans closer and says over the wind, "So how do you know him? Former flame?"

"Not exactly. He's Ryan's brother."

"Colby Kroft?"

"Have you met him?"

"No. Heard Ryan talking about him once or twice. Guess he won the Junior MMAC or something?"

"Right, last year. Wheel-kick to the other guy's jaw, twenty-seven seconds into it. Knocked the guy out cold."

"How'd I not see that?"

"It was two days after we won the Cup."

"Ah, right, right. I was chin-deep in fan pussy that week."

"Skank."

He grins. "If he comes with us at least he'll be invested in things working out. Guy probably wants to see Ryan almost as much as you do."

"I hadn't even thought of that, but yeah." We're almost at our destination now. "Hey, speaking of fan pussy," I say, glancing from his Warriors t-shirt to his trademark hipster 'stache, "we probably should've worn disguises."

"Why, where we going, anyway? Where's Colby work?"

"The most fan-tastic of all places, Clemente. He works at the mall."

We park and enter through two sets of big glass doors. Muzak greets us and my phone starts freaking out with alerts about coupons and sales. We're clear for a whopping ten feet before someone notices us.

It always starts slow, with a whisper or giggle or pointing finger — or all three. The bashful are usually the first to notice, but they're quick to tell the people they know will be more bold. The blushing girl tells her bossy sister, knowing the sister will drag her along for an autograph. The shy homo whispers to his hag, who's so eager to please him she'll drag him over for a sweaty handshake. And of course in addition to the fans of us there are the fans of the game in general, often over-friendly fratboys looking to have their t-shirts signed, their pictures taken, and most of all to share their particular wisdom about the game, about what we should've done, about how we got screwed. Some fans want to be signed or kissed; most just want to be heard.

Before we've passed the food court they've surrounded us.

"We'll get revenge for Kroft next season, McHenry," yells an oafish fratboy working the sunglasses kiosk, pounding his fist against his beefy chest in solidarity.

"Hell yeah we will," I yell back, forming my fingers into Ryan's old number. The fratboy hoots and then offers us free sunglasses. Even if we wanted to take them there's no way we could get over there.

Being surrounded means performing a slow yet hyper ballet: our arms reach in and out to receive and pass back pens and slips of paper (receipts, shopping lists, ticket stubs) from grasping fingers; we dip at the knees to pose for photos with children and arthritic oldsters; we use wide-armed tugs to pull faux-reluctant couples into cheesy embraces. We also make subtle backtracks from the weird or uncomfortable ones, like the one I'm looking at now: a teenage boy cute enough to give me pause, who in hushed whispers is offering, practically pleading, to suck my dick. Pretending not to hear, I autograph the palm of his hand and hope that'll satisfy him.

Clemente is better at this than I am, more a fan of the fans than I am, and perhaps because he's more at ease with them, he's better able to turn them away when the time comes.

"That's all we can do today, everyone," I hear him say over the din of squeals and hoots. And reluctantly the crowd parts enough for us to continue on our way. We still have to wave here and there, but at this point the most enthusiastic fans have been satisfied. Clemente and I can focus once again on our mission.

"So does Colby work mall security?" he asks.

"Not exactly. You'll see."

But before we can see, our roles must get reversed: we must become the fans. We wait in a long line to greet him, our potential recruit. He's standing at the front of a swanky, dimly-lit clothing store out of which the scent of pungent cologne wafts, surrounded by mannequins modeling the clothes he isn't actually wearing himself. He's wearing only boxers (though beneath them, he once told me, is a Speedo for security), flip-flops, and a blinding-white grin. He has shaggy blond hair that shows streaks of strawberry when he steps a certain way in front of the storefront lights. A scruff of blond hair fuzzes his chin and cheeks. In the heavy air-conditioning he should be cold but Colby is doing his own version of the fan-mob ballet, and in fact his shoulders and pecs sport a glistening sheen of sweat. At least I *think* it's sweat; it very well might be drool from any number of the girls and guys who've already had their moment with him and now are giggling on the outskirts.

"*That's* Colby?" Clemente says skeptically. We're standing in line behind two teenage girls, one of whom is fixing her make-up in a compact mirror; the other is futzing with her phone's camera. "*That's* the Junior MMAC champ?"

"Why?"

"Kind of pretty, no?"

"Don't be fooled. Colby could kill you with nothing more than those polka-dotted underoos he's wearing."

Clemente looks at me, then at Colby. "Hmm."

Colby's seen us by now and obviously gives the girls in front of us short shrift in his eagerness to get to us. When we step forward he grins and crosses his arms. My heartbeat kicks up a notch—I'm sorry, I can't help it. Some guys are cute and you want to pinch their cheeks and make sure they get home OK. Some guys are hot and you want them to bend you over a barrel and pound heaven into you. Colby is in an ambiguous place in between. I met him two years ago, when he was sixteen. He was the same way then, and at the time, even though I was only twenty-two myself, I felt like a dirty old man for thinking he was hot sometimes and not always just cute. At least now he's legal.

"Well if it isn't one-fifth of the Theban Warriors!" His smile's so bright I envy Clemente his sunglasses. Colby has an easy, just-got-out-of-bed beauty that no amount of primping or styling can match. "Looking for a modeling gig for the off-season? Or can I interest you in some underwear?" He tugs the waistband of his boxers, lets it snap back against his Adonis belt.

"Sorry, Colby, we're more interested in what's inside your underwear. Namely, you."

Colby's eyebrows pop up. I toss Clemente my phone, camera ready, and walk over to Colby, throw my arm around his shoulders. His muscles have the same density as Ryan's, which makes me sad but also reiterates my dedication to this mission.

"How are your parents?" I ask Colby as Clemente snaps a few photos of us to keep up appearances. "They doing OK?"

"They're in denial. My dad had a lawyer going over the NAPL contract looking for loopholes. It sucks but, like, whining about it's not going to help." His breath smells of bubble gum. "What'd you mean by what's inside my underwear? You thinking one Kroft's as good as another?" he teases.

"Sorry, kid, Ryan's the only Kroft for me."

He laughs.

I put my mouth to his blond-tussled ear and whisper, "Santiago and I want you to join us."

He mouths, nervously: "And become a Warrior?"

I laugh and clap his shoulder. He smells unnaturally good. Maybe the sheen on his skin isn't sweat or drool but some kind of candy-scented gloss to make him all the more iridescent. Whatever it is isn't coming off on my hand.

"Not a Warrior, Colby. We're planning a secret adventure I think you'd be interested in. And we could use your expertise." I look down at his boxers. "I mean as a martial arts champ, not a storefront model."

"A secret adventure?"

"That's what I said."

"How secret?"

"Top."

"Do I have to join up before you'll tell me what it is?"

I didn't think of that. I ask Clemente, who hands me back my phone.

"Nah, but let's not say anything here." To Colby he adds, after shaking hands, "Can you meet us? Let's say, tonight?"

"Where?"

Clemente looks at me. "My place is kind of small."

"My place, then," I tell Colby. "At seven."

"Hurry up!" whine a pair of tweens in frustrated unison. *"We're waiting!"* I'm sure they have no idea who we are; or maybe, next to Colby, we're just too dressed to be interesting.

"Watch your phone for any changes," I tell Colby before turning to the tweens. "He's all yours, kiddos."

Clemente and I walk fast through the mall and do a lot of waving and only have to stop a few times for autographs. When we get outside Clemente says teasingly, "He sure is a little stud-muffin."

"Shut up. He's all but my brother-in-law."

"Last time I saw you so hot and bothered, McHenry, it was because of *me*."

"Jealous?" I say, and he laughs. "Any time you want to get me hot and bothered again, Santiago, just say the word."

At this he laughs even harder and punches me in the arm. Does he think I'm kidding? After the other night, can he *possibly* think I'm kidding?

I drop him off at his house, wondering whether the house is intended to be ironic like his mustache or whether he really just can't part with it. Trooper is waiting behind the chain-link fence. As he's patting him, Clemente tells me he'll see me later.

Chapter 11

When I get home I realize it was a shitty idea to have the meeting here. It'll be like throwing a party in a graveyard. Maybe Clemente's little house and smiling dog have tuned me in to how dead and echoey my own place is. The housekeepers and pool guy have continued to come twice a week but there are lights I haven't turned on since Ryan left. The house is clean but it's an antiseptic clean. I throw open some windows and go out to the back patio, where I figure we'll conduct the meeting. Kneeling by the pool, which I almost forgot existed, I wiggle my fingers in the water. It's a perpetual eighty degrees even though I haven't been swimming since Ryan. I look at the water. *What the heck*, I think. I take off my t-shirt, shoes and socks, jeans, and finally my boxers. And with a running start that begins all the way back near the barbeque, I cannonball bare-ass through the glassy surface.

A stream of bubbles drifts up out of my nose. I'm hanging underwater watching the rippling foam on the underside of the surface, watching my pubes sway in the currents. Ryan always said I have the best pubic hair, though I'm not sure what's so special about it and he would never elaborate. *It's just the best*, he would say.

Goddamn.

I float to the surface, take a few breaths, wipe my eyes. Then I kick up my legs and swim, relishing the silky water flowing over my skin. I touch one end of the pool and then the other, and do it again, and again. When I'm tired I grab the diving board and hang from it idly, torso drying in the late afternoon air. "I miss you, Ryan," I murmur, watching the sunlight tinkling on the waves rocking outward from my legs. Remembering him, I drop back in and swim to the side of the pool, to the jet in the wall beneath the surface that blows in warm, filtered water. It was our secret thing: At night we'd swim to this spot naked and hold on to each other and kiss, letting the warm, smooth jet of water crash against our crossed cocks. In a rush of ecstasy we would come and shudder and clutch each other as the water blew against us. Ryan goofily referred to the jet as our boyfriend—once when there was something wrong with the filter he asked the pool man to check to make sure our boyfriend was clear. I think about that now and laugh and put a hand over my tearing-up eyes as the jet pummels my dick. It still feels good but it's not the same without Ryan, without his lips against mine. When I've finished coming I feel silly for having sex with a stream of water, because without Ryan that's all it is. So I swim very slowly, my pubes gluey with underwater sperm, back to the ladder, and get out.

Later, as I'm turning off the shower, my phone rings. Colby? Clemente? Hopefully not Piper. Dripping all over the slate floor, I pick it up off edge of the sink. It's none of the above—it's Marius Tumble, Ryan's replacement #9. I accept the video call and he appears on the screen.

"Oh, sorry," he says when he sees me shirtless and dripping. "Bad timing?"

"Nah, I was done." I'm naked but I'll keep the camera above shoulder level. It's nothing he hasn't seen in the locker room anyway. "What's up, Marius?"

"I'm just calling to ask. You didn't happen to empty out a locker near yours, by any chance, did you?"

"Yesterday. Why?"

"I think you might've taken my stuff by mistake."

"Your stuff?"

"I mean from my locker. The one near yours."

I stare at him. "Ryan's locker?"

"Well it was, yeah. But I moved my stuff into it before the last game."

In the thumbnail in the corner of the screen I can see my brow crunch in bewilderment. "Why would you do that? Where's Ryan's stuff?"

"I just moved it over to an empty one at the end."

"Why?"

"Well, because I— The lockers go with the uniform numbers, don't they? I wear #9 now, so—"

He's right, but still. "There are plenty of other lockers, Tumble."

"But only one #9."

"I can't believe this." I drop the phone to my side, accidentally giving him a face-full of my ass.

"Sorry," I say, bringing the phone back up, "that wasn't supposed to be a gesture or anything."

"It's OK." Then he adds, "I didn't take his stuff or anything. It's all still in that other locker, I checked this morning. You can go get it whenever. This is just a mix-up."

"Some mix-up, Tumble. I've been thinking that stuff belonged to my simu-dead *boyfriend*."

I'm not sure he understands the implications of that—of what a guy might do with the newly discovered clothing of someone he loved and lost. But maybe he does, because he seems to be speechless. Finally I say, "Do you want your stuff back?"

There's a pause. "Well, kind of, yeah. The practice jersey, at least. It's from my first practice on first-string, so...."

"Yeah. I understand. A souvenir." It was a souvenir to me too.

I flick Marius my address and tell him to stop by later to pick up the stuff. Then I end the call and slump down against the side of the tub. I feel rattled and sad. The underwear I held to my face last night. The fabric I pressed against my tongue. The scent I inhaled and loved for what I stupidly thought was its *familiarity*. The scent particles I imagined coursing through my bloodstream. None of it was Ryan's and I didn't even realize.

How is that possible? It isn't. It can't be. Tumble must be wrong. He must be mistaken.

I walk dripping into the bedroom and grab the trash bag full of our clothes and turn it upside down on the bed. Clothes spill out in a stinky tangle. I turn a pair of what I thought were Ryan's underwear inside out to show the label. Then I go to his dresser drawer, to the supply of underwear that's unquestionably his, and compare the brands, the sizes.

They're different. Shit. Marius is right.

I feel like I've been flipped upside down. This discovery is making me question everything about what I feel and want to do. Did I actually know Ryan so little that I can't even recognize his *smell?* Or am I so incredibly desperate for any piece of him that I didn't want to believe the stuff wasn't his? The second possibility is the one I try to settle on—because it makes me feel better, and because it makes the chimes at my front gate later that evening all the more welcome and needed. It makes the mission all the more urgent.

Clemente arrives first for the secret meeting. After buzzing him through the gate I hear his motorcycle coming up my driveway. He enters my house without knocking, which is weird, but maybe doing what we did together here the other night makes him feel a sense of entitlement to the place.

I hear him call from the foyer, "McHenry!"

"Kitchen," I yell, my voice echoing off the high ceiling, off the hanging, unused copper pans.

A moment later he enters the kitchen carrying a backpack and a six-pack of his hard cider. Most of his face is freshly shaved, and the absence of stubble around his mustache makes it more prominent. I like it.

"The kitchen!" he grins. "And not the bedroom!

You're making progress, mi amigo."

I ignore his teasing. "What do you think about food?" I ask, dropping a take-out menu on the countertop island between us. "I was thinking I'd order a couple of pizzas. Is pizza OK for a secret meeting?"

"Sounds good to me." He opens my fridge to put the cider inside. "Yikes, especially since you have like no food here."

"Too much trouble."

"Well that's not good," he says with a surprising amount of concern. "Where we're going, they don't make take-out."

"As far as we know."

"True. Kid here yet?"

"He texted. He's on his way." I'm looking at the menu. "Two large? That enough for three people?"

"Four." From his backpack he pulls his tablet and sets it on the counter. "Four people. I invited Piper to come."

My heart shudders. "Come where?"

He looks at me blankly, as though realizing he's made a big mistake. And unless he's fucking with me, he *has*.

"You didn't. Did you? Clemente!"

"I ran into him at the gym and he was talking about needing some adventure for the off-season and it kind of slipped out. I don't know."

"*Slipped out?* Great, Clemente. Nice work. Thanks."

"What's the matter?"

"Why would you do that? *Piper?*"

"Uh, because we're launching a secret mission and Piper is quick-thinking and he's a close-combat guy and he'd be a major asset?"

"We already *have* a close-combat guy, that's why we're bringing Colby. Why would you do this without asking me?"

"Didn't figure it would be such a big deal."

"You know about our history, Clemente. Come on. Would you want to do this kind of thing with an ex-girlfriend?"

He waves his hand. "Enough with your history, McHenry, jeez. From where I'm sitting the so-called history between you and Pernfors has led to one Cup and damn near a second one too."

"The drama is not *so-called*."

"Whatever romantic tension there was, I'm pretty sure you ended last week when you sucker-punched him on his couch."

"Ouch."

He holds up his hands. "Just saying."

"This is my trip, Clemente."

Suddenly he looks very serious. "No, McHenry. Let's get one thing straight up front. This is *my* trip. *My* idea. *My* coordinates. *My* trip."

We stand glaring at each other from opposite sides of the island while some incredible force ricochets between us; something that, if not for the presence of the island and cooktop separating us, may well have resulted in bloodshed. A challenge of wills that seems all out of proportion to the circumstances. It makes my pulse pound.

The buzzer rings.

Clemente turns to open a hard cider.

"This better not be him," I snarl.

It isn't, thank god; it's Colby. Colby, around whom it's impossible not to mellow out a little (possibly a secret to his success in the ring). And right now I could use a little mellowing.

When I get to the front door Colby's standing outside

with his hands in the back pockets of his jeans. A wisp of blond hair curls against his eyebrows. He's wearing a pink v-neck tee with a tear in the V that deepens it by an inch, and smells as though he's just been swimming.

Behind him in the driveway his red Jeep Classic is parked as though he slammed the brakes while dodging pedestrians. The front driver's-side tire hangs off the paving stones onto the otherwise pristine grass. My lawn guy will be livid but I don't care. Grass is just grass when it's being torn up by Colby Kroft.

"You don't have to knock," I tell him. I tell him every time.

"I always forget you guys are the only people who *live* here," he laughs, but the laugh drops when he remembers Ryan no longer does live here—or won't for five years. The flash of sadness makes me sure he was the right guy to invite on this mission; he has a stake in it too.

Just then Clemente appears behind me and grabs Colby by the shoulder, playfully yanking him off the porch. "Get in here. This is secret business."

Colby laughs but looks at me curiously. I know Clemente's playing and I wonder what makes him think he's earned the right. Doesn't he know we're still fighting? Straight guys!

"Anyone else coming?" Colby asks, looking around. Every time he comes here he seems amazed by the size of the place. I lead them both to the backyard patio, to the picnic table there. On the other side of the pool the muscular Poseidon continues spitting his everlasting chlorinated loogie.

"Apparently Clemente invited Piper Pernfors too," I grumble.

Colby frowns. "He invited your old *boyfriend?*"

"*Thank* you." I could kiss him for finding it weird. It's

important to me to have Colby in my corner. Things are sure to balance out when Piper arrives.

"Yes, I invited his old boyfriend," Clemente says. "I'm a horrible person, I'm sorry!" He flings the pizza menu at Colby. "Pepperoni or sausage?"

"Can we do both?"

"We can and must."

"So when are you guys going to tell me what I'm actually here for?" Colby says.

"Soon," Clemente says. "Soon as Piper arrives."

"We're going to exile island to see Ryan," I blurt. Clemente looks over at me, exasperated—but he shrugs, pulls out his phone, starts dialing the pizza place.

"You're joking," Colby says.

"No."

"You know where it is? How will we get there? Does he know we're coming?"

"Kind of. I don't know yet. And no."

Colby slaps his forehead. "Fuck, this is zilla cool, Boots."

"We thought you'd want to be involved," I say.

"I definitely do. So we're springing him?"

"Half an hour," Clemente tells us, dropping the menu back on the table, pushing his phone into his pocket.

"No," I tell Colby, "we're not springing him."

"We're getting Boots a goodbye," Clemente says. "And you too. Few minutes to sit on the beach or whatever with Ryan, and say what you need to say."

Colby thinks for a second. "What do I need to say?"

"That's up to you," Clemente says, poking him in the shoulder.

"And you don't know how we'll get there?"

"We'll talk about the details when Piper shows up," Clemente says, and this time I keep my mouth shut.

While waiting we nurse bottles of Clemente's hard cider in the backyard. Colby's pulled off his black espadrilles and is sitting at the edge of the pool with his jeans rolled up and his feet in the water. He doesn't know it, of course, but he's sitting directly above Ryan's and my boyfriend. I think of pointing it out—it's something Colby would get a kick out of—but before I have a chance the gate chimes ring.

"I'll go let him in," Clemente says after I've buzzed Piper through.

"I'll go," I say, stopping him with a hand against his chest. "My house."

He holds up his hands in a *Whatever bro* kind of way and backs off as I make my way to the foyer.

Piper is peering in through the door's prismed glass; it makes his sharp features look sharper and a glow of rainbow colors his skin. I open the door.

"Nice digs."

"Thanks."

"You opted for space over location, I see," says the owner of the Thebes Harbor condo.

"I like to think it has both."

"Yeah, well. Am I dressed OK?" He glances past me into the house. "Santiago wouldn't tell me much so I had no idea what to wear." He has on a yellow polyester polo with the all three buttons open. Yellow goes good with his hair, which has been freshly buzzed on the sides.

"You're fine. It's a meeting, not a party."

"Some kind of secret thing, he said?"

"Something like that. Come in." The door is open plenty wide but he brushes against me when he enters. It's unnecessary but I can't say I don't like it. The touch of polyester against my arm makes me tingle.

114

"So did you get my video message yesterday?"

"I got it," I tell him, carefully omitting the part where I jerked off to it.

"I wanted to clear the air or whatever."

"Yeah, I watched it."

After stopping at the fridge to get him a cider, I lead Piper out to the patio, where Clemente and Colby are skimming a frantic chipmunk out of the pool. Once it's scampered away we assemble around the picnic table. It isn't a round table but Colby's quick to point out the King Arthurness of it all—though it isn't clear who's Arthur since no one's at the head. Colby and I are on one side, Clemente and Piper on the other. Yes it's flattering that although Colby is beside me in all his young beauty, I'm the one Piper keeps looking at during Clemente's dramatic buildup. It's clear Clemente is enjoying unspooling the plan, but when finally he reveals that the point of this mission is to get me to Ryan, Piper's brow falls from an excited high to a disappointed crunch. He looks down at his hands and then quickly at me. Then his eyes drift along the hedge before being aimed, with some obvious effort, back at Clemente and the topic at hand. He clears his voice and fakes a smile.

And now I feel shitty. What has Piper done to me, really, except pursue me? Yes, he was a lousy boyfriend, but that was years ago. Maybe he's been too eager, but that isn't something a guy deserves to be demonized for. The real reason I've demonized him, of course, is to keep my mind off him. Ten minutes ago he probably thought he'd be going on vacation with me, if he even knew that much—and now he's finding out the vacation is to get me back into the arms of his replacement. He looks like he's been slapped in the face.

"Piper will be really efficient with that," I blurt, throwing a compliment his way just because, even though I was spacing on what they're talking about.

"I don't know jack about sea navigation," Piper replies.

"Um. Well, I mean you're a fast learner."

"Let's back up a second here," Piper says. "Why would I go along with this? If we get caught we'll get kicked right the fuck out of the NAPL. And likely sued, too."

"We're not going to get caught," Clemente says. "Even if we do, they're not going to fire us for getting caught. Or sue us. How could they fire three star players without causing a media firestorm? Everyone would want to know what we did to get canned. They'll only fire us if we go blabbing about it later. If we let the secret out. Which we're not going to do." He leans closer to Piper. "Plus, aren't you *curious*?"

"Who isn't curious?"

"Then come."

"Don't you want to see Ryan?" Colby says, with a touch of sarcasm.

Piper can't bring himself to say *Not really*, which is obviously what he's thinking. He looks skeptical. As Clemente begins another round of persuasion the gate chimes sound again.

"That'll be the pizza," I say, getting up and going inside.

But when I look at the monitor, the person idling outside my gate isn't wearing a Dominoes hat.

"Shit," I yell outside to the guys after buzzing the gate. "Marius is here."

"Tumble?" Piper says.

I'd totally forgotten about him coming over to pick up the bag of Ryan's stuff. *His* stuff. "Yeah, Tumble."

Clemente looks at me and raises his eyebrows and purses his lips as though to make a fart sound. It's a look that says: *You get mad at me for inviting Piper when you invited Marius?*

"I didn't invite him," I say preemptively. "He's here to pick up something. I forgot."

I run upstairs for the trash bag and I'm walking across the front lawn just as Marius is getting out of his BMW. A pizza delivery girl with a glowing Dominoes sign on her roof is rolling up behind him. Marius looks from the pizza to the other cars and says, "Sorry, do you have company?"

"Nah, we're just—"

"One of you boys order some pies?" shouts the pizza girl as she pulls a third box out of the heater compartment thingy in her back seat. "One of you *Warriors?*" A grin.

"Me," I say, taking the boxes. She's looking at a receipt on her tablet.

"You're all paid up, Boots. Can I call you Boots?"

"Yeah, of course." Pressing my chin against the boxes, I fish in my pocket for my phone and flick her some bills for the tip. I don't pay attention to how much goes, I just watch her face until it gets really bright.

"Wow, thanks!" As she's turning back to her car she adds, "Hey, zilla sorry about Ryan, Boots."

"Me too. Thanks."

At the mention of Ryan, Marius looks down, starts cracking his knuckles as though he's suddenly desperate for something to do. I suppose the subject of Ryan will always be an awkward one for him and me.

And on the heels of this awkwardness, and because Marius is still the new guy, and even though I have the bag he came for right here, I ask him inside for some pizza, etc. Because why not? I've seen him play. He'd be as much of an asset on this mission as Piper—and without the romantic drama.

"I could eat a slice," he says, so I hand him one of the boxes and show him in.

"We were having a sort of a meeting," I say.

Marius nods and looks around.

As we turn the corner into the kitchen I see Clemente sprawled face-down on the tile; Colby's sitting on top of him. One of his elbows is pressed into Clemente's back and with both hands he's clamping Clemente's left arm back into what looks like an excruciating position. Piper has found some paper plates.

"What are you guys *doing?*"

Colby releases Clemente's arm and stands up. "I was demonstrating a move."

Clemente turns his mouth away from the floor but doesn't move, not yet. "He was a good choice, McHenry. *Ach.*" Rolling onto his back, out of breath, Clemente notices Marius and waves. "Hey Tumble."

Now there are five of us at the picnic table, two on each side, and our King Arthur has apparently been determined, or more like self-selected: Clemente has dragged a lawn chair up to the head of the table. Can't say I'm happy about that, but I think things might balance out again soon. Because as we describe the mission and explain the details — as we go over the plan, discuss the map, the coordinates, the transportation, the timeframes, the *risks* — Marius becomes increasingly uncomfortable and I can tell, with growing certainty, that he's a no-go. He's still listening, but he's put down his slice and is punctuating his anxiety with the intermittent clicks of his knuckles cracking.

"We'll charter a boat," Clemente is saying, "and that's going to be fine, that's just going to be a matter of *getting there*. It's the *being there* we can't really account for."

"Are we going to have to fight?" Colby says, clearly

118

spoiling for it.

"There's no reason to think the island is *secured* in any way," I say. "Right? No one is there against his will, per se."

"Per se," Piper says sarcastically.

"Being there is basically a contractual obligation," I add. "They go and they do their five years because they prefer it to getting sued for VOC."

Colby: "VOC?"

"Violation of contract," Clemente says. "We hear about that a lot."

"So why would they need security?" I continue.

Marius is still sitting silently.

Piper adds, "What if they have security not to keep people on, but to keep people *off?*"

"Right. That's what we're thinking," Clemente says. "Whole point is we don't know. So we'll give it our best shot. I mean, worst case, we have to knock some dudes out, tie them up, make a run for it. That's why we have Colby, to hold back any muscle-heads who need holding back."

"I can break a man's leg, no sweat," Colby says. He grins; he's proud of this. If I could do it I'd be proud, too.

Marius leans forward, pushes his plate and his half-eaten slice away from his elbow. "So let me see if I'm following: You're going to charter a boat to an island you *think* is exile island, and you're going to, what, break Kroft out? Bring him home?"

"I thought we weren't breaking him out?" Piper says.

"Why *don't* we bring him back with us?" Colby asks.

"VOC," Clemente says, a little exasperated. "Look. There's not going to be any rescuing or whatever. This thing's not as glamorous as that. What this is, is— I don't know, McHenry, what is it?"

"It's just so I can—" And even before the words leave

my mouth I realize how incredibly selfish they'll sound. "It's just so I can say goodbye." I look around at them. "Or it was. Jeez. Now it sounds so silly."

"It's not silly," Piper says, more gently than I expect or probably deserve. "It's risky, it's not silly."

"It's romantic," Colby says. "It's zilla romantic. It's all for a goodbye. Plus I want to see my bro. So I'm in."

"OK," Piper sighs, grabbing a new slice of pizza, "I'm in, but for the record I think it's a bad idea."

"I've always been in," Clemente says. "It's going to be fun."

Marius sighs loudly. "I'm out." He leans back a little, then leans forward again. "Sorry guys. I appreciate the offer. I'm flattered you want to include the new guy. But I'm out." He looks around at us. "It's a nice idea, I just can't take the risk. I've only played in one game. I've worked all my life to get where I am. I can't jeopardize it now. What you guys want to do, it's like biting the hand that feeds you. It's not for me. I'm out."

I show Marius out of the house and walk with him across the driveway to his car.

"Going to be a nice night," I say. And then I add, "No hard feelings, right? But I'd appreciate it if you didn't say anything to anyone about what we talked about here tonight."

"I'm not going to tell anyone." He turns and sighs again. "I feel like a total dick, Boots, but I just can't risk it."

"Nah, it's cool. I understand."

"I know you don't like me, and hey, maybe it would make a great narrative: the dude who replaced your man helps you get a goodbye with him. Might even turn us into friends. That would be a sweet story." He pauses. "But I've only played in one game."

"Marius, seriously. It's fine. Here. Don't forget your stuff." I pick the bag up off the driveway and he takes it from me, tosses it in his BMW.

"There is one thing I *can* do for you, though," he says. "Got your phone?"

"Here." I take it out of my pocket.

He takes his out too, moves through a few screens looking for something, then flicks his index finger across the flexiglass. I accept what he's sent. It's a business card.

"*Marcus Tumble, Aquatic Tours*," I read.

"My twin brother," Marius says. "Give him a call. You said you want to charter a boat—well he's got a hell of a boat. He'll take you where you want to go. No captain better than him."

"You have a twin?" I say, thinking, *There are two of you?*

"We're not that close. Actually, we don't really talk anymore. But he's good."

"Thanks."

"Good luck."

As he's driving away I head back inside and share the info he gave me. Colby breaks into a grin.

"Thank god," he says, "I was bummed when he said he wasn't coming." Then he adds, "I have a thing for dark-skinned boys."

"I'm not dark enough for you?" Clemente teases.

Colby blushes, then recovers. "I could never have a romantic interest in someone so zilla easy to pin."

"Ho ho!" I yell, fist-bumping with Colby.

Clemente just shakes his head.

Piper clears his voice. "So how about we call this Marcus Tumble person and see what he says?"

"I'll do it," Colby says. I hand him my phone and he dials. "It's ringing."

HOMO ACTION LOVE STORY!

PART 2

Youth & Daring

HOMO ACTION LOVE STORY!

Chapter 12

On the morning our grand adventure begins I wake up with a headache and see, through the balcony doors, a sky full of gray haze. I push off the sheets and I'm rubbing my eyes when my phone rings. It's Clemente, making sure I'm awake. I tell him I am and he asks if I'm sure, then he laughs.

"Need to bring Trooper over to my mom's," he says. His mom is dog-sitting. "Then I'll meet everybody down at the wharf. Good?"

We hang up and I lay staring up at the reflected image of Ryan's empty half of the bed for another five minutes before finally hauling myself up. The sky's getting brighter by the minute and my headache starts to fade as soon as I'm upright; I can almost feel it slipping down the back of my neck and sliding off my shoulders. I stand over the bed looking at the hole Clemente's knees put in the sheet two weeks ago. It's time to say sayonara to that little memento, I guess. When I get home from the mission, I want a clean slate.

I ball up the sheet and carry it downstairs. The heavy silk fills the contours of a new trash bag, making it look like a big black water balloon.

That done, I make breakfast from the perishable food items that are left from what Clemente made me buy: a big plate of scrambled eggs, a banana, two apples. After I'm done I trash the remaining contents of the fridge. When I get back—whenever that is—I'll start fresh in the food department, too.

Next, with a swelling excitement I'm glad to be

feeling, I call the pool service and maid service and landscaper. I tell them all I'll be away on vacation for a while but to keep coming as normal. After that I program my checking account to deposit their pay on an automatic schedule. As long as I have my phone I could do all this from the middle of the ocean, but I don't want any of it on my mind while I'm gone.

Now I stand tapping my phone against my chin, looking around. Outside the haze is gone and the sky is a rich morning blue. Idly I slip my hand into my boxers and twirl my pubes. The maid will bring in the mail. Check. My bill-pays are automatic. Check. There's nothing in the house I need to worry about. Check. I packed my shit yesterday. All chores are covered.

I'm ready to go.

Thebes Harbor, where sunlight glitters like sparkly frosting on the waves. After paying the cabbie I check to make sure I'm at the right place—a big sign says Dandelion Wharf—and figure I'm just the first to arrive. There's no sign of Marius's brother's yacht, called the *Intrepid*, yet either. So I heft my backpack and stroll down the wharf.

At the end I sit down, dangle my legs over the edge and lay back, crossing my arms behind my head and using my backpack for a pillow. I'm glad I'm the first one here. Despite what Clemente said in my kitchen, this is my trip—we're going because of Ryan, and Ryan is mine. I'll welcome them all as they arrive.

In the meantime I'll just enjoy the quiet. The sun is warm on my skin but not bright enough yet to make me want to dig out my shades. I fill my lungs with the salty air, listen to the steady thump of waves breaking against the legs of the wharf. Even the *rrrrmm* of distant boat motors is peaceful, like white noise. Yes, this was a good idea, all of it.

Next thing I know—I guess I was dozing—the sun's much brighter and a train is bearing down on me. No, not a train, something else with a steady, growing loudness: feet pounding the wharf. I sit up quick, spot Colby sprinting in my direction, open short-sleeve button-down flapping behind him like desperate wings. He clutches a backpack by one strap and is waving with his free hand. "Wait!" he calls. "Wait! *Wait!*"

"Colby!" I yell and he skids to a stop in his black espadrilles and looks at me, baffled. Looks at me and then at a yacht leaving the harbor, then back to me.

"Oh," he says. "OK."

"You thought we left without you?"

"I thought I was late. I'm not?"

"No one else is even here yet."

"I slept through my alarm. I thought that was you guys leaving." He points to the yacht.

"Nope."

"Well good," he laughs. He drops his backpack next to me and sits down cross-legged, breathing heavy. I can see a white drawstring snaking out from under his butt.

"Colby, your shorts are on backward."

"Wha—? Oh." He blushes, finding the drawstring. "Told you I was in a hurry."

"Keep your shirt open like that and no one'll ever notice your shorts. Why didn't you call?"

"I did. I texted you like six times!"

"Didn't hear anything." I slip my phone out of my pocket and check. "Oh. Sorry." The last message reads: *DONT LEAVE W/OUT ME!* "Well you're here, that's all that matters."

"I'm here. *Whew.*" He gathers the flaps of his open shirt and casually does the bottom button with the nimble fingers of one hand. Then he lays back, using his backpack as a pillow too, and I feel the tiny thrill of being copied by someone younger. I lay back on mine beside him. From this angle I can see a flash of his blond armpit. His right ankle is resting on his bent left knee; casually he dangles an espadrille from his toes. His foot bouncing gently up and down reminds me of Clemente's doing the same thing on my couch right before we had sex.

"Heard from the other guys?" Colby asks.

"Clemente called to make sure I was up. Haven't heard anything from Piper. Maybe he'll miss the boat."

He laughs. "You really still have ex-boyfriend crap after all this time?"

"Always. And since your brother's been gone Piper's made it clear he's available for a rekindling."

"Zilla raunchy."

"Seriously."

"He's easy on the eyes, I guess." Bouncing the espadrille, he drops it, lets his foot go bare. His toenails are trimmed very low, which I think is regulation for Junior MMAC. "He's not my type though."

After a minute he sits up. "Ground's not as comfy as it looks." He stands, stomps back into his errant espadrille, walks to the end of the wharf, jokes like he's going to jump in, then jokes like he's going to *fall* in. Finally he yawns and stretches. "Hey Boots," he says, raising a hand to shield his eyes from the sun, "I think our ride's here."

The yacht, the Intrepid — it's bigger than I expected — slices across the waves like it's greased and glides up alongside Dandelion Wharf. The engine drops to an idle. The man who comes out and walks across the deck moments later is obviously Marcus Tumble — he's definitely Marius's twin, and not the fraternal kind.

"*Hello*," Colby murmurs under his breath, and when I laugh he looks at me, grins, and says, "*He's* my type."

After waving at us Marcus hangs a few scuffed red orbs over the side of the boat to keep the wharf from scraping the gleaming white hull. Then he tosses each of us the looped end of a thick rope, one for the front of the boat, one for the back; we fit these around the steel anchors on the edge of the wharf. That done, Marcus opens a gate in the railing and hops gracefully from the boat to the wharf, no gangplank needed.

"I'm Marcus Tumble," he says. "You guys order a boat?"

Marcus seems to be exactly my height but his feet are bare on the wharf, which means he's actually got at least a half-inch on me. His skin is darker than his brother's but creamier somehow, as if burnished under the sun. His short hair is highlighted here and there with the copper curls of someone who spends a lot of time in the ocean. He wears sharp khaki shorts and a blue polo shirt that has *Tumble Aquatic Tours* embroidered on the left pec.

"This is Colby Kroft," I say, introducing them (not soon enough for Colby, I'm sure). "He's Ryan's brother."

Colby is grinning as he shakes Marcus's hand.

"Shame about Ryan," Marcus says to us both.

I nod. "Got your brother off second-string, though."

"Shame about Ryan," he repeats. Then he smirks, just barely.

"Brotherly tension?"

"Just the inevitable when one's a superstar athlete and the other's a bookworm."

"Well we're glad he hooked us up with you. I thought transportation was going to be our biggest hurdle."

"Fate," Colby says. Without taking his eyes off Marcus he adds, "I like your boat."

"Thanks."

"Fast?"

"Well, it's a touring boat so it's not meant for speed. But it can get up there if I push it."

"I bet you're a great captain," Colby says.

I roll my eyes. I pray Marcus is a homo, for Colby's sake and for Marcus's own. Somehow I don't think Colby would take straight for an answer.

What finally breaks Colby's eye-lock on Marcus is a staccato *ka-thunk ka-thunk ka-thunk* coming down the wharf. I turn and see Piper dragging a wheeled suitcase behind him, one hand shielding his eyes from the sun. He's wearing tan corduroy shorts and a sleeveless Warriors tee, and I notice with surprise that his hair is gone—his trademark wild shock of blond mohawk has been buzzed down to stubble.

It makes him look very different, and very good. And it makes me gulp.

"You like?" he says, rubbing his scalp when he sees me staring.

"What happened?"

"Nothing *happened*. I just didn't want the wind slapping it in my face for three weeks. So you like?"

"It's different."

He grins. "Wanna feel?"

"No."

"Touch it. You'll like it."

"It was better the other way," Colby snorts.

Smirking, I change the subject by introducing Piper and Marcus.

"Just waiting for Santiago now," I tell Marcus, scanning the boardwalk for any sign of Clemente. "He said he had to bring his dog to his mom's."

"His mom lives in my building," Piper says.

"I know."

"I didn't see him."

"He'll be here."

"Well," Marcus says, "I can't stay parked here too long or I'll get a ticket. Someone want to flick him some urgency or something?"

"I will." I pull out my phone.

"Meantime," Marcus says, "if you guys want to come aboard I can start giving you the tour."

He jumps back onto the Intrepid, and with one hand on the railing grabs for Piper's suitcase to haul it aboard.

"Boots. Hey." Colby's giving me his backpack and espadrilles, and when I take them he rubs his hands together.

"What're you—?"

But before I can ask he's leaping barefoot from the wharf to the Intrepid's flat white railing, and without really stopping he pushes off the railing and rolls into a graceful somersault, landing in a crouching position with a squeak when his feet meet the glossy hardwood of the yacht's main deck. Straightening up, he fixes his shirt and drops his hands casually in his pockets, moseys over to the prow, and seems to check things out there. Smooth, but I know the little showoff's squirming to turn around and make sure Marcus saw the show.

Marcus did; his mouth is open a little.

Very smooth, I think. Except that Colby's still got a drawstring dangling against his butt.

After glancing again down the still-empty wharf, I join the other three on the boat. Immediately I feel the motion of the waves and remind myself I'll have to get used to it quick.

"You can set your stuff here for now," Marcus tells us, pushing aside a deck chair so we can line our luggage against the wall. "This here's the main deck," he says, rotating slowly. The big expanse of hardwood reflects sunlight that appears as glowing streaks on the railings and the enclosed cabin behind us. A cable running from a pole on the prow across the deck to the cabin roof swings a series of colorful square flags that look like Buddhist prayer flags. "Nice place for hanging out, out here," Marcus says.

"I imagine it gets pretty windy?" Piper says, looking around, hands on hips.

"When we're moving, yes, until— Hold on." Marcus presses a button on his phone and a big transparent windscreen grows up from against the prow with a mechanical whir. "That cuts most of it."

The main deck continues back at a width of about three feet on both sides of the enclosed cabin. Marcus brings us around inside, through a narrow doorway with a bottom lip we have to step over. In here the floor is soft tan carpet. Navy-blue vinyl couches run below the windows on the port and starboard sides. It looks like a living room.

"I guess this is technically called the *salon*," Marcus says, "but I call it the bridge."

"Aye aye, captain," Colby says. "Luxurious!"

"Over here's where the magic happens."

The front of the bridge is all windshield, and Marcus shows us the navigation stuff there. The dashboard is packed with video screens and instrument panels— levers and buttons. Two comfy, low-backed chairs are stationed in front of it.

"Looks complicated," Piper says.

"Looks that way," Marcus says, "but a lot of it can be automated. The boat can run on autopilot almost indefinitely."

"Almost?"

"Well," Marcus laughs, "certain disturbances will knock it off autopilot. Then it needs a real live driver."

I ask what counts as a disturbance.

"Like any significant change in ocean conditions. Hitting a rogue wave'll do it. Or like if we were to crash into a buoy or something."

"It can't avoid a buoy?" Piper says, incredulous.

Marcus shrugs. "It's not great at seeing little objects floating on the surface. It'll avoid another boat. It'll see, like, a sandbar or a reef. But stuff right on the surface, not so much."

"Ah."

"It's not foolproof," Marcus adds, "but it'll save a ton of time getting to Hawaii. We can drive at night. At reduced speed, of course."

"That's zilla cool," Colby says.

"Where do your tours normally go?" I ask. I look out the window for Clemente. He should be hearing this stuff. True, I was annoyed when I felt like he was taking over, but I'm freaking out without him.

"Up and down the coast," Marcus says. "Mexico to Canada. More often near Mexico."

"Ever gone to Hawaii?"

"Never been to Hawaii."

"Water's water, right?" Colby laughs.

"Well... Not exactly." Marcus grins. "But I'll get you there."

I feel my phone vibrate. It's a text from Clemente: *Scrambling. Almost there. Sorry.*

I relay it to the others. Marcus checks his watch.

In the floor at the back of the bridge there's an opening with a hatch that looks like a cellar bulkhead.

"Want to see the sleeping cabins now or should we wait for your friend?" Marcus asks.

I blurt that we'll wait. I don't want to pick beds

without Clemente here. If there's bunking involved I don't want to end up with Piper. Especially with his new haircut. That's more temptation than I need.

So instead Marcus takes us through the back door of the bridge, which leads down steep narrow steps to the lower deck. Unlike the main deck, the lower deck is only two feet above the water line. Here the railings are solid, more like walls to keep out the waves. Marcus pulls a handle in the back wall and a portion of it swings inward, giving access to the water.

"In places where there's no pier space we sometimes have to row ashore," Marcus says, "in those." He points behind us to two dinghies lashed vertically to the wall on either side of the stairs.

" — Anybody home?"

I look up with relief. Clemente is peering down at us from the main deck beside the bridge.

"Should I come down?" he asks, touching a sneaker to the top rung of the ladder that connects the main deck to the lower one.

"We'll come up," Marcus says. "Join us on the bridge."

"The *bridge!*" Clemente coos.

When we get inside he's standing near the steering wheel, perusing the instruments with his hands clasped behind his back, as if to keep himself from poking any buttons. He turns. His face and neck are shiny with sweat and his white t-shirt has gone transparent in all the best places — I can see his scorpion tattoo and his nipples through the fabric. He has on skinny jeans shorts and he's wearing Chucks, no socks.

"Haven't I seen you before?" Clemente teases, shaking Marcus's hand. "Sorry, you must get sick of twin jokes. Thanks for doing this."

"Thanks for hiring me," Marcus laughs. "You didn't

see any meter maids out there, did you?" He leans out the door to check the wharf. "Let me show you the downstairs quick so we can be off."

He leads the way down the hatch, followed by Colby and Piper.

"Made it, huh?" I say to Clemente.

"Wouldn't miss it, mi amigo." He squeezes my shoulder and we head downstairs.

The walls below deck are close and smooth and pink, and Piper is quick to joke that it looks like a colonoscopy. Marcus frowns.

"Just kidding," Piper adds.

Marcus shows us the galley, which is like the world's most efficient kitchen. There's a sink, microwave, fridge, stove—even a little clothes washer and dryer. Stacked against one wall are some cardboard boxes.

"Foodstuffs," Marcus says, drumming his fingers on the stack. "The stuff you ordered."

"Hey, nice, you got my hard cider," Clemente says.

Across from the galley is the bathroom, which I expect to be as cramped as an airplane bathroom, but it's spacious, with a full-size toilet and shower.

"You could fit three people in this shower," Marcus says, and coughs, adding, "I really don't recommend more than, uh, two."

Colby catches my eye and bites down on his knuckle.

"And fresh water is obviously at a premium on the Intrepid," Marcus adds, "so, short showers!"

He closes the bathroom door and leads us farther down the pink hallway.

"Now, it's up to you guys who sleeps where. I've got one cabin with bunks—that's the smaller one. The other one—well here, take a look."

He opens the door. The cabin holds a queen-size bed.

Against one wall is an upper bunk with a bureau beneath it.

"The big bed splits in half," Marcus says, "into two twins." He looks at us. "Any of you guys a couple?"

A loaded question if ever there was one. Piper and I *were* a couple and Piper sure would like us to be one again. Clemente gave me one of the best fucks of my life but he doesn't sleep with guys. Colby looks about ready to propose marriage to Marcus.

"No," I say.

"OK, so you can fight for the big bed or separate it. And back here's the second cabin," Marcus says, opening the next door.

Piper looks at me. "Boots, I was thinking we—"

"Boots and I will take this one," Clemente announces to Marcus, grabbing my shoulder and pushing me inside. He looks in after me. "Yeah, this is fine." He looks back at Piper and Colby. "You two can duke it out for the queen."

Piper looks at Clemente and frowns; Colby looks at Piper and frowns.

"That your room?" Colby says to Marcus. There's an old-fashioned galleon's steering wheel hanging on the door at the end of the hall.

"That's mine."

"Can I see it?"

"Um. I guess so? It's kind of messy...."

He opens the door a few inches but from where I'm standing I can't see much of the cabin. I spot a stack of laundry folded on the bed.

"Do you live here all the time?" Colby says. "Like on the ship?"

"Yup. Pretty much."

"Nice." Still looking into the cabin he adds, clearly trying to sound casual, "Do you date guys?" I don't know whether something he saw made him ask, or whether he simply could no longer contain it.

Marcus looks surprised — maybe. He sinks his hands in his pockets and looks at his feet. "Yeah. I do. Why?"

"No reason," Colby says, though he's blushing.

After Marcus leaves to let us get settled in, Clemente and I are alone in our cabin. It's the first time since boarding the boat that I feel an adventure is beginning. Maybe it's the glimpse of the Thebes skyline I can see through the high porthole — the circular view is like something you'd see through a telescope. It makes the city look far away even though we're still parked at the wharf.

I sit down on the spacious bottom bunk; I don't even have to duck my head, and the mattress feels comfy enough. Clemente is standing beside the beds digging in his backpack on the top bunk.

He takes off his sweaty t-shirt to trade for a fresh one he's pulled out of his pack. From where I'm sitting I can only see him up to his nipples and the bottom of his scorpion, so I can look with abandon at his appendix scar and fuzzy abs — a few beads of sweat cling in his belly button. I feel myself starting to get hard so I cross my legs and lean forward. Is he doing this to me on purpose?

"How'd you get so sweaty anyway?"

He pulls on the t-shirt and steps away from the bunks. He rubs his hair. "Ran from my mom's place. It was farther than I thought!"

"Ah. Trooper sorry to see you go?"

Sitting down beside me, he begins to unlace his Chucks. "Nah. He and my mom's cat are old buddies. Was like I wasn't even there. Fickle pooch."

I laugh. Going barefoot seems like a great idea so I kick off my own shoes. When I try to push them under the bed they clunk against some kind of storage compartment. I guess on the Intrepid there's no wasted space. It would be good for hide and seek.

"Hey, thanks for snagging me as a roommate before Piper could," I whisper, because the walls don't seem very thick and Colby and Piper are right next door. I've already heard Colby hooting about something once. "That would've been awkward."

"No sweat." Clemente gets up, peers through the porthole. "We moving?"

"I think I hear the engines."

"Yeah. —Well, I figured it was the least I could do. I brought him along, didn't have to make you sleep with the guy too." With a teasing grin he adds, "What do you think of the haircut?"

"I'd rather not say."

"You think it's hot, don't you."

I wave my hand. "*Pffft.*"

"Well if he gets you too steamed up you can always just toss him ov—" Suddenly Clemente grabs for the bunk and I reach out and push his hip to keep him from falling on me. "OK," he says, peering again through the porthole as the floor rumbles beneath our feet, "*now* we're moving."

When we get up to the main deck Colby and Piper are already there, standing with arms folded on the rail, watching Thebes drop away behind us. Our trail of wavy foam makes it look as though we're unspooling the city like a kite. Behind us in the bridge Marcus wears a determined grin as he pilots us around traffic buoys and anchored sailboats. He loves his boat, I can tell. I'll love it too, if it gets me what I want.

"That's my mom's place," Clemente says, nudging me and pointing. "See?"

"I see the building." It's one of many in the jagged skyline.

"Mine's a few floors above hers," Piper says, and he adds, "I had to go penthouse."

"I don't know about those fancy places," Colby says wistfully as the breeze slaps his hair around. "I think it would be more fun to live on a boat."

"You just want to live with our captain," Clemente teases, socking Colby on the shoulder.

"Don't make me pin you again, Santiago."

Clemente holds up his hands.

I smile, let the waves bump me against Clemente.

Colby turns to the port side, where ahead of us there's only blue all the way to the horizon's curve, and cups his hands against his mouth.

"We're coming for you, bro!" he yells, and the wind seems to pick up his voice and amplify it across the endless sea. *"We're coming for you!"*

Chapter 13

Alone on this boat we'd probably be swinging from the rafters. Balancing on the railings. Cooking up vats of bubble bath in the shower and playing slip n slide on the main deck with the suds. We'd be going the kind of crazy being on a kickass yacht like this makes a bunch of young guys want to go.

But Marcus—the captain, the owner—is here and with him around we don't quite know what to do with ourselves. It's almost like having the concierge sitting on one of the beds of your hotel room, watching you. You're not going to jump on the mattresses. You're not going to crank up the heat and walk around naked.

Marcus is cool but he's the boss, so we hang out politely on the bridge, keep our feet off the couches. I doubt this'll last long—we'll settle in soon enough—but for now it's here and it's palpable. A few minutes ago when Colby farted against the vinyl he actually said *Excuse me* rather than fanning it around the room.

We're shooting the shit. Warriors gossip, current events. Polite topics. Marcus explains a little more about the Intrepid. He's most proud of its engine, a top-of-the-line, hydrogen-powered beast that doubled the cost of the yacht.

"But it was worth it," he says, spinning around in the captain's chair, hands clasped behind his head. "Imagine: a boat that runs on water!"

His enthusiasm is contagious but you have to admit it *is* pretty cool. By now we're all used to putting hydrogen in our cars but that still requires a stop at the pump now and then; in that way modern cars aren't so different from the old-fashioned gasoline-powered road hogs of yore. But a boat that turns water into speed?

"Fuel-wise, we could drive 24/7 without stopping," Marcus tells us.

But humans are still humans, he says, and humans can't run on just water. So rather than cut straight across the Pacific, heading to Hawaii as the crow flies, he's put us on a course due south. There's a pit-stop he wants to make in Mexico, at a port where he's a regular, to refresh our food and supplies and to let us stretch our legs on solid ground.

"Trust me," he says when we groan about having to delay our arrival at exile island, "you'll want a break from my baby before long."

And as darkness falls I start to understand what he means. The clear sky turned cloudy long before sunset, and now that it's dark I can't tell if the water dotting the windshield is ocean spray or rain. I lost sight of the shoreline an hour ago, when the lights of civilization finally succumbed to haze and distance. It's easy to imagine the Intrepid is a spaceship hurtling through the void. And it's a little unsettling.

"All righty," Piper says, getting up off the couch, "I need a drink. Anyone else?"

I ask for a beer and Colby boastfully orders a Scotch on the rocks. Piper laughs and tells us he'll see what he can find in the galley. Clemente goes down with him to look.

When they're gone I kick Colby in the butt and make him get up so I can stretch out on the couch. He goes willingly but we both know the couch would be his if he wanted it.

"Can I drive?" he says to Marcus as he plops into the empty chair in front of the dashboard.

Marcus looks at him, grinning. He presses some buttons. "Sure," he says. Then he backs away. "All yours."

"No. Really?" Colby springs to his feet, clutches the wheel like he might have to wrestle it. "What do I *do?*"

"Drive. Like you said."

"I wasn't serious, Marcus!" His knuckles are white on the wheel. "Maybe this was a bad idea."

"You're doing fine. Bank us this way a little," Marcus says, gesturing.

"I don't want to flip us over."

"You won't flip us."

Colby turns the wheel, slowly at first, then harder, but the Intrepid doesn't seem to respond.

"Hey."

"It's on autopilot," Marcus laughs.

"Dope. I knew that." Colby spins the wheel like a

game-show host but it has no effect on our direction. "How do I get it off? Hit a rogue wave?"

"That'll do it. Otherwise you need my fingers to get it off."

I smirk but neither of them seems to notice that little double entendre.

"So you have magic hands?" Colby teases.

"Something like that."

I sit up. "Do you really need your fingerprints to take it off autopilot?"

"It's a security thing," Marcus says. "That way I can leave the bridge while the autopilot's on and no one who's chilling up here can screw with the settings."

"That makes sense. But what if someone else needs to stop the boat?"

"It'll steer around anything really dangerous. Some things I guess we'd just plow through."

"Like a buoy."

"Calculated risk," Marcus says.

"So will you ditch the autopilot so I can steer for real?" Colby says.

Marcus smiles. Colby's hooked him already, I can see it in Marcus's eyes—it'll only be another day or two before he's fully reeled in, if he can even hold out that long.

When Clemente and Piper return with a tray of drinks and a bucket of ice, we sit around the bridge and continue our small-talk. I'm not bored—the situation's too novel to be boring—but I do wonder if all Tumble Aquatic Tours are this quiet. Marcus keeps close to the captain's chair, as if he's not sure how much to participate. On other tours his role is probably mostly as pilot. We, on the other hand, have sort of made him a teammate. A bookworm among his brother's jock buddies. No wonder he's quiet.

But you can always count on Colby to supply some comic relief. A minute ago I noticed him put his Scotch down; there was a wary look on his face. Now he's bounding off the couch. The thrown-open door clangs the wall of the bridge as Colby jumps out to the main deck and pukes in a horizontal stream over the side of the fast-moving boat.

Clemente lowers his bottle of cider and says, "Nice to see that kid's human."

"You OK out there?" I yell.

Colby turns to face us, slumping against the rail. He drags his forearm across his mouth.

"Scotch-sick or seasick?" Clemente asks.

"Both-sick," Colby groans. He comes back into the bridge, closes the door, walks past us to the stairs. "I need bed."

"Thanks for getting it over the railing," Marcus says.

Colby just looks embarrassed as he disappears below deck.

"Don't throw up in my room," Piper calls.

Later, I'm in bed watching Clemente Santiago undress in the moonlight.

That sounds way sexier than it is.

With the motion of the boat and Clemente's alcohol-fueled tipsiness, he's already banged into the wall a few times peeling off his shorts. But now he's out of them, looking out through the porthole in nothing but a pair of his white square-cut briefs. The light makes him ghostlike. I can feel my heart pounding. He's a little bit drunk....

"Never slept on a boat before," he says, coming over to the bunks and looking down at me. Then he straightens up and grabs the top bunk, pulls himself up.

His hairy muscled legs dangle for a moment and his feet kick the air before finding purchase against my ribcage — his toes press hard into me and get enough traction to step him up the rest of the way. "Hope I can do it," he adds, creaking the mattress as he settles in.

I'm barely breathing. "Do what?"

"Sleep!"

"Oh. Yeah."

I don't know about him but it's pretty clear I won't be getting to sleep with the giant boner that's suddenly trying to tear through my underwear. I need to hit the bathroom for a quick jerkfest to get rid of it.

I snap my fingers. "Whoops, forgot to brush my teeth!"

"Don't want gingivitis," he says.

"Nope."

I pull back the sheet and it looks like I'm smuggling a paintball rifle in my underoos. No way I can leave our cabin like this. *Think of Colby puking, think of Colby puking.* I imagine the smell. I imagine he hadn't gotten outside in time. I imagine pools of it sloshing around the bridge.

That does the trick. I can be seen in public now. I get out of bed and leave our cabin.

Marcus's door is open, and he's sitting on the edge of his bed, poking at a tablet. He's still wearing his ironed khakis but his shirt is off. Great chest. Is there a gym on this boat I haven't noticed?

"G'night," I tell him.

He looks up. "Goodnight."

I turn back. "We're on autopilot?"

"Sure are."

"We won't hit anything?"

"Nah," he says. "Clear sailing."

"Cool. G'night."

I pass the galley. On the counter is the dishware we

used politely this evening. There's no dishwasher and we haven't discussed whose job it'll be to wash everything.

As I near the bathroom I begin conjuring the image of Clemente's bare legs and feel my dick springing back to attention. But never mind his legs. When I'm beating off I'm going to think of him pounding his cock into me—because however much that might feel like the memory of a dream, it *did* happen.

The bathroom light's on and my thought-bubbles quiver and burst. Fuck. It's Piper. Why has he not closed the door? He's standing at the sink wearing nothing but tight yellow briefs. Toothpaste foam covers his chin. He spits, looks out at me.

"Sorry," I say. "Uh. Forgot to brush my teeth."

He steps aside. "There's room."

"I'll come back when you're done."

"Kid took the queen bed," he says, holding out the toothpaste tube. "Can you believe that?"

"Colby?"

"This afternoon we separated the queen so neither of us would have to sleep on that shitty little bunk, right?" He straightens up and foam from his chin plunks onto his right pectoral; the motion of the boat makes it zigzag down his chest. He smears it away with his palm. "Anyway, I come down tonight and he's got the two halves pushed back together again. And he's sleeping all snug, dead center."

"Sneaky. So you get the bunk?"

"Lucky me, right?"

I lean in the doorway. Looking at Piper now, I realize why his new buzzed haircut is so sexy: with short hair it's more obvious how wide and broad his neck and shoulders are.

"You should've gotten into bed with him," I say.

"Seen what happened."

"Hah. Didn't think of that. He'd probably body-slam me out the window."

I laugh.

"You said you needed to brush your teeth?"

I shrug, grab my toothbrush, squirt on some paste. The brushing was a cover—my teeth are going to be double clean tonight. Standing beside me in front of the sink, Piper splashes water in his mouth, then dries his face on his forearm. This is far from the first time he and I have shared a bathroom sink, though we were always more likely to be naked while doing it, and the last time we did it was in a college dorm. We used to do that silly thing where we'd use toothpaste foam to draw beards and mustaches and hats and earrings on our reflections in the mirror....

He's remembering this too; I can see the nostalgia in his eyes. When he touches his finger to my lips to gather foam, I say quietly, "Don't."

"I wasn't."

"You were."

He smiles coyly. "I just didn't want it to drip."

Without actually having to look down, I can see in the mirror that he's hard. And I see that I'm hard. He sees it too.

"Let me touch you," he says, cupping my erection in his hand.

"No." I squeeze his wrist and hold it away from me. With the other hand I shut the door, closing us in.

He shakes his head, grins. "You want it, B. As much as you always used to want it."

"I'm trying to be good."

"It wouldn't be bad."

"Why did you come on this trip?"

"You invited me."

146

"*Clemente* invited you."

I feel his arm go limp and I let go of it. But he shrugs and grins again. He's unflappable. It's part of his so-called charm.

"So this means you're not going to let me give you the best blowjob of your life right now?"

I turn and look toward the shower curtain. "Yes, Piper, that's what it means."

He moves himself back into my line of vision. "You, Boots McHenry, are hereby turning down the most incredible blowjob of your life? I'd lick your balls, too. I remember how much you love that."

I roll my eyes.

He leans back against the wall, shakes his fist dramatically as I open the door.

"I'll get you inside me again, Boots McHenry. If it's the last thing I do!"

Faced with the double whammy of an unrelieved boner and the constant up-and-down motion of the Intrepid—both of which only grow more obnoxious the more I try to ignore them—I know that sleep is going to be near impossible tonight.

"Are you awake?" I whisper, in case he isn't.

"Oh yeah," Clemente laughs, fully alert. I hear him shift in his bunk and then his head drops over the side—I can see the top of his head and his two brown eyes. "And sober enough to know I'm going to be awake for a while."

"Waves bothering you?"

"Yup."

"Me too."

He pulls his head back up and sighs.

"Want to go up on deck?" I ask. "Check out the stars or whatever?"

"That sounds positively romantic, McHenry."

We pull on some sweatshirts and as we pass the galley we can't help but grab another six-pack of his hard cider.

"Feels so naughty," Clemente whispers.

But when we get upstairs we find there's no reason to be sneaking around, because the others have had the same idea. Colby is on the couch playing a game on his phone, and Piper is outside on the main deck, leaning against the rail with another beer. He looks deep in thought, and I suspect he's coming up with new ways to try to get me back.

"Can't sleep either?" I say to Colby.

He shakes his head.

"Still feeling pukey?"

"Nah. Better."

"Want some more *booze?*" Clemente grins, holding out a hard cider.

Colby smirks, shows us a bottle of water with something foamy, like Alka-Seltzer, on the surface.

"We're having a seasick party," I say. "Come sit outside with us."

"Do, but swing down and wake up Marcus first," Clemente tells him, "and bring him with you. And ask him to put up the windscreen thing on your way out. We'll save you a seat."

With folding chairs arranged in a loose circle and a storage trunk in the center covered with bottles of beer and hard cider at various levels of emptiness, the five of us shoot the shit (less politely already), give Colby crap about his weak stomach, and run through a bunch of crazy ideas about what we might find at exile island. The windscreen is up and it's so effective at shielding the main deck that the prayer flags overhead are barely fluttering.

And when we've exhausted everything except our intolerance for the waves—which Marcus promises we'll get used to soon enough—and when the night is as deep as the ocean around us, Piper suggests we play First & Last as a way of getting to know each other better. My pulse quickens and I glance at Clemente.

"What's First & Last?" he says, looking from me to Piper.

"Anyone else ever played?" Piper says.

"I've played," Colby replies. "You tell about your first time and your most recent time."

"I've played," I say. *Played* isn't quite the right word, though—First & Last is more of a conversation kick-starter than a game.

"First and last time getting laid, you mean?" Clemente says.

"Of course," Piper replies.

"All right," Clemente says, sounding to me surprisingly willing in light of the two hours we clocked in my bed. Is he really OK with telling everyone his last time was with *me?* Assuming his last time *was* with me.

"Guys," I say, wanting to give him an out, "Clemente doesn't want to hear about a bunch of teenage homos going down on each other. Let's talk about something else."

"It's OK, McHenry," Clemente says, waving dismissively with bottle in hand. He seems to know what I'm thinking, because he winks. "All good."

"You sure?"

"Zilla sure. Am I not a player?"

Oh. I guess that means our night together, at least for *him*, has been bumped into the giant middle-ground this game leaves uninvestigated. And I'm—what? Relieved? Disappointed? Both?

Rubbing his hands together, Piper, who's always liked talking about sex, asks who wants to go first.

"I'll go," Marcus says, and by the looks on our faces he's surprised all of us. I was expecting we'd have to drag him in at the end. And he isn't even drinking.

"Details, remember," Piper says.

"Lots of details," Colby adds.

Marcus looks down at his water, rubs condensation off the bottle with his thumb. "OK, so my first time—"

"It didn't involve your brother, did it?"

"Uh. No."

Colby smirks. "Sorry. Go on."

Marcus clears his voice. "My first time— So are we doing first actual intercourse? Or first sexual experience?"

"Whichever one you liked better," Colby says.

"First sexual experience," Piper says.

"OK."

Colby leans forward eagerly. I notice drops of condensation from his water making a wet spot on his lap. At least I *think* it's condensation.

"We were in Teen Mountaineers," Marcus begins. "On a camping trip."

"Awh, you were a Mountaineer?" Colby gushes.

Clemente rolls his eyes, smiling. "Let the guy tell it."

"And, um, it was nighttime," Marcus continues. "We were all in our tents. I had to pee. So I crawled out of mine, and I didn't want to wake anyone up. It was the middle of the night. I was pretty freaked out—we'd seen a mountain lion earlier. But I went to the latrine and was peeing and something tapped my shoulder and I screamed. Actually, no, it was more of a *choke* than a scream. And my pee stopped short. My heart too. But it wasn't a lion, it was this other Mountaineer named Kale. And he must've seen how freaked out I was, because he just looked so sorry for scaring me. He kind of turned me to him and hugged me, and of course I was still, like, hanging out of my drawers, and you know, before long it was poking him in the belly. So he touched it and I thought I was going to explode right there, and then he told me he wanted to—"

"*Wanted to what?*" Colby interrupts.

Blushing, Marcus makes a quick motion with his fist and cheek.

"Jesus," Colby gasps. He looks intoxicated again.

"But, you know, he didn't want to do it near the latrine because that's gross, so we walked to the river. He used his phone for a flashlight. The moon was out and it almost sounds romantic—and I guess it would've been if not for all the mosquitoes. So we were kind of just standing around on the shore with our pants down, and we took turns—" Again he makes the blowjob motion. "And after we finished and talked for a while we went back to our tents. Next day we both had mosquito bites on our butts but that was kind of our funny secret."

Colby sighs.

"So this guy," Clemente says, as though trying to piece together the logistics of guy-on-guy hookups, "he just walked up to you one night and started sucking on your dick?"

"No," Marcus laughs. "We'd kissed a few times before that. It wasn't out of the blue."

"OK."

"Did you get with him again after that?" Colby asks.

"A few times." Marcus thinks about it. "He was a year older than me. He went off to college. And that was that."

"So nice," Colby swoons.

"Now your last," I say to Marcus.

"Last was nothing special. This guy I've dated off

and on lately. Paul. In his apartment. In his bed. While his hedgehog watched us. It was weird."

"So this guy Paul," Colby says, obviously trying to sound disinterested. "Nothing serious?"

Marcus looks at him and smiles. "Nothing serious. Why?"

Colby purses his lips and looks at the sky. "No reason."

"Jeez, you guys," Piper says. "All right, who's next?"

I tell them I'll go. Piper grins.

"First time. Let's see.... It's not as good as yours, Marcus."

"Mine's really not *that* good."

"I *assume*," Colby teases, "that your first time was with my brother. Right, Boots?"

"Sorry," I laugh. "My first time wasn't even with Piper."

Piper shrugs. "He was a slut before I met him."

I continue: "Mine was freshman year of high school. His name was BJ. My first boyfriend."

"I never get tired of hearing this," Piper says.

"BJ Macintosh," I continue. "It was a typical school-kid relationship where it's so dramatic and important. We hung out a lot and I liked him but the whole thing was more about being seen together at school, to round-out our coolness or whatever—I was jock-popular and he was musician-popular. Anyway, we were at the movies holding hands and I reached over and started rubbing his crotch. I felt him get hard. After like twenty seconds, tops, he came. I felt it through his pants. I practically fainted from thinking it was so great, that I'd made that happen to him. But BJ started freaking out because he had on these skinny tan pants that were sporting this huge dark spot now. He couldn't go around the mall like that, obviously. So I ran out of the theater to buy him new pants. I had about ten minutes before the movie ended. I looked for the same kind he was wearing but I only had enough money to buy these flimsy sweatpants shorts. He wore them home."

"That's sweet," Marcus says.

"Not exactly. He was embarrassed and so angry. We stopped dating after that. We had our official break-up in the cafeteria and he moved to a different table."

"Harsh," Clemente says.

"And then my last one —"

I don't think it's just my imagination: they all tense up, probably expecting a tearful recollection of Ryan. But Ryan wasn't my last. And I'm not about to tell them my last was Clemente, especially if his last wasn't me. To have someone be your last and to not have been their last too can be zilla awkward — which is really why this game's a hit in big groups. No, I'm not going to say Clemente.

"My last sexual encounter was actually with a swimming pool jet in my backyard."

They all laugh, thankful for a joke rather than tears.

Piper gently rubs my shoulder. Then he leans and whispers in my ear, "Didn't have to be."

"What if the jet pulled your boner right off, though?" Colby says.

"Not the sucking one," I tell him, laughing. "The blowing-in one."

"Ooh. Oooh, I never thought of that...."

"It'll do in a pinch. OK, Colby, you go next."

"Me? OK. My first was last year." He says it bashfully. "So it's still fresh in my mind."

"Wait," Marcus says, leaning forward, "how old are you?"

"Eighteen."

"Why did I ho— Why did I think you were older?"

"How old are *you?*" Colby says.

"Twenty-four."

"Barely a difference."

"I guess so. Never mind. Go on. Sorry."

Colby glances at me and wiggles his eyebrows; the kid's not very subtle.

"So you didn't lose your big V until age seventeen?" Clemente says. "Isn't that old, especially for a homo?"

"Well I was training pretty much *all* the time," Colby says. "Didn't leave tons of time for dating. But yeah, my senior year, I was at a tourney in Seattle."

"Tourney?" Marcus says.

"Uh. Tournament? Junior MMAC. Mixed martial arts?"

"... You're in the MMAC?"

"*Junior* MMAC," Colby says. "For now."

"He was the Junior MMAC *champ* last year," I add.

Marcus leans back in his chair, touches the water bottle to his chin. "Hence the somersaulting onto my boat."

"I guess," Colby says.

Piper says, "Did you fuck a teammate?"

"Let me get to it!"

"Let him get to it guys, jeez," Clemente teases.

"I had a few matches already and it was the night before my big one. We're in this big hotel, this fancy place. I'm supposed to be resting up or whatever. My coach: all business. Some of the other guys who were done their fights got to go out on the town. But for me it's house arrest. I'm watching videos of the guy I'm going to be fighting the next day, and I'm starting—"

"Videos?" I say.

"Videos. Like of his previous matches. So I can get a sense of his moves."

"I *bet* you were getting a sense of his moves," Piper

says. "Those MMAC boys are banging."

"I really was," Colby laughs. "Because you're right, he was zilla hot. I'm popping the biggest boner watching this guy. He's really heating me up. But Coach told us all: no sex for at least one week before the tourney. Supposedly being horny improves a guy's fighting instincts or whatever? I don't know."

"Sex releases hormones that mellow you out," Marcus says.

"Right," Colby says, "so no sex. And no jerking off either. So when I'm about ready to pop from watching this guy I stop the video and walk around the hotel for a while scoping things out. I end up on the roof-deck. To cool off. There's nobody up there at first and then I notice one guy leaning against the railing. I recognize him right away because I was just watching videos of him. This guy's my opponent."

"Oh god," Clemente laughs.

"So I go over and we start talking or whatever, and eventually he says something about how I look even better in person. So obviously he's been studying my moves too."

"So to speak," Piper says.

"And the guy's like, *To be honest your videos were turning me on a lot so I thought I would come up here to try to focus.* Then he tells me how his coach told him the same thing about the no-sex policy. And I'm like, *Bummer, me too.* And by now we're sort of standing really close, and I can smell his breath, which smells really nice like coconut or something, and I have this boner slamming around in my pants like a battering ram. And I go, *I can't believe I would meet such a cute guy and be stuck with this stupid rule.* And he's like, *I know, it sucks.* But then he puts his hand under my shirt and touches my abs and I feel my boner start singing *opera* practically. But I get mad, too, because it's like, this guy's trying to make me come so I'll get mellow and he'll have an advantage in our fight tomorrow, you know?! What a jerk! And I'm like, *Back off, bitch!* But this dude's wise, because he's like, *Well if we both get off together neither one of us will have the advantage tomorrow.*"

"Clever boy," Piper says.

Marcus is sitting very still with his hands folded on his lap, looking like he's trying to hide something. Colby has some innate storytelling abilities, for sure, because his use of present tense is making this way more immediate.

"And I'm like, *Yeah, actually you're right aren't you.* So we kind of start making out on the roof, and then we go back to my room and have sex."

There's a finality in Colby's tone that suggests that, with this abrupt ending, his story is finito. Meanwhile the rest of us, even the resident straightboy, are leaning toward him gaping.

"You *went back to your room and had sex*?" Piper cries. "What does that even mean? What kind of sex? What *happened?*"

"I don't know," Colby says, "we went back to my room and started making out on the bed, and then we took off our clothes and I fucked him."

"You *fucked* him? You fucked during your first-ever sexual encounter?"

Colby shrugs. "I fucked him until he came (I kind of wanted to make sure he went first, to make sure he wasn't trying to trick me). And then I pulled out and he licked my butt with his tongue while I jerked off and then I came too."

"Hold up, kiddo, hold up," Piper says, raising his hand. "Your very first time out, you fucked and rimmed? You sure jumped into the deep end, didn't you?"

Colby shrugs. "Came pretty natural, I thought."

"I know what a rimjob is," Clemente interjects proudly.

"Maybe you were just making up for lost time?" Marcus suggests.

"So this was last year," Piper says, "and how many guys have you been with since then?"

"Two since then. After Jack there was Matthew, then Tré."

"You remember their names, so sweet," Piper says, daintily patting Colby's knee. "So should I go next?"

"Wait a second, wait a second," Clemente interrupts. "Who won the match?"

"Oh. I did, of course," Colby laughs. "I had him pinned and he knew it, but he wouldn't tap out. He was a tough one. So I ended up having to dislocate his shoulder. But even still—"

"Wait wait wait," I say. "Ryan and I were at the match where you dislocated the guy's shoulder. *That* was the guy?"

Colby laughs. "That was him."

"You dislocated a guy's shoulder?" says Marcus.

"It happens," Colby says. "I've broken two guys' arms and one guy's femur when they wouldn't tap out."

"Yikes," Clemente says. "A femur? That's the thickest bone in the body."

"This's why I wanted to bring him along, remember?" I say to Clemente. Then I add, "I think Colby wins for best story."

"Clemente and I haven't even *gone* yet," Piper complains. "Although Clemente's is going to involve pussy, so one of us'll win by default."

"Go, Piper," Marcus says. "Actually, hold on." He gets up and goes to check something on the bridge, and returns a minute later. "OK."

"All right," Piper says. "So first. First was pretty scandalous. I was hanging with this guy Eli, who was a few years older than me. And gorgeous. And straight. I jerked off to him like fifty million times. Ever since I was capable of getting horny, Eli was the guy I was horny for. Sometimes I even opened video of his face on my tablet and set it on my pillow so I could gaze into his eyes while I fucked the mattress. Anyway, one day after I got home from driver's ed, Eli came over and took me out skateboarding at this park. Only I totally suck at skateboarding, surprisingly enough, so I mostly just watched him. And at one point he took off his shirt while he was on the half-pipe and threw it to me. Probably meant for me to stow it in his backpack or whatever but I held on to it, and kept holding it to my face smelling it, but pretending like I was just trying to hide my eyes when it looked like he might wipe out. Which of course he never did."

"Of course," Clemente says sarcastically.

"So I'm smelling his shirt. Watching the sun on his shiny back. And I just decide that whatever happens, *no matter what happens*, I need to get something going with him ASAP. Regardless of who he is. His pheromones were messing with my mind. So anyway, we went back to his house after that. His roommate's band was practicing in the basement, but Eli and I were just chilling on the couch watching TV. And drinking Cokes. And I think, *Now's my chance*. So I lean over and start kissing his neck, and at first he's like, *What the fuck, Piper!*, and he pulls away. But I just went along with him, and then started licking his neck. And he was like, *Piper, dude, no*. But then I started licking his collar bone and I could tell he liked that. He was sitting pretty stiff, like tense, but he wasn't pulling away anymore. He was in that paralyzed place between freaking out and wanting to see what was going to happen next. Just rigid. I noticed him close his eyes. Then I lifted up his shirt and started licking his nipples. I could see he was getting hard. He had on these loose shorts that were super easy for me to get down to let his dick out. He was breathing heavy and had his hands against the couch cushions as if he might jump up and run away at any second. When I took his dick in my mouth I remember being surprised by how intense the sweat smell was. I was repulsed for a split second before getting even more turned on by it. I heard him whisper, *Oh my god.* Half whisper, half laugh, like he couldn't believe this was happening. I remember feeling so psyched that he was enjoying it. I thought, *Fuck yeah!*"

"Then what?" I ask. I know the story—I've heard it a bunch of times—but I figure I'll help it along. "Did you swallow?"

He smirks at me. Maybe he's happy I'm playing a role. "I didn't blow him to completion. I wanted to but I didn't know what it would taste like or how much there would be. I didn't want to choke or anything. So no. But I jerked him off the rest of the way."

"How'd he act afterward?" Clemente asks. "Did he need some kind of cooling-off period?"

"He pulled up his shorts and just sat there for a minute. He had jizz on the front of his shirt. I wanted to jerk myself too but I didn't, I just sat there. Then he got up and went in his room. Came back a few minutes later with a new shirt but didn't mention anything about what happened. We went out skating again."

"Did he ever mention it?" Colby asks.

"Few days later, he said, *What happened on the couch shouldn't happen again.*"

"So who was this guy?" Clemente says. "You said

this was scandalous. Were you related to this guy?"

I smirk, and wait for it.

Piper grins. "First cousins."

"Oh oh!" Clemente claps his hands. "So wrong!"

"Hey," Piper says, "in most states you can marry your cousin."

Colby says, "That's so hot and so gross all at once."

"So he said it should never happen again," Marcus says. "Did it?"

"Yeah. Lots of times. Always on my terms."

"Nice," Colby says.

"It was nice in the sense that he was cool to me. He could've been a cocky jerk about it when he realized how much I wanted him. He could've been a dick because he had all the power. But he never was. He was kind and sweet. Which meant he broke my heart in the end."

"What happened?" Clemente asks.

"Nothing, really," Piper says, shaking his head, his voice softening. Are his eyes welling up or is that just the salt air? "I was young and silly and I started to think he was my boyfriend or whatever. He was straight, never felt the same way, just liked the physical part. So when he moved out of state, for him it was probably just a bummer, for me it was the end of the fucking world." He pauses. "He's like thirty now. Married to a woman. Just had their first kid a while ago. Still gorgeous, too."

"No chance your first was also your last, eh?" Marcus says gently.

"I wish. No." Piper glances at me. "My last was with some photographer guy in the Warriors locker room. We were doing a shoot and one thing led to another. Great ass." Again he looks at me; I know he's talking to me. "But it didn't mean anything. It was just a fuck. So that's that."

For a while the only sound is of waves and the

rumble of the hydrogen engine. Piper is wiping his eyes, and it seems that the game of First & Last is about to drop away before Clemente's told his tales. That would be OK with me even though I'd like to hear what he says. But then Marcus, perhaps feeling it's his duty as captain to salvage the mood, says, "OK Clemente, you're up. You sat through ours, now we'll sit through yours." He laughs.

"Oh, great," Clemente says, tipping his cider bottle and taking a swig. He leans forward in his chair.

"It's funny," Piper says, "we're always bombarded with hetero media, and yet, sitting here right now, I can't imagine any possible scenario where a guy and a girl would have sex."

"Believe it or not," Clemente says, "it does happen from time to time."

"Educate us," Piper laughs.

"OK. So I got in this big line near city hall, and when it was my turn I was paired up with this naked girl and I put my ding-dong in her hoo-ha and wiggled it around and then I went home."

Colby's jaw drops.

"I'm kidding, Colby."

There's nervous laughter.

"I was afraid you were serious," Colby says sheepishly.

"No, child, no." Clemente takes another long swig and settles back in his chair. "Her name was Sabrina. They tell of her in old tales passed down from father to son. She smelled of passion-fruit ice-cream and the sun followed her wherever she went like a puppy in love. She liked yellow and dancing and she called me Clemmy."

"I like this one," Colby says.

"She was the twin sister of my best buddy in high

school, Stefano. She was always around and I'd been noticing her *that way* since I met her. Had no idea if she was noticing me too, though. So anyway, in addition to liking yellow and dancing she was prone to terrible migraines. One weekend their parents went out of town so they threw a big bash. I got ready for that party all day. Planned to ask Sabrina out during it. Haircut, new shirt, tacky little bracelets like everyone was wearing back then. For an hour beforehand I did pushups so I'd look imposing when I told Stef I was going to ask out his sis. But when I finally worked up the courage Stef didn't even care, told me to go for it, told me I was a good guy, told me he thought she'd say yes. I stalked around the party working up the courage, but in that crowd of kids it took me a while to find her. Eventually found her in a corner in the upstairs hallway, squinting and rubbing her temples. I was like, *Oh shit, migraine?* She just nodded. I felt bad because I couldn't ask her out when she was sick, and I thought it was bad to add to the noise even by *talking* to her. So I just stood there with her. Finally I made a motion of pills and she said she'd already taken some. Then she took my hand and led me down through the house, through the kids, to the cellar. Brought me into the basement. She didn't turn on any lights but she knew where to go. Pitch dark. But I swear there was light coming off that yellow sundress of hers somehow. She brought me to this little hiding place behind a tarp-covered lawnmower or something, and we sat on the floor on this foam mattress thing like for in pools. *This is where I come when my head hurts,* she said. Because it's always so cool and quiet and dark. My eyes finally adjusted and I could see she had hers closed. I took her hands and started massaging her palms. Must've heard it can stimulate blood flow or something. Did that for a while. I thought it was really nice, being with her there, touching her. Then she started kissing me. I could tell she was still hurting but maybe kissing me was a distraction? Maybe it even made her better? We took off all our clothes and kissed and hugged and I kissed her all over her body, up and down, everywhere. I ended up squirting but it wasn't even over after that— we just kind of snuggled and hugged. I think her medicine started working a little while later."

"You know, headaches are usually used to get out of sex," Piper says. "She used one to get *into* it. Not bad, straightboy."

"I don't even know what to say about how sweet that story is," Colby says.

I look around and they all have dreamy grins on their faces. I must too. I want to touch him.

"Oh *pfft*," Clemente says, "a couple days later I totally fucked her hot wet pussy and blew buckets of jizz on her tatas." We laugh. "But no, seriously, we dated until college. She was my first love."

"Your first," Colby says. "Now tell us your last, *Clemmy*."

"My last, huh?" For a second he seems to be looking into his cider bottle. "The last time I had sex...." He's about to unspool a story about getting with a fan. Some chick he met at Yon's Kneecaps. An old girlfriend he ran into. Someone he met online. His neighbor. The lady at the supermarket. No way is he going to say me. No way. Then he glances at me and says, "It was with Boots."

The contents of four mouths are symbolically, if not literally, spewed toward the center of the circle.

He said it casually. Matter-of-factly. Without embarrassment and without humor. He looks from me to each of the others, one by one. Their faces are frozen in various states of blankness or open mouth. Colby's is the first to melt into a smirk.

"No way."

"Zilla way," Clemente nods.

Piper looks from Colby to Clemente to me, confusion spreading over his face. "Wait. Seriously? You guys slept together?"

"Seriously," Clemente says.

"Yeah, seriously," I confirm.

Piper looks down at his beer bottle, rocks it on the arm of the chair. "Oh." He seems frozen in a moment the rest of us have continued through. He looks at me again. "When?"

"... Couple days after the last game."

"Oh. I see." He looks away at the sea off the side of the boat. "Why?"

I look at Clemente and shrug, then back at Piper. I say, cautiously: "Shits and giggles?"

"It was just for fun," Clemente adds.

"Ah. Just a lark. I see. Why not, right? No one else available." Piper looks into his beer for a moment. "Excuse me." He puts the bottle on the crate and steps out of the circle, clutching the rail to steady himself. He goes inside through the bridge where we can't see him.

"Why he's so angry?" Marcus says. "Uh, if I can ask?"

"I think he's just feeling seasick," I say, getting up.

Marcus looks at Clemente, almost says something. Colby, who of all people has a right to be offended by the idea of Clemente and me hooking up, doesn't look offended — there's an amused smirk on his face.

I tell Clemente to tell Colby and Marcus the rest of the story if they want to hear it. Obviously they want to hear it.

I push my chair back and as I'm crossing from the deck to the bridge I hear Clemente begin, "Well Boots was feeling pretty wrecked about Ryan, and he just...."

A boat this size isn't a great place to be when you want to storm angrily away. There are only so many places you can go. You can lock yourself in your cabin, or in the bathroom, or, if you're really dramatic, you can threaten to throw yourself overboard. Piper hasn't done any of these things. I find him on the lower deck, sitting on the bench with his arm hanging over the port side, chin on his bicep.

"Piper, I just wanted the sex," I sigh. I can see lights in the black distance — another boat, or it might even be the shoreline, the tip of some peninsula. "He was in the mood to be experimental or something. Things just lined up."

"This was after the night you and I went out for pancakes?"

"Yes."

He doesn't reply.

"You're mad?" I say, standing beside him but not sitting down. I wish I didn't care how he felt, but I do.

"I'm not used to feeling stupid," he mumbles into his bicep.

"And why would you feel stupid?"

"I'm used to snapping my fingers and getting what I want. OK, maybe I'm spoiled. Whatever. But I snapped my fingers and you weren't interested. I figured maybe you were playing, though. Playing hard to get. So I threw myself at you a million times, and you still weren't interested. And *how* not-interested were you, Boots? Turns out you were *so* not-interested that when you wanted to get laid you turned me away when I literally already had my *pants down*, and you found a clumsy, know-nothing straightboy to go to bed with instead. I feel really stupid."

I shrug.

"He *is* straight, isn't he?"

"Yes."

"Then yeah, I feel totally stupid."

"He was just easier."

"Easier? Bullshit. My dick was out, Boots. What could've been easier than that? How much coercing did it take with him? How drunk did he have to be? Did you pay him?"

"No I didn't *pay* him."

He smirks. "I'm beginning to think you just don't want me!"

"*Beginning?*" But my voice sounds so outraged, even to my own ears, that to try to take the edge off I lamely add: "I just like you too much."

"Oh, you like me so much you won't touch me again with a ten-foot pole? Your Spock-like logic is airtight!" He's quiet for a minute. "Am I bad in bed? Is that it? I was a kid back then, Boots. I've learned a thing or two."

"Honestly, Piper? I didn't want to deal with the drama of getting with you again. I knew there'd be drama. And look: drama!"

I expect him to flip me the bird but he doesn't. For a minute we just watch the white waves spewing out behind us and sucking into the black hole of darkness beyond. As I'm turning to go back up the stairs he adds, "He must've been *horrible*. God, he moves like an ox."

I should just walk away, I know. And I almost do. But the better angels of my nature aren't always the ones in control.

"It was the best sex of my life," I say. "Aside from Ryan."

He doesn't seem as hurt as I want him to be, but of course he never is. Instead he says, "Well then it worked out just perfect for you. How many times?"

"Just the once."

"Huh. Must not've been quite as mind-blowing for him if he didn't come back for more."

"Doesn't matter, once was all I wanted. The whole point of this thing, Piper—this boat, this mission—is to get me to Ryan. It's all about Ryan. Clemente doesn't matter to me." Those last words make me cringe and I regret them immediately. Not only are they untrue—of course I care about Clemente—they're vicious and the viciousness is meant for Piper. I've used one Warrior to hurt another. I don't like how that feels. I don't want to be a person who would do that.

Suddenly this boat, which seemed so big earlier today, feels as small and tight as a scratchy sweater. And the days ahead loom both empty and cramped. I look down at Piper's buzzed blond head and then out at the sea, while beneath my feet the boat's hydrogen engine continues its endless drone, taking us south.

Chapter 14

Like cats we find our comfortable places on the boat and we gravitate to those places during the long and idle days that follow as the Intrepid makes its way south.

Marcus obviously spends most of his time on the bridge; Colby is in there a lot too, flirting with Marcus and sometimes getting steering lessons. I don't know if they've slept together, but that probably means they haven't. On a boat this size, in cabins with walls this thin, it would be tough to hide any boinking. How two guys so obviously into each other can keep their hands to themselves—especially when there's so little else to *do* on this tub—is beyond me.

Piper has a favorite chair on the main deck, where he

sits reading romance novels on a tablet he rolls up when anyone comes too close or tries to read over his shoulder. He and I haven't been full-on avoiding each other, but we haven't talked much since Clemente's big reveal. Piper's not one to let go of what he wants, though, so I suspect he's biding his time to see what happens as we get closer to exile island.

Clemente's been sort of quiet too. I don't know if telling the guys about our night together left a sour taste in his mouth, or what; I don't know if he's embarrassed. He assures me he isn't, but he seems to have something on his mind. He spends a lot of time by himself on the roof of the bridge, the closest thing to a crow's nest the Intrepid has to offer. Maybe he likes the height, or the unblocked ocean breeze, or just the solitude (he even sometimes, playfully or not, pulls the ladder up with him). What he does up there, I don't know. Most of the time he's out of view. Sometimes only his legs are visible, hanging over the side, bare feet swinging with the motion of the boat while the rest of him daydreams or whatever. I often see only pieces of him: legs when he's up in the crow's nest, hand when it sometimes dangles from the top bunk while he sleeps. Pieces of Clemente when in these long empty days I would like to have the whole thing, in whatever capacity he might be willing to share it.

And me: I like the front of the boat, especially when the windscreen is down. I like leaning or sitting at the sharp point where the railings and sides of the prow come together—the furthest point, the one closest to our destination, to resolution. I like the rush of the wind and the pounding of the waves as the Intrepid lifts out of the water and crashes back down. Sometimes I'll spot a dolphin or two surfing alongside us. Most of the time I just look ahead, literally and figuratively.

At night the darkness, the boat's warm yellow lights, and dinner-related chores pull us from our places and bring us together—and only then does it feel like we're sharing the same trip. But for all the other hours of the day, we kill time in our own ways.

All in all, Marcus was right about us being glad for the stop in the Mexican port. What seemed like a needless detour when he first told us about it has become, by our third day at sea, a welcome break on the horizon. A half-time, as Clemente said. Something to look forward to.

One afternoon, from where I'm lying on a towel at the prow, I watch Clemente lower his ladder and climb down out of the crow's nest. He skips the last two rungs and drops with a thump on the deck. Piper looks up from his book as Clemente pads over to me. His skin is darker than ever these days—a golden brown the color of caramel—and he's wearing nothing but baby-blue boardshorts.

"Come with me," he says. "I want to try something."

With a flash of excitement I get up and follow. I feel Piper's eyes on us until he forces them back to his book.

Clemente leads me across the deck and through the bridge, past Marcus and Colby.

"Naughty business again, boys?" Colby teases.

I swat at him but hope he's right. Can he possibly be right?

Clemente brings me out to the lower deck, the loudest part of the ship, and I wonder whether that's because he has something to tell me. What something, I have no idea.

"Stand here," he says, pulling me close until our bare shoulders touch. The salt air has made our skin sticky, and the motion of the boat rocks us apart with a pinch and then glues us back together. All the visceral details of our night atop the shredded sheet come into my mind.

"Now breathe in," he tells me, inhaling deeply just as a cloud of engine vapor wafts over us. I'm so fixated on him, I don't understand what he's doing and I fail to join him in his deep breath. Suddenly his eyes look wider. "It's the oxygen exhaust," he laughs. "Pure oxygen."

"Ah," I say, catching on. The engine sucks in sea water and separates the hydrogen out of the molecules to use as fuel. Meanwhile the oxygen is left behind and discharged as a steady stream of thick white vapor.

"From up there I noticed," he says, nodding to the crow's nest, "that sometimes when the wind's right, the exhaust blows back this way."

I breathe in deep like he did, and feel stronger almost immediately. I imagine my blood rich and red, coursing through stretched arteries.

"Feel like I could lift a truck," Clemente says, flexing his biceps. "Grrr!"

"I feel like I could fuck an entire army," I say. I mean it, too. Or maybe just him. For the first time, the very first time, I start to regret we had sex—simply because our one-and-done is done and relegated to the past. I should've waited. *Now* could've been the one-and-done. We could've been heading to our cabin right *now*, dropping our shorts to our ankles on the way.

After a few more breaths he claps me on the shoulder and leaves me there, climbs the first ladder up to the main deck, then the second one up to the crow's nest, all fuzzy limbs, sturdy feet, rough hands, jet-black hair, colorful scorpion as he rises rung by rung toward the sky. I watch him until he climbs over the edge of the roof and pulls the ladder up behind him. Clouds of oxygen surround me and my heart feels like it might explode.

At sea there isn't much of a dawn or a dusk. The sun drops behind the horizon and bursts up from it later with very little transition in the light aside from the pink-orange firework of color that tints the sky during those brief moments. Night's like a light-switch flipping off, and morning is like one flipping on. It's a transition that never fails to wake me up. One moment it's dark in our cabin, and the next, the porthole is a glowing white circle through my eyelids. Clemente seems to have no trouble staying asleep; maybe in the top bunk he's shielded from the glare. But I've been up at dawn every day.

Marcus is an early riser too, so we sit together on the lower deck, pouring each other coffee and hunkering into hooded sweatshirts against the morning wind. I like these mornings with Marcus. I like him. He's getting over his shyness, and good company. And the oxygen drift is a waker-upper, better than coffee.

This morning as we sit sipping and breathing, Marcus tells me we'll be in the Mexican port by nightfall if the wind stays at our back.

"I thought not till tomorrow?"

"Well, I like to under-promise and over-deliver," he says. "Keeps the troops in good spirits to get a surprise."

"It's a good one. No offense to the Intrepid but I'll be happy to get my feet on dry land for a while."

He smiles, sips his coffee. "Told you."

"What's the plan for when we get there?"

"In Puerto Natan? No plan for you guys. I have to see about supplies for the boat. But you guys can go exploring or whatever. It's a beautiful little town. You'll like it."

"And we'll spend the night?"

He nods. "We'll get back on the road tomorrow afternoon."

For a few minutes we slurp our coffees in silence.

When I notice a cloud of exhaust blowing back I inhale. Marcus must too—a moment later he adds boldly, "I'm going to ask Colby to have dinner with me in port."

"Like a date?"

He rests his coffee on one of his bare knees crossed beneath him on the bench. "Think he'll say yes?"

"Is the sky blue, Marcus?"

He smiles. "You don't think it's like weird at all?"

"Weird? Why? Kid's smitten with you."

His smile brightens. "Weird because of the age difference, I guess. I don't want to feel like I'm taking advantage."

"Twenty-four and eighteen is nothing."

He's quiet for a minute. "I wonder if I'm hung-up on his age because I'm really just intimidated by his looks. I mean, is Colby not the most beautiful guy you've ever seen?"

"I don't know about *ever seen*. But you're pretty easy on the eyes yourself, Marcus. Don't sell yourself short."

"Yeah, well. I do all right." He takes a sip of coffee. "Even if I'm not a *Warrior*."

"Like your bro?"

"Like everyone's favorite Tumble twin."

"Ah. Marius does have the moves."

"It's probably why I'm so *gahhh*"—he makes a strangling motion with his hands—"about the boat, you know? This is my thing and I take it seriously. I want to grow this business, maybe buy a second yacht soon. So I'll still be successful long after Marius is maxed-out at thirty or whittling sticks on exile island."

"These seem like serious family issues," I say, laughing into my coffee.

He shrugs.

"I've only played one game with your bro and I barely know him, so take this for what it's worth. But he

172

seems proud of you. Said you were the best sea captain around when he gave me your business card."

"Oh. He did?"

I nod.

"Hmm. Interesting." He goes quiet again. He takes a sip of coffee and watches the waves.

"So with Colby," I say coyly. "You guys haven't done anything yet?"

"Physically, you mean?"

"Sure."

He shakes his head. "I've *wanted* to. But every time he makes it pretty clear he wants to—you know—"

I nod.

"—I get nervous and start checking the sonar or whatever." He laughs. "I mean, the boy's hobby involves putting other guys in the hospital. What if he brings that kind of aggression into the bedroom? I like my shoulder joints intact!"

"Nah, I bet he's a kitten between the sheets. Although now that you mention it, his first time did sound pretty intense."

"I know!"

"But if he's anything like his brother, he's into the pretty standard stuff."

He smirks. "Ryan never shattered your pelvis in bed?"

"Not once," I laugh. "So take him out when we get to Mexico. It'll be fun."

"What'll be fun?" says a voice leaning out of the bridge. Piper. He's usually the next one up after me but his arrival always has me yearning for Clemente and Colby, too, to help dilute his presence. Among me and Marcus, Piper seems the third wheel. Among anyone, actually.

I look up at him as he's coming down the narrow

stairs, but I defer to Marcus on the answer.

"I'm going to ask Colby out," Marcus says.

"Praise the lord," Piper says, raising one hand to the sky. He's brought a mug with him from the galley and I fill it from the coffee pot Marcus and I have nearly polished off. "Someone on this ship needs to be getting laid. Cut some of the sexual tension around here. When's this happening? In Mexico?"

"Tonight," Marcus says. "Mexico's tonight."

Chapter 15

Mexico. Puerto Natan, to be more specific. One glimpse makes me want to write a song about Puerto Natan. Marcus wasn't kidding about it being beautiful. That's obvious from the moment the Intrepid cruises into port at the pinkest, orangest time of day, a time for fairy tales and travel magazine photoshoots. Sailboats by the dozen bob in the champagne-pink waves of the bay. The four of us stand spellbound at the prow while Marcus, with a cheerful yell of "Keep your eye out for a parking space," pilots us into port. Excitement seems to crackle off each of us, and the wind that blows through our hair and t-shirts makes us look like we're in an ad for youth and daring.

Here and there fishermen are parking their boats for the day. We pass a young shirtless fisherman covering the motor on a twelve-footer with a tarp. Surrounding his bare brown feet are glittering, silver-scaled fish in a jumble of blue nets. A sheathed knife hangs from a belt around his waist. His thick black hair hangs in his eyes and his skin is like mocha. He looks up at the Intrepid with indifference at first but then begins waving wildly.

Clemente's the first of us to wave back. Sometimes I forget how widely known we Warriors are; even when I remember I can barely believe it. Colby starts waving back too, happy to ride the coattails of our fame.

"Ahoy!" calls Clemente.

"Warriors!" the fisherman yells, putting his hands on his hips and rocking back with a laugh. "*Bienvenidos!*"

Piper whispers to me with a grin, elbowing my ribs, "Threeway?"

We continue past and the shirtless fisherman has to grab on to the side of his boat when it rocks in our wake.

The sun-bleached pier, with its legs wrapped in seaweed, has no room for us.

"Looks like we'll be rowing in," Marcus says as he navigates the Intrepid to the middle of the bay. We drop anchor and soon afterward Piper, Clemente, and I open the gate on the lower deck and push one of the two dinghies onto the waves.

Before hopping in with them I grab my shoes and phone. Then, careful not to tip it, the three of us arrange ourselves awkwardly in the little rubbery craft. When a big wave rolls underneath us Piper grabs my upper thigh to steady himself. I push his hand away. Clemente sees but doesn't say anything.

"You guys cozy?" Colby calls, looking down at us from the bridge. He's ditched his usual tee for a dressier button-down that's half-open against his tan chest.

"Coming with us?" Clemente says.

"You guys go. We'll head in a little later."

Marcus, who's been shutting down the Intrepid, comes to the door too and looks surprised that we've already disembarked.

"You landlubbers are itching for dry ground, aren't you?"

We laugh and nod. The land is drawing us toward it, a horizontal gravity.

Marcus looks at his phone before dropping it back in his pocket. "Go have fun. You can come back here to sleep if you *have* to, but you shouldn't have any trouble finding a great room in a really nice guesthouse." From his tone this seems more demand than suggestion, though I can't imagine why he and Colby would want the Intrepid all to themselves, ahem. "We'll be at sea for a while after this, so get your fill of land."

"What time should we be back?" Clemente asks, squinting up.

"I'd like to be on the road by sunset tomorrow."

"Sunset it is," Clemente says.

"What time is sunset?" Piper whispers into his phone, which tells him.

"Have fun, Marcus," I say, shooting him a wink.

Colby sees it and flashes me his *I'm so innocent* grin.

Then, fixing the small paddles into their slots, Clemente yells, "Land ho!"

Land-sick is more like it, though. Wouldn't have believed there *was* such a thing, but the solid, unmoving ground that beckoned to us from afar is making me dizzy now that I'm on it—and not just me. After beaching the dinghy, Piper, Clemente, and I walk like Martians in clumsy steps across the beach. But by the time we've reached the boardwalk and stop to shake sand out of our shoes, my inner-ears and stomach have mostly adjusted.

"Well isn't that pretty," Piper sighs, pointing.

The street beyond the boardwalk sparkles with colored lights and pulses with the quiet rhythm of drums and the springy melodies of classical guitars. Brightly-painted shops and restaurants line the cobblestone street, their windows open, apparently doorless. Shirtless guys and women in bikinis pilot bikes around moseying pedestrians.

After our encounter with the friendly fisherman I imagined being swarmed by fans in town but no one seems to pay much attention to us. Maybe Puerto Natan has too much else to offer. Three guys who shoot paintballs at people for a living fade into the vibrant scenery, just another sight among many.

From among the crowd a raven-haired woman in a low-cut, flowing pink dress dances down the street calling out the name of a restaurant and enticing passersby with intimate recitations of tonight's dinner specials. Clemente follows her hungrily with his eyes.

"Think I want a taste of that," he says, tightening his hoodie around his waist and smoothing his mustache. "Later boys. Have fun." And he trots along after the beauty in the pink dress—our resident straightboy in action.

At first I think he's only joking, that he'll come sauntering back any time now with his hands stuffed in his pockets and a bashful grin on his face. But when he dances around her and in front of her and says something that makes her laugh and brush back her hair, I realize with a stab of disappointment that he's a goner.

I never thought about us going our separate ways in Puerto Natan but he seems never to have considered we'd stay together. I guess that's OK. Why would we? We've seen enough of each other on the Intrepid. Still, I'm left to look awkwardly at Piper, not sure what to do or say now that it's just the two of us.

"Looks like you failed to convert him, B," Piper smirks, watching Clemente work his magic.

"Whatever."

"How about you?" he says. "Planning on sampling

the local fare?" By *fare* of course he means the dudes. "What happens in Puerto Natan stays in Puerto Natan, remember. I won't tell, promise." He mimes locking his lips with a key.

"We'll see. Maybe."

"Wonder if we can find that fisherman," he muses. "I'd ride that guy in a pile of fish guts if that's what it took." He slides his arm around me. "Oh come on," he purrs, "you would too."

I look at his eyes, six inches from mine. He's feeling bolder than he has since the game of First & Last, I can tell—probably because Clemente's chasing after a female and I've been left in his dust. Piper tips his head closer to mine. The sun has brightened his buzzed hair and his skin's turned a golden brown. "Or," he says, "we could skip the fisherman and get straight to business ourselves."

"Piper, seriously."

He laughs.

"I need something to eat," I say, looking away, looking around, pulling out from under his arm. "So many restaurants."

"Me too. Let's find something."

"Actually, Piper, I'd rather explore on my own for a while."

"Oh." He frowns. "Really? You're bailing on me?"

"See you back at the boat."

"Boots—" He clearly wants to say something more but then just sighs. He looks bewildered and I don't see how that's possible. "OK. Fine. When? Tomorrow?"

He's rolling his eyes before I even have the chance to answer, but when I tell him "Whenever," he adds, "Sure, whatever Boots, whatever. Later! Bye! Adios!"

Determined not to look back while he continues to chant various farewells, I walk down the street opposite the way Clemente chased after the woman. I wonder how long Piper will stand there looking at me, but I tell myself not to worry. He's a big boy; he'll find something to do.

It feels better being away from him. Maybe he was right: maybe what happens in Puerto Natan can stay in Puerto Natan—and if that's the case maybe this would've been the perfect place to get with him and get it out of my system. But maybe what I've pinned on the moral urge not to betray Ryan is actually just a flat-out lack of interest in reigniting anything with Piper. I mean jeez, I broke up with the guy for a reason, and it wasn't all that long ago.

I take a breath of the fragrant air, feeling a rising happiness. I let the lights play over me, enjoy the people flowing past. Distractions are a dime a dozen here. The music, the food, and of course the sex. But it's an innocent type of sex. While everyone is in some state of undress, it seems without insinuation, more about comfort in this climate than an attempt to turn heads. Still my head is turned. Young fishermen my own age, trust-fund surfers from the States—they all mingle. Perfect bodies, sun-kissed skin of all shades decorating lovely muscles.

It suddenly occurs to me I can do whatever I want. It's a novel feeling: whatever I want.

In fact, Puerto Natan seems to beg to satisfy all appetites, and I realize as the cooking smells waft over me that my telling Piper I needed something to eat wasn't just an excuse to get away: my growling stomach needs to be satisfied before I can think about anything else.

I buy a hotdog from a mustachioed oldster with a cart, and sit down to eat on a bench half-occupied by two young handholding lovers. The boy, thirteen or fourteen with a boastful rash of black fuzz on his upper lip, seems annoyed at first by my sitting here and encroaching on him and his girl. But then with a twitch he recognizes me and his frown becomes a bashful smile. He holds out his hand for me to shake and then, with a heavy accent, asks me to put a kiss on his girlfriend's blushing cheek. After wiping mustard off my lips I lean over and oblige. Giggling, she cups her cheek as if to preserve the kiss, and speaks to the boy in Spanish. Among the words I hear *Ryan*, and the boy, translating, says, "We are sad your Ryan goes away from you."

Despite the humidity, goosebumps flash across my skin and Puerto Natan feels less like a blank slate than it did a few minutes ago.

"Thank you. I'm sad too."

The girl subtly moves her hand from her cheek to her lips, as if she's moving the kiss.

"*Buenas noches*," I say and, getting up, start walking.

Even in this little town, the news of Ryan has spread. Hell, those kids probably watched the events unfold live—the events that are the reason for my being here now. A vacation from it may not be possible after all, not even here. Ryan is all around me, in the memories of everyone I meet.

It makes me feel lonely and disoriented. I look around, wondering what Clemente's up to, where Piper's gone, whether Colby and Marcus have started their date. But most of all I wonder what Ryan is doing right now, and whether any part of him senses that I'm on my way to him. And that I'll be there soon.

In the meantime Puerto Natan is opening its arms to me, and all of a sudden I want more than anything to fall into them and get carried away.

Clubs seem to me like shooting fish in a barrel, and I've

always preferred, on the paintball field and in the dating scene, to stalk my prey. But there's a time for everything, so when I spot a trio of gorgeous locals heading through a strobe-lit doorway, I follow them. I pay the cover charge and get my hand stamped, then doff my shirt and hook it through my belt. Inside is a glittery mass of glistening bodies — like a blown-up view of cells under a microscope, dividing, growing, quivering pieces of a larger, happy whole. I step into the mass and let the bare skin envelope me. The transplant takes — I'm one of them. Almost immediately I'm dripping sweat and my dick is hard from a thousand smooth, sensory-overloading touches. Scenesters with razored haircuts mix with bearded beach hippies, mouths lock with mouths, hands clasp hips, all move in near unison. Arms like a cell's flagellum come around me and lock against my belly and I don't care who they belong to, I'm just happy they're there. They could be Ryan's arms or the arms of any of the millions of people who know him from TV and were sad to see him go. They could be Clemente's arms. That thought gets me even harder. I want to divide.

I dance and dance until I can feel sweat running down my legs and my shoes are squishy with it. I'm pretty lost in the lights and the music but I can always sense when I'm in someone's cross-hairs. Facing me in the jostling crowd, a fair-haired twink dyed yellow and blue by the lights is looking at me with the ecstatic grimace of what I'm sure is an O face. Another twink dancing close behind him rests his chin on the front twink's bare shoulder and, grinning, looks down. Other dancers suddenly scramble away from the pair. And sure enough, the O-faced twink's fly is down and his exposed erection, clamped in the fist of the twink behind him, is pumping jizz onto the dance floor. Slipping will inevitably follow, as will spotted pants, which explains why other dancers are dodging the orgasming pair. Call me a prude but this kind of thing makes me feel slimy, especially because the twinks were using me to fuel their jerkfest. So I make my way to the edge of the floor, float there for a while and sip a drink in the less-dense crowd, then put on my shirt and leave the club.

The night air is cold at first but I acclimate fast as my sweat dries in the breeze. I put my hands in my pockets and mill around, not sure what to do now. Part of me wants to just go back to the Intrepid — that's the most comfortable idea — but Colby and Marcus deserve a night to themselves. Maybe I'll find a room and hit the sack. I check my phone. It's only ten but none of the guys would have to know I crapped-out early. A shower would be good, and a cushy robe while I have my clothes cleaned.

So it's decided: shower, robe, bed.

As I return to the main street, out of the corner of my eye I see a flash of familiar pink dress, the one worn by the woman Clemente followed away like a puppy. She's dancing, slow and sweet, and dancing behind her is none other than Clemente. He has one hand on her flat belly and the other's resting on her hip; she's reaching up and back and seems to be gently guiding his face into her hair. They wear the same little grin. There's something beautiful about the way they're moving. He hasn't known her more than two hours and yet they seem to move as one, in a natural, musical rhythm I can remember only ever experiencing myself with... him, actually. Clemente. During our night together.

In a flash I feel both sadness and pity. Sadness for myself, for the realization that Clemente Santiago must generate this kind of chemistry with whomever he's with. And pity for this woman who probably thinks they have something special going on—in fact it's so un-special he can conjure it up with a dude. I'm envious that she doesn't know she's un-special. I wonder if he's hard against her back.

Of course he is. Look at her. *I* would be.

I look down and turn to leave in the other direction, but I haven't gone more than a few steps before I hear my name. The voice is Clemente's, of course. *Dude,* I think, *if you won't fuck me again then just leave me alone.* But I turn and wave and he beckons me over. He whispers something to the woman and she squints at me and nods and smiles as I approach.

"This is Madelena," he tells me.

"Mariana," she corrects, pinching his chin. Gallantly I kiss her cheek.

"I like this town," he says mid-breath, like someone recovering from a hearty laugh.

"Looks like you're doing OK here."

He grins. "Seen the other guys?"

"Piper and I split up too after you bailed on us."

Now he frowns, ever so slightly, and his eyes seem to dig into me with something resembling regret. "You heading back to the Intrepid?" he says.

"Hadn't thought of it. Why?"

"No reason. You look kind of bored."

"Guess I'm not used to all this dry land! It's messing with my constitution."

"Maybe Mariana knows somebody we can hook you up with for the night." He turns to her. "Know any cute homos in town?"

She waves dismissively. "I know *all* the cute homos in this town. Walk up to any one you like. I'd tell you to tell them I sent you, but you, all you need to give them is a smile."

"I like this one," I say to Clemente. "Can she come

with us?"

"Working on it." He winks.

Mariana rolls her eyes. "I have a man on every ship," she says, tracing a fingernail down Clemente's throat.

They'll sleep together tonight, I know. It'll be his first time since me, and I wonder if it'll be as good for him. If he'll gasp the way he did with me, and laugh the way he did with me, and get as sweaty as he got with me. If he'll shred the sheet to ribbons beneath her.

I say goodbye and continue down the street. At a little guesthouse with important-looking columns out front, I book myself a room.

With my clothes hanging near the a.c. vent to dry, I shower off my sweat and flop naked into bed. The sheets are soft and white and the headboard is made of bamboo reeds. Googly-eyed tiki masks line one wall. I laugh that I've ended up in a Polynesian hotel in a Mexican port.

I stretch out, roll over, tuck my arm under the pillow and pull it against my chest.

Would my fans be surprised by how sulky and broody I get sometimes? It wouldn't match the persona they see on their floor-to-ceiling TVs. On the field I'm always swinging around like an action hero, making careful aim and taking decisive shots. They see me win games and strut around in my skintight uniform and give confident interviews in front of splashy graphics. They're used to seeing me with a rifle in my hand. Would they be surprised that on this night in beautiful Puerto Natan, I'm lying limp-dicked in a hotel room looking up at cheesy masks?

Pffft. I should be out partying the night away like the action hero I am. Or at least getting drunk. Or at least finding something better to eat than a hotdog.

So I put back on my jeans and t-shirt, lock my room,

and head down the stairs, dragging my hand over the tubes of bamboo nailed decoratively to the wall.

"*Thought* it was too early for bed-time, Warrior," says the old woman at the desk as she looks up from painting her nails. The vibrant pink suggests that she too is getting ready to go out.

"Just had to get myself cleaned up," I say.

Outside the night is darker and the colorful lights brighter, or maybe I'm just more ready to see them that way now. I do a quick loop of the boardwalk but don't run into any of the guys. Seems I'm still on my own. For a while I watch a pair of women grooving to a guitar player's tunes, and then, through an open window, I spot a familiar face working in a restaurant across the street. So he's not only a fisherman, but a cook too. I flick a few bills at the phone in the guitar case and head across the street.

The restaurant is small with a handful of tables, almost all of which are filled. It's lit dimly by strings of pink and yellow lights woven like fishnets across the ceiling. The rosy glow is zilla cozy; it feels like being inside someone. This is an order-at-the-counter place and at the counter I stand looking up at the menu on the wall, written in both English and Spanish. A thin, pretty woman with gray streaks in her black hair and a floral apron asks in English if I have any questions.

"Hard to decide. Everything sounds good!"

"Have the baked cod," she tells me. "Caught only hours ago by my son, here." And she gestures behind her, where I see the fisherman rinsing what looks like seaweed under the tap. He has on a tight-fitting red soccer jersey with a white apron tied around his waist. He looks up and grins, more bashful now than he was in his boat.

"Yes, please," I say.

After paying and receiving a number on a square of paper I find a free table near an open window. From here I watch people passing outside, all with some spring in their step. It isn't a holiday as far as I know, or any special day; maybe every night in Puerto Natan is like this. If so there are worse places to live.

Before long a paper plate containing the cheese- and salsa-covered fish (with a side of fries) is lowered to the table in front of me and the fisherman, hands folded behind him, asks if I need anything else.

"Company?" I say, gesturing to the chair opposite me at the little table.

"Ah," he says indecisively, looking back at the kitchen. "What's the time?"

I glance at my phone. "A little after eleven."

"Good, then officially we're closed." He grins. Untying his apron and dropping it over the back of the chair, he sits down.

"Mind?" he says, reaching out to snag a few fries. His hands look rough and his cute biceps strain the sleeves of his too-small red jersey. Judging by how wash-worn the shirt is, the small size isn't a fashion statement—he's simply outgrown it. He's younger, actually, than I thought at first; he looks about twenty.

"I remember you from earlier today." I take the first bite of steaming baked cod. "Ah, this is good." And it *is*, but it's so hot I have to keep it away from my cheeks with my teeth. "You were in your boat, probably with my dinner?"

"I was hoping you wouldn't remember. Me waving like a dope. I was star-struck. So many Warriors. My favorite team." He has a trio of freckles that form a straight line, like Orion's belt, from his cheek to his chin. He looks down at his hands. On his right hand a solid black star is tattooed between his thumb and pointer finger.

"Don't worry about that," I say. "I liked it. We all did." I laugh. "Feeds our egos."

"A cook is good at feeding." He grins, watches me blow on the next bite, grabs another fry off my plate. "And Pernfors? Santiago? The new guy? Did they come ashore too?"

"All gone," I say. I realize it was vague so I add, "All gone off, searching for love. Or lovers."

Looking across at me with big hazel eyes, he says: "And are you looking for a lover too?"

I laugh. He's more right than he knows. "I guess you could say that's why I'm here."

He laughs too, looks down again. But this time he's looking at my hands, not his own. I watch his gaze travel up my arms.

"So you catch the fish and then you cook it, too? Doesn't that make for a long day?"

He shrugs and meets my eyes. "Here no one pays us for paintball."

At some point while I'm eating, and while his mother silently (but with an air of approval) sweeps the floor around our feet, the roles of customer and cook fall away and it begins to feel that the fisherman and I are on a date. A good one. And this of course is a new feeling—at least a forgotten feeling. I like it. And I like that when I finally stand up, he stands up too and we leave the restaurant together. The lights blink off behind us.

"What's your name?" I ask as we stroll the boardwalk, the nighttime party only fully getting underway now that midnight has come and gone.

"Natan."

I laugh. "Your name's Natan? Natan from Puerto Natan?"

He smiles. "The town and me, we are one."

"You're both very beautiful." (The things a guy can say when he's leaving in the morning!)

"Let me show you around." He takes my hand. It's as rough as it looked, but dry and cool. I touch my thumb to the star.

"Around you or the town?" I ask coyly.

"I told you, we are one." And he smirks.

He does show me around the town, places I already walked by once or twice, and then he brings me back to his place—a room he rents in the back of a bigger house—and shows me the other Natan. He pulls off his too-small jersey and pushes down his jeans. He kicks his worn Adidas across the floor—"My stinky shoes," he grins—and falls on his back onto his narrow bed.

He's sweet and gorgeous. As I drop my shirt and pants on the floor I quietly thank myself for finding the motivation to come out.

Naked now I climb over him lengthwise and kiss him, suck at his lips, kiss his Orion's belt of freckles, press my tongue into the ridges of his ear. He tastes salty and good, and despite his work in the kitchen he smells of the natural freshness of one who spends all day in the sea breeze. His fingers trace my shoulder blades, then move down my spine to squeeze my ass cheeks and tug me against him, pulling my boner against his and into the stiff tight curls of his pubic hair. We trade breath as our mouths crash together. I'm rolling in waves of that tingly, numbly-great feeling you can get from scratching a terrible itch. As I grind my pelvis against his I feel my dick thump back behind his balls. I want to fuck him but first I want to suck him, so I shimmy down across his squeaking bed. His crotch smells sharp and bitter and good and I work my mouth down around his cock until my lips touch its base and hair tickles my nose.

After a few minutes he slips a rough hand under my chin and tugs me up.

"I want to do something."

"Anything," I tell him, touching my lips to his ribs.

He rolls away from me and drops to the floor and, on hands and knees, starts digging around under the bed. Only as he searches do I begin to notice the room. It's a boy's room—the particle-board walls are painted bright blue, with posters of soccer stars and comic book heroes held up with thumbtacks. The linoleum floor is covered with colorful fraying rugs and there's laundry everywhere, tossed about in the same carefree way he kicked off his shoes.

When Natan stands up he has a big bottle of lube, a grin, a fantastic erection that's still glistening with my spit.

"Do you want me to fuck you?" I say.

"Maybe later," he says, but he shrugs, and I can tell that isn't what he has in mind. He taps his fingers on the bottle. "I want to put this all over you."

"And wrestle?" I say, giddy.

"And wrestle *so much.*"

He motions for me to get off the bed and then with a swoop he clears the mattress of all but a single sheet. Then we jump back on. We're facing each other, he kneeling, me cross-legged. Starting at my head, as though he's shampooing me, he begins working the lube into my hair and down the sides of my neck and across my shoulders. I can't help it: I lean forward and lick his lips again.

Smiling, he pushes me back with a slick hand. "Lift," he says, and I oblige by raising my arms so he can smear lube into my pits.

It tickles and I squirm.

He smooths a blob of lube across my ribs and belly

and then clutches my cock, gives it a few intense yanks. The sensation makes my eyes roll up. With hands that shine in the low light he lubes my balls and thighs and knees and calves and even in between my toes. I feel slippery and warm all over. Then he crawls behind me and lubes my back; he starts at my shoulders and when he gets to the small of it he pushes me forward by the back of my head—I rock over on my knees and present him my ass. His fingers slip along my crack and dabble my hole and he laughs. When he pronounces me finished he pushes the bottle toward me (his hands are too slick to pick it up) and says, "Now you do me."

"Gladly."

I pick up the bottle and squirt into my palm. Like Ryan used to do to me in the shower I shape Natan's hair into a mohawk and then into a giant rhino horn that sticks off the front. Laughing, he holds up a hand and touches it. Then I lube up his neck and shoulders and armpits. His muscles are small but hard. I squeeze coils of the clear, glistening stuff onto his belly like soft-serve ice cream and spread it around—I fill his belly button with it before smearing it around to his back and bum and along the significant girth of his erection. When I'm done he sits looking at me with an eager grin, silly with the flaccid rhino horn drooping against his forehead.

We are gleaming.

I'm reaching down to put the bottle on the floor when suddenly I feel a slick silken slap against me. Beads of lube fly out from us and tap the posters on the wall. I gasp and laugh and the bottle clatters to the linoleum. He's upon me, lubed lanky limbs everywhere, entwining me. I open my arms and embrace him.

"Thought we'd do a countdown or something first," I laugh, kissing him. We're tightly entwined lengthwise on the bed, straining against the lube's determination to slide us right apart. Our chests are pressed so tightly as we kiss that I can feel lube running down my sides, like jelly squirting from a flattened peanut-butter sandwich.

"I couldn't wait!" he laughs.

His voice is so filled with glee, I realize that this isn't actually wrestling; there's no competition here. This is about sensation. He pushes off with his feet against the wall (leaving two shining footprints there) and slides across the length of me. And as my cock skims his belly and burrows through his pubes and slips down between his sweet clenched thighs, I realize there's nothing better. The lube hasn't just made us slippery, it's awakened every nerve, primed every pore for pleasure. It's made us explorers of touch. The bed thumps the wall as we slide into topsy-turvy positions. We clutch each other, belly button to nipples, in a sixty-nine, a tight human yin-yang. Then I pull myself headfirst past his cock and through the ring of his legs, and come up around the other side of him, dragging my chin through his ass-crack and passing my pecs and then my belly across his balls. He has a trio of stars, like the one on his hand, tattooed across the small of his back, I'm only noticing now. My cock snags his and then pulls through behind him as my face buries in his hair. I spoon him for a second, pressing the front of my thighs against the backs of his, and then resume my journey across his body. I drag my crotch up along his spine and rub my balls against the fuzzy back of his neck and my cock through slick coils of his thick black hair. Grabbing my ankles from either side he pulls my legs around him so that it must look like I'm sitting on his head (though we're horizontal), and, pressing my feet together between his hands, he begins fucking the tightness between the soles of my feet.

No, this isn't about wrestling, this is about enlisting a

band of formerly neglected body parts into a symphony of sex. Positions like these have never been as practical or as wonderful. He fucks the space behind my ears; I fuck (and very nearly come into) his armpit. And, when I have him pinned on his belly and am lost in the up-and-down slide of my cock between his ass-cheeks, I begin to fuck his ass. It isn't planned; I don't know if it's on his agenda, but when my erection has snapped into him as if it belongs there, I don't pull it out. In fact I don't move at all; I would come.

"This OK?" I whisper, trying barely to breathe lest I fall over the edge.

"It's OK. I want it."

When I feel myself draw safely back from the point of no return, I begin thrusting gently and slowly. Slowly is all I can do—between us there's no friction to aid harder thrusting. My slick thighs can find no purchase against his slick thighs, nor my slick groin against his slick bum, nor my slick belly against his slick back, nor my slick chin against his slick shoulder.

"Maybe like this," he says, pushing up on hands and knees and backing into me, onto me.

I gasp something that's meant to be, "That's perfect," and cover two of his stars with my thumbs.

Now I can get traction against the mattress of the little bed.

"Boots," he's saying, "more," and even when I give him more he still says "more." Droplets of lube spatter out every time my groin smacks his ass. And when he yells for even more and begins to gasp I know he's already coming—I reach around and grab his cock in time to feel the sticky heat flow across my knuckles. Just another few hard thrusts and I go over the edge myself. My orgasm tears through my body like a knee through a silk bedsheet.

From the clouds, from the fucking *stars*, I drift slowly back to Earth.

For a minute we're still as statues. The only sounds are of our breathing and the irregular *ploop* of lube dripping off us and hitting the mattress. Then I gently pull out of him and dry his bum with a corner of sheet. Slippery and spent, we collapse across the bed.

Later he leads me naked out of his room to an overgrown patio out back, where a pipe running up the wall ends in a spout above our heads. Shrouded by bushes with wide, drooping leaves, we clean off there. He doesn't seem to mind the cold water but I have to jump in and out of it, and he laughs.

"Was it fun for you?" he says when we're huddling on the patio in wash-worn beach towels illustrated with cartoon characters. Piles of soapsuds landscape the concrete around us like fake snow.

"Zilla fun. Never gotten so lubey before!"

"My favorite thing," he grins. He rubs his face dry with his towel-covered arm. "Will you spend the night?"

"In that little bed?"

"Little? How big's *your* bed?"

I think of that big silvery thing so far away and don't respond except to say OK. I assume I won't be getting much sleep, but I can make up for it in the lazy days of travel ahead.

I use his bathroom and then join him, still naked, in the little bed. He swapped the lubey sheet for a blanket that at first is itchy on my skin, but the smoothness of his back and bum against me makes up for it. What I thought would be a long night collapses into almost instant sleep.

Chapter 16

I awake with a flash—literally—and the sound of a camera, and then a giggled whisper, "Mierda." I open my eyes and see Natan's long brown arm holding a phone above us. He's photographing us in bed.

"Forgot to turn off the flash," he says, turning his head on the pillow we're sharing. "Caught!"

"Oh."

"I can delete it," he says, blushing. "Do you want me to delete it?"

"Let me see it."

"I'll delete it."

"Don't delete it, let me see."

Leaning up on one elbow so that his cute armpit hair dapples the pillow near my cheek, he shows me the phone. The photo is fine, shows me from the shoulders up sleeping, him from the shoulders up grinning cheesily. Getting photographed unawares is inherently creepy, but this one's proof he's done nothing worse: He wouldn't be scrambling for G-rated photos now if he'd hidden a video recorder somewhere in the room last night. And, given my teammate Rufus's steady supply of tabloid fuel, this kind of photo isn't likely to interest anyone other than Natan's friends, or go anywhere further than the wallpaper screen of Natan's phone. "Keep it," I tell him. "A souvenir. It's a good one of you."

"To remember you," he says, putting the phone to sleep and dropping it into something muffled on the floor, "to prove I was with the one and only Boots McHenry."

The one and only.

Stretching is difficult in Natan's cramped bed but I

manage, rub my nose in his spicy armpit as I do, and let out a yawn. Our legs are entwined.

"Do you always wake up this early?"

"The fishes wake up early," he replies. He untangles himself from me, sits up, swings his legs out of bed, runs a hand through his hair. "So it's time for you to get on your way. Or you're welcome to come out with me."

"Sounds fun, but I can't. I've got the other Warriors to deal with."

"Ah, yes."

He stands up—revealing again the three stars tattooed across the small of his back—and goes outside naked. For a while I hear water running from the shower spout on the other side of the wall. By the time he comes back wrapped in the towel he used last night, I'm dressed and tying my sneakers. I think about yanking off his towel and throwing him back into bed, but I don't want to make him late for the fishes.

"Got any food around here?" I say, half-joking.

"Never anything much. Usually I swing by the restaurant on my way to the pier. It's not open but I pop in."

He puts on a faded blue swimsuit (letting the mesh liner suffice for underwear), a sleeveless yellow t-shirt, and some sleek black shades, and then, grabbing a backpack and stepping into his Adidas, he shows me out of the apartment.

"And what are you and your Warriors up to today?" Natan asks as we walk. "Something fun I hope."

The town, so boisterous last night, is engulfed in sleepy silence now, and the salty moist air has a chill that reminds me of mornings on the Intrepid.

"We're leaving town later today, actually."

"Ah, already you're leaving me?" he says. "Then this was a one-night stand?" Before I can reply—because for a second I'm speechless — he jabs me teasingly in the ribs. "It's OK, I had only one night to spend with you too."

"Only one?"

"Well, only one with my boyfriend's blessing."

"A boyfriend. I should've known. He gave his blessing, huh? Nice guy."

"He has to. You're on my *list*."

"Your list?"

"My list of celebrities I'm allowed to get with if I ever get the chance. I never expected to get the chance!"

I laugh. "Who else is on your list?"

"No one. Brody Jackson. Alfonso Connors. You."

"Hot company. So your boy won't be mad?"

"Not mad. Jealous. Not mad."

"You should've invited him over," I tease.

He laughs. "I didn't want to share you!"

As we walk he waves at a young woman opening up a little shop selling t-shirts and beach towels and stuff, but he doesn't make any special gesture to call her attention to me.

"So what brought the Theban Warriors to Puerto Natan, anyway?" he asks.

"Just a pit-stop on the way to somewhere else."

"Then for me it was a lucky stop. Where's somewhere else?"

"Honest truth, I don't know! Somewhere near Hawaii."

"Oh. Hawaii?" There's a cloud of nervousness in his eyes. "Then from Puerto Natan you'll catch a plane the rest of the way?"

"No, we're going by boat. The Intrepid. You saw it yesterday."

"I saw." He shakes his head. "By boat isn't a good idea," he says firmly.

"What? Why?"

"From here to Hawaii takes you straight through the Trash Vortex," he says, pointing out at the ocean. "The territory of the plastic pirates."

I laugh. "Are those guys for real?"

Natan isn't laughing, not at all; he reaches out and stabs my forehead with his thumb.

"Ow."

"You need to play less paintball and watch more news. The plastic pirates have an island out there, built from the plastic and shit that swirls around in the ocean." He moves his index finger in a circle on his open palm. "Area as big as my country. The pirates like to raid ships and take whatever they can't scavenge from the sea or out of the trash."

"I'm sure our captain has a plan." But I wonder, assuming he knows about it, why Marcus hasn't mentioned the plastic pirates to us.

"I hope so," Natan says.

"The Vortex is as big as Mexico?"

"Bigger."

"Then there's not much chance we'll run into any pirates, right? A small band of people in such a big area?"

"Not a small band. Thousands."

"But still. In such a big space?"

"Sure, a small chance if everything goes OK. It'll feel like a big chance if you get raided, though." We've arrived at the restaurant. Through the cracks in the closed shutters I can see it's dark inside. "Wait here," he says.

He goes in and comes out a few minutes later with a paper bag, and from this he gives me a banana. I peel it and bite into it, squish the sweet paste through my teeth. "Tastes almost as good as you did last night," I say, trying to restore the morning's glow. But when Natan only smiles I know the mood has irrevocably changed — a victim of the plastic pirates, I guess you could say. In Natan's eyes I've probably gone from glamorous paintballer to dumbass tourist in ten seconds flat.

"I'm trying to find Ryan," I blurt to Natan. Yes it's classified info, but I tell it because hopefully it sounds good and noble and worthy of whatever danger awaits. I want Natan to respect me. "We think exile island is in Hawaii. That's why I'm going there. It's top secret. So please don't tell anyone."

He shrugs. "I don't say you shouldn't go, I say you should take a plane."

I sigh. "Can I walk with you to your boat?"

"OK."

At a pavilion at the top of the pier he stops at a locker and pulls out his fishing equipment. The net, folded and tied up with straps, is obvious, but the rest is a jumble of plastic and metal I would probably recognize in its assembled forms but which now looks technical and intimidating. Natan swings the load over his shoulder and we walk slowly to the end of the pier.

"How do you swim all this stuff out to your boat?" I ask.

"*I* swim," he grins, "*it* doesn't."

After setting it all down he slips off his shoes and pulls off his shirt, hands me his sunglasses, and drops backward into the water. He's a clean, pretty swimmer, with movements that seem to work with the waves rather than fighting them. Before long he's gripping the side of the boat we saw him in yesterday, and then with a splash he heaves his glistening body — his lean, starry back and strong legs — up out of the water and over the side of the rocking boat. I watch him shake out his hair and get to work pulling the tarp off the motor.

I stand holding his sunglasses. I put them on, look

around, take them off. Before long he motors up beside the pier. I pass his gear down to him and he arranges it around the boat.

"So I guess this is goodbye," I say.

"It happens," he says with a smirk. "Be careful, Boots McHenry. I had fun with you. I want to see you on TV next season so I can point to you and tell my friends and boyfriend I was with you. So be careful."

I start walking back down the pier before he's motored away, but when he's zooming out across the bay I turn and watch him. Sunlight winks on the back of his boat, which I see is named *Miguel*. Then I put my hands in my pockets and continue across the beach to the boardwalk.

I go back to my unused hotel room and shower and then check out (the old woman with the pink fingernails looks bleary-eyed this morning). Standing on the street with a breakfast burrito and coffee, I watch the town waking up. Yawning shop-owners push open shuddered windows, vendors roll covered carts along the boardwalk.

When I'm done eating I head back to the rocky beach where we parked the dinghy. Technically I still have plenty of time to spend in Puerto Natan, but I've had my fun and I'm eager to be back on the Intrepid. Maybe I can help Marcus with the supplies.

On the beach I find our dinghy, and find it occupied. Barefoot blond legs that can only belong to Piper Pernfors are hanging over the side, dangling toes half buried in the sand. That's all I can see as I approach so it's not clear whether he's dead, passed out, or just lying around daydreaming. I hope he didn't get murdered or something.

As soon as I can see the rest of him it's clear he's not

dead, and equally clear he's not just daydreaming. He has one arm covering his eyes and the other is bent in an uncomfortable-looking angle between his back and the floor of the dinghy. I kneel down beside it and cup my hands and yell his name. You'd think he'd be surprised, but he slowly moves his arm and gazes up at me with red-rimmed eyes.

"Boots. Time is it?"

"Almost nine. Been here all night, Piper?"

He frowns. "Does it *look* like I've been here all night?"

I can smell the fumes on his breath and know he was busy somewhere else, probably until a little while ago. I ask him what happened.

"This place was like Mardi Gras and they say it's like that *every night.*"

Things were hopping when I was touring around with Natan but I wouldn't call it Mardi Gras. Makes me wonder what went on outside while we were in bed — not that I would trade it.

"Well did you have fun?" I ask. I don't think there was any particular tone in my voice, but he snarls.

"I don't need you to lecture me, Boots."

"What would I be lecturing about?"

"Oh I can hear it in your *voice.* I know what you think of me."

I sit down beside the dinghy and drag my fingers through the sand. "Then you know I think you're still drunk."

"That must fit right in with the picture you have of me now, I bet. Poor pitiful drunk-ass Piper. Pitiful washed-up ex-boyfriend. Not even worth another glance, not even when you're so lonely you'll accept a know-nothing straightboy."

"I glanced, Piper. I glanced for years. Jeez."

"Wait'll you find out, Boots. Just wait'll you find out that this was *all* because of you. And then you're going to feel so fucking stupid."

The way he swooped his hand through the air to emphasize *all* sends a shiver up my spine, as though I'm responsible for all the misery in the world and not just his feelings of rejection. And I don't feel responsible for those either. If he wanted to spend his night in Puerto Natan piss-drunk because I'm not charging headlong into Boots-Piper 2.0, that's his problem, not mine.

"I'm going back to the Intrepid," I say. "I can either tip this dinghy over and dump you out, or you can shut up and I'll take you back with me. Your choice."

He doesn't respond.

A receding wave and a running start are enough to get the dinghy back in the water; Piper doesn't even have to move. My sneakers get soaked when I'm hopping back in, but everyone goes barefoot on the Intrepid anyway and soon I'll be able to ditch them again.

"What about your precious Clemente Santiago?" says Piper, still lying on the floor of the dinghy, looking up at me as I paddle. Now he does seem truly pitiful. "Can't forget about *him*."

"I'll come back for him later. He's probably off with Mariana still."

Piper closes his eyes for a moment and then opens them. "Ever run into our fisherman boy?"

I don't respond right away. I could really hurt him now, and he's put me in the mood to do it. I could tell him all about my night with Natan—all the vivid, slippery details. How great it was, how sweet. How this time when I wanted intimacy I passed over Piper in favor of a complete stranger.

I look down at him lying there—and I can't do it to

him. "No," I say finally. "I never did."

The Intrepid is a flurry of activity as we approach. Another boat is anchored beside it and there's a corrugated steel bridge connecting the two vessels. My first thought is *pirates!*, but it's clear that this boat, bearing the stenciled name *Diego Bros. Supply*, is here to stock our larders, not raid them.

With a thump we bang into the Intrepid's lower deck and I reach a hand out to hold us there. Piper gets to his knees and crawls clumsily past me out of the dinghy, nearly swamping us. After we drag the dinghy out of the water, Piper goes downstairs through the bridge and I climb the ladder up to the main deck. Marcus is there with a tablet in hand, directing traffic.

"All this stuff!" I say, marveling at the crates and boxes being hauled aboard by workers in navy-blue t-shirts that match the name on the other boat.

"It's cheaper to stock up in Mexico," Marcus says cheerfully. "Thought I'd do you guys a favor since you're the ones paying."

I see food supplies, fruit, water and beer and hard cider; chilled stuff in Styrofoam coolers. These are the things coming onto the boat. A row of black bags of garbage and blue bags of recycling are waiting to go off.

"The bags remind me," I say to Marcus. "I ran into a guy in town. He was telling me about the Trash Vortex pirates. Have you heard of them?"

"Yeah. Supply guy was talking about them too."

"My guy didn't seem to think it was very smart to be going where we're going. Just so you're aware."

"I'm aware. We'll have to make some changes to steer clear of trouble, but we'll talk about it once we're underway. Clemente back?"

"Still ashore. When are we leaving? Still sunset?"

"I'd like to get going sooner," he says. "But it's up to you."

"Where's Colby?"

"Sleeping." After a second he adds, "In my cabin."

"Nice."

Smiling, he goes back to directing the suppliers for a moment, then turns to me. "I think I'm in love with him."

"Easy now. You've got the whole trip ahead of you, Cap."

"Thank god for that."

After kicking off my squeaking shoes I go downstairs for what I want to be a quick nap, but the sounds of Piper puking in the bathroom reverberate down the hallway. The noise has also woken Colby, who leans into my cabin wearing striped boxer-briefs and messy hair.

"Who's sick?"

"Piper."

"Gross." He stands on his toes and peers up into Clemente's empty bunk. "Everyone back?"

"Clemente's still out partying."

"Oh."

"He met a girl."

"Fun." He turns and disappears from the doorway.

"Colby," I call. He comes back. "Marcus is busy with the suppliers. Piper's basically dead. I need to go back anyway to get Clemente. Feel like hitting the beach with me?"

"Beach? Cool. Let me get on my swimsuit."

I get up and put on my own swimsuit, stuff a towel, sunblock, and water into a backpack, and head upstairs. A wooden crate of bananas sits on the floor of the bridge waiting to go to the galley; I start to pick it up but one of the Diego brothers tongue-lashes me in Spanish so I put it down and back away slowly. Apparently there's a system here I'm not supposed to mess with.

Colby's already on the lower deck, pushing a dinghy off the Intrepid. He's dressed in a red mesh tanktop with orange swim trunks cut well above the knee, and checkerboard flip-flops—an ensemble that makes me wonder if he's taken one too many blows to the head in his fighting career. But if anyone can pull it off, it's Colby.

We get in the dinghy and each take a paddle, and after a minute settle into a rhythm that, if not exactly efficient, seems like it'll eventually get us somewhere decent. We find a small sandy beach a little ways down from the rocky one where we parked last night.

For a while Colby and I play in the warm, clear waves, and we partake in the age-old joy of throwing rocks into water. Most of the time when I'm with Colby it's easy, even automatic, to act he's my little bro or something. He says little-bro things, often seems to look at me in a little-bro way—laughing easy and always ready to learn something. He even seems little because he's so much shorter than me. Most of the time we have brotherly vibes. But here on the beach his bare chest and orange trunks with the slits up the sides blur things a little, and I have flashes of desire to pull down the trunks, bend him over, and lick his taint like an ice cream cone. I can't help it! For a million good reasons nothing like that would ever happen between us, of course—and now there's a million plus one.

"So my night with Marcus was zilla great," he says in a sing-song voice as we settle on towels side by side on the pink sand. He puts on some shades and smooths back his wet hair.

"He told me he wanted to take you on a date."

"We did go out," he says, and then he laughs. "Eventually."

I pop my eyebrows.

Still laughing, he adds, "We were in bed before you three even got ashore."

"Surprise surprise."

"I was throwing everything I had at the guy all week!" he says. "I was getting *frustrated*."

"He must've just been waiting for the right time."

"Well, us being alone was the right time, then."

"It was good?"

"*So* good, Boots."

"Details."

"Oh jeez. Well, we rolled around naked and stuff. Made out. I like his bed."

"Nice."

He puts his hand to his lips and whispers, "I really wanted him to fuck me, too."

"Yeah?"

"We *tried* to. I was really embarrassed." He's quiet for a minute and then he adds, "I couldn't, like, *take* him. Is that normal?"

"Is he big?"

"Not zilla huge or anything. I guess I was just tight?"

"Happens to the best of us, Colby." I reach over and playfully smack his shoulder. "Life's not a porno. In the real world it doesn't happen every time. It happens when it happens."

"Does my brother ever have trouble? Like, taking it?"

"Yeah, sometimes. So do I, sometimes."

He seems glad of that. "I just really wanted it to happen."

"You'll have other chances. Marcus isn't complaining. He looked on Cloud 9 this morning."

He smiles. "Anyway, then we got cleaned up and took the second dinghy and went for dinner. We had ice cream for dinner."

"Yum. I had baked cod." I'm not sure if I should tell him about Natan, because he's Ryan's brother and might not be thrilled about me fooling around with yet another dude, and because I wanted what happened in Puerto Natan to stay in Puerto Natan. But he confided in me enough about his night with Marcus that I want to share something too. "And I had a fisherman," I add.

"*Had* a fisherman? You hooked up?"

I nod and wait for his reaction.

"Zilla cool."

I smile. "It *was* zilla cool."

"The fisherman we saw coming in?"

"Actually, yeah. Natan."

"*Natan.* Sweet."

"Think Ryan would be cool with that?"

"He knows the difference between your heart and your junk, Boots," he says matter-of-factly. He rolls over onto his back, giving the sun his smooth belly. "And how about Piper?" he says. "We saw him wandering around by himself with a martini."

"I think Piper hooked up with a whole gangbang of martinis."

"That guy needed to get plastered and get something out of his system. I mean I barely know him, but he's sure been hung-up on something."

"He's hung up on me," I say. "I'm not interested, obviously. But it's complicated."

He's quiet a moment. "He's got nothing on my brother."

"No, he doesn't. Plus, for some reason it really threw him for a loop when he found out Clemente and I messed around together. So if he's been extra sour since the First & Last thing, that's why."

"I think you made a good choice," he says after a moment.

"Dumping Piper?"

"Duh, but I mean picking Clemente to hook up with when you needed a release or whatever."

"Think so?"

"Well, Clemente thinks so."

That catches me off-guard; for a second I think I've heard him wrong, or misunderstood, or something. "Has Clemente talked about it? How do you know? What did he say, exactly?"

Colby seems to realize he's set my expectations high and looks nervous about delivering. "Well I mean, he told me and Marcus, after you left to go talk to Piper."

"Yeah. What did he— Uh. What'd he say about it?"

"About your sex?"

"Yeah, Colby, yeah!"

"That he— That you blew him on your couch and then he topped you? Is that what happened?"

"Yes." I roll onto my stomach to hide a burgeoning erection. "That's what happened."

"Yeah, so there was that. And then he mentioned it again when we were up in the crow's nest."

"... You've been in the crow's nest?"

"Just once, I guess. Like three or four days ago."

"He invited you up there?"

"Nah, I just went up. But it was before he kind of took it over."

I lean up on my elbows. "So up in the crow's nest— That's when he said he liked having sex with me?"

"Um. I don't think he said *like*. He said he thought it was a good life experience or something like that."

"A good life experience like trying something and finding out you don't like it? Or a good life experience like trying something and realizing you *love* it?"

"I don't know, Boots, really. It's so windy up in the crow's nest, I could barely even *hear* him."

"Ah, Colby, you kill me."

He rolls onto his stomach again. "You like him, don't you?"

I look down at the sand under my fingernails. "I love your brother. But I'd be lying if I said it wasn't hot turning a straightboy to our team, if only for one night."

After completing the swimming-sunning cycle a few more times we roll up our towels and put on our shirts, and in all that time we've seen no sign of the aforementioned straightboy. My phone is in my jeans back on the Intrepid and I don't know Clemente's number so Colby's is of no use. Reluctantly we paddle back to the yacht.

It's after noon now, the Diego brothers have departed, and Marcus is eager to get back on the road. Piper is sitting in his usual chair on the main deck with a hoodie covering his face.

I go downstairs to get my phone, and when I discover my jeans pocket empty I remember, in a flash, the exact place I left it in Natan's apartment. *Shit.* I remember balancing it on the edge of a plastic stacker when I sat down to tie my shoes. Then Natan came in naked from his shower and drew my attention like iron filings to a magnet. That whole string of events means my phone is now locked away in Puerto Natan. So a photo's not the only souvenir Natan will be getting from me.

I trudge back upstairs. Colby's phone is still useless because it doesn't have Clemente's number. Marcus's would have his brother Marius's, who in turn might have Clemente's, but the easier solution is to ask to borrow Piper's, even though I'm reluctant to ask him for anything now, ever.

I do, though, for the good of the team and stuff, and

without saying anything or even removing the hoodie from his face he fishes in his pocket and holds up his phone. I pinch it out of his hand so I don't have to touch him.

Clemente answers after a few rings. He sounds tired. I suppose Mariana is equally tired this morning. I listen for her voice in the background but don't hear anything.

"We're ready to go," I tell him. "We're all waiting for you, Santiago."

"Am I late? Thought we weren't leaving till sundown! It's only one."

"Marcus needs to make some course changes so we're leaving earlier."

He sighs. "OK. Are you on the Intrepid? Where should I meet you?"

"Beach where we parked yesterday. I'll pick you up."

I'm sitting on the side of the dinghy when he comes sauntering across the beach. He has his hoodie balled-up in one hand and one of its drawstrings drags a delicate line in the sand behind him. For reasons unknown I want to slug him.

"Fun night?" I say.

"Above average. Couldn't get her to come with us, though. You?"

"Fucked a fan." I realize, almost as if I'm observing myself from outside my body, that I'm going to try to make him jealous. "Ass as tight as a hummingbird's. A tongue like candy."

"Sweet," he says, frowning. His shirt collar looks stretched-out. He puts a hand to his brow and looks toward the bay. "Everyone's on board already?"

"Yup. All morning."

We push the dinghy into the water and jump in with minimal splashing. I hand him a paddle. Once more we cross the bay of Puerto Natan, meant to be a pit-stop but actually a tangled web of intrigue all its own, or something. I'm even leaving behind a piece of myself, if only in the form of a phone. But I like the idea of Natan getting home tonight and finding it there in his room.

After banging against the lower deck Clemente and I climb aboard the Intrepid and haul the dinghy up behind us. The engine hums to life and Marcus greets us from the captain's chair as we enter the bridge. Soon the bay is receding with growing speed into the distance. And ahead of us is the wide Pacific.

PART 3

Vortex

Chapter 17

The Great Garbage Patch, often known more dramatically as the Pacific Trash Vortex, is a floating continent of plastic shit, accumulated over decades and held more or less stationary by ocean currents, the way a hairball will surf the drain of an emptying bathtub. Depending on the strength of the currents and the time of year, the Vortex can cover an area as big as the continental United States. Even at its smallest and densest, when the currents are strongest, it's bigger in area than the state of Hawaii. And like a spinning spiral galaxy it drags mile-wide arms and tendrils of plastic around and around with it.

"We're lucky," Marcus tells us on the first night of the second leg of our journey, when Puerto Natan is nothing but a glowing pink haze on the dark horizon, "because this time of year the Vortex is pretty small. Well, *relatively* small." With the Intrepid on autopilot we've gathered on the bridge to go over the plans. "That's the good news. The bad news is that it's a little farther south than I'd like."

"Then what's the issue, Mar?" Colby asks. "I'm sure the Intrepid can plow through that junk."

"Going through too much could wreck the propellers," Marcus says, with a smile I assume is for the nickname, "but that's not our real problem."

"Our problem is pirates," I say. "Right?"

"Pirates?" Clemente says skeptically, looking at me and then Marcus. "For serious?"

Marcus nods. "Unfortunately. They have a

settlement in the Vortex. They use the plastic to make rafts sturdy enough to build whole shanty-towns on. It's like a floating ghetto."

"Guess I've heard of them," Clemente says. "But barely. How dangerous can they be?"

"Dangerous enough that we'll be steering clear," Marcus says, picking up his tablet. "I changed our course. Guys in Puerto Natan gave me a pretty clear latitudinal safe zone, but I'm going to be extra careful and go even farther south. So we're not heading to your coordinates as the crow flies anymore. We'll go in a curve, like a *U*, to give the pirates plenty of breathing room." He holds up the tablet, showing us a finger-sketched line on a map.

"Drawbacks?" I say.

"Well, the main one is that this new course adds almost a week to the trip."

"So like three days each way?" Clemente says.

"Each way? No. I'm only calculating one-way here. Once we get to Hawaii all bets are off. From there we're playing it by ear."

"Hey, an extra couple weeks on the Intrepid," Colby says, looking at Marcus, "I'm not complaining."

"This is silly," interjects Piper, who's been quiet until now. "It is. I'm sorry."

"What's silly?" Marcus says.

"Colby might not have anything better to do with his life, but, uh—"

Colby is glaring. "Watch it, Pernfors."

"—But we're adding two weeks to this mission just so we can avoid even the *potential* of running into a few malnourished trash-pickers? Seriously?"

"They're hardly a *few*, Piper," Marcus says. "There are hundreds of them, maybe thousands. Shanty-town was the wrong word; it sounds too small. *Favela* is a better one. And we wouldn't be the first boat they've taken. Diego was telling me they've taken ships plenty bigger than the Intrepid, with plenty bigger crews."

"Crews made up of professional athletes who shoot guns and dodge bullets and outrun other professional athletes for a living?" Piper leans forward, clasps his hands. "Look, I'm not saying we should fly welcome banners and ask them aboard for tea and cookies. Just that a week is a long time, and if worse comes to worst we could handle ourselves against a bunch of scrawny sea-rats."

"When you put it like that," Clemente says, "it basically comes down to a cost-benefit analysis."

"Exactly. An extra week to avoid a negligible risk," Piper reiterates. "It's a waste. Would we even have supplies for that?"

"I stocked the Intrepid with that time-frame in mind," Marcus says.

"Dude, no offense," Piper says, "but we hired you, we're in charge here. Maybe we should put this to a vote." He stands up. "All in favor of —"

"Excuse me," Marcus says, dropping the tablet on the couch and standing up, "there won't be a vote. This isn't a democracy, Pernfors. The Intrepid belongs to me, it responds to my fingerprints, and all the rules are mine, and while you're on board you'll follow those rules. If you don't like that, Piper, you're welcome to grab a life vest and jump overboard. There won't be a vote." He sits down again. "You hired me to do one thing: to take you to a set of coordinates in Hawaii. I told you up front I couldn't guarantee a definite time-frame. And now, I'm sorry, but that time-frame is going to be longer than we thought. But I intend to get you there safe." He looks around. "I apologize if anyone thought this was an open meeting. I didn't call you together to discuss this — I called it to inform you. We're avoiding the Vortex. Either that or we head back to Thebes. Your call."

"Well we can't turn *back*," Clemente says.

Piper not-so-subtly rolls his eyes.

"You heard the captain then," Colby says. "We avoid the Vortex."

Chapter 18

The next few days feel like a montage. Hours and even whole days seem interchangeable. Order isn't important. Time is fluid. The only constant is the hum of the engines and the unending crash of waves against the prow.

I spend a lot of time sitting up near there, thinking of Ryan, replaying his last game over and over in my mind. Wondering if there was anything I could've done differently, wondering what he said to me from the chopper, when his hair was obscuring his mouth. Wondering what I'll do and feel when I see him—if the coordinates actually bring us to the right place.

I wonder too—honestly, more—about what Colby told me Clemente said to him in the crow's nest. About sleeping with me being a good experience. What made Clemente say that? How does he really feel about it, deep down? And why is getting one night with him starting to feel more like missing out on a thousand?

And what does that mean for Ryan and me?

Sometimes I flat-out daydream. Blame the dolphins for that; there are lot of them. One afternoon Colby and I spend hours watching them surf beside the boat— they're hypnotic and serene and make me feel content, primed for daydreaming. I daydream about Natan, chilling in his boat with the boyfriend I didn't meet, the boyfriend who graciously allowed Natan to have a list I was lucky to be on. I daydream about living in Puerto Natan. I could never give up paintball, but it's fun to imagine moving to a place like that—a place with less, but also, kind of, *more*. Clemente seems happy in his tiny childhood home, and Natan even happier in a one-room pad. It would be nice to have some of that. Maybe when I get home I'll sell the house.

"There's another pod at one o'clock," Colby says from behind a pair of binoculars, pointing. Sleek gray dolphins soar, and their speed stops time.

That day or another day, I'm washing dishes in the galley. Someone has to do it, and my tolerance for a sink full of crusty clutter is the lowest of anyone on board.

Clemente is sitting on the countertop near the sink, keeping me company and nursing a hard cider. There's a ring of condensation on his knee where he's been resting the bottle, and the black hairs on his leg, normally so springy, are slicked flat there. The glances I keep sneaking at his swaying legs are making my dick tingle. He's been on my mind more than usual lately—the way I felt seeing him with Mariana caught me by surprise. But the more I think about it, it's less a surprise than a confirmation of a feeling that's been nipping at my better judgment for a while now.

Sudsy runoff has drifted across the countertop and crept under his bum, but he doesn't seem to care that his shorts are getting wet.

He's too busy missing his dog.

"Just hope ol' Troop doesn't kick off before we get home," he says with a nervous laugh. He puts the bottle to his mouth, takes a swig, rubs the back of his hand against his lips. "Don't know what I'll do when he *does* go."

"It would be like losing your best bud," I offer, though it's speculation—I've never had a dog.

He nods. "Don't even like to think about it."

"You could get another dog."

"*Pfft.* Nah, never. Wouldn't be the same. Me and that mutt go *back.*"

After a minute I say, "Is it weird that I like doing this?"

"What, washing dishes?"

"It's soothing or something."

"You just like it because I chill with you while you're doing it," he says, and he's right—I like everything about him sitting there, from the hollow thumping sound his heels make against the cupboard door, to the smell of his sunblock, to the tone of his voice in this small, pink-walled space.

"Whatever, Santiago. It's soothing for you, too."

"Actually it's a little painful for me, McHenry, watching a fellow sniper's trigger finger get all dishpanny."

"Seriously." I hold up my finger. Suds run down my forearm.

"When we're done with this whole thing," he says, handing me a fork that's surfed away from the sink, "you're welcome to come to my house and knock yourself out on my dishes any time."

"Let's not get carried away."

After taking a final swig he puts down the empty bottle and hops off the countertop. A spot on the left butt cheek of his shorts is wet and ringed with suds. For a second I think he's going to leave, but he just stretches and ends up closer to me than when he started.

"I'll dry," he says, pulling the towel off my shoulder.

"Jeez. Watching you do this all, it kills me."

"I'm tough."

"Yeah. Still." He takes a plastic plate I've just finished scrubbing dried ketchup off of. "Need to remember to bring a bag or something up to the crow's nest. There's quite a collection of cider bottles building up up there."

"You shouldn't be drinking in the crow's nest. You might fall out."

He laughs. "Whatever."

"What do you do up there, anyway? You're up there so often, it seems like I barely ever even see you sometimes."

"It's just my secret place. I like high places. It's the sniper in me."

I smirk. "You like to watch?"

"Hey baby, I like to watch." He snaps the towel.

"You won't let anyone else up there."

"What? Sure. Everyone's been up."

"No one's been up there, Clemente."

"Colby has."

"Colby. No one else. You pull up the ladder. It's not very welcoming." I push out my lower lip.

He rolls his eyes. "It clangs against the wall, makes things less peaceful."

"Sure it does." I hand him a mug to dry.

"What, you'd prefer we chill together all day long? You'd get so sick of me."

"Whatever, you can do what you want."

I straighten a plate he's put in the drying rack incorrectly — by which I mean, not how I would've done it. He observes this and moves it back to its crooked position and then pokes me in the ribs with his thumb.

"Don't touch me."

"I'll touch you. I do what I want."

I laugh. "Maybe you should do what *I* want, Clemente."

For a second he looks at me. Then he resumes drying. "I don't take orders from you, dork-ass." He gives me a wry smile and, without taking his eyes from mine, reaches and returns the plate in the drying rack to the position I like it in. "There. Now don't say I never did nothin' for you, McHenry."

My heart is pounding and the water is swirling around the drain when Marcus comes downstairs and leans into the galley.

"There you are," he says. "Hey, we're in a warm spot, if you want to go for a swim. Colby and Piper are already overboard."

Only then do I realize the engine's roar has quieted to near silence and the floor has leveled out—something I would've noticed right away if not for Clemente's distracting presence.

"Awesome," Clemente says, and he throws the dishtowel on the counter. "Let me get my swimsuit!"

"Actually," Marcus says, blushing, "the other guys went in naked."

"Naked?" I say.

"Naked it is, then," Clemente laughs, sliding past Marcus and dashing up the stairs.

When I get to the main deck I see him doffing his t-shirt on his way toward the prow and then, barely breaking stride (but dropping my jaw), he yanks down his shorts and underwear and hops free of them. Naked as the day he was in my bed, dick flopping against his legs and belly, he hops the rail. There's a splash and moments later I hear him hooting joyously. With my own shirt in my hand and my shorts unzipped, I run to the side and look over. He's looking up at me, a brown blur among two blond ones in the shimmering waves.

"Coming in, you baby?"

It's all the coaxing I need to get naked and dive.

Deep underwater I open my eyes, the salt sting totally worth this view of hanging legs, hair waving out from crotches and legs like seaweed. Colby's legs, Piper's, Clemente's. I want to swim up beneath Clemente and break through the surface and kiss him. The joy with which he jumped off the boat makes me want to kiss him. This trip has stirred so many mixed emotions so far but this one is clear: I want to kiss him more than anything.

"Elegant dive," he says when I finally surface. His hair and mustache are so richly black that the water dripping down his face seems to take the color with it, and almost looks inky.

Colby is saying, "OK, ready?" in the tone he and Ryan both use when they're goofing around. And then after taking a breath he somersaults under. He's a blur beneath the waves and a moment later his feet push through the surface and his legs begin scissoring rhythmically like a synchronized swimmer.

Laughing and looking down at us from the main deck where he's undressing, Marcus says, almost to himself, "Colby," and shakes his head, smiling.

With a mischievous look, Piper swims close and grabs Colby's ankle and clutches it above the surface.

"Piper, stop it," I say.

He's reaching for the other one when suddenly he groans "*Ooof!*" and lets go. Colby bursts up gasping, pushing hair out of his eyes.

"Pernfors, what the fuck!"

"I was just *playing*," Piper says, dodging an angry splash from Colby, "you didn't have to punch me in the dick."

"I couldn't breathe! I don't have *gills*, asshole!"

"It was only one second," Piper says, laughing but putting some distance between himself and Colby and trying to make it look casual. "Come on." If we were on dry land we all know Piper would be in a choke-hold right now.

For an awkward minute we all tread water and the only sound is of the hum of the idling engine, the water lapping the sides of the Intrepid, and Colby blowing seawater snot out of his nostrils one at a time. Marcus disappears from the railing.

I swim alone over to the boat's starboard side, where a patch of cool shade clings like oil to the waves. I drag my hand against the smooth hull, wiping away globs of furry seaweed. When I'm halfway to the lower deck I feel something lash against my thighs, soft but strong. I look around but don't see anything.

"Something's swimming around me," I call out nervously. Saying it makes it real, makes my skin crawl.

"Did you get bitten?" I hear Clemente ask.

I'm turning to answer when I feel it again: a soft but powerful thump against my thigh. This time I notice bubbles foaming up against my chest—and I realize what it is, and laugh. It's no sea monster, no shark, no bloated corpse, just water shooting from the idling boat, an extra-large version of the jet in my pool at home. A gigantic new boyfriend, Ryan would say. I put my hand on the hull and center my dick in front of the stream.

"McHenry, did something bite you? Answer me!"

"No." I close my eyes, feel them roll back. "Clemente, come here a sec."

"What is it?" He swims toward me, looking at me funny.

"Closer."

He comes, but cautiously, as though I'm going to

222

spring a trap. I move back enough to share the stream. When it hits him he says *"Whoa!"* and splashes backward. "What *is* that?"

"My new boyfriend."

"Your what?"

I grab him and guide him back to the right place. "It can be yours too."

"Oh," he says. And then, when he's realized what the fuss is about, he says it again in a totally different way: *"Oohh."*

For a minute he floats with his eyes closed, bubbles foaming around his chin like a white beard. He has a little grin. I watch him. The stream is wide enough to pummel me too—we're in it together. Is this becoming something?

When I'm about to touch him, but before I've moved to do it, he laughs and shakes his head and swims out of the stream. Treading water, he says, "OK, I think that's enough."

"What? Did you come?"

"No," he says, blushing a little, "no."

"Don't you want to?"

"Want to what?"

"You know."

He just looks at me. Then he looks back over his shoulder; the other guys aren't in sight. He claps his hand over his face. He's grinning. "Will you go make sure no one comes around?"

"I can do that," I say, disappointed.

"Because you're right," he adds, "I'm sick of jerking off in that tiny bathroom."

I laugh, but really I'm surprised by how hurt my feelings are.

Our shoulders and outer thighs brush together as he swims past me. I watch him from behind as he looks for the stream, can tell by the way his shoulder muscles contract and then relax, that he's found it.

Reluctantly I turn and swim back to the others.

They're on the sunny port side. Piper is floating on his back. Marcus is with them now and he's brought a few foam kickboards down with him.

"Where's your other half, Boots?" Colby teases.

"Giant squid pulled him under," I reply, grabbing a kickboard. "Nice here in the sun, huh?"

Piper looks at me, turns his mouth up at the corner as if to show he suspects Clemente and I were up to something, then lies back and resumes floating. Horizontal atop the waves, his penis hidden just beneath the rippling surface, he seems to be daring me to look at him, daring me not to want him. And Clemente is on the other side of the boat, 300 million miles away, getting off with my boyfriend without me.

We play in the water for an hour or more until a brewing storm on the horizon makes everyone feel chilly and ready to get out.

"Crazy lightning," Clemente says, leaning on a kickboard pressed under his belly. He doesn't realize it, I'm sure, but the water is lapping his bare bum halfway up, sectioning it horizontally across the vertical crack into quarters of firm brown skin.

The air has grown cool and misty while we've been swimming and I keep having to wipe beads of water from my eyelashes. The sky, though it's still blue above us, gets steadily darker as it nears the horizon, where a patch of black rainclouds is lighting up here and there with the glow of hidden lightning. Every so often a jagged streak springs out and zaps the water.

"*Pfft*," Piper scoffs, "that's a baby storm." He laughs, looks around. "But just for the sake of argument, what happens if that baby storm comes our way?"

"We'd be tossing our baby cookies," Marcus laughs. "But don't worry. We're heading the other way. And we should get a move on."

One by one we climb, dripping and goosebumpy, onto the lower deck, and then up the ladder to the main one. Clemente climbs ahead of me and I steal a glance up at his bare inner thighs, at the plump, fuzzy mounds where they merge with his bum. He seems the most relaxed with his nudity, the most mellow, maybe because he just emptied himself into the Pacific. The rest of us run hooting and jeering around the main deck, scrambling to find our discarded clothes like embarrassed participants in an aborted orgy. Colby, lean and curiously free of tan lines, hops across the deck, downy butt bouncing and making me think of peaches. Piper's body brings to mind my better memories from when we were boyfriends. And Marcus, tall and smooth as a glass of iced coffee, has, surprisingly, a big old anchor tattooed on his butt.

Soon the Intrepid's engine roars back up to full power, and we're off.

Our course, Marcus has said, will be shaped like a U—which, as Colby reminds us when the storm is safely far behind, is also a zilla big smile.

Chapter 19

"This better not take them *two hours*," Clemente groans in a disembodied monotone three feet above me, in the dark.

"You love it."

"Definitely rather be sleeping," he says.

"I think it's hot."

"You would." He's quiet for a minute while we go on listening. "Jeez, they should be finishing soon, no?"

"Sounds like they might be getting close." I roll onto my stomach and tilt my head just-so, to better hear the fucking that's going on in Marcus's cabin.

Over the fucking I hear Clemente sigh. "Forget it, I'm not sleeping anyway." His legs drop over the top bunk and he hops down, all dark skin and white underwear in the moonlight that gleams through our porthole. He leans against the opposite wall near the door, arms crossed over his chest, head cocked. "Should I open our door a tad?"

"Evil."

"Heh."

Quickly and casually, as though it's pure accident, he reaches out and tugs the door handle, setting the door ajar three or four inches. The muffled sounds of bed and bodies and breathing grow louder.

Clemente whispers conspiratorially, "Who do you think's the— Who do you think's doing, you know, what you did? And who's doing what I did?"

"Who's fucking who, you mean?"

He nods, presses the sole of one foot against the wall.

"Sounds like Colby's on bottom," I say. "Which is a big deal for him. —Oop, oop, Colby's going over the falls!"

Clemente leans closer to the door, knuckles of one fist brushing back and forth against his mustache. Then he turns and looks at me with a mischievous grin. "Now Marcus."

We listen for the couple's final yelps and satisfied laughter and then wait through a full minute of silence. Clemente steps away from the door, head down, rubbing the back of his neck, listening.

I say, "They didn't sync their orgasms as well as we did, that time. Remember?"

He looks up and gives me a little smirk before returning his attention to the other cabin. Under the covers I've gotten rock-hard listening to Marcus and Colby, and I want Clemente to throw me at least a bone of acknowledgment of our super-sexy fun-time. More than a smirk.

"It was like clockwork when you pulled out of me and grabbed my — "

Suddenly Marcus's cabin door opens and the couple's voices grow louder.

Clemente drops to a crouch. "Shit shit!" Creeping away from our door on hands on toes, he springs up and belly-flops onto my bunk beside me. I stop breathing. "Did they see me?" he whispers, chin pressed into my pillow.

I have no idea what they may have seen; with Clemente this close they no longer exist.

"Think they're going to the bathroom," he adds. Then quietly he rolls from his belly to his side, which puts his smooth shoulder blades against my pecs. His arms and one of his legs are hanging off the bunk. My left arm is bent somewhere underneath me; my right hand is hovering over his ribs and I'm not sure whether to rest it on them. We listen. Colby and Marcus seem to be standing in Marcus's doorway but I can't make out what they're saying. Clemente laughs. "What are they doing just standing around?"

"Beats me." Finally I bend my arm back and rest my hand on my neck, out of the way.

"Boots, why'd you make me open the *door?*"

"*I* didn't make you. *You* opened it."

"You *made* me." He laughs. "Shit, here they — *Sshh.*"

The hallway lights up, sending a three-inch beam

across our floor, a spotlight that very nearly touches Clemente's dangling foot. Like a comedy prison-break he slowly pulls it away from the light and back onto the mattress. We can hear their muffled voices. Clemente is vibrating against me, laughing.

"Shut up," I whisper, and then I do touch him—but just a hand on his shoulder to keep him still.

He shushes me, and adds, "Feels like we caught our parents boinking."

"Seriously." But no, it's nothing like that. It's like listening to two gorgeous guys fuck and having another gorgeous guy all up against me. Can he not feel my boner stabbing his butt-cheek? Because it is. Stabbing and ready to pop.

After a minute the lights turn off and we hear the hallway creak as bodies move along it. Then the bathroom door closes. The shower begins to run. After a clink of shower-curtain rings the falling water takes on a varied sound as it hits bodies on its way to the tub floor.

Clemente turns onto his back, his elbow dragging across my chest, and clasps his hands against his sternum. "Think the show's over now." And yet he isn't getting up.

"Yeah?" I pass my hand lightly over his knuckles where they're resting between his pecs, and then lay my open hand on his abs. I can feel his skin and muscles react to my touch—quick, subtle rises and falls, as if he's ticklish but can hide it.

"Yeah," he says. "Think so."

"Doesn't really *have* to be, Clemente," I whisper. "If you don't want."

He doesn't say anything—I can only hear his breathing. Gently I lower my hand to his crotch. I'm surprised but happy to find hardness already beneath the white cotton. When I start squeezing his shaft through his briefs he closes his eyes and opens his mouth as his lungs empty with what I take as glad surprise. For a minute I trace the shape of his erection through the fabric, then slide my hand down his treasure trail and under the elastic waist of his briefs. His cock feels smooth and hot and moist. *One and done—maybe not.* I stroke it up and down, squeeze it, rub my thumb over the tip. He pushes his head back into my pillow, breathing heavy.

"Feels good?"

He doesn't reply.

"Clemente. I'll suck it again if you want—"

But all of a sudden, like a startled cat, he's bolting off the bunk. I get an elbow in the ribs and a toenail scrape across my shin. The blankets whisk off like a tablecloth trick. It takes me full seconds to realize someone has knocked on our door. Clemente must know he has no chance at his bunk so instead leaps to a pile of laundry on the floor—a fake task as a disguise. He stands up with his phone in one hand and a pair of shorts in the other as Colby pushes open our door and peers into our cabin.

"You guys awake?"

My heart is pounding. I want to fucking murder him.

"Yeah," Clemente says, calm. He drops his shorts to the floor and then casually tosses his phone onto them, as though he's done checking what he got up to check. In the same motion, he turns to the bunks and climbs up into his—fast, but not so fast that I don't glimpse the lingering erection straining his briefs, or the tip of pink cock peeking out near his belly button.

"You awake, Boots?"

"Yes, Colby, yes." Boy I'd like to use this kid for target practice right now. "I'm awake."

With that he bounds into our cabin, falls to his knees with a happy sigh in front of my bunk, and smashes his face dreamily into my mattress.

"Good sex?" I say, monotone.

He turns his head and peers up at me and nods, cheek mashed against the sheet. "You heard us?"

"The dolphins heard you."

He laughs and swoons back, arm flopping out dramatically, and falls to the floor, rolls to the middle of the cabin, sprawls out on his back, sighing. He has on boxer-briefs and Marcus's *Tumble Aquatic Tours* polo.

"Come on, Colby, no sex is *that* good."

"I took him, Boots," he says, still gazing dreamily at the ceiling. "I did it. For the first time." He curls into a ball just long enough to burst out of it, like some kind of horizontal cheerleading move.

I sit up on my bunk, pull a blanket across my lap. "We thought it sounded that way."

He sits up too, shimmies across the carpet to lean against the wall. "You were right. Patience is key. Patience and lube."

"Told you."

"I can still feel him inside me," he laughs, standing up, giving his butt a wiggle. "I wanted you to know."

"Thanks."

"I need to go to *sleep* now," he says. And plucking the crotch of his underwear, he wanders back out to the hall, pulling our door shut behind him with a flick of his foot.

While I'm trying to decide what to say to Clemente I listen to Marcus finish up in the bathroom and return to his cabin. Colby says something and then their door closes and it's quiet.

All this time Clemente's been quiet too.

Finally I whisper: "Hey. You awake?"

From the top bunk: "Yes."

"Clemente. If you want— We can finish what we

were doing. We can keep going."

He's quiet for a long time. I start to wonder if he even heard me, but finally he says, "Think I'll pass."

"Oh."

"Yeah. G'night, McHenry." I hear him roll over.

"Really? Seemed like you were enjoying yourself."

He sighs. "Maybe I'm just not in the mood to service you tonight, Boots." He mumbles it into his pillow.

"Wow, *service* me? Where'd that come from?"

"That's what it was that time, right? You asked, I obliged. One and done, we said. A service."

"You felt like you were servicing me? That's all? Nothing else?"

The voice comes clear but the tone is vague, noncommittal: "Yeah."

"*Pfft.* I don't believe that."

"Don't know what else to tell you, Boots."

"I saw how hard you came, Clemente. You weren't just servicing me; you got something out of it. Maybe it wasn't romance. Maybe it wasn't palpitations of the heart-strings or whatever. But you got something out of it. I saw you come." He doesn't say anything but I can hear him breathing up there. It feels good to say this and it's making my boner swell, as if it knows this is all it's going to get. "I saw how the cords in your neck and shoulders stood out like you were being *electrocuted*. I saw every *fiber* of your muscles clenched under your skin—as if your skin was just *painted on*. That's how *hard* you came, Clemente. So don't tell me you felt like some kind of human dildo that I used and tossed aside and never cared about."

There's a thump—he punched his mattress. I can hear him breathing fast. Is this escalating? Will we get so angry the only thing to do will be to stop and kiss?

"Boots, did you ever think that maybe you shouldn't

be asking me for a re-fuck when we're days away from finding your *boyfriend?* Where's your mind at?"

I'm quiet for a second—his invoking Ryan startled me—and then I say, "Wouldn't be any different from the first time."

"Would too."

"And the whole one-and-done thing was all you, Clemente. If it was up to me, maybe Ryan wouldn't even be involved anymore, maybe you and I would just alwa—"

His pillow falls past me and plops on the floor. Only when a blanket follows it do I realize he's throwing them down. Then he drops down in his white underwear.

"Don't even say it, McHenry." He kicks his balled-up shorts out of the laundry pile, pulls them on, zips them up. "Don't. *Do not.*" He looks at me for a second before bending down to gather the pillow and blanket into his arms. "Don't tell me that. Not when we've gotten so close."

And with that he pulls open our door and I can hear him bang away up the stairs.

"Oh fuck," I whisper in the dark when it's clear he's not coming back.

I've crossed a line. I don't think I even said very much, but he knew, knows I want more than a one-and-done, and that means I must've been sending out signals. For how long? I stare up at the underside of his bunk and every shard of explanation that comes to mind would only cut worse if I said it to him.

Just be chill, I tell myself, just be chill. Give him some space for a few days so he knows I'm not going to push it. So he knows I won't make things weirder. Not on purpose, anyway.

Just be chill.

If Clemente can sleep with me and brush it off as a good life experience then he's not likely to hold it against me just because later on he learns I want more. Is he? It'll be OK. Things will be OK. Just be chill.

Chapter 20

A whisper brings me suddenly awake. A gentle caress along my jaw makes my eyelids flutter. I'm lying on my back in my bunk. The pre-dawn glow from the porthole illuminates the underside of Clemente's bunk; I have some sense from the lack of bulge that he's still not in it. So this must be him beside me now, caressing me, not angry anymore, ready to slip into my bunk with me again, this time leaving his briefs on the floor, to finish what he wants to finish. I can feel the heat radiating off him, the nervous sweat on his fingertips. I'm ready for him. I open my mouth for a kiss, and inhale.

What?

This is not Clemente.

The smell. What's that *smell?* Clemente has never smelled this awful a day in his life.

"Wakey wakey," chortles a deep phlegmy voice like the bark of a decrepit Rottweiler—only the sound is *vakey vakey.* A foreign voice. It's not from my team.

I scramble but the sheet slips across the mattress, coils around my legs. Hands, rough and callused and long-nailed, close around my throat and start to choke me. Thumbs pound like pistons against my windpipe.

My eyes bulge open, from surprise and from the pressure that's exploding up through my face. My dry tongue lashes out of my mouth. I open wider but there's no air to scream. I can't even gasp.

With my fists I pummel the hands locked around my throat; when that fails I try to pry the greasy fingers apart but their grip is vice-like. My vision's starting to blur—through a growing haze I see yellowed eyes, a thin-lipped mouth, beard-hairs dangling some kind of black trinkets. There's nothing to kick except the wall and the end of the bunk. I feel my legs thrashing, all on their own.

Calm down, McHenry. This isn't the first time your life's been on the line. Use your brain.

I imagine Lucinda Skullcrusher in my ear, that guiding voice. *What are your options, McHenry?* There aren't many; my legs feel dead against the wall. Dead. I use that, and go limp, play possum, make him think he's got me. Maybe it's stupid but it's the best I can think of right now.

The pirate pulls away a little, starts dragging my head and torso across the mattress as though he's trying to get me onto the floor. Of course that's what he's doing—better leverage for choking my guts out. But in the meantime he's put himself face-level with Clemente's bunk. When my hand springs out I expect to grab the pirate's shirt but my fingers slide through a mat of greasy chest hair. I roll to one side; with my other hand I grab his hairy shoulder and, with everything I can muster, yank him hard toward me. His nose and mouth slam the steel edge of Clemente's bunk—I hear a crunch and he screams and lets go of my throat and lurches backward. I kick away from the wall, roll onto the floor, and sit up gasping, pulling sheets off me. In the dark the blood falling out of the pirate's face looks black as squid ink. He's screaming a silent gurgly scream, his bloody, sunburned face a haunting grimace in the moonlight. I'm up before he staggers back against the porthole wall.

He's probably down for good already but where

there's one pirate there's got to be many and I don't know if he has a gun, or a knife, or what. I don't have time for anything less than a knockout. I punch him in the face once, twice, his head bouncing against the wall, and I think I must be doing it wrong. Should it hurt this much? It's a joke to believe I'm trained in combat. I'm trained in fucking *paintball*.

Where is Colby?

Where's Marcus? Piper? Clemente?

My heart pounds faster. *Clemente.*

Something heavy slams against the wall of the cabin next door — Piper's cabin. The mirror in my cabin falls off the wall and shatters, flinging shards across the floor.

I press my forearm against the pirate's throat and clavicle as hard as I can. Frothy blood bubbles from his hanging-open mouth. To seal the deal I knee him hard in the nuts. He doesn't have enough breath to scream. *See how it feels?*

"*Clemente!*" I call out, but it comes as a croak. Rubbing my throat, I step away from the pirate and he crumples to the floor like a masterless puppet. But no pirate is going to raid a boat alone — there have to be others.

I start for the door but pain shoots up my right leg and I realize I've stepped on a shard of broken mirror. There's no time to check the damage, not now, but it feels like the last thing my sanity can handle at the moment.

God help me but I want to cry. I put my hands over my face for two seconds that I know will seem like an eternity when I examine this moment for the rest of my life.

Cheer up, McHenry — you just waylaid your first plastic pirate! Now focus on your team.

When I've caught my breath I slip into the hall.

Near me, Marcus's door hangs open. I creep closer with my back against the wall and look in. There was a fight here—the sheets are ripped off the bed, a lamp is broken on the floor—but the cabin is empty.

As I'm making my way toward Piper's cabin a pirate comes around out of the galley. He jumps when he sees me and then charges me, a gleaming knife raised like a steel nightmare. My balls leap into my gut. *Fuck.* I turn and run and duck back into Marcus's cabin, get behind the door and whip it closed when the pirate's barging in. It clobbers his face. The tip of the knife pops through my side of the hollow door, six inches from my eye, as the pirate's weight crashes the door into me. It's like getting hit by a car but I'm able to get clear fast enough to avoid getting pinned against the wall. I jump onto Marcus's bed, ducking the low ceiling beams. From here I think I can jump right over the pirate, as if he's a barrel in the Industrial Zone, and land in the hall. But barrels don't reach and grab like this fucker's reaching and grabbing. He catches hold of my right foot, the bad foot, and twists it trying to yank me off the bed. I grab the cabin door, slam it closed against the pirate's ribs again and again until he lets go of my leg. He's disoriented on the floor and now I jump clean over him, pulling the knife out of the wood as I pass, and land in a painful crouch in the hallway.

Nice one, McHenry!

I wish I could get the pirate fully into Marcus's cabin and lock it somehow, but I know that's not in the cards. I turn and kick him hard under the chin with my bloody foot, but it's bad aim and even though I think it turns his lights out it probably hurts me almost as much as it hurts him. It makes me drop the knife.

Behind me, down the hall, there's a crash and I turn in time to see a pirate tumble backward out of Piper's cabin. Then Piper enters the hallway. He's in his underwear, same as me. His mouth is contorted in a snarl and the right side of his face is dripping with blood. But he's alive—it's the first proof I have that I'm not alone.

Screaming, he jumps onto the pirate and rains punches on the guy's face and gut. When it seems he's about the kill the guy I call his name.

He looks up, surprised; the rage in his eyes changes to desperation when he sees me.

"Boots," he says, "thank god. The others?"

"I think Marcus and Colby are captured—or gone. Clemente— I don't know."

"Captured?"

"We're being raided, Piper!"

He must know that's what's happening—the unconscious pirates littering the floor make it pretty fucking clear—but still, hearing it spoken out loud is a shock for me too.

I drop to my haunches and feel around for the knife. Got it. As I'm standing up I hear a nauseating crunch— Piper has stomped on the face of the pirate struggling to get out from under him. Piper's barefoot, but still. I don't know if the pirate's dead. I don't want to know.

I'm already moving past Piper when he tells me we need to get out of here.

I agree but I don't answer. I'm already near the end of the hall. There's a smear of blood on the bathroom door. I tell Piper to find us more knives from the galley.

"Wish we knew how many more are up there," I whisper, peering up the stairwell. There are footsteps on the bridge—I can't tell how many people they belong to—and I can't see anything except the occasional shadow bending across the top few stairs. "Think they've got guns?"

Piper stands beside me, a steak knife in each hand. "Risky to shoot on a boat."

"Down here, yeah. Which probably explains the choking. Not so much up there."

"Fuck."

"The Intrepid's still moving. I don't think we've ever stopped. They'll need Marcus's fingerprint to get the autopilot off and take control of the boat."

"What if they cut off his hand?"

I cringe, feel anger surge from my belly. "A bunch of pro paintballers against a few malnourished trash-pickers—I believe those were your words, Piper. Shouldn't be any match for us, right?" This isn't the time for sarcasm and I shouldn't be trying to make him feel guilty, but I can't help it.

Pain shoots up my leg as I place my cut foot on the first stair. My back is against the pink wall. I'm squeezing the pirate's knife with white knuckles. Piper is beside me.

"Boots," he says softly, leaning closer and touching one of his knife-wielding hands to my chin in a way that would be gentle if he weren't rushing it, "I'm sorry, for all of this. If this is my last chance—"

And he kisses me. I recoil at first, partly because he's kissing me at all and partly because I can taste the hot metal of blood on his lips.

"Now what do we do?" he says, looking up the stairs.

"No way to know until we're already there. Just need to be fast, get our hands on a better weapon than knives if we're going to have any chance."

Side by side we creep up the stairs. I can hear pirates talking—English interspersed with fragments of other languages. Strange accents. I think they're talking about the autopilot.

I'm focused on the voices, trying to determine numbers, ages, strength, when a cold steel rifle barrel springs like a cobra into the stairwell and presses against my temple. Time stops and I begin to inhabit my whole life, all at once. Childhood, high school, the first time I slept with Piper, the day I was drafted to the Warriors, the day Ryan and I bought the house. And among all these moments and memories it's not much of a surprise to me at this point that my favorites are the ones that involve Clemente.

And then I'm back, and everything is *now*.

There's a pirate on the other end of the rifle, no less nasty-looking than the gun itself. He's about thirty. His head is shaved, teeth gray. He wears a torn yellow t-shirt featuring a palm tree and the word *Miami*; the fabric sports dozens of small cuts, and through these cuts are woven what looks like ancient videotape. It gives the shirt a weird chainmail quality. He wears denim shorts and combat boots.

He's aiming the rifle at the small no-man's-land between Piper and me now. Then it jumps back toward me. I squeeze the knife but it feels like a dinner accessory now.

"Nighty night," the pirate says—a disgusting bookend to the *vakey vakey* I awoke to. But there's something in his voice—perhaps a hint of recognition—that makes him appear less committed to blowing our heads off than he was just five seconds ago.

"That's right," I say, "you know me. I'm Boots McHenry, of the Theban Warriors. You like paintball?"

He squints at me.

For a second I think he's lowering the rifle. But then he's swinging it and things just go dark.

Chapter 21

Gentleness isn't exactly these motherfuckers' MO. When I come to, the back of my head is throbbing and it takes all my strength just to raise my eyeballs enough to look around. The first thing I know is that we're still moving. My vision clears slowly, like a widening pinhole. I'm sitting on the main deck against the port-side railing, legs stretched out in front of me across the wood. Behind me my hands are tied with what feels like plastic rope.

Piper's beside me, in the same state except his ankles are tied too. My right foot is lying across his shins, as though we're playing footsie. I wonder if we've been posed this way. I leave my foot where it is; I don't want any pirates to know I'm alert.

Six feet away with their backs against the wall of the bridge are Marcus and Colby. They're tied up too, and both are naked. My stomach twists in a knot: their nakedness makes them seem even more vulnerable, but it's also evidence of the sweet coziness these plastic pirates violated.

Colby's legs aren't tied, though, and I know that if Colby's got his legs we still have a chance to get out of this. I make eye contact with him and Marcus and then lower my aching eyeballs.

Clemente's the only one unaccounted for. It's the scariest part of this whole situation—even considering that I count six pirates on this deck, and among them are at least five rifles. Two pirates are in the bridge, an older man and a teenager; I can see them through the glass, looking like they're trying to figure out the navigation system. There are two standing near Colby and Marcus, facing Piper and me—one of these is the guy in the Miami shirt, the other is a skinny black man with a nose ring. Another is at the prow looking out through the windscreen like a dumbass, holding his rifle nonchalantly across his gut. The sixth is at the narrow back end of the main deck; he seems to be talking to someone on the lower deck, so there must be more I can't see.

As I take in the scene I realize my ears are ringing. Or maybe they're not, maybe it's just unusually loud out here. Without moving too much I roll my eyes toward the rear of the Intrepid. Beyond the chatty pirate, who's begun climbing down the ladder to the lower deck, I see a black speedboat, sun-faded and salt-crusted to a sickly gray, trailing us from about thirty feet. There are six or eight pirates on it. A cable is stretched from the speedboat to the railing of our main deck. I can't see how it's attached but it must be with some kind of grappling hook. Dangling from this cable, climbing hand over hand over the frothy ocean streaming between the two boats, is yet another pirate. A rifle swings from a strap around his torso. He's ten feet from being able to drop onto the Intrepid's lower deck. This must be how they all got aboard without us ever stopping.

The older guy comes out of the bridge, trailed by the younger guy who, despite moving with the lankiness of a teenager, looks sunburned and dehydrated like a beachgoing meth addict. When the older one approaches, Miami and Nose Ring grip their rifles tighter and stand more aggressively—I take it this guy's their leader. He has thick gray hair woven into a dozen long braids that swing from his scalp like dreds. Against his shirtless muscled chest dangles a necklace made of flattened and serrated bottle caps, painted multiple colors like a tacky lei. With his back to me he turns and looks down at Colby and Marcus. His bare legs are

241

hairless and his seersucker shorts are smeared with grease. I look up at the idiotic braids thumping against his leathery back. I want to rip them off. As my gaze travels upward, I lift my head for the first time since coming-to—and there, peeping over the edge of the crow's nest, is Clemente Santiago, looking right at me with what's rapidly becoming a smile, the most crazy-beautiful smile I've ever seen. My eyes fill up and I almost call out in happiness—but he puts a finger to his lips so I lower my head again. I'm trying to keep calm but my pulse is pounding so hard you can almost see my skin thumping.

Bottle Cap kneels down in front of Colby and Marcus and says, almost politely, "I think I need the captain of this tub to give me a *hand* with the autopilot, so to speak." He laughs; all the pirates within hearing distance laugh. "Now which one of you Warriors is our captain?"

Warriors. So they *do* recognize us.

"I am," Colby blurts.

"*I* am," Marcus says coolly, giving Colby a glare.

Bottle Cap laughs again. "Co-captains, eh? You look a little young to be captaining a boat this nice." He slaps Colby's foot. "Barely even got any hairs on your nads!" He reaches forward and gives Colby's scrotum a little *coochy-coo*; Colby silently grits his teeth but Marcus's face turns gray with rage. Then Bottle Cap looks up at Miami. "Let's try the black one first. I think he's our captain."

All this time Colby's legs have been stretched out beside Marcus's but suddenly he's got his heels under his butt. With a squeaky upward thrust against the side of the bridge, he's on his feet. He doesn't even need time to get his balance before swirling into a wheel-kick; he's a blur as he spins, a downy blond blur. His foot rips the air so fast I expect thunder; it's got more than enough power to make a full 360, but it's interrupted three-quarters of the way by Bottle Cap's grizzled jaw. It's the move that won Colby the Junior MMAC title, and it's just taught Bottle Cap to keep his hands to himself. Instantly after the cracking collision Bottle Cap's body goes rigid and he pinwheels like a mannequin face-first into the railing — not that he even feels it by then. Colby's scored a knockout.

I look up past Colby just in time to see Clemente — butt on the roof of the bridge, dangling backward out of the crow's nest — slam an empty cider bottle against Miami's skull and then perform an epic sit-up, heaving himself as well as Miami's rifle back into the crow's nest.

The teenager starts wailing a high-pitched animal yell while Miami is dazedly wiping glittering brown glass off his shoulders, as if he has no idea how it got there. Nose Ring, following the teenager's accusing finger, swings his rifle toward the crow's nest just as Colby runs headlong at him, bends at the waist just before contact, rams his shoulder into the pirate's distended gut. Nose Ring's rifle clatters against the teenager's boots and he goes down backward on the deck while Colby somersaults across his chest and face. Colby lands on his feet with Nose Ring grimacing up between Colby's feet.

The move is a sight to behold, and it's almost fitting that Colby's done it naked — it makes him seem even more of an animal, a force of nature.

Miami has run to the prow, is grabbing the rifle away from the sea-gazing pirate, who seems paralyzed by the fighting.

Meanwhile Colby's got the teenage pirate, who had picked up Nose Ring's rifle probably planning to be some kind of action hero, in a death grip like the one he demonstrated on Clemente in my kitchen: the teenager is face-down on the deck and Colby is on top of him, twisting the kid's arms between them like the bow on a birthday present, pressing his forehead into the base of the kid's skull, and clamping the kid's legs into immobility with his own. This is no mere demonstration. Tendons in Colby's neck stand out thick; the muscles in his butt and legs look like they're about to split his smooth skin. And then there's an echoey, hollow crack, followed by the most blistering scream I've ever heard.

Like lightning somehow following a blast of thunder Colby's off the teenager and back on the skinny black pirate, has his heel on the underside of the pirate's chin, as though he's tipping the head back to clear the pirate's airway before ramming his foot down his throat. That's when there's a shot and the bridge windshield spider-webs.

I turn and Miami is aiming for another shot.

In almost that same moment a quieter shot rings out and a portion of Miami's shoulder splatters across the windscreen. Seconds later at the other end of the Intrepid a bullet removes the chatty pirate from the ladder just as he's returning to the main deck.

One of the rear bridge windows bursts. I press against the rail and struggle to my feet.

"Clemente, look out!"

They're shooting at him from the speedboat. He fires back and one pirate drops and draws a red smear across the floor of the speedboat while other pirates leap out of the way. Clemente's standing up now, shirtless with a band of cordless headphones around his neck. The blanket from his bed catches the wind and opens behind him like a stage backdrop for an instant before kiting away. His shorts snap against his thighs. He's pumping round after round into the speedboat—not at the pirates themselves anymore, I realize, but at the smooth, water-pounded surface of the speedboat's prow. The pirate climbing the cable drops onto the Intrepid's lower deck and another is close behind.

When Clemente fires yet another bullet into the speedboat's prow a stream of seawater springs up from inside, arcing through the air over the surprised pirates like the stream of a lawn sprinkler. Another few rounds and the stream becomes a torrent that spills the frantic pirates around the boat. Still more rounds and the prow of the speedboat breaks open completely to the pounding sea, sending a cascade back into the boat that washes out all but the most stubborn pirates. The speedboat is beginning to wobble, all off-balance now but still connected by cable to the Intrepid. Like a can dragged by a string from the back of a car, the speedboat careens wildly back and forth across our wake. The wrecked front end has begun to submerge, sending a jet-stream a hundred feet into the sky. And then the boat starts to capsize and spin—the remaining pirates go flying into the sea—and the smooth black hull turns out of the waves and rolls upright again, lifting an empty wet deck back into the air.

With a thunderous *thwong* the twisting cable suddenly snaps, lashes through the air like a whip; I hear pirates on the lower deck screaming. The speedboat rears up like a breaching whale, turns end over end over end, and finally scrapes upside-down and sideways through the surface with a foamy blast in the growing distance.

I look to the crow's nest. Clemente is looking at me. And his face is just breaking into a smile when a pink fog, almost pretty, opens up behind him in the morning light. It would be terrible enough if it were a paintball rupturing against his skin, but it's not. He seems to take flight then, and drops out of sight off the far side of the crow's nest. There's a white crystal splash behind us as his body enters the sea.

I don't breathe. I don't think. What do I do?

I lean back, kick up my legs, and tumble over the rail.

And it's when my body is in the air between the main deck and the waves that I realize I've fallen in love.

Chapter 22

I hit the water sideways in the Intrepid's churning wake, feel my legs turn over my head and slap painfully into the water again and again, like the stones Colby and I skipped on the beach in Puerto Natan. When I finally do get my bearings I'm deep underwater. Frothy bubbles from the wake tickle me but also help to buoy me up. Without them I'd be too stunned to find the surface. My arms are still tied behind my back. I use them as much as possible but that isn't much; my legs need to do all the work. I follow the bubbles up to the air and break into it, gasping.

Already I can barely hear the Intrepid. I turn myself around and spot it vanishing into the distance. Panic over being left alone out here in the middle of the Pacific Ocean ignites like fire in my blood—I start to feel dizzy—but then I remember Clemente, who might still be alive. Who *has to* still be alive. And I remember why I jumped, and why I'd jump again.

Blurry-eyed, I scan the round, bulging waves. They lift me and drop me in their hills and valleys. I don't see anything on the surface, just bits of plastic shit and seaweed floating here and there. I take a breath and drop beneath the surface, peer into the murk, but I can't see anything from here either. When I come up again I notice a pin-sized spout—someone gasping—a hundred feet away. It's either Clemente or one of the overboard pirates.

I call his name. No response, at least not one I can hear, and I lose sight of him, too, as a wave bulges in front of me. The waves are so disorienting; I don't feel like I'm pointed in one direction for more than two seconds before they turn me another way. I find the ever-shrinking Intrepid on the horizon and try to orient myself. A wave slaps water up my nose.

"Boots!"

I'm coughing and the voice is so faint I'm sure I've imagined it. I try to call out but my voice is a saltwater croak.

Soon I hear it again—"Boots!"—but it's even weaker this time. I put my back to the sound and try to kick myself closer. Swimming backward seems to be the easiest way to swim with my arms tied behind me.

"Keep yelling, Clemente!"

"Boots! Here!"

If there's any blessing at this point, it's that swimming backward allows me the most wonderful surprise: the sudden soft connection with Clemente here in the middle of the lonely ocean. It doesn't last more than a second or two but the relief that comes from touching him, from finding him alive, feels like it will get me through whatever's coming next.

I turn around. He looks dazed, gray, his mouth tight with a grimace, his eyes bloodshot from seawater. On his shoulder, right through his scorpion tattoo, is a black hole that seems to grow and contract with his pulse—the wound oozes blood as fast as the waves can wash it away. At its smallest the hole looks the size of a dime.

"It come out?" he asks, teeth gritted.

I look at his back and find that yes, the bullet made an exit wound too: the hole on the back of his shoulder is uglier, ragged, the size of a quarter.

"It's out, out—" My mouth keeps slipping underwater; my legs are getting tired. "Need to get my hands—out of these ropes—ropes soon."

"Yeah." He seems exhausted, is processing things slowly. But finally he says, "Let me look."

He drops beneath the surface and I can feel him pulling at the rope that binds my wrists.

He comes up gasping. Bloody water drains out of his wound. "Not ropes," he says, "some kind of webbing made from those old soda-can rings."

"Can you break it?"

"Yes." He moves behind me; I feel him squeeze the webbing. "When I start pulling," he tells me, "pull with all your might."

Again he drops beneath the surface. I can feel his hands on my wrists, and when he starts pulling them apart I pull too. The pain is explosive but I'm not free yet. He bursts up again, coughs water in my face.

"It cutting into you?" he says.

"Yeah."

"Fuck. Stuff's too strong for my arm like this. They've got the plastic reinforced with wires or some shit."

I don't reply. I'll be in trouble if we can't get this off me. I know Clemente would try to hold me up somehow but he can barely swim for one person, never mind two.

"OK," he says, steeling himself for another go, "I'm going to see if I can take some of the weight with my foot. Pull when I pull."

He drops once again beneath the waves and I feel him grab my left wrist. His toenails scrape across my lifeline and along my wrist as he forces his toes under the webbing. He's hanging sideways in the water, ribs and hip breaking the surface. Now he's got his fingers through the webbing of my right hand and he's pulling. I pull too. Even through the water I can hear him screaming; bubbles that seem to contain his agony break around my ears.

Suddenly something gives and my wrists fly apart and his belly smacks the small of my back. And then he's splashing to the surface, gasping through clenched teeth.

The strain has torn his wound open even further and his shoulder is pouring blood now, making the water cloudy around us.

I don't know what else to do so I put my newly-free arms (and the webbing still attached to my right hand) around him and hug him.

"The pain is zilla major, McHenry," he whispers, his mustache bristly against my shoulder.

"I'm so sorry."

"What about the others?"

"I don't know," I say. "I don't know."

Again I lose track of time, but it's not like those days on the Intrepid—it's no place for a montage. I'm busy pressing the heels of my palms into both ends of Clemente's wound to slow the bleeding. Otherwise, mostly I stare. I stare at the rivulets of blood still seeping down his scorpion tattoo. I stare at the plastic junk floating around us, watching for anything big enough to grab onto.

It might be fifteen minutes, it might be two hours.

The sun comes up, hot on my hair. We drift a few feet apart. I can see him struggling.

I ask if he wants to hold on to me so he can take a break from treading water. A few seconds pass before he nods, and I think he needed that time not to decide, but to understand me. I swim closer, and as the space between us narrows, the water takes on that tinkling, musical sound it gets between two bodies on the verge of touching. Then we touch; he wraps himself around me. Our bellies together, his legs crossed against my bum, his chin on my shoulder— Before any of this, back when life was lighter, I probably would've joked that, hey, if I have to die, I wouldn't mind having the gorgeous Clemente Santiago wrapped around me when I go. But now that it looks like we may die here just that way, I only feel sad that my friend is in pain.

With his good arm he swooshes the water at our side, making an effort to help keep us afloat.

"I can do it," I tell him. "Take a break. It's OK. Just rest."

He puts the arm around my neck, exhales heavily, sending a cool breeze past my ear.

"Warriors forever?" I say to the superstar sniper in my arms.

He smiles. "Warriors forever."

In the sky above Clemente I think I see a bird, and I don't know if it's meaningful. From the hole in his shoulder the blood seems to have stopped running. The goosebumpy skin around his wound is licked steadily by the waves bobbing over us. Is seawater good for a wound, or bad? I can't seem to remember ever knowing for sure. It's one of those age-old mysteries: Does the salt sterilize or does the fish poop infect? I wonder if we'll have time for it to matter.

I'm pretty sure it's a bird up there, but before I can decide, before I can show him, Clemente is letting go of me and slipping down into the dark water. It covers his shoulder, laps at his jaw and ears and nose. There's a look of blank surprise on his face that I think means he's gone into shock. Coldness fills the growing empty space between us, slaps icily against me.

Struggling, I reach for him.

"Boots, no. I think it's in my pants!"

It isn't shock; he's taken on the tentatively stunned look of someone who has four of the right lottery numbers and is waiting to hear the fifth.

He's feeling around underwater but he grimaces, rubs his shoulder, falls under, kicks back up, spits water. "Shoulder's so tight."

"What— What are you doing?"

"McHenry— My phone."

"... You have your *phone?*"

He looks at me for a moment, unmoving, as though afraid of jinxing it. "Please god, I think I had it with me."

"Let me."

"My pocket. Thigh. Left thigh."

I push through a patch of Velcro on his leg. My heart's in my throat—

—and good god damn, his phone's in his pocket. When my fingers touch the flexiglass hugging the shape of his thigh I cheer right into his ear.

Laughing, some of the grayness drops out of his face and pink lights up his cheeks.

When I'm confident of my grip I bring the phone to the surface. Water beads on the rubbery screen. It's 10:42 a.m. and the phone is playing an old Frank Ocean song through headphones that are god-knows-where by now.

"Don't drop it." He holds up his good hand and I put the phone into it. "Thank god for flexiglass," he adds, drawing his passcode lines to unlock the phone. "Good to 120 feet."

"Before you get my hopes up any higher, Clemente: Do you have signal?"

"Five sat-bars. Yup. And plenty of battery!"

Before I even realize what I'm doing, I'm cupping his

rough cheeks in my pruney hands and kissing his salty lips.

"OK," he laughs when I let go of him. "Now who do we call?"

"Nine-one-one?"

"Think we might be outside their jurisdiction."

"Um. Coast Guard?"

"If we call the authorities we're looking at an international incident here. Uh. Be tough to explain what we're doing way out here. And it'll put the kibosh on the rest of the mission."

I feel my brow pop in surprise. "You still want to go ahead with the mission?"

He laughs. "After all this? I took a bullet for this mission! And you know, lately I feel like it's even more important. We need to rescue the boys and the Intrepid first, though — somehow."

I don't know what to make of all this. I think he might be crazy. He doesn't look crazy, but he's lost a lot of blood. That's got to have some effect, right?

But because he's smiling and looks so alive all of a sudden I can't not go along with him.

"I think I know someone who can help us," I say. "He's a fan. He lives in Puerto Natan. And he's got my phone."

It's weird choosing myself from Clemente's contacts, though I'm pleased to see I've made it into his favorites. And it's weird seeing the video background he uses for me displayed across the screen while the call initiates (it's a clip he recorded during a practice, of me leaning against a faux-ganic tree casually tapping my foot). But it's just frustrating when there's no answer. I try again; same result.

It makes me doubt everything. Maybe I didn't

actually leave my phone at Natan's. Maybe he hasn't noticed it yet. Maybe he's out fishing.

"Maybe he's just afraid to answer someone else's phone," Clemente says. "Text him."

"What should I say?"

"SOS?"

Natan, I poke out with water-logged fingers, *it's Boots McHenry. I'm in major trouble. Please answer the phone.* And send.

"How long should we wait?" I say.

"Give it a few —"

But before he can finish, the phone lights up and an animated me is tapping his foot impatiently.

"Answer it, McHenry!"

I press *Go*.

"Natan?"

His sweet accent sounds nervous: "Boots? What kind of trouble? Are you OK?"

Clemente's smile is full of relief; he opens his mouth, tips back his head, laughs. I take a deep breath and continue.

"I'm in pretty dire straits, Natan. Check this out." I select Clemente's GPS icon and flick it through the airwaves.

"Got you," Natan says a moment later. "Oh. Good. You went way south, huh?"

"Not south enough, apparently. There's been a — thing. Clemente and I are overboard. We're treading water."

There's an epic pause. "You're not in your boat?"

"No."

Another pause. "Plastic pirates?"

"You told me so."

"I want to help. How can I?"

"Where are you?"

"Fishing. About two kilometers outside the bay. I brought your phone along—you have some great music. I can come and give you a ride back?"

I look at Clemente, who shakes his head.

"We don't actually want you to bring us back to Mexico, Natan. We need to rescue our friends. Can you bring us a boat?"

"We could do an ad campaign for BNA when we get back to Thebes," Clemente says. More color has returned to his cheeks and apparently he's starting to have enough peace of mind to daydream. *"With Bank of North America,"* he narrates, *"I can flick $2 million to a Mexican's phone while floating gunshotted in the middle of the Pacific with my teammate."*

"Gunshotted?"

"Gunshot? Gunsheet? I don't know. I don't write the stuff, I just read it and smile."

"There's a whole bunch of commercials in this. *With my Deus Ex flexiglass phone I can dial underwater and send the gorgeous fisherman I banged money so he can buy supplies to rescue me with."*

"You mean, *With which to rescue me."*

"Smart guy."

We're quiet for a long time after that as waves break against us. Reaching Natan was exhilarating but I think it's starting to dawn on us just how long we'll have to wait for him to get here, even with the hydrogen speedboat I gave him the money to buy.

"How are you doing?"

"Hanging in there," Clemente says with a little smile. "Getting hot, though, huh?"

It's early afternoon and the sun is beating down, making the bulging water-hills look white as snow with reflected light. We've been in the water seven hours, give or take a couple, and for the past few hours we've been keeping watch for any floating crap to keep the sun off us. For a while Clemente tried to balance the back of an old computer keyboard on his head, but it kept falling off.

When all this squinting is starting to give me a headache, I tell him it's time to get naked.

"Naked?"

"Yup." I doff my underwear, wring them out, and fit them over my head. "Don't want to get sunstroke."

He laughs. "Looks like a cross between a shower cap and a turban." I tell him he should do it too. "Don't want to have the phone separated from me," he says. It's back in his shorts pocket, set on vibrate. "How's your head feel, though?"

"Cooler," I say, touching my drying boxers. "Wonder if I can stiffen it with salt and fashion a visor...."

"Think I *will* try it," he says a minute later. After wriggling out of his shorts he gives me the wad of fabric to hold. "Careful of the pocket."

I hold his pants while he takes off his underwear, the same pair of white square-cut briefs I reached into last night—which seems like a distant, vaguely-remembered life at this point. He hands me his underwear in exchange for his shorts, and when he's clumsily gotten back into them commando-style he realizes he can't do the fly and button one-handed.

"Let me," I tell him, plopping his dripping briefs on his head. Treading in front of him while he looks over my shoulder into the distance, I carefully do up his fly, even going so far as to reach in and hold down his floating pubes with the back of my hand to keep them out of the zipper teeth. He's clearly far less comfortable with my touch now than on the night we had sex, and I wonder if I really screwed things up last night by putting the moves on him again. One and done—I should've respected that. "There you go."

"Thanks," he says sheepishly, pulling his underwear down to his eyebrows.

"You two really are Warriors, aren't you?"

"Holy shit!" Clemente cries, briefs dropping off his head as he splashes backward.

"Theban Warriors," the pirate says. "Hah."

He's bobbing in the waves twenty feet from us, clinging to a small white Styrofoam cooler. An Asian guy, young, accent plain American English, hair done up in short braids laced through with plastic beads and shit, face pink and peeling from layers of sunburn. Across his jaw is the same frost of salt Clemente and I both have.

"The other guys were talking but I didn't believe them," he went on. "Recognize you with my own eyes anywhere, though. Hah."

"Don't come any closer," I warn, because even if he's armed, his stench is the bigger threat—and he's only in the air from the shoulders up. How can these guys live on the planet's biggest body of water and be so against bathing?

The pirate raises one water-logged hand in a gesture of peace and brotherly-love or whatever. "I'm a fan, really." He laughs, a little deliriously.

"Where'd you come from?" I say. "You were with the fuckers who raided us?"

"I was in the speeder you *sank*, actually." He looks at Clemente. "Nice shooting, by the way." He coughs, spits something dark into the water. "Never saw anyone capsize a speeder with a few bullets before."

"You asked for it," Clemente says in a low voice. "We were minding our own fucking business."

"Yeah, well, any business out here is our business.

Especially when the business is a hydrogen-powered engine. That would be an offering, for sure. How could we *resist?*" Another laugh.

"That's why you raided us?" I say. "For the engine?"

The pirate crosses his arms sardonically across the cooler. "You think we were after your autographs?"

Clemente and I look at each other. If the engine is the treasure I don't know what that means for Colby, Marcus, and Piper.

"Guess the guys would've just killed you," the pirate goes on, giving me the willies, "but someone must've recognized you before the knives went in."

"But how do you know who we are?" Clemente says.

"We're pirates, not cavemen. We have TV." He spits again.

"Which I'm guessing you power with hydrogen engines," I add.

"We *might.*" He laughs, rubbing at black residue on his lip. I can't help but marvel at the irony of us getting raided in part to power the plastic pirates' NAPL addiction. "That's why it's such a fine offering," the pirate continues. "And we know enough to know you Warriors will fetch a pretty ransom too. Another offering."

"What's this *offering* business?" Clemente says.

The pirate rolls his eyes. "Gifts. Bribes. I don't know. See, our head guy Brogan"—I gather he means Bottle Cap—"and the rest of us tried to force a little, shall we say, *exchange of power.* And it didn't exactly *take.* That time, anyway; but it *will.* We've been on our own since then, boo hoo, and believe me that gets old out here. Us bringing your cute little engine along will pave our welcome back into the clan." He puts his mouth against the cooler and mumbles, "Or theirs, I guess." Then he looks up at us with dark, hateful eyes.

"Your friends must know you're out here," I say.

"*Pffft.* They'll assume I went down with the ship. Like the others." He throws Clemente another glare.

"Well, we have help coming. If you shut up we won't leave you out here."

"So kind," the pirate whispers sarcastically, and crosses his arms over the cooler.

"What's your name, anyway?" I ask a little later, more from boredom than curiosity.

The pirate takes a minute to respond. I decide he's not feeling chatty anymore. Then he says, "Ryan. Ryan Kroft."

"Fuck you."

Laughter. "Psych!"

"I should drown you for that," I say.

"Fagballer can't take a joke?" He spits again and drags his hand across his mouth and laughs.

Clemente swims closer and asks me, in a normal voice making no effort to be discreet, "What do we think's in his cooler?"

"Could be anything," I say. "Could be empty."

"Wouldn't mind having it even if it's empty. Seems to float pretty well. And my legs are tired."

"Yeah." I look at the pirate bobbing solo over there. He's drifted a little farther away but it wouldn't take us long to get to him. "You thinking what I'm thinking?"

"Yeah, I am," Clemente admits with a guilty smirk. "But how close to being evil would that be?"

"Given that he and his fellow scallywags tried to fucking murder us? I'd say we're justified in making him swim."

"What are you two yakking about over there?" the pirate demands. He spits more of his dark inner goop into the water.

"Just debating whether to take your cooler away from you," I say matter-of-factly.

The pirate's sunburned face blanches. "It's empty."

"It floats," I say, shaking my head. "That's all we care about."

"You hurt?" Clemente asks the pirate.

"No!"

Clemente points underwater, says to me, "See if you can see if he's hurt."

"Why's it matter?"

"Want to know how much sympathy to have for the scumbag."

"... OK."

I drop underwater. It's easier to see now that the sun's beating down through the waves. Shimmering streaks slice diagonally from the surface and fade down into the depths.

The pirate's wearing sneakers. They've got to be weighing him down so it's hard to fathom why he hasn't ditched them already—but then again a matching pair must be tough to come by on a floating junkyard. His rolled-up khakis are torn open up one leg; the fabric fans around his thigh like a fin. I might take it for pirate fashion if not for the billows of blood clouding the water around the tear. There's no telling what part of the speedboat he may have sliced against on his way out.

I return to the surface.

"—come any closer I'll just crack it in half. Hah!"

"Your choice," Clemente says to the pirate. "But if you do we'll use *you* for a raft instead. Until you sink, anyway. *Hah.*"

The pirate shakes his head; the beads in his hair tink together. "You wouldn't."

"*I* would," I say. "For that thing about Ryan."

Clemente, at least, can tell I'm dead serious. "We

might need him," he whispers. "He would know where the pirate settlement is."

"Yeah. Good news for him." More quietly I add, "But we'll be lucky if he lives long enough to show us."

Turns out we're not that lucky. The pirate's cooler is offered up to us as the sun is setting, and it happens out of nowhere. Not with a trickle of dwindling blood but fast, amid a torrent of roaring water.

In the movies the victims always see the fins in plenty of time to add dramatic tension to the scene. *Ba da. Ba da. Badabadabada.* This is nothing like that. There's no warning. One second he's scratching some design into the top of the cooler with his thumbnail, the next he's getting enveloped by what seems like living water — swallowed by a torpedo-shaped mass of cold gray flesh as it bursts out of the sea all around him. Water clings to its skin like a layer of rippled glass and frothing foam sheaths it like an inverted waterfall. The triangular fin on its back comes fully out of the water as the shark banks, twists. The cooler tumbles along the shark's smooth back, opening and spilling out a dozen water bottles. The pirate is in the shark's mouth up to his waist, his upper half flopping limply against gills the size of sewer grates as the creature twists and writhes. On his face is a look of mild surprise, nothing more. I see his arms flail up like windsocks as the shark crashes back down through the surface.

My mouth is hanging open and fills with the shark's splash. Clemente's eyes are bugging.

"Did that really just happen?"

It was so quick it would've been easy to miss if I'd been looking in a different direction. I almost wish I did miss it.

After the pirate's gone there seems to be an empty

space in the air above the pink foam footprint in the water. And even that is quickly dissolved by the waves, as if the pirate has simply been erased from existence. And the same thing could happen to either of us at any moment. My legs suddenly feel like a kicking buffet.

Instinctively Clemente and I come together with as little motion as possible. Lightly he touches the back of my thigh and I pull my legs up into a less appetizing ball.

We stare at each other wide-eyed, just holding our breath so we can float without moving too much.

Despite the threat of being eaten, the Styrofoam cooler is a temptation we can't resist for long. So slowly, still huddled together, we swim over to it. On the way, we get our hands on a floating water bottle. I had no idea how thirsty I was until I've finished my half.

Now we cling to the little cooler, one to a side, face to face. Beneath it I'm squeezing one of his legs between mine and he's doing likewise. It seems the best way to keep from dropping our feet any farther into shark territory.

"Guess it's good we already slept together," he says with a laugh that seems giddy with attempt at self-distraction. "This would be awkward otherwise."

"Don't tease."

After a pause, he says, "You liked it, didn't you?"

"Liked what?"

"... That time we went to bed."

"I told you I did."

"But, *really* liked it." He pauses. "Didn't you?"

"What would it matter if I did, Clemente? And what would it matter if it wasn't just teammate solidarity that made me jump in after you? How would that be relevant to either of us? I don't want to replay last night."

He's quiet for a long time, as though digesting what I just said, and then he smirks.

"Maybe I'll take you to a lighthouse and kiss you like in that book about the cranberries everyone has to read in high school." He has a sort of twinkle in his eye and I can't tell whether he's making fun of me.

"Fine. Hey. I'm going to close my eyes for a while. Wake me up if we get eaten by sharks."

Sleep is impossible, though. Out here darkness equals sensory deprivation. There's no light in the cloudy sky except for a few pin-pricks of stars, no sound except the slap of waves against the sides of the hollow cooler, no feeling except the cold numbing sea. We're hanging defenseless at the top of two miles of monsters that could swim up and eat us at any moment. But that terror feels distant, and I have to accept it on faith, because right now my world is no bigger than twelve inches around me. The only things in it are Clemente and a Styrofoam cooler.

One of them is keeping me afloat, the other is keeping me alive.

I whisper to him. "I did really like it, Clemente."

"Like what, Boots?"

I'm quiet for a second. "That night with you."

He tilts his head and looks at me. "Yeah, Boots. Yeah. Me too."

I'm not sure I heard him right. His face is inches from mine but it's so dark I can barely see him. I can only feel his breath on my skin.

Then his hand squeaks as he lets go of the Styrofoam, and I feel it moments later on my ear. His fingers rub the back of my wet hair in little circles. His thumb brushes gently across my eyelid, my eyebrow, and he smiles.

He barely has to move to kiss me, just has to let his

lips touch mine. It feels very natural when it happens. His lips are chapped and hard and his mustache is stiff with salt but it's the sweetest kiss, and if a shark were to choose this moment to end our lives, I would notice nothing but Clemente, and I'd be happy.

But no shark comes, and when the kiss is over our foreheads touch and we stay that way unmoving except in the bob from the waves.

"Did I dream it, Clemente?" I whisper, remembering the touch of his lips against mine.

He's quiet for a long time. "Let's say you dreamed it," he whispers finally. "For now, let's say you dreamed it."

It must be after midnight now, which means we've been in the water for more than eighteen hours. Clemente's head is resting on his good arm on top of the cooler. Every so often I put a kiss on his ear. I don't know what's happened between us in these last hours — whether something long unspoken has been acknowledged, whether we had nowhere else to go so we arrived at each other — or whether it's just fear and desperation creating a sense of intimacy that daylight will soon reveal was false. I'm too unsure to ask, and really too tired to wonder. It's easier just to put another kiss on his ear and to keep scanning the dark horizon for light.

Before I see any light, though, I hear voices. And then a splash.

Then there's more splashing, and someone is taking away our cooler and replacing it with a red rubber donut attached to a rope.

"The catch of the day is two Theban Warriors," someone says gently. It could be another plastic pirate.

Could be, but the voice is familiar, the accent is sweet. "Funny running into you guys out here."

"Natan," I croak.

"Let's get you dried up."

I force my eyes open. My lashes are grainy with salt. Natan is bobbing close by in a red lifejacket studded with strobing yellow LEDs. There's light on us, a beam of it, aimed by someone holding a flashlight, someone standing in a speedboat fifteen feet away. The speedboat's headlights cast misty bars over the surface, make it seem like we're coming up from underground, being birthed out of a watery grave. My mind registering things slowly but I don't have to think anymore. After twenty hours in the ocean, Clemente and I are being tugged toward a boat.

Chapter 23

I'm halfway through my third chocolate PowerBar and water from the bottle I'm holding to my lips is streaming down my chin and throat. It's slicking my chest with chocolate grime and making splotches on the brand-new swimsuit I've got on.

I'm too hungry to care. I shove the last chunk of PowerBar into my mouth.

"You, uh, might want to take it easy," says Miguel, the boyfriend of Natan. He's kneeling beside me, awkwardly holding out a napkin I'm too busy stuffing my face to bother with. His eyes are dark but gentle, if a little hesitant, and his hair is shaggy brown with sun-streaks of red. He's wearing a bulky hoodie but his bare legs are lean, a surfer's legs. Miguel is *hot*. Natan did well. Miguel looks at me, shrugs, tucks the napkin in his hoodie pocket, and stands up.

I look over at Clemente, who's sitting in the captain's chair with his teeth gritted and eyes squeezed shut. Natan is standing beside him with a tube of BodyGlue and a glistening finger the same color blue as the tube's contents. Clemente's scorpion sports a blue blob where the front bullet hole has already been sealed.

"Should keep you OK for a while," Natan says, wiping off his finger against Clemente's back and then screwing the cap on the tube.

"Thanks," Clemente replies, fanning his shoulder with his good hand to help the BodyGlue dry.

"Boots," says Natan, "you said you had something with your foot?"

"A cut on my heel," I say. "But I can do it."

"I'll do it," says Natan.

"*I'll* do it," says Miguel, plucking the BodyGlue from his boyfriend's grasp. He kneels down, grabs me by the ankle and aims a flashlight beam at the sole of my foot. And I remember why Miguel probably isn't completely thrilled by me.

"Miguel, I was on his *list*."

"Mm." He puts down the flashlight, uncaps the BodyGlue.

"Right?"

"The point of a celebrity sex list, Boots McHenry, is that there's supposed to be no chance of it ever *happening*."

I shrug. "He got lucky?"

He gives me the hint of a smirk. "*You* were the one who got lucky."

"Heh."

He has to squeeze the tube from the bottom up; Clemente's wound took nearly all the BodyGlue.

"You must have a list of your own, Miguel. Who's on

yours? Maybe I can help make it happen. Anyone in the NAPL?"

"I'm not much of a sports guy," he says, then he jabs a blue finger into the gash on my foot.

It hurts, but a few minutes later when the BodyGlue's dry I'm testing it out, walking around the small, misty space of the idling speedboat. It seems OK.

Meanwhile Clemente's been messing with his phone, trying to get a location on the other guys.

"Piper's still online," he says, rubbing salt off the flexiglass with the leg of his new swimsuit, "but he's not accepting my request for a location share. No surprise there."

"Let me try Colby," I say. "Colby's location is public to his friends. All 5,000 of them."

"Public? All the time?"

"Ryan used to say it would get him in trouble one of these days."

"Funny if it ends up saving his life."

I ask Natan for my phone and he fishes it out of his pocket and hands it over. I open my address book. Beside Colby's name (in green to show he's online) is a globe icon. I touch the globe and the screen changes to a map. An animation of Colby doing a backflip appears on an expanse of blue. When I zoom in enough to get details it tells me Colby's phone is a whopping 904 miles away from mine, moving at forty-seven miles per hour. I take it as a good sign that they're still traveling. Hopefully we still have a chance to retake the Intrepid before our mutinous pirates can use it to bribe their way back into a clan full of reinforcements. A handful of them is one thing; a thousand is quite another.

I zoom back out until we're visible on the map too, then I stand the phone on the dashboard.

"Miguel," I say, "do me a favor and aim for this Junior MMAC champ / storefront model, will you?"

Maybe he's eager to finish this errand and get his boyfriend away from me as quickly as possible, or maybe he's wrapped up in the adventure of it all, but never mind, Miguel is *flying*. The boat's barely touching the water. According to the speedometer, which I've been peeking at with terror and glee, we're doing 220 over open ocean. Feels even faster. It's the kind of speed that makes you hunker down low, with bended knees, as though if you lose contact with the floor for even a second it'll get out from under you and leave you in the dust.

Or in this case in the water. Which I've spent more than enough time in today already, thank you.

Miguel keeps glancing at my phone. The blue dot that represents us is growing steadily closer to Colby. We're moving five times faster than the pirates but it's hard to relax when we don't know where they're headed, or how far they have left to go. Satellite images don't show any pirate settlements, only the miles of tentacle-like plastic peninsulas curling off the spinning Vortex. The Intrepid is rounding the tip of one now. We might have plenty of time to reach them, or it might already be too late.

I give Miguel a wary thumbs-up. He shrugs, looks at the instruments, looks at my phone, shoots me a cautious grin, and punches us up to 250.

Behind us Clemente and Natan have spread out the gear Natan and Miguel bought for us on their pre-rescue shopping spree. Natan is filling a utility belt with a knife and a length of rope. On the floor between them are two paintball rifles and a box of ammo. Clemente is trying on some aqua shoes, which look like a cross between espadrilles and ballet slippers.

I sit down on the bench beside him and pick up a rifle. I'm eager to start shooting.

"Guys," Miguel calls back, "we've got a lot of smooth water ahead. I'm going to try 270."

He's grinning, loving this speed, but Natan is staring at his boyfriend with a look that says, *Are you crazy?!*

"Two-seventy," I say, bumping my knee against Clemente's. "Almost beats your motorcycle."

"Next time the paparazzi are after us, Miguel can drive."

Then he stands up, lifts his rifle, and fires a practice shot at the waves. We're moving way too fast to see anything, but whatever he was aiming for, I'm confident he got it. I wish I was as confident about everything else.

"Colby, Marcus, Piper," I whisper into the wind, "I hope you're OK."

Chapter 24

"I've got visual," Miguel says gravely, pointing out through the windshield.

Natan laughs. "Did you just say, *I've got visual?* You act like you're in an Alfonso Connors thriller, Miguelito!" Natan rubs the back of his boyfriend's sun-streaked hair and kisses his temple. Their affection nearly makes me pop a stiffy.

But Miguel's right. On the horizon, growing fast, is Marcus Tumble's pride and joy and my home away from home.

"If we don't slow down we'll hit them in less than a minute," Miguel says. "So you're sure about this? You trust me?"

I nod. Obviously we can't just pull up alongside the Intrepid and jump aboard, not without getting our heads blown the fuck off. It's daylight now, plus we're throwing back a tailfin of water fifty feet high; the pirates know we're coming. That means we need to be creative. And hope Miguel has the chops to pull this off.

Clemente, who's buckling a clunky black utility belt that contrasts bizarrely with his floral swimsuit and bare chest, looks at me. "This's one of those moments you wish you had Lucinda Skullcrusher in your ear, you know?"

"I was just thinking the same thing."

"We're flying solo now."

"*Pffft*. Not solo. I've got your back, Santiago. Same as always."

He nods, smiles, picks up his paintball rifle. I do the same, and check my ammo—enough bullets for a hundred pirates, hopefully. Back when the newly-*gunshotted* Clemente said no more real bullets, I happily agreed we should use something more familiar. But now that we're facing down a pirate ship I'm hoping we made the right choice.

Clemente takes a breath. The quiet before the storm. He looks to Natan. "How you doing with the water cannon?"

Natan nods; Clemente nods back.

"OK, Miguel," I say. "Just like we planned."

Nothing against our faithful Intrepid, right, but when we approach we're like an F-16 chasing down a bumble bee.

A bumble bee with guns, though. Lots of guns. A half-dozen flashes of rifle-fire glint from various places on the main deck. I'm afraid the incoming fire is going to scare Miguel off, but he only floors it harder.

We're on a collision course, and there's no stopping it now. Natan closes his eyes and Clemente turns his head, but I want to see every detail.

With what looks like only inches to spare us from total destruction we zoom across the Intrepid's path. Miguel hits the angle so clean, so beautiful, like something out of a physics textbook, that you just want to kiss him. Our wake and our fifty-foot tailfin swamp the Intrepid's main deck, even more than we hoped. Water crashes against the spider-webbed bridge windshield in an arcing torrent, scooping up pirates and pinning them to railings like laundry on a line. I see three pirates—at least—swept clear overboard, their rifles along with them.

In a blink we're past, leaving the Intrepid rocking like a bathtub toy in our wake.

"That took care of a few of them," Clemente says, looking back with a hand up to shield his eyes from the sun. "I'd call Phase 1 a success."

"Didn't slow them down any, though," I say, watching the back-flipping Colby on my phone.

"What we really need is to get in the bridge," Clemente says, pensively touching his tongue to his mustache.

"Phase 2 now?" Miguel says.

"Go for it."

Miguel spins the wheel hard and the speedboat banks, our port side lifting clear out of the water and spraying a splashy curtain into the air. The ocean surface on the other side's a blur as we tip down close to it. I feel dizzy. The Intrepid is in our sights again and we're closing in fast, and Miguel's not letting up on the turn.

"Those pirates love a vortex," he says, "we'll give them a vortex."

Blazing a tailfin of water we circle the Intrepid again

and again, tighter each time, an orbiting tetherball wrapping a pole. Natan has the water cannon going and he's plucking stragglers off the main deck. Nose-Ring goes overboard; others, too.

Despite the efforts of its pirate driver to maintain course, the Intrepid's starting to catch in our swirling current and turn, if not quite spin—until a bullet punctures our windshield and Miguel ducks away from the wheel. Like a wayward missile we careen away from our target. Natan and I go skidding across the floor and bang painfully against the back corner in a twisted pile of limbs much less fun than the one we got in on his bed. I'm afraid he's knocked his hip pretty good but he's already crawling back to the cannon. I scramble to get my hands on my rifle again.

"You OK, amorcito?" Miguel yells to Natan while he wrestles the speedboat back under control. Natan nods. Miguel turns to us. "If I'm going around again, guys, I better start seeing some of this fancy shooting you get paid so zilla much for."

Clemente nods. I brace myself beside him.

Moments later we're resuming our vortex, dragging the Intrepid into an unwilling spin. Natan is swamping it with a steady blast from the cannon, making it tough for any lingering pirates to maneuver on the main deck. I spot one who must've been crouched near the prow making a mad dash for the bridge, and fire a bullet at his ankle that sends him sprawling.

"Another one coming out on the back, Natan," I say, pointing, while I tag my sprawled pirate's crotch with another paintball.

Natan hits his square in the gut, pinning him to the low railing. A back-up shot to the shoulder from Clemente tips the pirate backward over the rail, into the sea. And then the cannon's stream is dragging across the

Intrepid's hull as we swing around toward the prow again.

Suddenly a bullet—the non-paint kind—punctures one of the bench cushions behind me with a muffled thump that blows a cloud of foam into the air.

"Pretty sure that came from the bridge," Clemente says, looking at me and grinning. "Know what that means?"

"The door's open now?"

"Which means the driver is what we call a sitting duck. *Ka-ching.*"

As Miguel brings us around again Clemente and I kneel side by side on the floor, torsos braced against the bench, rifles resting on the rail.

"Almost—"

Miami is in the open doorway of the bridge, shooting at us. Bullets spout fountains around us but nothing lands. I spot Bottle Cap, the boss, that fucker who touched Colby, behind Miami at the wheel. Then Miami puts a bullet in the side of our boat—luckily above the water line—rattling the floor beneath my feet.

"Now," I say, and before Miami can squeeze off another shot, his jaw and cheek splash blue and his head snaps back from the blow. Then he drops face-forward onto the deck.

"Feels so naughty, aiming for the face," Clemente giggles, full-on *giggles.* "We'd get sidelined for that in a game," he tells Natan.

Natan laughs, still hosing the main deck, though it seems to be clear now. Coming around again, we see Bottle Cap inside the bridge, frantically trying to kick the unconscious Miami across the threshold so he can get the door closed.

Clemente smiles at me. We are a team, a matched pair, a duo, and I'm happy to be beside him.

Simultaneously we stand, brace a knee against the bench, and squeeze our triggers.

One bullet misses, hits inside the bridge and plasters the spider-webbed windshield; the other finds its target, gets Bottle Cap on the cheek, bucking his head back and whiplashing his braids. His face is awash and he's flailing. He slams the steering wheel with his elbow as he scrapes at his eyes. The Intrepid lurches, hull groaning like an injured whale, and banks, a storm of foam rumbling up around it.

Bottle Cap, already off-balance, trips over Miami's body and smacks face-first into the railing outside — in almost the exact place Colby wheel-kicked him into it yesterday.

Miguel gently widens our circle to avoid a crash but his job is done — the Intrepid is stopped.

Chapter 25

Sitting idle in the waves, the poor thing looks like a ghost ship. There's no sign of life on the main deck. Long John Paint-Face, as Clemente has just called Bottle Cap, is still lying in a heap on top of Miami. If there are any conscious pirates left aboard, they're downstairs. That's got to be where our boys are, too. I can't bear to think they've been dumped overboard.

As Miguel steers us closer to the drifting Intrepid, Clemente, Natan, and I keep our weapons aimed. It reminds me of sitting up in that faux-ganic elm, watching the field through my image-linked scope — only now the stakes are higher than any five-year exile.

"See anyone?" I whisper to Clemente.

"Nope."

With a scratchy, screechy thump the speedboat rubs against the side of the Intrepid's hull. Miguel lets us drift around to the lower deck, then keeps us there with short bursts of the engine.

Clemente gives him and Natan a thumbs-up and jumps aboard the Intrepid, his rifle darting tensely between the bridge entrance and the main deck above.

Before I step off the speedboat I toss Natan my phone. "We'll be in touch."

"Hopefully," Miguel says.

Clemente keeps licking his lips. Maybe he misses the lollypop he usually has in his mouth during games.

We're on the lower deck, looking up. I don't like the idea of heading into the bridge just yet—too confined, too dangerous. First I want to make sure the main deck is clear.

"Cover me," I tell him as I grab a ladder rung, and he nods. As I head up I'm painfully aware that a pirate could point a gun down and blow me away, wouldn't even have to show his face to do it. It's the same unseen terror I felt hanging naked in the water a few hours ago.

When I reach the top Clemente says "I got you" in a steady, confident tone that relaxes me a little.

Like a dude in a foxhole I peer over the floor of the main deck. Then I climb onto it, straighten up slowly, press my back against the railing, all while sweeping the rifle back and forth. The bridge is a mess of food containers and broken glass, and Miami is still in a heap in the doorway, but he's alone. Bottle Cap is gone. My pulse pounds.

In the reflection on the smeared glass I can see Natan and Miguel drifting twenty feet away. I turn and signal them to back off, and the speedboat's engine rumbles.

Then I reach through the rail and gesture to

Clemente that it's clear to come up.

It takes him a while—he's climbing with his bad arm—but I feel so much better when he's with me. Every word Skullcrusher ever preached about being on a team is true, and it's all the better when your team includes Clemente Santiago.

"Uh. Where'd Long John Paint-Face go?" he says.

"MIA."

"Shit." Then: "We'll find him. Just like a game."

"Except he's got a real gun with real bullets."

He grins. "Nothing a little BodyGlue won't fix, right?"

"BodyGlue can't fix dead, Clemente."

"Ah. True."

"Let's check the front deck."

Before the raid, from where we're standing we would've been able to see straight through the bridge, but now the windows are cracked and cloudy with paint.

We step over Miami, and Clemente nudges the pirate's head with his aqua shoe. No response from Miami—he seems pretty stone-cold.

"Touch his eyeball," I tell Clemente. Just saying it should cause a reaction if Miami's just faking, but there's nothing.

Clemente kneels, pulls up the pirate's eyelid, pokes, pokes, pokes. "Ew. Nothing. He's really out."

We slide along the bridge to the front of the main deck. Being back aboard feels weird. The places that were so familiar—my place at the prow, Piper's place in the deck chair, the inside of the bridge—seem alien now, like footage from the wreck of the Titanic.

The place is creepy, but it's pirate-free.

"Wait," Clemente whispers as we're heading back to the bridge entrance. He points to the crow's nest.

While I cover him, he climbs the ladder until his calves are level with my face. Then with an upward thrust he peers rifle-first over the edge. I can tell by the way his back muscles relax that the crow's nest is empty.

Descending the narrow pink stairway flashes me back to when I was here with Piper, after the kiss and before Miami started wagging his gun in my face. It almost makes me forget my stint in the water and makes this feel like one continuous moment. Clemente and I proceed slowly down the hallway. The galley is a wreck—the pirates tore into our food supplies like rats at a banquet (the bathroom, on the other hand, looks oddly unused). There's a bloodstain on the floor where Piper took down his pirate, but that pirate is gone. The one I left in Marcus's doorway is gone too, and the door's closed. All of the cabin doors are closed except ours, which is ajar a few inches.

I mouth to Clemente: "Trap?"

He purses his lips, shrugs, mimes a kick.

My breath tight in my chest, I kick the door hard. It screeches inward over broken glass. I lean in, rifle ahead of me. Piper is lying on his side on the floor, hands tied behind him to the leg of the bottom bunk. His face is half-covered in flaking blood, and he's gagged with a t-shirt, but he looks up at me with bright eyes.

Another person is scrambling. At the end of my bunk the emaciated teenage pirate is wrestling with his pants, struggling to get them up over a flimsy erection. He's clearly been beating it, using the bound-and-gagged Piper as his personal 3D porn.

Twisted fucker, and yet it's funny, the kind of funny I've needed all day. Barely stifling a grin, I motion for the twerp to get down on the floor. "You're in for some major blue-balls," I add.

The kid—red-faced and boiling with rage from the double whammy of being both caught and captured—growls that he can't, because of his arm. I remember that Colby blew it out yesterday.

"You'll do just fine."

Sneering, he hauls off and spits at me, but it lands mostly on his own leg. Then he does as he's told, brushing glass away before he presses his cheek to the floor. I step on his shoulder to hold him down while Clemente unwinds some rope.

"You look kinky, Piper," I say, but I'm just about passing out with relief as I slice free his ankles with the knife from my belt. Clemente is tying up the pirate when there's a slam from above, and Clemente, after yanking the knot tight, jumps up and runs from the cabin. Something is being dragged across the floor upstairs and then there's a thump that echoes down the hall.

I free Piper's wrists and he pulls out the gag. There are tears in his red eyes. "I thought you were dead, B."

"Just went for a little swim," I say with a grin, but he's not smiling, he's hugging me.

"Shit," he whispers into my neck. "Shit, Boots."

"You OK?"

"Yeah." He looks down at the tied-up pirate. "But that twink's been wanking to me since yesterday."

Clemente returns to our cabin for just long enough to tell us we're locked in down here. Then he disappears again, swearing.

I shake my head. Being locked in feels secondary right now. I say to Piper, "The others?"

"I'll get them." He takes my knife. "Go help Santiago."

He pushes into his own cabin while I scramble up the stairs and join Clemente against the bulkhead door. His breath is hot and nervous on my face.

"Bottle Cap?" I say.

"If not him—" He raises a finger and starts moving it toward my eye; I jerk my head back before he can make contact. "—then Miami has some incredible reflex control."

"Where was Bottle Cap, then?"

"No idea. Some random storage compartment? I don't know. Dammit, we should've looked better."

"No time for woulda-coulda's. On three?"

We stand sideways, bent low at the knees so we can push up against the bulkhead. He's got his back to me. The blue smear of BodyGlue on his shoulder has peeled up a little but seems to be holding. On three we slam our shoulders and backs into the door but it's a lousy hit— the stairs are steep and there's no space to get momentum. Nothing more than a quarter-inch of sunlight opens around the bottom edge of the bulkhead before it snaps tight again.

"Hands?" Clemente says.

We try pushing upward. The door dimples under our palms but doesn't budge. Clemente drops his arms, wincing and grabbing his shoulder.

Another voice: "Where's Colby?"

I turn. It's Marcus—Piper has him free. He's still naked and looks like hell. His left eye is swollen shut and he's cradling his ribs with one arm. I suspect Marcus, as captain, put up the toughest fight. When he sees Clemente and me he looks relieved, but when Piper says "Gotta be in your room," Marcus turns to the captain's cabin, the only door still unopened.

"Again, Boots," Clemente says to me, raising his hands to the bulkhead door again. "On three."

"Ready."

But we only get to two. That's when the Intrepid's hydrogen engine flares to life and the ship turns hard to starboard. Clemente slams against me — his bare back meeting my belly makes a stinging slap — and I get my arm under his armpit fast enough to make me think, for a second, that we'll keep our footing. But when the boat lurches again we both go down hard. My tailbone pounds the step; Clemente's utility belt rams my groin and his stubbled cheek burns across my forehead.

Piper's pulling himself out of his cabin, which the movement must've knocked him into, and Marcus's cabin door is swinging on its hinges.

"Sorry," Clemente says, grabbing the handrail and pulling himself off me, "you OK?"

"Think so."

"Fucker's on the go, huh?"

From behind us: "That was zilla *fucked up*."

Clemente and I turn and look to the end of the hall. Colby is wrapped in Marcus's arms, and over Marcus's shoulder he looks up and sees us. His face breaks into a surprised smile, and I feel mine do the same.

We're all standing in the galley, in the dark, unwilling passengers on a runaway boat that Bottle Cap is racing to deliver to his clan as one gigantic offering. He cut the power down here — maybe he thinks the darkness will chew at our nerves — so the only illumination is from the portholes. And when all we can see are those circles of light, they begin to seem like the answer.

Piper and I toss the tied-up teenage pirate into the top bunk to clear some floor space. Then Colby, who's been stretching and doing jumping jacks in the hallway to warm up, enters the cabin. Like a prizefighter he walks across the carpet of blankets we've laid out to cover the broken glass. He's wearing black boxer-briefs and the calm, determined smile I'm used to seeing on him when he's in the ring waiting for the bell to start a fight.

"You're *sure* about this?" Marcus says, clearly looking for any excuse to nix the idea.

But Colby looks at him and nods. With one hand on Marcus's shoulder and the other on mine, he steps up into our hands.

Through the open porthole we can hear the hull cutting the waves as the boat zooms along under Bottle Cap's command. The low roar of water ominously fills the cabin liked a thousand anxious gasps.

Colby is sweating. Beads of it dot his belly. His bare foot is slick on my palm. I squeeze my fingers tighter across the top of it.

"Col, if you fall—" Marcus begins.

"Junior MMAC champs don't ever fall, Marcus. Now lift!"

So we lift, very slowly, while Colby tells us "OK, OK." Then he reaches behind himself for the frame of the dripping, inward-opened porthole. He's going through backward so he'll be able to grab the floor of the main deck once he's outside. At least that's the plan. "Bye," he says before popping his head outside.

When he's through the porthole to the bottom of his ribcage, I try to steady him with my other hand on his butt, my imagination flashing with terrible images of dropping him backward into the sea.

We push his feet up closer to the porthole as the silver frame swallows his hips, thighs, knees. Then the quivering weight in my hands lightens and lifts away and I know he's got a hold of something outside. With a kick he pulls his feet through the porthole.

Marcus gasps at the finality of the empty window, which shows us only blue sky and the occasional white splash. He peers out, cranes his neck. "I think he's up."

We look at each other nervously, tell each other he'll

be fine, he can handle this, he's Colby Kroft, Junior MMAC champ of North America.

Clemente, who's sitting on my bunk, crosses his arms and leans forward. Piper is biting his lip.

"I'm praying this wasn't stupid," Marcus says. "I'll never forgive myself."

"He can take out a sea rat," I say with a smile.

"A sea rat with a gun?"

It makes me break Marcus's eye contact. Smoothing the floor-blanket with my aqua shoe, I listen at the porthole but I can't hear anything except the rush of waves. We're moving really fast. Bottle Cap is straining the engine. If Colby succeeds, the Intrepid will become suddenly driverless, and Colby can't steer for crap. I'm bracing for the lurch.

Then we hear a voice. Colby's voice, taunting: "Love what the Warriors have done with your *face*. Zilla chic. Blue suits you. Come here."

Bottle Cap laughs and seconds later lets out a surprised yelp, and then there's a crash; small plastic objects clatter against the floor above us.

"Jeez, you fucking stink."

Clemente and Piper scramble to join Marcus and me at the porthole. Clemente is squeezed against me, head tipped.

"Are you *telling* me," Colby says, voice straining—I wonder what position he's got Bottle Cap twisted up in. "Are you telling me that—that in all this water, you can't find—one bucket—to take a *bath with*?"

Marcus's face erupts with a grin. "I'm in love with him," he says. "There's no question."

Colby again: "No, no, Cap'n. No tap-outs for *you*." Something hits the deck and we hear a muffled scream. "Normally I'd break your hands for touching me like you did. But you'll need them to swim and I'm a nice guy." There's another clatter of plastic, of a string of bottle caps. "Bath time! But first I take *this*."

Then there's a slam against the railing. One second Colby's roaring and the next the boss pirate is tumbling past our porthole on his way to the black waves— But a lucky hand catches the frame of the porthole and the four of us are suddenly staring at five fingers' worth of hairy knuckles and yellow nails.

"Uh," I say, looking at the knuckles, "moral dilemma?"

Marcus and I are reaching to grab the boss pirate's wrist—it's a reflex, I guess—to haul him inside, or at least to try, even though there's no way he'd fit through the porthole, when Piper steps forward and punches the knuckles flat against the sill.

"There's *no* moral dilemma," Piper says.

The hairy fingers go rigid and disappear, and we hear a splash we quickly speed past. We must all be looking at Piper because he says, "Oh, OK," reaches into the compartment under the lower bunk for a life-vest and pushes it through the porthole. "There. Happy?"

"Anyone notice we're still, uh, moving?" Clemente says.

That's when the hallway behind us bursts with sunlight. Colby is jumping down the stairs.

"Little problem!" he says. His cheeks are flushed and he's got a pink scrape across his left pectoral—otherwise he looks as fresh as a Sunday morning. Around his neck, like a trophy, is the boss pirate's bottle-cap lei. "He has us on autopilot."

"I thought they couldn't do that?" Piper says.

"I think I can turn it off," Marcus says, pushing past us and running for the stairs.

We follow him to the bridge, where it's clear right away that Bottle Cap somehow replaced the fingerprint codes and locked Marcus out of his own boat. He punches the chair.

And suddenly Clemente's getting a phone call.

"Where are *you?*" he says, turning around, looking out to sea. The speedboat is pulling alongside us, close enough to spray water across the main deck. Natan has my phone. Miguel is pointing. I step out of the bridge and look ahead of us. There's a fuzzy line on the horizon.

"They say we're heading for the Trash Vortex— No— An arm of the spiral or something," Clemente says to us. "A tentacle. Fast."

"It won't take a new fingerprint while it's on autopilot," Marcus says. "It's a basic security feature. Fuck!"

Piper says, "But won't the boat see the plastic and stop?"

"It doesn't see it." Marcus is shaking his head. "It must not be deep enough or tall enough. The autopilot doesn't see floating things! I told you!"

Colby puts his arm around Marcus.

"I don't know, Natan," Clemente is saying. "Can Miguel work some of his whirlpool magic and try to catch us in a spin again?" He lowers the phone and says to Marcus, "Would that be enough of a sufficient disturbance to disable the autopilot?"

I can see Natan yelling something to Miguel and Miguel yelling something back to Natan. Miguel's shaking his head, gesturing wildly.

Clemente says to us, "Doesn't matter, they say there isn't time for a whirlpool."

"I think we're going to crash, Marcus," Colby says.

Marcus looks at him, looks down to the instruments. "Just let me think for a second."

"I say we jump," Piper says. "Sorry, but—"

"Jump if you want," Marcus says. "Captains don't

jump."

"Neither do boyfriends of captains," Colby adds.

Marcus looks at him with a smile overtaking his worried face. I wonder if they talked about being boyfriends before this.

Piper sighs.

"How thick is the trash island here?" Clemente says. "How much damage are we looking at? It's just plastic, right?" He looks at me. "I mean, how bad can it be?"

We decide the safest place to be when a boat crashes into something is lying flat on our backs on the main deck, where nothing can tip over and crush us, where we won't get stuck underwater in a blown-open hull. So like people making snow angels we lie down side by side on the gleaming wood.

I look over at Clemente. "This is going to hurt, I think."

"Little bit," he says, "but it might be pretty fun, too."

"We never had a chance to talk about what happened between us, in the water."

He smirks. "You mean with the shark?" I stare at him for a second and he adds, "We'll talk about it, McHenry. I promise. But it all depends on what happens in Hawaii."

Hawaii. I'd forgotten all about Hawaii. Somehow the whole point of this mission has become an afterthought, at least for now—something we'll do if we ever get the chance. Right now I don't see how we're ever going to get the chance.

The Trash Vortex must be close. I can't hear Natan and Miguel tailing us anymore.

They must've let us go.

I reach out and take Clemente's hand. He doesn't squeeze it back.

And then we hit.

Or maybe it's more accurate to say we *enter*. We penetrate. We are subsumed. There's very little impact — not like what we braced for. Instead a barrage of plastic flotsam scooped heavenward by the prow and windscreen soars through the sunny sky above us. It's like being behind a waterfall of translucent, multi-colored plastic. And to be honest, it's beautiful. Up close it'd all be junk, but so far overhead, and in such quantity, the objects — pink shampoo containers, green and blue soda bottles, orange sunglasses lenses, yellow headlight covers — glide between us and the sun and dance thousands of colors upon our bare skin. As we're sliding on our backs across the wet deck I turn and Clemente is already looking at me, and his face and his smile and his eyes are a prism of colors.

And I feel him squeeze my hand back.

Chapter 26

Turns out if you have to crash into something in a boat at sixty miles per hour you can do a lot worse than this plastic island we're lodged in. The gathered plastic acted like the stacks of cardboard boxes used to break stuntmen's falls.

The deck is strewn with plastic bits that after their moment of beauty are back to being trash (and after we appreciated its beauty we had to scramble around dodging it like people caught in a hailstorm). But we're stopped, and the autopilot, apparently having considered this a disturbance worthy of human attention, has released the boat, and the engine is quiet.

Clemente's phone beeps in the silence. He pulls it out of his pocket, smiles, hands it to me. I accept the incoming video call.

"That was a heck of a money shot," Natan says. He and Miguel are idling in the open water a few hundred feet away.

"Should've seen it from here," I laugh.

"You're all OK?"

"We're all good."

"And can you get out of there now, do you think?"

I look to Marcus. He nods in a *no sweat* kind of way, kicks a toothbrush back into the water, and heads to the bridge to replace his fingerprints as the rightful captain of the Intrepid.

Still, just to be safe, I ask Natan and Miguel to stick around until we've extracted ourselves from the Vortex.

While Marcus is busy coaxing the boat backward along the long path we carved during our entry, Piper and I tie up Miami, who must've been jolted by the impact back into something resembling consciousness.

"What if more come?" Piper says to me as we lead Miami to the lower deck. "These guys must've had friends."

"Actually, I don't think they did," I say. "They were banished. Some kind of attempted coup or something. So I think we'll be OK."

"Well *I* won't be OK until the little shit downstairs is off this boat," Piper says, and he heads below to get him.

Marcus soon has the Intrepid back in open water, rocking gently on the waves while he performs various systems checks. We use that time to push Miami and the teenager—all that remain of the band of plastic pirates— adrift in one of the dinghies. They have paddles and some water, and I guess they'll navigate up the coast of the Vortex to wherever their pirate shanty-town is. Maybe they'll pick up the floating Bottle Cap first, and use him as an offering to bribe their way back into the clan. To be honest I don't care what happens to them—I would've been content to roll them all overboard with weights in their shoes. But Clemente says it's important to stay human, and he's right.

Clemente's phone rings again in my pocket. I look out at the speedboat, a little blotch of red in the distance, and accept the video call.

"Looks like you're clear," Natan says.

"Couldn't have done this without you guys."

He grins. "So if things are good with everything, I think me and Mig are going to head home."

"Things are good," I say. "Thank you both. We owe you our lives. Take my phone with you, just to be safe."

"If he keeps the phone," Miguel says, leaning over to fill more of the screen, "I want to keep the boat. You owe me double, McHenry."

I smile. "It's yours, always has been. Now go find a place in safe water and make some sweet love in the back of your new boat."

"Boots," Natan laughs, "what do you think we've been up to while you guys were stuck in the plastic?"

I just assume he's joking but then he aims the camera down, giving Clemente and me a flash of the nakedness below their shirts. Miguel's already grabbing away the phone—"Amorcito, jeez!"—when Natan says, "Alfonso Connors eat your heart out, I have my own action hero!"

Clemente laughs out loud.

Moments later the speedboat begins to hum, grows a long tailfin of arcing water, and races away in the direction of Puerto Natan. I watch them until I can't see them anymore. And then Colby, who I realize has been standing beside me, says, "Ryan would say you picked a good one for your fling."

I look back once more as we return to the bridge, but the speedboat has already gone over the horizon.

"Systems report shows everything's looking OK on the old tub," Marcus says, lovingly clearing a smudge on the steering wheel with his thumb and some spit. "So, you know, if you guys are still intent on Hawaii and everything," he grins, "we're good to go."

"I'm still intent," I say.

Piper looks over from cleaning the windshield, his brow furrowed. He doesn't say anything, just nods.

"I'm still intent," Colby says. "I want to see my brother."

"You still intent?" I say to Clemente.

He nods and licks salt from his upper lip; his black mustache is white with it. "More than ever," he says. "This isn't over until we find Ryan Kroft."

While the Intrepid gets up to full speed I notice Clemente walk to the prow and rest his elbows on the rail. For a long time he just stands there, looking into the wind, out at the sea. His bad shoulder curves in a little, almost a hunch, and in spite of his young body, glossy and firm, it's enough to make me think of a maimed Captain Ahab. Exile island is, for whatever reason, Clemente's white whale. I think back to the night of our planning meeting in my kitchen, when, with only the countertop island between us to keep us from coming to blows, we argued about whose trip this really would be. I watch him at the prow now, rubbing his shoulder, massaging the ache, and realize he was right. This is *his* trip.

But why?

Chapter 27

Things don't go back to the usual. And by that I mean we don't retreat to our own quiet places anymore. This has become a team endeavor. We spend the days cleaning the Intrepid — it's a particular bitch scrubbing the paint off the bridge windshield without crumbling the spider-webbed glass. And as for the nights, we spend those camped on the main deck, rolled up in blankets scavenged from our bunks. Ostensibly this is because our cabins are still too torn up to be livable, but I know the real reason is that none of us likes the idea of sleeping down there just yet. It's too easy to be caught off-guard down there. Better to sleep up here, where the moonlight is bright and the air is open — where even the smallest sounds are like foghorns in the night.

Sounds like the cute little groans Colby and Marcus make when they alternate inside-spoon and outside-spoon. I heard them having sex in Marcus's cabin once while I was sweeping broken glass out of my own. The sound of their muffled grunting behind the thin door made me happy — it was proof that we won. Those plastic pirates can go fuck themselves.

And it's probably good that we're all sleeping outside on the deck, because I'm not sure that I'm ready to be alone with Clemente yet. We haven't been alone since our last moments clinging to that cooler — a topic he and I still haven't discussed but that the other guys won't let up on. Colby and Marcus, at least. They tease us mercilessly about it.

"What'd you boys *do*, clutching on to each other for all that time?" Colby keeps asking. "Any repeats of your super-happy fun-time?"

They're pretty easy to distract, though, when we start

talking about the shark. Clemente has an old cider box he uses to represent the cooler when he does his impression of the pirate getting eaten.

"Dude was like, *Yaaarrrr, me legs! Me fuckin legs arrre gooone!*"

"He was not," I keep correcting. "He didn't make a single peep."

But the truth doesn't stick. It's better the way Clemente tells it. And maybe if he and I can remember it that way it's less terrifying. We'll keep the real truth about what happened between us.

So we continue uneventfully to Hawaii, free of pirates, free of sharks, but with heavy hearts—at least for me, and for Clemente too, I think. As I watch him, shirtless and blue-shouldered, jumping around the deck, zinging the box comically in the air as he flops to the floor, my feelings about getting there, about seeing Ryan, grow ever murkier. In some way that makes the mission even more important—for closure, for an ending. But as I look at Clemente and see how he sometimes looks back at me, I think that what I want from Ryan isn't his goodbye at all, but his blessing.

I just don't want to break anyone's heart.

PART 4

Exile Island

HOMO ACTION LOVE STORY!

Chapter 28

At night we arrive at the coordinates.

What we believe is exile island is one of a pair of islands separated by an inlet a half-mile wide. It's too late and dark to do anything now, so Marcus finds us a nice little cove on the second island, and under cover of darkness he parks the Intrepid and drops anchor. I stand on the main deck looking at shadows stretching across the rolling waves, waves that after so many miles finally have a sandy beach to break on. As the windscreen rattles down, sweet-smelling air rushes over my face.

In the dark Clemente comes up beside me, leaning with the rail against his belly. He's close enough that our arms are touching.

"Got so used to the smell of sea air," I say. "All this greenery. Wow. Smell it?"

He inhales, lifts his shoulders, stands on his toes — a full-body breath. "Like sticking your face in a salad," he says.

"So romantic."

He laughs.

"Think it's the right place?" I say, meaning the other island.

"I don't know, McHenry. Sure hope so."

"What if it ends up as empty as this one? What if it's not exile island at all?"

"We didn't come all this way for nothing." He squeezes my shoulder and as he steps away he lets his grip slide smoothly down my arm and off.

Alone again I look up at the stars, take a deep breath,

and try to feel Ryan. I try to feel if he's close by. But the only thing I feel is the fading tingling sensation on my arm where Clemente touched me.

Morning reveals the cove to be something straight out of a romance movie. Aqua-colored water laps a black sand beach; beyond the beach is a tangled wall of green—vines and flowers and leaves as big as bicycle wheels. There's no trace of civilization—it's like the land time forgot. I wouldn't be surprised if a brachiosaurus head on a long slender neck rose out of the canopy, chewing plants lazily with flat teeth.

Here and there wisps of volcanic steam seep from among the trees. The bird-calls are a relentless music. It seems like paradise. For us it's merely a way-station.

"We're down a dinghy since we decided to play Good Samaritan," Piper says, standing on the bridge with hands on hips. "So we'll put what we need in the one we have, and swim it ashore."

"I don't know about you guys," Colby says, coming upstairs, tying his swimsuit drawstring in a bow against his belly, "but I'll be swimming in anyway." His chest is bare and it's the first time since his brawl with Bottle Cap that I've seen him without his prize lei. "This water is zilla beautiful. I need to be in it. Now." He glances around at us mischievously. "Like. Right. Now." Then he bounds out of the bridge, horse-vaults over the railing, and lands with a splash in the blue waves. We hear him yell: "Oh my god, it's gorgeous!"

Piper sighs. "Is he bringing anything? I'm not carrying his stuff up."

"Don't worry about it," Marcus says, heading downstairs.

I pick my backpack up off the couch and, after maneuvering its awkward shape through the narrow doorway, bring it out to the lower deck. Piper joins me there with a backpack of his own, and after dropping it on the bench he helps me unlash the remaining dinghy from the wall.

"So we're just going to watch?" Piper says.

"We're going to survey. I don't want to make any moves until we know what's over there."

"Spoken like a sniper, Boots." He pauses. "So we're going to survey. And then what?"

"Then we raid exile island."

"*Raid* seems a rash word."

"Thought it'd be more your style, Piper." I push the back gate open, dip my foot in the warm water, wag it around. Colby had the right idea—I want to be in it too.

"Have you decided what you're going to say to him?" Piper says.

"To Ryan?"

He nods.

"Assuming it's the right island? And assuming we find him?"

"Assuming those things. Are you going to, like, wait for him?"

"No. I'm going to tell him goodbye."

Piper's face lights up a little. "A permanent goodbye? Like you're breaking up?"

"Yeah."

I can see he's trying to keep himself in check, trying not to let his face light up any more than it is. Because this, I suppose, is the news he's been hoping to hear since the day I met Ryan. He must think he'll have an opening now. I don't mean to give him false hope, but what can I say that I haven't already said?

"B, if you've come to that decision," he says, "we can just go home. Can't we?"

I look up to the bridge. "Are they coming?"

"I mean, if you came here to decide and you've already decided, can't we just—?"

"Go tell them to hurry up."

He sighs and walks into the bridge.

Alone on the lower deck, I sit down and put my feet in the water. I can feel the peeling BodyGlue dragging in the current. A hundred feet away I can see Colby on the black beach, stomping through the last inches of frothy waves, then crawling dramatically like a shipwreck victim across the hard wet sand. He turns to me and waves and then falls to his knees and spread-eagles on his back. With a glance he checks to see that I'm still watching, then he laughs and folds his arms behind his head. I wonder how he feels about being so near to his simu-dead brother. The situation is less complicated for him, but it must still be weird.

Clemente joins me on the deck with a backpack slung over his good shoulder. He winces a little when he puts it down. His BodyGlue has turned gray but seems to be holding. I ask if he'll be OK getting it wet again and he brushes me off.

"All right," Piper says, returning to the lower deck, "I've got extra clothes, water, PowerBars, flashlight, blanket, binoculars. What else?"

"A partridge in a pear tree?" Clemente says.

Piper frowns.

"I've got those things too," I say. "Plus my paintball rifle and some ammo. And some other crap."

"Kickboards!" Clemente says, snapping his fingers. "We'll need kickboards to cross the inlet with." He hops to the third step and looks up into the bridge. "Marcus. Kickboards?"

"Compartment under the bench out there," Marcus says from inside.

I turn and lift the seat. "OK, so five kickboards."

"Four," Marcus says, leaning out.

"Four?"

"I do boats, I don't do islands."

He goes back into the bridge and I follow him there.

"Are you really not coming?"

"My job was to get you here, Boots."

"Well yeah, but— You may have started out as our transportation or whatever, but you're part of the team now. If you want to see how this ends, I'd like to have you with us."

Marcus sits down in the captain's chair, swivels gently with his long legs stretched out.

"Well first off," he says, "someone has to keep an eye on the Intrepid. I'm not cool leaving it here alone." He's facing the window now, watching something—I realize he's watching Colby splash around on the beach. "Second, no offense Boots, but for me this thing doesn't end with whatever happens on exile island between you and your boyfriend. For me this is just beginning, and the journey and destination are both *him*." He points to Colby just as he flops onto the sand again. "Hah. Little did I know, right? I thought this was just going to be another job." He turns and looks at me. "So go do what you have to do. I'm going to finish cleaning up my boat. And when you're done over there, I'll take you home."

As Piper, Clemente and I drag the dinghy up the beach, Colby comes and gives us a hand. His skin from head to toe is gritty from rolling in the black sand. He looks like the boy-god of volcanoes.

"Your boyfriend bailed on us," Piper says to him before sitting down to wipe off his feet. It strikes me as a jerk-ass thing to say given everything Marcus's body and boat went through to get us here.

"Nice, Pernfors," Clemente says, shooting him a

frown.

"I was just *kidding*," Piper says.

I would love to see Colby pile-drive Piper three feet into the sand right now, but Colby shrugs it off, adds that someone needs to stay with the boat.

We gather up our gear after weighing down the dinghy with a few black rocks to keep it from blowing away.

Entering the dense forest feels like pressing through a green force-field. Leaves scrape my bare arms and chest and drag against my backpack and the kickboard strapped to it. I thought it would be cooler in here than on the beach, but it's warmer, or maybe just moister.

Clemente is leading, navigating with his phone, and I'm following him. A canopy of trees towers over us and the undergrowth is thick and mossy and rampant with vines and flowers. It would've been nice to have a machete but Clemente seems to know where to go, what paths to choose, when to climb over and when to slip under—in fact he seems more in command in this forest than I've seen him anywhere besides his motorcycle. I wonder what in his life has prepared him for this; I never took him for a nature boy. There's so much I want to learn about him. So many questions I want to ask. But his answers, he has said, will depend on Hawaii—whatever that means. So instead I watch him in silence, watch the muscles of his bare arms, watch the sweat gathering at the small of his smooth back, darkening the waist of his swimsuit.

Colby starts to hum. Clemente picks up the tune. Piper is whacking leaves with a stick. We're heading to a cliff on the other side of the island, and from there we'll be able to spy on the place Clemente's coach's coordinates have ultimately lead us.

When we get to our lookout spot it's sunset. The waves far below are glowing orange the way they did the evening we pulled into Puerto Natan. I can hear them crashing against the bottom of the cliff, what must be a hundred feet below the ledge we're on. While the other guys are sipping water and chewing PowerBars I get out my binoculars and peer across the inlet to the other island, seeing it for the first time. In the dying light it looks exactly like the one we're on now. Same black sand, same thick forest—and by all appearances just as uninhabited.

"Anything?" Clemente says, wiping chocolate off his mustache with the back of his hand.

"Nah."

"Imagine if we've come all this way for nothing?" Piper says. "That's a long way to swim just to make sure."

"Cool it, Piper," Clemente says.

I adjust the focus so it's even sharper, scan back and forth across the barren beach. I raise the binoculars to the line where the trees meet the orange sky, looking for signs of campfire smoke—but there's nothing. The island looks as it did in all the satellite photos. Maybe there were no image scramblers being used here after all. Maybe the island is as empty as it's always appeared. Despair starts leaking into me, I feel it in my gut; it feels like I'm filling with that black stuff that pirate kept coughing up before he turned into shark bait.

"We'll try looking again in the morning," Clemente tells me, holding out a PowerBar. "Here, have something to eat."

"Yeah."

But as I'm lowering the binoculars I spot movement. It takes me a minute to find it again. Someone—a man, who must've been sitting rocklike on the beach—is standing up. He's stretching. My heart starts to pound. I zoom in on his face, just as he ducks out of frame. I zoom out a little. He's bending over to pick up something. A stone. He winds up, pitches it, watches it, grins as though he's satisfied with how many times it skipped. Then he kisses his fingers and holds them to the sky, a remembering smile on his face. He's a man who misses someone. A man alone. A man in exile?

Tears spill from the corners of my eyes. The binoculars are wet when I shakily hand them to Clemente.

"Who's that on the beach?" I say.

"What!" He takes the binoculars, thumps them against his brow. "Where?"

"Far left." I wipe my face. "Near the big sandbar."

"Is it a paintballer?" Colby shouts.

"Well I'll be damned," Clemente whispers, standing up, rubbing his finger across the focus wheel. "That there is Xavier Bonenfant, of the Montreal Poutines. This would be his, uh, third year in exile." He lowers the binoculars and looks down at me, smiling hugely. "We found it, McHenry."

I can tell by how I feel sitting on this ledge, looking across the inlet at exile island, that I never believed we *would* find it. Because I'm in shock. The hypothetical—the purely whimsical, the imagined, the daydreamed—has become stark reality. My hands feel heavy and my chest is tight with some type of pent-up vocalization—a laugh, a sob, a gasp, something—that I think would be easier to release if I knew what it actually was.

Around me the guys are setting up camp for the night, gathering leaves and fronds to cushion our space-blanket beds. But all I can do is sit and look and try to make sense of the feeling in my chest. Sometimes I look through the binoculars. Sometimes I just gaze out with my own eyes.

"Clemente," I say when I can't take it anymore. The moon is high and bright and he's lying folded in a cocoon of silver space blanket, good arm tucked under his head for a pillow. With his bad arm he's playing with his phone. "Come for a walk with me. I want to talk to you."

He shoots a glance at exile island before responding. "Now? But it's almost tomorrow."

"It can't wait. Come on."

Reluctantly he gets out of his crinkling pod, drops his phone into the folds of the blanket. He's wearing his swimsuit and nothing else, same as me.

"Don't get lost," Colby says as he pulls his space blanket tighter around him.

"Famous last words," Piper grumbles before rolling over to face the waves.

Clemente looks at me and shakes his head a little, and finally gestures to the tangle of shadowy green.

As we leave the breezy ledge the air turns hot and humid. The dirt and leaves are soft and squishy between my toes and I can feel drops of dew clattering on my head and shoulders as I push my way through the thick growth.

He follows me for fifty yards or so before finally asking where we're going.

"That's what I want to find out, Clemente. Exactly that."

I've imagined having the conversation I want to have in a flower-filled clearing, with a canopy of stars and an audience of colorful, sleeping birds with their heads tucked under their wings. But after leading him another twenty yards I realize the moss-covered flow of ancient lava we're standing on now is probably as picturesque as it's going to get. I sit down, breathing heavy, and pull a thin broken vine from between my toes.

He sits down next to me, dropping with a tired *oompf*. The moss that covers everything here is thick and soft, like fur. A big fern at the edge of the lava flow droops its fronds above his head. His face and hair and shoulders are dappled with dew drops lit silver by moonlight.

"All right now, McHenry," he says, and there's a resigned tenderness in his voice. "What's up?"

"I'm going to break up with Ryan." He looks at me, eyes big and brown, expression vague. After a pause I add, "I wanted you to know that. And I want to tell you why."

"Boots—" He's shaking his head. "You should see him before we get into this. I brought you all this way. There's a proper order."

"I don't need to see him, Clemente. Because that means I'd have to take my eyes off of *you*."

Dew runs from his shoulder down his arm. I catch it on my finger, flick it at him. He smirks, and I continue:

"Maybe I'm way off-base here, and if I am, you can laugh at me. But— Do you want to *be* with me, Clemente? Because I feel like you *do*. I know that's not the norm for you, and I'm not saying you've been hiding or anything before but, with me, I think, with *me*, you *do*. But you hold back and I don't know why. Or am I wrong? Am I just another homo in a long line of homos who's fallen in love with his straight best friend?"

He looks at me with surprise, or with something more like relief, a subtle happiness, and for a second I think he's going to kiss me. But then his face stiffens up and he says, "I don't want to tell you anything before you see Ryan." He reaches up and plucks at a fern, dropping more dew on the moss-covered flow. "That was the mission."

"Clemente, I've already told you I'm leaving him. Nothing you say will change that. Because I can't feel this way about someone other than him, even if it's not requited, and stay with him. I can't. So forget about Ryan. I want to talk about you and me. Am I wrong that you have feelings for me?"

"McHenry, you're not wrong. God. You're zilla right." He's quiet for a long time. Then he reaches out and touches the side of my face, rubs his fingers in the back of my hair the way he did when we were lost at sea. His fingers are wet and dirty with threads of moss, but they calm me, quiet my heart. "I am *so into you*, McHenry," he says. "And I want you. All of you, in every way—have for a long time now. Never felt that way about a guy before though and at first it was crazy, surprising, different. I don't know. But there's no doubt I feel it."

"I'm glad you do."

"Believe me, I'm glad you're glad. Never really dared to think you'd go for me until you jumped in after me after I got hit."

"I'm not sure I really knew until then either. It's easy to trace it back, though. I mean, when we slept together, it wasn't just—" I put my hand on one of his, rub my thumb over his dirty thumbnail. "Did something change for you that night?"

"It was already there," he says, shaking his head. "Just talked you into the sex because I wanted to be sure. Test it out, I guess."

"What? You didn't talk me into— That's silly. It was my idea."

He smirks. "You thought so."

I stare at him for like fifty years before he continues.

"McHenry, look: I wanted you, but what I *didn't* want was to be the guy who just pops onto the scene when you were sad and lonely and fucks things up between you and Ryan if there was still something between you guys you needed to see through." He squeezes my hand. "So I did as much as I felt like I could do and still be a good guy. I thought, if I could get you and Ryan face to face, you'd decide what you wanted. You'd decide what was best for you. Either stick out the five years, or make a clean end."

"And you'd just watch and wait patiently until you saw the right time to make your move?"

"I guess so. Yeah. Exactly." He smiles bashfully. "If you and me end up getting something going, it's going to be pretty new for me. And that's great, that's awesome, I'm not afraid of it. But I didn't want to start something new on a sour note. Wanted to do this right, set things in motion and then head up into the trees or whatever and hope I got a clean shot at you at the end."

"Spoken like a true sniper, Clemente." I lift his hand to my mouth, hold his knuckles against my lips for long seconds before actually putting a kiss on them. "I loved Ryan and he was a good boyfriend and I wish him the best but— I don't think I've ever had any intention of waiting for him. It's crazy, but I've been waiting for you. So take your shot already, you silly sniper," I laugh. "Or better yet, come down from the trees and tell me hello."

He grins and tells me, with his mouth but not with his voice. His lips brush against mine, moist and sweet; he turns his face side to side, his eyes moving back and forth, locked on mine, lets his mouth slip across mine, his nose rub against mine. Then he stops and parts his lips and closes his eyes and it fully becomes a kiss. I lean into him and lace my fingers against the back of his neck. His tongue pushes past my lips and feels like silk against mine.

After a while we part, but our foreheads are still touching.

"So are you bi?" I ask.

"I'm a Bootsmosexual," he laughs. "Yeah, I must be a little bi."

"But you never experimented with a guy before?"

"Never wanted to. Until you. Never a lot of things, McHenry, until I met you. I don't know what it is, but it is."

He pulls me to his mouth by the back of my head and the kiss is deeper and fuller and more erotic than before.

"Did everything I could to be patient till this thing played out. Hid up in the crow's nest as much as I could. Distracted myself with Mariana. But man I want you so fucking bad, McHenry."

He leans back into the dewy moss and pulls me along with him so that I'm lying on top of him. Through our swimsuits our erections grind together and I know it's going to feel like a miracle when we're not wearing them anymore. Without taking my mouth away from his I slide a hand between our bellies and try to push my suit down. I expose enough of my cock so that I can feel his treasure trail tickling against the head.

"You're packing some heat down there," he laughs.

"This time it knows you want it."

Just as I'm pressing Clemente's hand against my cock, a flashlight beam lashes my eyes.

"Guys, I was starting to think— Oh. *Oh.*" It's Colby, quickly dropping the beam, lighting up the foliage around his sneakers as though he's standing in green fire.

I roll off Clemente, hitch up my swimsuit, rock up on one elbow. "Colby, what are you doing?"

"You were gone for so long and you don't have your phone, Clemente, and—" He stops. The flashlight beam is on us again. Behind its light he's a dark silhouette. "Boots, you're—" His voice is quivering with some mixture of surprise and anger. "You're seeing my brother in the morning. *In the morning.* You're doing this *now*, when he's right over there? What are you *doing?*"

"Colby, dude," Clemente says.

"We can explain," I add. My face is hot.

In the darkness I can't be sure where Colby is looking but it *feels* like he's looking at me. "I'm not the one you owe an explanation to," he says. "In fact I don't want to talk to you at all."

Then the light swings a wide arc across the lava flow and Colby becomes a dark shadow as he follows it away into the forest.

I rub a hand down my face as though to pull away the shock. I'm lying on my side, and after a minute Clemente puts a hand under my arm and traces circles on my back.

"We should've waited," I tell him. "We should've done this right."

"That's what I wanted. See? Sometimes you need to just chill in the trees, let things play out."

I sigh and drop my head back on the moss.

"Look on the bright side," he adds, head resting on his bicep, "at least he didn't break our femurs, right?"

"Yet. We should probably give him some space tonight, though."

"Agreed. Better safe than sorry. After all that hiking we did today, I can sleep right here." He turns onto his back and laces his fingers against his sternum, looking up at the dark sky beyond the trees.

"Know something, Clemente? If it had been *you* who got simu-killed, I wouldn't have needed a friend to push me to find you. And I wouldn't have gone back and forth about Piper in the meantime, or dallied with Natan, no matter how cute he is. If it had been you I would've been swimming to exile island, and nothing — not sharks, not pirates — nothing could've kept me from you. And I'm so glad you want to know it."

He doesn't say anything but I can see his sweet smile.

"Come here."

He reaches out and pulls me firmly against him by the back of my shoulder, and rolls onto his side in the same motion, giving me his back to spoon. He squeezes my fist against his belly and yawns once, twice, his back expanding against my chest. I focus on the feel of his skin against mine. It's the last thing I'm aware of before I fall asleep.

Chapter 29

Amid sunbeams we wake up looking like lizards or sea monsters or something, for all the scaly imprints the night on the moss has pressed into our skin.

"You're a mutant," I whisper, tracing the squiggles on his ribs. He laughs and bats my hand away.

Even as I brush moss off my skin, and even though my toenails are black with soil, I don't feel dirty. Lifting my arm, I find I don't even smell. My hair is wet with dew and my fingers are almost as pruney as they were after our stint in the ocean. I feel clean and fresh and awake. And ready to finish the mission. Clemente is too; I can see it in his eyes.

We walk back to the camp. On the ledge Piper is rolling up his space blanket and Colby is sitting beside a packed backpack, looking out at the inlet and at his brother's island on the other side.

He turns, throws a PowerBar at me hard enough to show me things aren't cool. But I catch it and thank him and tear open the wrapper.

"I don't know why you liked the humidity over this nice breeze," Piper says. "Did you actually *sleep?*"

His tone makes it clear he thinks something's up between Clemente and me, but he doesn't appear to know what. I try to make eye contact with Colby, to pass a signal of thanks for keeping quiet about what he saw last night, but he's already putting on his backpack and walking away.

As we make our way slowly down to the water I rehearse my speech to Ryan in my head. It sounds dumb and trite, but it's honest. Honesty will give us the clean end Clemente wants.

While I'm resting on a rock outcropping thirty feet above the waves, Piper climbs over beside me and says, in a whisper, "You don't have to do this, you know, B."

"Do what?"

He gestures toward the island. "Go over there. Stir things up. Look, you made your valiant effort to find him. It was commendable, it was brave. These are the things I've always loved about you. But this should be the end."

"Why would I come all this way and not go the last mile?"

"What good can it do? The last time you saw him should stay the last time. Maybe it wasn't ideal, but it was what it was." When I just look at him, he adds, "The only goodbye you need to say to Kroft is the one you've already said in your heart. It's time to move on. Start living your life again."

"I'm not the only one looking for him. Colby is in this too."

"Then let him go on. You don't have to."

"Piper, just— I wish once and for all you'd get it into your head that we're never going to get together again, Ryan or no Ryan. And that you're just really fucking up the way I used to feel about you."

He frowns and looks away and takes a swig of water.

Below us Colby and Clemente have stopped on a ledge twenty feet above the white-capped waves, and they're shrugging off their backpacks to untie their kickboards. I join them and peer over. I'm eager to jump, I'm ready for the thrill, and after throwing my backpack and kickboard down, I make the leap. But when I hit the water it's less thrill than terror, because it reminds me of jumping overboard after Clemente. I can tell by the look on his face when he surfaces beside me that he's had the same thought. But he does the same as me: pushes it away, fakes a grin.

"It's cool," he says. "No sweat. All good."

Colby plunges in with a great splash near us, and Piper eventually follows. He'd been dawdling up on the ledge and I was starting to wonder if he was pulling out. I wish he would.

"All of a sudden that island looks zilla far," Colby says, treading in the waves with his wet hair slicked back.

"Come on, Colby," I say gently, trying to smooth things with him, "you took down Bottle Cap like a champ, you can conquer a puny inlet."

He smirks. "I guess I can conquer an inlet."

"Santiago's beating you to it," Piper says, lifting his chin.

I turn and see that Clemente has already started swimming. He's like an eager black-haired motorboat, churning out a wake of white foam.

Chapter 30

We're sixty yards offshore of exile island. Fifty. Forty. Thirty, twenty, ten.

The water recedes down my body as I stomp through the surf. I tuck my kickboard under one arm and watch pools of tide-tugged sand stream around my ankles. When I look up at the island I can't help but smile and wish I had some sort of statement prepared. *One small step for Boots McHenry, one giant leap for paintballer kind.* Because it feels that momentous. The fabled, mysterious place every pro paintballer jokes about nervously— The place that haunts us and fuels us even as we wonder whether it truly exists— I'm *standing on it.*

Piper comes out of the surf and walks a little way across the sand, looking around warily and reaching back to tug his rifle out of his backpack.

"Think we'll be OK without the weaponry, Pernfors," Clemente says, coming up beside me. Piper ignores him, though. To me Clemente adds, "Seems silly to think we'd need them."

"I hope so."

Colby, after emptying his swimsuit pockets of water, holds his backpack out to Clemente. "Carry this for me?"

"Why do I have to carry it?" Clemente asks, taking it.

"I want to be free in case I need to do some ass-kicking."

"I think we'll be OK, Colby," I say.

"Still," he says, scoping the forest, "this is the main reason you brought me, right? I need to be zilla ready."

"Be zilla ready, then," Clemente laughs, slipping the backpack over his good shoulder. Colby talking to us is definitely welcome after last night; I'm sure Clemente feels it too.

There's a weird peacefulness here, maybe just because it seems so far from our worst fears. No barbed wire, no electric fences. Now that we're here I know how silly it is that anyone imagines exile as a prison. It's not designed for punishment. It's merely a waiting room, a cog in the machine of a trillion-dollar sports-entertainment industry based on the drama of disappearance.

Piper is scouting farther up the beach. He lowers his rifle to his side, and turns. "What now?"

"Now we find Ryan," I say.

Piper sighs. "And how do we do *that?*"

"We find someone to ask?"

"I don't like the idea of getting too far from the beach," Piper says. "I don't want to get arrested."

"Then you can stay here," I say.

"Over there," Colby says, pointing. "Looks like a trail."

He's right. Farther up the beach there's a big gap in the trees—nothing paved or anything fancy, but the packed earth suggests it gets regular use.

I'm in the lead and I've seen no signs of civilization except for the possible whiff of a barbeque on the breeze.

"You know," Clemente says from behind me, "I just thought of something. A lot of the guys here—a good number anyway—they were simu-killed by *us.*"

"Right."

"How would *you* feel, coming face to face with the dude whose trigger finger got you exiled?"

"I'd probably want to strangle him."

"Just saying."

"That's why I'm here," says Colby. "To protect your sorry asses."

I'm still grinning when I turn back to the trail, but the

grin freezes when I see someone approaching. Branches and big leaves bend around him, sunlight glints on his shaved scalp and black sunglasses. I'm not sure how to feel about someone from exile knowing we're here.

"It's Bonenfant," Clemente whispers to me.

Xavier Bonenfant, who we saw blow a kiss at the stars last night. He's shirtless with a Montreal Poutines towel slung over his meaty shoulder.

We stop to do the awkward dance of negotiating passage on the narrow trail. As I stand with branches stabbing into my back to let Xavier pass, it's right on my tongue to ask if he knows where Ryan is. But when he says a quick bonjour and keeps moving I realize I've clammed up.

Clemente hasn't, though. "Xavier," he says, "bonjour!"

Bonenfant is a good six inches taller than Clemente, and since they're standing chest to chest Xavier lifts his sunglasses and peers down at Clemente's upturned face.

"Clemente Santiago." He holds his hand up for Bonenfant to shake. "You don't know me, I was still playing college ball when you got sent here."

"OK." He looks at each of us. Something about Colby makes him smirk. "You are just arriving?"

"Just this morning," I say, trying to put on the type of frown I imagine a paintballer newly exiled would be wearing.

"I'm a sniper too," Clemente says proudly to Bonenfant, still pumping his hand. "Learned so much from watching your moves. *So* much."

"Merci, thank you." He's finally released from Clemente's grip. "But I do not know how good a teacher I was if we have both ended up *here*."

We all laugh. Maybe everyone here will just assume we got simu-killed, too—one big happy family or something.

"Beach is good today?" Bonenfant asks, moving past us to continue on his way.

"Xavier," I say. "You don't know where I can find Ryan Kroft, do you? He got here about, oh, six weeks ago."

"Kroft, yes, I think." He points up the trail. "You are going in the right direction, mes amis. Keep going."

Before long the trail widens, and soon after that it opens on a grassy plaza, two acres or more. Footpaths are worn through the grass in curling lines. In one corner of the plaza is a big pavilion covering lawn chairs and a few pool tables.

"Image scrambler, McHenry," Clemente says, pointing to the tall, multi-pronged antenna stemming off the pavilion's roof.

At another corner of the plaza there's a basketball court; four guys are having a game.

"This looks like summer camp," Colby mumbles beside me.

He's right, and the nearby barbeque only adds to that effect. Flame-licked hotdogs are being tended by a shirtless man I recognize immediately as Clemente's most recent simu-kill: Gerry Swift, of the Icebergs.

"Don't look now," I say to Clemente out of the corner of my mouth.

"What?" He looks, of course. "Yikes, he's one of mine. Let's move along, shall we?"

But it's too late.

"Santiago? Is that Clemente Santiago?"

Clemente makes the mistake of turning toward the voice rather than grabbing a big head-start.

"Clemente Santi-fucking-ago? Well well." Swift is looking at us, banging a greasy fork against his palm.

"How the mighty have fallen!"

"Uh. Gerry. Hah. Hey! How you doing and stuff?"

"Luck finally ran out on you, hey Santiago?"

"Guess you could say that...."

Swift rocks back on his bare heels, laughs a weird laugh. "You fucking asshole, Santiago. I *had* that game and then you just had to come out of nowhere, didn't you?" He drops the fork on the back of the grill and stalks toward us, hand curling into a fist at his side.

A sleek-muscled man in a chaise lounge near the barbeque looks up from a book and says, in the thickest of Mexican accents, "Gerry, your wieners are going to burn."

"Only one thing round here's going to *burn*, Manuel," Swift says, eyes on Clemente. He's breaking into a trot now.

"Uh, Colby? Colby?" Clemente laughs, but with a rising lilt that reveals a touch of panic. He's turning and sprinting across the grassy plaza before Colby has time to reply. Like an angry bull Swift plunges past us. Colby takes off after him.

"Come back here and put em up, Santiago!" Swift yells. "Let's see how tough you are when you don't have a trailer truck to shoot from!"

"Ouch," Piper coughs.

"Boots!" Clemente yells, turning mid-stride. He's laughing again. "Remember me always! Go find Ryan! Good luck! Godspeed!"

He's running through the pavilion, tipping plastic lawn chairs into Swift's path. Colby is hot on both their heels — the three-man chase curls across the plaza before plunging into the jungle beyond.

"How ugly is that likely to get?" I ask the man in the chaise lounge with the Mexican accent.

He laughs. "Gerry's happy here, so not very ugly."

His answer surprises me. I never imagined anyone being happy in exile. "Are *you* happy here?"

"Have to say I've been in worse places." He looks us up and down. "Just getting here?"

"Just today," I reply.

"All four of you at once? Rough days in the NAPL!"

The grill coughs a cloud of black smoke. The guy makes a little grimace—"Told him, didn't I?"—and gets up, lifts the lid, pokes at the sizzling hotdogs with Swift's fork.

"I'm trying to find Ryan Kroft," I tell him. "Do you know him?"

"Sure I know Ryan. I was his orientation guide."

"Orien— Jeez, this *is* like summer camp," Piper says.

"Ryan a friend of yours?"

"Boyfriend, actually. Or— Yeah."

"You must be Boots, then," Manuel says, lowering the lid and turning down the flame. "Talked my ear off about you."

That's not exactly what I was hoping to hear—it won't make what I have to do any easier—and I don't know how to respond.

"Do you know where I can find him?"

"Don't think I've seen him yet this morning. But his place is just yonder." He gestures to the far side of the grassy plaza. "That's your best bet. Unless he's at the beach. He likes the beach."

"Thanks."

While we're crossing the plaza Clemente and Colby, running side by side now, tear out of the forest, try to ditch Swift with a few crazy corkscrews like something out of an old Warner Bros. cartoon, and then plunge headlong back into the forest.

"Maybe they'll just wear each other out," Piper says.

We reach the boundary of the plaza and a wide dirt

trail leads us to what I assume is the residential part of the island. After walking for a minute we begin to see little huts nestled in thick foliage, each one isolated in a cushion of green that makes it hard to see how dense the neighborhood might actually be. Smaller even than my pool-house, the huts are round with cone-shaped grass roofs and doors of colorful fabric.

"How do you think we'll know which one's his?" I ask.

"Beats me."

A while after I've passed a hut with a blue striped door curtain, I realize Piper has stopped. He's about twenty feet back, gazing into the hut.

"Was that Ryan's?"

He shrugs and beckons me over.

When I'm beside him it's clear right away what he's so hypnotized by, but I have to keep moving my head to see past the fluttering door curtain. Inside on a thick mat on the tile floor, two naked paintballers are making love—very clearly making love and not just fucking. They're in a kneeling spoon position; the top has his brawny arms crossed against the smooth chest of the shaggy, brown-haired guy in front, who's arcing his head back to suck the top's ear. The kneeling spoon position was one of Ryan's favorites; we did it all the time.

Oh man. Is this—?

Before I can be sure, the breeze lets up and the curtain falls back over the doorway. My heart is in my throat. But really, what am I afraid of? This will be so much easier if the shaggy-haired guy *is* Ryan; I might even be able to turn around and leave and feel satisfied.

Again the curtain flutters and we can see inside. This time the shaggy-haired guy is looking at us. And although he looks a lot like Ryan, he isn't Ryan. He tips his head back and rubs his cheek against the other guy's jaw as they continue making love.

I find I've been holding my breath.

"One of them probably knows where Ryan lives," Piper whispers. "We could, uh, go inside and ask...."

I start walking up the trail again and reluctantly he joins me, coming out of a jog when he reaches my side.

"I was only kidding, B," he sighs. "Hey, ask them."

Coming our way are a man and woman carrying between them a big basket of what looks like white bed sheets.

I ask if they know which house belongs to Ryan Kroft. The man shakes his head and the woman says, "No, sorry," and they continue on their way.

I watch them go, then turn to Piper. "Should we just, like, yell zilla loud and hope he hears us?"

"I don't think we should be yelling, Boots. The less people who know we're here, the better. I mean, it's fine that they assume we're here for simu-death reasons, but they're all going to wonder where the fuck we've gone when we leave."

I look at him. I look down at my bare feet on the packed-dirt path and feel a renewed leak of that black bile of despair.

"We gave it a try," Piper continues. "I just don't think it's going to work. Let's go make sure Clemente and Colby are OK." He slips an arm around my shoulders. "What do you say?"

The truth is I'm about to say yes, when something squealing and hard slams my heel. I kneel down and pick up a flipped-over remote control car, set it down right-side up in the dirt. It scrambles back and forth a few times before going still.

A guy in white soccer shorts is jogging up the footpath. He looks familiar—I must've seen his image all over the news recently. He's young, has to be a fresh simu-kill.

"Sorry," he calls, "I saw your leg and panicked and forgot how to stop." He laughs. On his face he wears remote-control goggles. He lifts them up over his hair. "Still getting the hang of this thing. Did yours go off the cliff? Seems like everyone's driven theirs off the cliff already."

"Uh, yeah." I make a falling gesture. "Right over."

"Zilla tragic," Goggles laments. "All right, let's give this another whirl." He lowers the goggles and bugs out his eyeballs. The little car leaps forward a few inches.

"Hey, dude," I say, "you can't point me toward Ryan Kroft's place, by any chance?"

"Kroft? Definitely." He starts gesturing along the path. "You want to continue up this way about a quarter mile," he says. Even though he's no longer paying attention to his car, it's still reacting to his eye movements, racing maniacally back and forth across the trail. Piper is finding this hilarious. "There'll be another path on your left, right? Take that."

"The path on the left? Uh!" I have to hop out of the car's frantic path.

"Yes. Sorry. On the left. Follow that for like, oh, a few minutes or something. You'll come to a row of shacks. Kroft's is the one with a big smiley sun on the door. Can't miss it. Well, bye!"

He turns and the car zooms full-speed into a tree stump, releases a spritz of sparks, and starts smoking.

"Awh, shit."

Goggles was nuts but he was right. In front of us is a hut that looks like all the others except for the smiling sun design on its door curtain. The curtain is billowing gently in the breeze. Beyond it I can see blue tile floor and pieces of furniture, the edge of a bed—but I don't see Ryan.

As I take a step toward the smiling sun I hear a peal of laughter come from the other side. Ryan's laugh. He's here, and when I hear no other voice I realize he must be alone. After all this, he's just on the other side of that curtain. Suddenly I wonder how I look. I hope I look OK. I haven't shaved in days. My feet are black with dirt and sand. My heart is pounding. But none of it matters. None of it has any bearing on what I'm here to do. I take another step and Piper seizes my arm.

"Don't go in, Boots." His eyes look scared. "I never thought we'd really find it. I thought I would've been able to make you forget about it long before now. But if I haven't, let me tell you friend to friend: You don't want to go in there. Please."

"You have to know that every time you try to talk me out of this it just makes me want to do it even more."

He shakes his head dismissively. "If I ever meant anything to you, Boots, think of that and trust me that this is for the best."

He did mean something to me once. For a time he meant everything to me—and during that time I gave him my body, all the most delicate parts of it. I put my balls in his hands, I put my lips between his teeth. I trusted him to treat my body with love and care and he always did. I never imagined he would actually try to hurt me. Which is why, here on Ryan's doorstep, I am totally unprepared for the punch.

I go down hard in a row of yellow flowers. Holding my jaw, testing to make sure it still opens, I see him standing over me, tears running down his face. I understand that he wanted a knock-out and didn't get one. He's looking at his hand, looking down at me. He comes at me again, raises his fist as he's dropping to one knee, and in the second he hesitates I grab his hand and wrestle him down. I manage to get on top of him — Colby would be proud — and I'm winding up to return the punch when I decide I don't need to. The point has been made.

"I'm going in."

I push into him hard as I stand up, and he slowly lifts his hands in resigned surrender. I expect him to offer one last protest, but instead he just sits up in the little yard and tells me he'll wait here.

Shaking, I turn to the curtain and push it aside.

The hut is all one room, round with a white fan rotating gently at the top of the cone-shaped ceiling. The bed is strewn with yellow pillows and a fluffy floral blanket; a corner of white sheet hangs out from under the mattress and touches the blue tile. Across from the bed is a yellow couch and a TV and a desk. There's a kitchenette with a sink, fridge, and cooktop. On the same wall as the bed a pink curtain closes off what must be the bathroom. It looks like a nice hotel room, pretty but anonymous. On the opposite wall from the door I've just come through is a wide patio doorway, its curtains tied back to reveal a striking vista: it must be the cliff Goggles mentioned — this hut is perched on the edge of it. Beyond, far below and miles away, is an old volcanic valley carpeted in the greenest of greens. But the valley, however beautiful, isn't the sight that's taken my breath away. Stretched between two trees just outside the doorway is a pink and yellow hammock, and in this hammock, bare legs crossed comfortably, holding an old-fashioned paperback novel in one hand and a glass of lemonade in the other, is Ryan Kroft.

Chapter 31

Whatever I was going to say, whatever it was I had planned, I've forgotten it. *Poof*—just like that. Even the pain in my jaw is gone.

After standing in silence watching him read for I don't know how long, I finally whisper his name.

"Oh!" he laughs, startled. He turns casually, lowering the lemonade from his lips. When he sees it's me he flinches. The hammock swings; lemonade sloshes from the glass and patters his bare chest, turns his gray underwear a darker gray. "Boots...."

My mouth is dry.

He's staring at me; I'm staring back. Absently he reaches down and puts the glass on the patio floor. "You— You got hit?"

He's clumsily trying to get out of the hammock. The book falls to the ground with a ruffle of pages. When he's finally standing I'm surprised by his body. He's thinner than when I saw him last, but it's just because he's stopped weightlifting and his thick muscles have melted away. He looks healthy and beautiful and has a serenity I can't remember ever seeing on him before. And now that I'm seeing it I wonder why I never noticed its absence.

"I didn't get hit, Ryan, I— We came to find you."

His eyebrows sink low, his lips form a thin line. "Find me? What do you mean?"

I can only look at him. Part of me—a part that runs on habit and nostalgia—wants to run to him and pick him up and carry him to bed and make love to him until the sun sets across that far valley. But at some point in this flash of daydream I begin to realize he's just looking at me, too. Isn't running to me, isn't throwing his arms around me, isn't covering my lips with his. Shouldn't he be happy to see me? His brow is creased. He's confused.

"What do you mean, *find me*, Boots? You didn't get simu-killed?"

"We sailed here. We found the coordinates."

His lips begin to form a question, then he looks away and rubs his chin nervously. "Who's *we?*"

"Clemente Santiago. Colby—"

"You brought my brother *here?*"

"He wanted to see you. And Piper Pernfors."

A blankness wipes his face clear of all Colby-related emotion and he says icily, "*Piper is here?*"

I can feel the same blankness creep onto my own.

"Oh god," he says. Still I'm unable to respond. He's never liked Piper and would never be thrilled to see him. But now it's more than that. "Then you know."

I feel like I've wandered onto a minefield and I'm afraid to step in any direction. I look down at the floor.

"Why'd you have to come here, Boots? Why'd you drag Colby into this?"

"Just to see you," I say. "To see you and— So we could talk about how you left. So we could discuss it, make peace with it. That's all."

"Boots, there's nothing to say about how I left. I did what I did and there's nothing to say about it."

That throws me off-guard even more.

He puts his hand on his forehead and rubs it back over his hair. "Boots, please don't tell me Colby knows what happened."

I'm starting to feel really nervous but I'm also afraid he'll clam up if I let on that I have no idea what he's talking about. "Colby doesn't know. Only Piper and I— Only we know."

"Are you and Piper back together?"

"What? No. Not since college. You know that."

"But he tried, though."

"Of course he— I mean—"

"And you said no?"

"Of course I did."

"So let me guess: he told you for spite."

"Ryan, I'm—" I hold out my hand to slow him down; it feels cold in the air and I realize I've been squeezing it in a sweaty fist. "Why are you asking me about Piper?"

He sighs. "I told him that if he helped me he'd have a chance at you, and—"

"Whoa, hold on. What do you mean, a chance at me? Helped you to do *what?*"

He looks at me blank-faced, and I can tell it's dawned on him that I don't actually know anything at all, and never did. He swallows hard, turns, looks out at the valley.

"Awh fuck, Boots, you shouldn't've come. I told you, when I was on the helicopter, I told you to let me go. Didn't you see?"

"*Helped you do what?*"

He looks at me and then down at his hands; he's wringing his hands. He seems to be running a thousand different explanations through his mind looking for one that might fit.

Quietly I say, "Just tell me the truth. I came a long way. I fought pirates."

He looks at me, timidly now. "Pirates?"

"Pirates. Nasty ones." I look at his face, see how the anxiety in his eyes has obliterated the serenity that was there when I arrived. I'm afraid I know what his answer is going to be but I take a deep breath and ask again: "Helped you do what, Ry?"

He looks away and then back at me. There are tears in his eyes when he says, "To come here."

I thought I was ready for it. I thought I was ready, but it feels like a punch in the gut. A punch and a twist and a shredding rip.

"You self-inflicted. *Why?*"

He closes his eyes for a second and then opens them, takes a deep breath. "I don't know."

"Of *course* you fucking know."

"Ah, fuck, Boots, it's just that when I joined the NAPL," he says, "everything started happening so fast. You know, you were there. Like life went into warp speed. And it was great. A lot of it was great. But the rest was just too much. Too much, too fast. The money, the everybody knowing my business, the interviews, the tabloid bullshit, the pressure...."

"And me?"

"Yeah, Boots. And you. I loved you. I *love* you. But it went so fast. We met and then *bam!* I wanted to get out. Get away."

"Ryan, there's this little thing called *breaking up*. People do it. I came all this way to do it to *you*." He flinches. "You could've broken up with me. You didn't have to fucking *kill* yourself."

"Boots, you aren't listening. It wasn't just you. It was everything—our relationship was a tiny part of it. I wanted out of *everything*. Out of the NAPL, out of that house, *out of people's consciousness*."

"You're so selfish."

It stings him. I'm glad.

"I thought it would be easier on you this way, Boots. I'd be gone and in the meantime you could move on."

"I *have* moved on. But I wanted to grant you the courtesy of letting you know it. While you were chilling in paradise with your fucking lemonade, I was almost getting killed by pirates. Numerous times!"

"I didn't ask you to do that."

"I didn't ask you to be a selfish prick." I step back, turn around, press my forehead against the cool wood of the door frame. "I cannot believe you self-inflicted. How the fuck did you even *do* it? With all those cameras?"

"It doesn't matter."

"It does. I deserve an explanation. Apparently the two guys I've loved in my life have been lying to me. I deserve an explanation. You said Piper helped you. Did he steal the Panthers' paintballs for you?"

"He shot me for me."

"Piper shot — ? I don't believe you."

"It's the truth. You asked for it."

"Why would Piper help you do that? Piper never even *liked* you, Ryan. Why would he risk his paintball career for you?"

"Think about it, Boots. He didn't like me because I was with *you*. With me gone, you'd be a free agent. And he wanted you back since the day you dumped him."

"And so he shot you? How did you not get seen?"

He sighs, sits down on the edge of the hammock; it curls up against his back like a hood. "That whole thing was going down with Rufus and the guys from the Panthers. Rufus fucked one of the Panthers' wives or something, and — Everyone was shooting. Piper had the other team's color in his pistol. We took advantage of the chaos and he pulled the trigger."

"Simple as that," I murmur.

"It wasn't *simple*, Boots. I thought about it for a long time. Almost got my chance naturally the week before, but Piper fucked that up when he pushed me out of the way."

"That's when you told him you wanted out?"

"Our team was too good to have it happen naturally."

"Our team is a sham."

"Boots, it's a fucking job. It's all it ever was. *Rah rah* team spirit will always run a distant second to money and love."

This all seems like such bullshit; I can feel everything I've cared about crumbling. "I can't believe this. I feel like such a fucking stooge."

"Not everything is about you, Boots."

"It is about me. It's *all* about me." Even as I'm saying the words I remember Piper telling me almost the exact same thing on his drunken morning in Puerto Natan. "So the gist of this whole thing is, you sold me to my ex-boyfriend for a ticket out of my life."

"No, Boots. I sold you for a ticket out of *my* life."

For a long time I just stare at him. He looks like a stranger. I want to punch his teeth down his throat.

But my god, it's a throat I have kissed so many times.

"I came all this way to tell you goodbye, Ryan. I just had no idea how glad I'd be to say it when the time came." I turn and walk back into the hut. "Enjoy your little island paradise or whatever. Goodbye."

My heart is pounding and I feel sick. As I walk by his desk I pick up the chair and hurl it at the wall above his bed. One leg punches through the plaster and keeps the chair hanging there for a second before the wall crumbles and drops it onto Ryan's pillows.

"Really mature," Ryan says from the patio doorway, arms crossed.

"Your brother is here somewhere," I say, holding back the smiling-sun curtain. "If you don't tell him what a coward you are, I will."

I let the curtain fall back behind me.

Piper is where I left him in the yard. I point at him with a finger that feels like a sizzling lightning bolt. "Is it true? Did you shoot him?"

"B, I only did it because I—"

"Why the fuck did you come on my trip?"

He searches my eyes for a second before saying, "So I could explain?"

"I know all I need to know, believe me, you two-timing asshole."

Then I hear my name and look up. Clemente and Colby, both shining with sweat but otherwise apparently unharmed by Gerry Swift, are coming up the dirt path. Colby breaks into a jog, leaving Clemente slumping behind.

"Is this his house?" Colby shouts. "Did you find him?"

The sight of his happiness is what brings the first tears to my eyes. I clear my voice. "He's inside. Yeah. He's here."

We pass each other in the yard. He pushes through the curtain and I hear him laugh. I don't want to be here when he learns the truth.

Leaving the yard, I break into a run.

"McHenry," Clemente says, looking at me from where he's doubled over on the path, hands on knees, "what happened? You OK?"

I'm running toward him and he probably thinks I'm going to stop when I get to him, but I don't. I run right past.

"Awh, Boots, no," he moans, "I can't run any more today!"

But before long I realize he's running anyway, trying to catch up, and I run faster to outpace him. He can't have been involved in this, right? No, he was with me in the tree when Ryan self-inflicted. He can't have been involved. I love him too much for him to be a part of this. But I loved Ryan too and look what happened.

"McHenry, c'mon, stop!"

I run harder, bare feet slapping the earth; each

pounding step pushes dirt up between my toes. I make a skidding turn, hoping I'm choosing the right path, and soon I'm in the plaza again, pounding across the stiff grass. I run right through a soccer game, spot Manuel laughing at a worn-out Gerry Swift, and soon I'm on the narrow trail that'll take me back to the beach.

To my surprise, Clemente is still on my heels, gaining on me.

"McHenry, I'll chase you till my heart explodes. Just saying!"

When my feet hit the black sand I stumble crazily. But I catch my balance and moments later foamy water is smashing against my thighs and chest as I plow into the surf.

"McHenry, your backpack! The kickboards!"

I look back and see Clemente rooting around in the bushes where we hid our stuff. Fuck kickboards. I'm chest-deep and my feet have already left the coarse sand. I'm swimming now, arm over arm, legs fighting the tide. I want to be off this fucking island. I want to be home.

I've gone a few hundred yards when I hear Clemente again. I look back and spot him, double-humped with our backpacks, two kickboards skimming beneath his hands.

"Let me give you a kickboard before you drown, mi amigo," he calls.

Eventually he catches up to me, not because I let him but because I'm tired and can't swim any farther. He's floating in front of me with a kickboard under each arm—they look like wings.

"Will you tell me what happened in there?" he says.

"Clemente— You weren't a part of it, were you?"

I can tell by his face he has no idea what I'm talking about.

"McHenry, I would never be part of anything that

hurts you."

I look at his eyes, at his nose, at his mustache, at his lips. He lets go of the kickboards and puts his arms around me. I am held and I am OK and I sob against his hair while the kickboards drift away from us in separate directions on the waves.

Clemente and me, just the two of us, once again lost at sea.

Chapter 32

The back of the Intrepid slides against my belly as Marcus gives me a hand out of the water and pulls me onto the lower deck. Clemente tosses our backpacks up after me as I roll coughing across the floor. Then Clemente is kneeling over me, little crystal waterfalls sliding off his swimsuit and spreading out beneath his knees.

"Can we get a towel for him, Marcus?"

"I'm *fine.*"

But Marcus nods and heads into the bridge anyway.

Clemente sits down and stretches out his legs. When Marcus returns and hands him a towel he shakes it open and flops it across my shoulders.

I look up at Marcus. My whole head feels full of water. "Colby's not going to be a happy camper when he gets back, Marcus, so be ready."

"Have you heard from them?" Clemente asks.

"Colby called," Marcus says. "And you're right, Boots. They're on the beach somewhere. We'll swing by and pick them up."

Soon after Marcus goes into the bridge again, the engine hums and our drift gains direction. The two islands on either side of us look like they're floating. I almost expect to see them rocking gently in the waves like big green buoys.

Clemente stands up, picks up our backpacks, shakes water off them. "I'm going to go change," he says. "You should too."

After a minute I get up and follow him downstairs, not because I care about changing, but because I don't want to see Piper when he comes aboard — or necessarily ever again.

When I enter our cabin Clemente is stepping out of his swimsuit. He has a towel across his shoulders but otherwise he's naked. His penis has been made small from swimming and it's caught in a clinging net of black hair.

I wrap the towel around my waist and sit down on my bunk. After drying his hair, Clemente folds his towel in half and places it on the top bunk. Tan lines slice him below his belly button and across the tops of his thighs.

"Are you ever going to tell me what happened with Ryan?" he says.

"What happened could jeopardize your future career in the NAPL if it ever comes out that you knew about it. So no, I'm not going to tell you."

He sighs. Naked still, he kneels in front of me, laces his fingers against my calf. He touches his nose to my knee, almost as if he's smelling it, then touches his chin to it and looks up at me. "I'm not asking you to tell me as a coworker, McHenry. Tell me as someone who loves you."

I look down at him and cup his ear in my hand. "I'll tell you this: I told him goodbye like I planned, and it was a forever goodbye. Just give me a little time to deal with the rest first, OK?"

He nods, reluctantly. When he stands up again I see

that his penis has pushed its way through his clinging pubic hair and returned to normal size.

"When you're ready," he says, "I'll be here."

After changing into dry clothes I take a quick hard nap, then spend a wakeful eternity staring up at the underside of Clemente's empty bunk. The engine is quiet; we're idling somewhere but no one's told me where and I haven't gone to find out.

I'm like this when Colby slumps into my cabin, the usual lightness in his footsteps dulled, I'm sure, by Ryan's big reveal. Wordlessly and without turning on the light he lies down beside me, facing away from me on his side with his arms hanging off the bunk. I feel like maybe I should put my arm around him.

"I'm sorry I yelled at you when I found you in the woods with Clemente," he says, voice soft and raw.

"Never mind about that."

"You were right to fall in love with Clemente. You picked the good guy."

"Colby—"

"I can't believe he did this," he says, lifting his head off the pillow and dropping it back with a thump that bounces mine.

"Neither can I. I guess he had his reasons."

"I can't ever tell my parents. They'd *die*."

I do put my arm around him then. It feels good because he knows how I feel. We're brothers in this; we've both been deceived.

"If I had any idea I never would've invited you on this mission," I say.

"I have no regrets about coming," he says, clearing his voice. "I wouldn't have met Marcus."

The cabin door opens and Clemente comes in.

"You boys sulking together?" he says. Standing in

front of the bunks, he crosses his arms over the Warriors logo on his shirt. He looks at me. "Colby told me about Ryan, McHenry."

"I couldn't hold it in," Colby says, shrugging beneath my hand.

"It's OK. Aren't a lot of secrets between Clemente and me these days, anyway."

"So I've seen," Colby smirks. He sits up and gets to his feet. "I'm going to go dislocate Piper's other shoulder now." He closes the door behind him and Clemente and I are alone.

"He's not kidding," Clemente says. "At least about the first shoulder." He sits down on my bunk, leans against my leg. "I'm sorry that my need to bring you here ended up in you finding out so much crap. It's not what I wanted. I hoped you'd break up with him but I never knew any of this was going to happen. I'm so sorry, McHenry."

"Don't apologize for doing the right thing, Clemente. Never apologize for being the good guy."

He sniffs hard. "In the morning we're heading to Honolulu," he says, running his hand along the underside of the upper bunk as if inspecting its construction. "Piper wants to catch a plane back to Thebes—I figure that's for the best. Also Marcus doesn't want to drive all the way home with a broken windshield, especially since we're going about a zillion miles out of the way this time. Guess a couple other things need fixing too, after all the pirate craziness. Says the repairs'll take a few days. Ever been to Honolulu?"

"Where are we now?"

"Just parked back in the cove again."

"You can tell me what Honolulu's like. I'm going to stay here."

He turns and looks at me. "Where? On the island?"

"I need some time alone. That's all."

"On a deserted island all by yourself? No. I'll stay with you."

"Don't take this the wrong way, Clemente. There's something great between you and me and I'm happy about it and I want to roll with it. But right now I just need to be alone."

He looks about to say something. Instead he reaches a hand back and gently cups my heel, the one that shed its last gum of BodyGlue in the sand on exile island.

"Think about letting me camp on the beach," he says. "You can go off and do your thing, take all the time you need. But just so I'll be around."

He drops a kiss on my shoulder. "Think about it," he says again, and then he leaves the cabin.

Chapter 33

I wake to the sound of zippers and snaps—Clemente is packing. When I open my eyes I see him kneeling on the floor, guiding a backpack strap through its buckle. He has on boardshorts, his Warriors tee, and a blue and white bandana tied around his black hair. The bandana looks zilla sexy and I don't know why he hasn't worn it before now. He stands up, yawns, sees I'm awake.

"Marcus wants to get going soon," he says. "If we're hopping off, now's the time."

"I'm up."

He puts his hands on his hips. "Don't know what you plan on bringing. I'm just bringing the same shit. Colby packed us a box of food."

"OK. Let me pee."

Getting up, I straighten the sheets with a quick tug,

feeling a little dazed. He's watching me. He looks so cute in that bandana and I know he wants a kiss, a hug, something — but I'm still feeling too raw to be affectionate, even with him.

In the galley Piper is scraping a thin smear of butter across a slice of burned toast. We make awkward eye contact and he starts to say something, but I keep walking and shut the bathroom door behind me. I pee, brush my teeth, take a quick shower, and realize I didn't bring a towel. I dry off as well as I can with my own underwear, then put them back on wet. It feels gross. I feel gross.

If Piper had any smarts at all he wouldn't still be in the galley when I come back through, but he is, standing at the sink banging crumbs out of the toaster.

My plan is to ignore him — that's what I'll be doing for the perpetual future, so why not start now? But when he says my name I stop. I didn't notice before how red his eyes are. He looks haggard. But fuck, knowing him it's probably stage make-up.

"I'm sorry," he says. "Just— I'm sorry. For all of it."

I start walking again, then I stop. "How many times in my life are you going to break my heart, Piper?"

Clearly it isn't what he was expecting. He probably braced himself for anger and he's surprised by the hurt. His head drops.

"When we get back," he says, "when we see Skullcrusher. Am I done?"

"I haven't decided yet. Guess we'll find out, won't we?"

Colby is helping Marcus unlash the dinghy from the wall. When they have it down, Clemente and I stand aside while they swing it into the water. Clemente tosses our backpacks into it.

"You're sure you won't get zilla bored?" Colby says, incredulous.

"Kind of the point, dude," I say. "After everything, I want a little boring time alone."

"How about you?" Colby says, looking coyly at Clemente.

"Let's just say there's a lot of sandcastles in my future."

We climb into the dinghy. We're old pros at it now — our first wobbly boarding in Puerto Natan seems ages ago. When we're settled Marcus lifts down the box of food supplies Colby packed for us.

"Bury the cider in the sand," Marcus tells Clemente, "to keep it nice and cold."

"Right on! Sandcastles and hard cider. All a man needs."

"No more than a few days, now," Marcus adds, "then we'll come back for you. We'll be in touch."

I let Clemente take the paddles. We push away from the Intrepid with a jerky swoosh that feels like an umbilical cord cut. I look up and spot Piper standing in the bridge looking down at us through a cracked window. He waves but I don't return it.

I think Clemente thought I wouldn't actually leave. That I'd change my mind once we got ashore. Because once we've beached the dinghy he stands looking at me, arms slightly spread, palms up, and he says, "Really now?"

"Really," I tell him, and with a gentle smile I step forward in the sand and put a kiss on his temple.

"Get out of here then, McHenry," he says, brushing me aside. "I won't stop you. Got a whole case of ciders with my name on it, anyway."

He plops down in the sand with his back against the dinghy, still with the clear expectation that at any

335

HOMO ACTION LOVE STORY!

moment I'm going to drop the act and crack open a cold one with him.

"All right then."

"All right." I lean down and kiss him again, this time on the top of his head. As an afterthought I pull off his bandana and fit it around my own head. Then I turn and make for the tangled green forest at the edge of the beach, and let it swallow me whole.

I don't head back to the ledge on purpose — maybe I do — but by dusk I'm back where we set up camp two nights ago. The mattresses of ferns are still here, albeit a little dried-out and wind-strewn, and there's a gallery of doodles in the dirt near where Colby slept. I imagine him scratching them in angry silence after catching Clemente and me on the lava flow.

I slip off my backpack and, sitting down on Colby's ferns, make myself a luscious dinner of Gatorade and granola bar. I sit chewing, looking out. I can hear nothing but wind and waves and the flutter of foil against my chin. It's peaceful. The quiet is nice. No one is observing me, and that's nice too. I look over at exile island.

Everyone always says, about anyone close who dies, *If only I had five more minutes.* But I would tell them to be careful what they wish for. Five minutes can ripple back through years.

What makes Ryan's abandonment of our life together so painful is that part of me understands why he did it. Part of me almost agrees — not with the follow-through, but with the desire behind it. As I sit here looking out, and when I think back to our day in Puerto Natan, I can understand the allure. The simplicity. The freedom in giving everything up, the bliss of walking away. There's a beauty in it — or at least there would've been if he'd achieved it some other way. But he had to cheat and lie to get here. And that's left me rattled, and doubtful, and afraid. You think you know a person, etc.

But I don't have the luxury of bitterness. I can't afford to stomp around, develop trust issues, throw myself into my work to try to compensate. I need to get over this quick. Like *now*. Because a sweet, mustachioed sniper loves me, and I love him back, and I really don't want anything that happened on exile island to fuck that up. Not when he came all this way to get to me—the best, fairest, truest way he knew how.

So this time alone is my time. My time to feel deceived. My time to be angry about it. To rage over it. And when the purpose of this aloneness becomes clear my emotions rise to fulfill it. Everything I feel about the sham of Ryan and Piper erupts within me like a new volcano and, dropping my face into the cold brown dirt, I cry like I've never cried before.

When I'm done—it feels like hours have passed—I pour the remaining contents of a water bottle onto Clemente's bandana and use it to wash myself, clean myself up. Then I ring it out, roll it back up, and tie it around my head.

It's too dark to walk back to him now, and I'm too exhausted to try. But I don't want to spend the night on this ledge, either. I gather up my things, and after some searching by flashlight, I find the mossy lava flow where he and I slept. Stretching out on my back, I pick up the phone Colby lent me.

"Guess where I am, Clemente?"

"Colombia!"

"What?"

He laughs. "Where are you, McHenry?"

"At our lava flow. I'm going to spend the night

here."

"Ah, you mean Blue-Balls Mountain!"

I laugh.

"What are you wearing?" he asks.

I laugh again, this time because I realize he sounds a little drunk. "Me?" I look down at my grimy clothes. "Nothing at all."

"Hey, nice."

"What are *you* wearing?"

"Hmm. A sharkskin leisure suit."

"Did you catch a shark? Is that what you've been up to?"

"Ha. No. Got drunk and been skipping stones."

"No sandcastles?"

"Maybe tomorrow."

"Yeah. Speaking of tomorrow — I'm going to start back in the morning."

"So soon?" I can hear the smile in his voice. "You do what you needed to do and stuff?"

"*Pfft.* Sure. No sweat."

"Good." I hear him sigh, a content sigh. Then there's a pop as a cider bottle leaves his lips. "Nice night," he says. "Starry and stuff."

"Sure is."

His voice lilts into cuteness. "When you get back tomorrow, howzabout we finally do some more sex together?"

I laugh. "The second I see you."

"Right on. —Hey, I need to tell you about this crab war I saw on the beach this afternoon!"

"Crab war?"

"These two angry sand crabs. Epic. Looked choreographed. One of them climbed up on a chunk of driftwood and totally jumped off and pile-drived the other one."

"Tell me." I close my eyes and reach into my pants and focus on the sexy melodies of his voice.

"I was just sitting on the beach and I feel this tickle on my foot. I look down and it's a full-on crab war!"

"Go on. Tell me everything."

Chapter 34

When I wake up the sky is a high blue ceiling sparkling beyond the holey green canopy. I roll over on the cushion of thick moss and yawn. The phone is lying beside my head.

Today the leaves and trees seem to part for me while I make my trek back to the beach, as if they're eager to hasten my reunion with Clemente. I'm glad for any help. I walk fast all day, and mostly run the last mile.

When I finally get back to the beach, though, I find it empty, and the fire Clemente tended is nothing but a bed of glowing coals. I look around, drop my backpack near his sand-covered space blanket.

Just as I'm about to call his name, I hear the soft twangs of his voice. He's making that electric guitar sound, the signature *bawoew bwow* he makes when he's on his motorcycle.

I follow his voice through the forest and come upon a waterfall. It's not a serious waterfall, more like a run-off, but Clemente's working it. He's standing naked on a rock beneath the sputtering stream, rubbing his black hair, making his guitar sounds as though he's the last man on Earth. His eyes are closed. Water skims his brown muscles in ribbons that whisk off his elbows, hands, penis, and clatter on the smooth domed rock beneath his feet. *Bawoew bwow*, he sings, raising one arm and rubbing an armpit clean; then he switches and does the other one.

"Got a date tonight with #6, *bawoew bwow*, that awesome dude who drives me wild, *bawoeeoow bwow*, he loves me back, how fucking nuts is that, love his bod because it's his, *bawoew bwow*, he's mine all mine all mine."

His voice gurgles in the water. He shakes his hair, rubs his chest, inspects his BodyGlue. I laugh when he leans back to let the water hit his crotch, and when he holds back his foreskin I glimpse his pretty pink head.

I'm about to go join him when, while bending over to rinse his ass, he almost slips off the rock and has to swing his arms to catch his balance. Laughing, I clamp my hand over my mouth to keep from blowing my cover.

A little Colby sitting on my shoulder tells me, *Get down there and make love to that boy so hard it makes the flowers bloom!* And I want to do what he says.

But on my other shoulder there's a little Marcus who shushes us both. *There's time for that. Just watch this, don't disturb him, just enjoy this because it's magic.*

It's Marcus I choose to listen to, at least for now. Looking at Clemente in that waterfall, it would be hard to deny he's the most beautiful man I've ever laid eyes on. It's like he's got my breath on a string and every move he makes takes it away even further.

While I watch, he carefully sits down on the rock and hops off into the shallow pool surrounding it. The water comes up to his knees and he stands stirring it with one foot while he looks at something—a bug, maybe a flower—with a cute smirk. Then he wades out and lays down on the bank and crosses his arms behind his head. His eyes are closed. He raises one knee out of the water and rocks it, sending waves rippling across the surface and lapping his belly. He mumbles something I don't catch. Then he lifts his leg out of the water and playfully lets it fall back with a big splash. He smiles and does it again.

Suddenly Colby's advice seems best.

I pull off my shirt, step out of my sneakers, unbutton my pants.

It's true I have no assurance that Clemente Santiago won't one day break my heart. That he won't lie to me or hurt me or make me cry the way Piper and Ryan have made me cry. But still—

I burst naked through the trees and splash into the pool and, surprised, he pulls his legs up to protect his jewels. But when he sees it's me he laughs and opens his arms and says "*Ooof!*" when I tumble onto him. His skin is like warm silk and as I press my mouth against his I feel his hands slide down my back and over my bum to my thighs. He leans up and rocks me backward into the pool with a splash but doesn't let me go under. I'm floating, looking up at him, my legs around him. He smiles at me and whispers my name. I take his hand and cup his palm and fingers around my balls; with my other hand I reach up and pull his face to mine, and put my lips between his teeth.

No, I have no assurance that he won't someday hurt me or break my heart. But my god, just look at him.

He's worth the risk.

HOMO ACTION LOVE STORY!

EPILOGUE

Changes

HOMO ACTION LOVE STORY!

When our lips are red from kissing he guides me out of the pool and lays me down on the bank so that only my legs are still in the water. Crawling up between them he takes my erection in his mouth. At first he's gentle, hesitant, learning the feel of this thing he's never done before. But he's a fast learner. He hugs my thigh with one arm, reaches up along my chest with the other, so far that I'm able to bite his cool wet fingers while he sucks me. He rubs his tongue and face against my balls and I dig my heels into the sand to lift my hips and give him access to the space behind them. He presses his lips there and then, opening his mouth, motorboats my taint. *Pppbbbtbtbtbb.* He's laughing between my thighs and I'm laughing around his fingers, and, spitting them out, I tell him, "Get up here, you dork."

"McHenry, so demanding."

He kisses his way up my belly and chest. Right before he's about to meet my lips he looks up and past me and his expression changes.

"*Seriously?*" he says, shaking his head in apparent disbelief before pressing his face to my chest.

"What?" I ask his ink-black hair.

"Just look," he laughs.

I arch my head back so I can see what's behind me, and looking upside-down through the tops of my eyes I spot, through the green trees, the most epically pink and orange and purple and yellow and gold sunset I've ever seen in real life.

"You've got to be kidding," I laugh.

"So zilla precious, isn't it?"

"Clemente Santiago and Boots McHenry, Warriors both, snipers both, together in a flower-filled tide-pool on a deserted tropical island during the most beautiful sunset this good clean world has ever seen. What do we *do* with a landscape like that, Clemente?"

"We live up to it, McHenry," he laughs, pulling my hand across his hard bum and pressing my fingers there.

And my goodness, we do. We do.

"We do what, McHenry?"

I open my eyes and for just a second I think the grizzled yellow lab on the bed is speaking to me.

"Live up to the sunset," I say, smiling and rubbing my eyes.

Clemente laughs. He's wearing a towel around his waist and his hair is still wet. He thumb-pops the cap on a stick of deodorant and applies a layer to each armpit as the scent of peppermint fills the room. His scorpion tattoo sports a shiny round scar with a mate on the other side.

"You had the dream again?" he asks.

"Does it count as a dream if it really happened?"

"Believe me, McHenry, it was a dream *while* it was happening." He turns from his bureau and flops down on the bed, one arm around my waist, the other around Trooper's neck. "But it's good to know I rocked your world so hard in that tide-pool to engrave it on your memory like that."

"*Pfft*, the landscape made it memorable."

"Smart guy." He bites playfully at my nipple. Then he rolls off the bed, the towel lifting up enough to give me a flash of his bum—the bum he let me do wonderful things to again last night. "Up, McHenry, we need to go. It's game time."

"Thank god, my trigger finger's itchy as a motherfucker."

I reach and give Trooper's head a rub. He closes his eyes and flops out his tongue in appreciation. Then I push back the covers and get up. The carpeted floor is strewn with laundry, most of it Clemente's. I find my pants behind a chair and pull them on. I don't even know where my shirt went last night — I look around for a minute and then pull on one that smells like Clemente.

As I'm leaving the bedroom to join Clemente in the kitchen, I notice Trooper standing at the edge of the bed, pawing the mattress. I walk over to him and lift him in my arms.

"Up, up, and away, Troop!" I say as I guide him to the floor. After touch-down he follows me out to the kitchen, where the kettle is whistling and Clemente is filling the French press with coffee. His tanktop is tucked into his underwear — something he sometimes forgets should never be done — so I stand behind him and fix it.

"Before I forget," he says, "can you flick me that affidavit thing for Marcus? Do you have it?"

"Already flicked it."

"What do I have to do?"

"Just needs your thumb on the last page."

"I don't know why his insurance won't just pay up the full amount. Does the Intrepid look like it was hit by vandals? Of *course* it was pirates. Forget my sworn testimony — I'll just show them my bullet holes."

I kiss his head and sink my hands into his briefs, clutching handfuls of his fuzzy bum. "I love all your holes," I tell him.

He laughs. "You fucker."

He kick-starts his motorcycle and we're off, zooming across Thebes on our way to the stadium. We pass what'll soon be my new home: I bought a condo in some new construction near the harbor—just a small place, four rooms, but the views of the ocean are killer. It doesn't feel bad to have sold the house I shared with Ryan. He's happy where he is, apparently, and that has nothing to do with me anymore. Still, I *will* miss my swimming-pool boyfriend.

My human boyfriend will make up for it, though. I told him he'll get a key, but we haven't even joked about him moving in. For one thing, Trooper doesn't like elevators. For another, there's no need to rush things— I've learned my lesson about rushing things. And it'll be nice to have Clemente's place to escape to when the paparazzi turn up the heat on us. They're obsessed with our new romance, of course, but they never follow us to Clemente's neighborhood. They probably figure people wouldn't believe it.

When we get to the stadium the parking lots are already packed—the first game of the season is always a biggie. But we cruise into the VIP lot and Clemente parks in his #4 space. I'm happy to see the red Jeep Classic over in my own space—Colby and Marcus must've had no trouble getting in.

I let go of Clemente and hop off the bike. Demetri, unlit cigar dangling from his lips, gives us a wave as we enter the building. And Rufus Wong is just beyond the locker-room doors, flirting with a good-looking reporter he'll probably bang after the game. I have to laugh. Some things never change.

A lot of things *do* change, though.

For one, when Clemente looks over at me from his locker with that cute little smile, I know that what I took for a full season to be a *yo dude* teammate grin is actually the kind of love you cross oceans for. Maybe I should wonder why he feels this way about me—why with every other man he's as straight as can be, but with me, when we're together, he's *more*. Maybe I should wonder, but I don't—I don't ever remember to. It feels too natural. We're just *us*.

Another change: The locker near mine and the #9 uniform now belong indisputably to Marius Tumble, who's sitting on the bench putting on his game shoes, joking with his brother Marcus. Marcus looks at me and smiles, visitor ID dangling from his shirt pocket. I hear they've started hanging out a little bit here and there, the athlete and the sea captain—that's yet another change. A little flick of a business card, when it leads to the love of your life, goes a long way toward mending fences.

Lots of things change.

But there's one thing that, after a lot of thinking, I decided not to change. Piper Pernfors is at his locker suiting up, still #5, still a Warrior, still rich and famous. I've never said anything to Skullcrusher or to anyone else about what he helped Ryan do, and I told Colby and Marcus and Clemente to let it go too. What would be the point? Justice? Maybe. But Piper did what he did because he loves me, and I can't bring myself to squash him for that.

Still, we don't talk unless we have to; we haven't interacted much during practices. But on this day of our first game he looks over at me as he's zipping his uniform and gives me a nod. I return it.

Then I hear my name. Colby is walking toward me, ID tag swinging from a lanyard around his neck. He's cracking open a soda.

"You made it," I say, glad to see him. On the trip back from Honolulu, the nicest few weeks of my life, the four of us got really tight—Colby and me especially. He hugs me and I feel a new layer of muscle under his t-shirt. Since we've been back he's been training hard, getting ready to make the MMAC his bitch—no more junior division for Colby Kroft. They root for him at Yon's Kneecaps. "Have you checked out your seats?"

"Not yet," he says, taking a swig of soda. "We'll head out while you're gearing up." He looks over at Marcus. "Nice to see my man talking to his bro, huh?"

I nod. "Maybe you're getting closer to that twinsy threeway you've got your heart set on."

"I promise you'll be the first to know," he laughs.

He looks at Marcus and Marius again, and I notice his eyes lingering on Marius's #9, and I can see in those eyes that the number makes him sad. He turns his head and clears his voice and takes another swig of soda.

"Looks like Clemente's drafted you a new recruit," he laughs, pointing.

I turn and see Clemente near the doors. There's a little girl standing on his foot, arms locked tight around his uniformed waist. Clemente has one hand on her back and is touching his mustache with the other, listening intently to the gesturing, wheelchair-bound old man in front of him. A dog sleeps on the old man's lap, oblivious to the strategy session.

"Last-minute advice from his old coach," I say to Colby, and he laughs.

"Kid's cute."

"Ready to go find our seats, sexy?" Marcus says, bending down for a sip of Colby's soda.

With a few last good-lucks, they clear out of the locker room, followed by the humming wheelchair and its three passengers. I turn to close my locker and an arm slips around my shoulders, a mustache touches my ear.

"McHenry," Clemente whispers, "we're on."

I stand in a line with my arms and legs spread while my

handlers load on my gear. Rifle, goggles, belt, pistol. The earpiece is pressed into my ear with a familiar crackle. Lucinda Skullcrusher's voice comes on, psyching us Warriors up with a curse-filled rant that welcomes us to a new season. I smile as I squeeze my rifle, as I run my fingers through the smooth cascade of bullets that hang in a pouch on my hip. Part of the reason I've spared Piper is because, in spite of everything, I love this team. I love this game. And I want to win again. I want that Cup. The way certain people were made for certain things, I was made for this game. It's no less true now than it's ever been.

But I know I'm not invincible. Never was, never will be. None of us is invincible. This game is life and death — I know that firsthand. I've seen it and felt it and dealt with it. I can be hit. I can be exiled. And so can Clemente. From any direction. At any moment. In a multitude of colors.

But one last thing has changed, one last zilla important thing:

From now on, if anything ever goes wrong, if any sudden burst of paint means that the worst has come to pass, I'll know where to find the guy I love. And more: He'll know where to find me.

SPECIAL THANKS

To Maggie for planting the seed that grew into this book. To Chris for putting up with all of the guys in my life, even if they're just fictional. To Tom for helping me tame the synopsis-beast once again. To Halex and Tiffany for test-reading this book, and for helping to make it better. To Ivan for the military-grade fight moves. To Heather, Josh, and Ethan for their perpetual encouragement. To my family, even though we're never going to acknowledge this one! And to my faithful readers.

ABOUT THE AUTHOR

Ben Monopoli lives in Boston with his husband, Chris.